Explorations

Explorations

The long journey of James Duffield

JULIAN DOLMAN

THE CHOIR PRESS

First published in the United Kingdom in 2014 by
The Choir Press

ISBN 978-1-909300-64-4

Contents

List of Illustrations

Glossary

Assegai	Spear
Biltong	Strips of dried edible animal flesh
Boer/Boor	South African resident, not British – often an emigrant farmer
Boyalwa	Native beer
Bogale	Brave, aggressive
Boguera	Manhood initiation rite
Fore-clap	After clap, a canvas or similar, hung across the opening into the wagon
Fore-slok/after-slok	Parts of the wagoner's whip
Furlough	Leave from the army
Fynbos	Scrubby heathland vegetation
Gentoo	A prostitute
In-span/out-span	Yoking and unyoking oxen
Jambok	Big whip
Kagn	Some natives' Supreme Spirit
Kapenaar	Cape Town resident
Kaross	Blanket/wrap of animal skin(s), of varying size
Kuil	Water hole
Lambele	Hunger belt, worn tightly to depress hunger, a form of gastric belt
Leina	Morning poetic praise/oration
Litupa	Small whip of rhino hide
Macooa	White/civilised/European

Maseka	Bracelet of iron, copper or brass
Mutti	Mother
Pitso	Council of war, native/tribal parliament
Poola	Blessing/rain
Poorte	Gate or mountain pass
Receipt	Recipe/instructions
Rheim	Strip of leather, or chain, often used for fastening
Roer	An antiquated, heavy long-barrelled rifle commonly used by farmers/Boers
Sable dam, a	A coloured/native woman
Sadak	"Sadak searching for the waters of oblivion" was a painting by John Martin hugely popular in Victorian times
Salted horse	A horse that has recovered from a bout of deadly horse disease and is now immune, and hence very valuable. The disease carriers were midges, not the tsetse fly
Sibilo	A shiny, powdery iron ore that feels greasy and soils what it touches
Soopje	A tot, usually of Cape brandy
Spoor	Track of man or animals
Stoep	Step/platform/verandah
Tebogo	Thank you/thanksgiving
Trek	Journey
Trek-touw	Plaited leather rope by which yokes of ox are fastened to the wagon
Tsecha	Animal skin loin cloth/strips
Veldt	Plain, grassy or not
Veldt-cornet	Mounted local policeman
Vrouw	A Boer houswife or widow
Zuur	Hardy, strong, healthy

1

Trinity Hall, Cambridge, 1849

THE AIR WAS STILL and warm. Motes moved almost impercepti-
bly, caught in the glancing shafts of strong sunlight from twin
sash windows. The windows overlooked an immaculately green
college lawn, which lay basking in the light-aired high summer's
day. Inside the room, the tone of the light made the pale panelled
walls glow. The room was silent and empty, although voices could
be heard approaching, but for a last few moments, the room itself
was totally tranquil, as if expectant.

Decorating the walls of Charles' college rooms were pictures in
black and gold frames of sporting teams, and sporting trophies,
ranging from a college oar, on which Charles' name appeared as
stroke of the college eight, to an elegant mounted head of an
antelope. An ancient and elaborately carved leather-topped writing
desk, piled high with books and with papers scattered over it, and a
pair of worn leather armchairs were the main furniture in the room.
The mantelpiece over the ornate carved wooden fireplace was
cluttered with objects from two shining sporting trophies to a
silver-mounted ostrich egg, along with many cards of invitation and
folded letters, and some unopened envelopes. On a small octagonal
table by one window, a lone clear cut-glass vase, tall and elaborate,
filled with fading flowers spilling out of it, provided a bright
summer-filled purple splash of colour. The gleam from the highly
polished brass handle on the old painted door was reflected in a
silver tray lying on a wide mahogany side table next to it. On the
tray were a number of full glasses of champagne (with not a few
unopened bottles underneath the table) and from the door an

excited and noisy group of young men without exception helped themselves to brimming glasses as they entered.

The first person in, leading the way, happily and proudly, was the host, Charles Duffield. Many people had said of him that he was a good-looking young man, if a little florid in the face. He was a touch over six feet tall, of broad-shouldered build, with a mop of too long unruly fair hair with unusually pale, clear blue eyes. He was wearing a white silk, pleated, open-necked shirt, and he had a college rowing club tie around his waist as a belt for his immaculately crumpled white trousers. He was laughing a little loudly, and plainly in high spirits. He was a little breathless.

The calm stillness in the room soon ceased with the arrival of Charles' guests. Indeed the room was quickly full of their conversation. They were all young men of about the same age and with their animated talk were boasting, laughing and drinking. The young undergraduates were going to be leaving university in the coming days, so this was the end of their time together and they seemed keen to enjoy Charles' usual generous hospitality right up to the very last minute. One or two were smoking the newly fashionable cheroots, someone for an unknown reason was declaiming what he said was Latin poetry, although that seemed doubtful, and some were fiercely drinking, although that did not stop them laughing and talking to each other at the same time. Most were happily talking loudly about what they had done and about what they would do. One was wearing a college blazer, a strongly coloured striped garment, while several had carried gaudily beribboned boaters which they casually threw down onto a chair near the door as they entered.

Charles himself was talking to a tall, very dark, upright and slightly older but striking-looking man with piercing, very pale blue eyes, who was, it was to be assumed from his suntanned appearance, newly arrived in Cambridge from overseas. He was nevertheless personally well known to Charles, as a family friend, and as a man who had seen a lot of the world. He had been to many wild and dangerous places on the frontiers of the unexplored world. Places which lay at the edge of the known world – wild, unmapped places, where it was well known that only savages and dangerous animals held sway.

Charles was talking with this older man, by name Harry Vardon: Captain Harry Vardon of the loyal 25th Madras Light Infantry to be precise (as Charles said when introducing him to one or two fellows), who was on extended furlough. Charles, and some others in a small group, were enthralled by Harry's vivid accounts of big game hunting, the animals he had encountered, the people he had met and the places he had seen. He talked with reticence, and that made his account all the more authoritative, and so attractive to his young listeners.

"You need a good steady salted horse that stands as fast as a rock when you fire, and is not afraid of either the noise of the discharge, your movement on his back from the recoil, or of the charging rhino. You need a good dog, with a sound nose, and a native with you to carry your traps on his own horse. It's all very simple really, you just have to get a very good rifle before you go, say at Blissett's or somewhere like that, and all the rest you get when you arrive there. You can't get a decent rifle out there. The Boers don't have such a thing as a decent rifle. Their antiquated rifles, or roers as they call them, would be put to shame by a north-west frontier tribesman's weapon, for length and inaccuracy. And you will need to learn all you can about how to survey and measure distances and so on. But the Royal Geographical Society will help with all that, if you go to them first.

"Before you set out, fix a trocheameter on your wagon to be certain of distances – expensive but accurate, and that's the point. Accuracy, that's what matters. You only have one chance in the interior. Take it or you may well die. The important thing is to prepare your technical abilities here in England first. Learn what you can, and as well, get just a few basic necessities, like the rifle, and then get all the rest of what you need for an expedition like the trocheameter – and the wagon to go with it of course – out there in Cape Town. It will be far cheaper to do that than take all your equipment out to the Cape." He paused for breath and looked around at his listeners grouped near him. Young men, all in the prime of youth. No one said anything, they all waited for him to continue. The babble of chatter in the rest of the room was ignored.

"Take a look at that antelope over there," he said, waving his hand elegantly towards the trophy over the door, and nearly spilling his glass as he did so. "It was a long day and then I came across this spoor, as it is called, which was quite new to me, so I followed it. I had to do a lot of tracking through some pretty tough bush to get to it, and then when I had bagged it, I found I was separated from the wagon, and I could not find or see it. Either the wagon or I were completely lost in the middle of nowhere. By then it was the end of a long and pretty tiring day and I was in real need of a drink of water and a sleep. But because the light goes so rapidly, all you can do in a situation like that, is sit and wait. If you tried to find it in the dark you could wander miles off track.

"I knew what would happen when the darkness was complete so to speak, as I had some good boys, and they fired off rockets as soon as the light was gone, to guide me on what turned out to be quite a long ride back. Without those rockets I would never have found them and the safety of the wagon. That would have been curtains for me, the place was stiff with lions. I could hear them all around. My horse was in bad way. In fact, only a few weeks before in a similar situation the lions had had a go at Oswell when he was trying to find his wagon. He had a pretty bad time of it. Mauled, and all that." He paused, and looked at Charles and the others, appraisingly.

"Young lads like you," he turned slightly to face Charles, "adventurous, plenty of money and even more time to spare, have you ever thought about trying your hand at this life out on the veldt? It's very good sport out there. The best in the world. There are herds of buck, wildebeests, buffaloes and zebras, and so on which are so vast you can't see them all at any one time. Why not?" He laughed, openly. "With proper training and the right kit, and I can help you with all that, you could go out to the Cape. From there, with luck in a very short time you will be right in the middle of the very best first-class hunting. And you could bag a load of ivory at the same time which could well pay for your trip. Indeed, it could make you rich. So you would not need to ask your old man for the funds for this either!

"And if you had a bit of luck in the exploration stakes, and with a lot of hard perseverance as well, you might even find the great lake which is said by the natives to exist somewhere right up country beyond the Boers. The natives talk about this lake sometimes, but no white man has ever seen it, and perhaps you could find it and maybe name it after someone, your old man perhaps. Or the queen. People have got a knighthood for less, you know.

"You are lucky Charles, you have no ties. No lady has engaged your affections, you are single and free. You could just get up and go. I am sure your old man would give you the tin if you asked nicely. You could say you would repay him when you got back."

Charles was following what Harry was saying closely, and signs of enthusiasm were writ large upon his face. Flushed with champagne, Charles' imagination was fired by Harry with his tales and advice. He had known Harry for a few years as an excellent man to invite to shooting parties on his father's estate in Devon (where he was very welcome) not just as an excellent shot, but also as a colourful raconteur, as a friend and adviser, and although older, as a confidant. Charles was of a mood to take the advice he was being offered by Harry, but he needed to talk to his father, Sir Marshall Duffield, who would doubtless have an opinion, which would usually be offered pretty straightforwardly and quickly. It seemed to

Charles then that he should present a scheme like this and try to give it some sort of a slant that would appeal to his father. After all, his father had offered him a continental tour when he went down, so perhaps Charles could suggest a trip to the Cape as an alternative. His father had clearly been disappointed when he said no to the Continent, so if he played his cards right, maybe the Cape, with no mention of danger, apart from the voyage of course, would satisfy the old man. But the possibility of danger was what really attracted Charles. He thought he needed to feel alive and this was the way to achieve that. Nothing banal for him.

The conversation which Harry had started became more general and more animated now, with Charles' friends joining in, making haphazard suggestions, some of which were of doubtful usefulness. Someone asked Harry if he had any pictures of the sort of places he was talking about. But Harry quickly shook his head.

"What you need is a good artist who can paint a decent watercolour. The problem is that without such a chap you have to try to paint the scene or draw it for yourself, and then you have to explain the miserable thing to someone who has never seen what you are talking about, and I simply can't manage it. No. When I get back to London I show my rotten sketches to a real artist, and he then has to try and interpret the daft paintings or drawings. But really their pictures are just a travesty – looking at them you get no real idea of the heat, the smell, the stillness, the light, the animals and the amazing space everywhere. What is really needed on all these expeditions is a good artist. That is what would save you all the embarrassment."

A voice from among the group around Harry called out, "James can draw, and he can paint. He's your man."

"Yes," said Charles. "Of course, the very chap. My brother James is a very fair artist. I will get him to show you some of his work. He is in the room somewhere." He waved an arm around, boastfully and a little vaguely. "At least. He was with us just a second ago."

Charles' face was flushed with drink now, and he was slightly slurring his words occasionally. Harry looked at him closely, and wondered if this young man he knew to have too much money was quite the person he seemed. He had noticed James in the room earlier, and wondered how two brothers could look so physically alike, but apparently be so different in temperament.

Charles and James were due to go down to Devon to see the family in a few days' time, and Charles now saw the visit as a chance to talk to his father about Harry's suggestion. But he had also received a letter from his mother saying she had someone she would like him to meet. Happy and confident, he told Harry he would have to leave for now and start packing his kit.

The party started to break up. Taking their cue from him, a couple of young men came up to Charles, and said they were off, a quick slap on the shoulder was all, no thanks as such, just a familiar farewell gesture between young, but good, if careless friends. The room was soon emptied, and the guests' clattering departure receded rapidly down the emptiness of the stone stair. After Charles and Harry followed the last guests out, the air in the room gradually stilled. Apart from empty glasses and a few bottles on the floor by the table, only the dancing movement of the motes remained as evidence that anyone had been there.

2

The Homecoming

THE FAMILY HOME in Devon was rather a grand place. Sir Marshall had been for many years a lawyer with a very fashionable practice in London, and he had made a considerable fortune. He had even been made a baronet for services rendered (although what those services were, was not known generally) and was justly proud of his status as such. In Devon he and his wife Lady Eleanor lived in some state with a large staff, both indoors and out, in the elaborate, almost ostentatious house they had built on the edge of Dartmoor, to which they moved some four years or so previously from their house at Clapham Common. The new house, proudly called Highsteignton, was constructed out of heavy, thick grey granite, and the family crest was carved on a granite shield which had been built in over the front door. Within, the large high rooms were extremely comfortable with fine, rich dark oak panelling, and heavy warm-coloured mahogany furniture. There was a good-sized smoking room, with a jockey's weighing scales to one corner for some reason, a gun room of course, an enormous library with a few thousand old books (purchased by Sir Marshall as a "complete" library), and then as he liked to put it to his friends, the usual offices. "Like the dining room, wine cellars, and so on," he liked to say.

He and Lady Eleanor had decided that as they were getting on a bit, the years advancing and all that, as they put it to themselves but not to Charles, that it was right that their elder son Charles should get married to someone of whom they approved, who would herself be happy to wed him. Charles was, they thought proudly to themselves, a fine catch for some lucky lady. He had a title to come in the hopefully distant future, and what would be a very good fortune. Preferably that lady would be someone like the daughter of a friend, or someone they knew who would simply be suitable in some unspecified way for their son. This point of view was not intended to be anything other than helpful to Charles; they had not the slightest thought that he might have plans or even wishes of his own. Charles being in receipt of a good allowance from his father which they both felt was very adequate, would happily accept, so they fondly imagined, whomsoever they suggested to him as a suitable match. With this objective in mind Lady Eleanor had long been conducting a clandestine but detailed and very private examination of possible candidates for the match. They had ended up picking a rather charming girl they, or rather Lady Eleanor, thought, called Francesca Trevanion. They knew of her father of course, although sadly, as she said to herself, the girl's mother was dead.

The Trevanions were an old landed family who lived not too far away, whom they did not know all that well socially, being relatively new to the county themselves. But the Trevanions were respectable, and that mattered. She had a brother called Lewis, and it was true that Lewis was not altogether what they would have wanted as a possible relative, reputedly being a bit of a spendthrift, and with a poor reputation. But Francesca herself was completely charming, everyone said the same, and she was certainly a very beautiful young woman. She seemed the perfect match, thought Lady Eleanor. Francesca was bright, and as well educated as they thought she should be. She was an excellent horsewoman and they had been told she rode to hounds regularly, which was important socially. Her manners, social connections and deportment were impeccable, and in fact the only difficulty about her from their point of view was that her father, Richardson Trevanion, had no money. But his was indeed a very old local family, and in the eyes of

Charles' parents, that counted for a very great deal. Francesca, they kept telling themselves, was beautiful, and that was enough. They had the money, and Francesca's lack of prospects in that respect was not thought by them to be important. She would, they decided, although really they hardly knew her as a person, make an excellent wife for Charles. They kept this objective of a marriage firmly to themselves, in case it should not work out as they wished. If they had to drop the idea of Francesca as a suitable wife for Charles, they did not want it to be known that it had been dropped. They never gave a thought to their younger son James in all this. The Estate, quite considerable, would go to Charles, and James was expected to make his own way.

The Duffields had the idea (which seemed a good one to them at the time) that when Charles (and James of course since they were to travel together) returned from Cambridge they would arrange for Francesca and her father to stay for a ball which they would give. They would invite all the county families for the purpose, and a few friends of course. They both hoped that Charles and Francesca, when they met, would find each other sufficiently attractive to make their marriage seem a likely prospect, at least to both their parents. Francesca's brother Lewis was, apparently, out of the country travelling somewhere, and had indeed been away for some time, so that was all to the good. They did not have to take him into account. They were to discover very much later that that was exactly what they should have done.

When Charles and James arrived home on the Friday evening, they were met as usual by Coleman, the butler, who as soon as he saw Charles, said, "Oh, I am sorry Mister Charles, for everything being so upside down. It's because of the ball being tomorrow, and I am having to send people here and there doing things, and making sure they do things, and I don't know what all myself besides."

"What ball?" asked Charles.

"Ah, there you are, I thought you were never coming," said his mother, ignoring his question as she darted at him from out of the morning room. She wanted to stop Coleman from saying any more. Her remark was patently untrue. She had clearly been lurking, waiting for Charles to arrive. "Good. I need someone strong like you to ensure that the ropes holding the marquee, have been properly pegged in. You never know with these people, you have to check everything." She gasped for breath. "All the time. And we are told by McGregor it may be windy, but I doubt that."

"Mother, how nice to see you, and how well you are looking," said Charles, taking no notice of her or what she said at all. She had taken no thought of him as a person, as her son, so he told himself he would take none of her.

They clutched each other in a brief formal and sadly unwanted embrace, then Charles stepped back to look at his mother. She looked harassed he thought, tired and older, but he could see she was still imperious of manner and appearance, even perhaps petulant in approach.

As if carelessly she said, "We have got a few guests staying for a few days for the ball, which is in your honour of course." She halted, as if aware for the first time that she had to be careful of precisely what she was saying. "Friends of ours, of course, so please be nice and polite to them. That nice Mr Vardon you know will be here, and your father wants to talk business with some of the others. So, it would be nice if you could be around, and if for once you could be helpful at the same time. You know what I mean. My goodness, you are looking a bit tired from the journey, and a bit untidy as well." She looked at Charles encouragingly. Winningly, as she imagined. Charles of course had no idea at all of what she meant or what she had in mind, but he knew he wanted to go to the kitchen and see Dorcas, and get a quick bite to eat, and a drink.

The kitchen was a high-domed, stone-flagged room with a large fireplace which had a huge cast iron stove set in it, and a spit in an open fire alongside. A large, very well scrubbed, old deal table covered with food in various stages of preparation, occupied almost the complete centre of the room, and a plain wooden dresser laden with mugs, plates, drinking glasses and bundles of herbs stood to one side. Beside Dorcas, the cook, who was hard at work by the lead sink preparing piles of vegetables, stood a young woman Charles did not know, but she did not appear to be doing anything. They both turned and looked at him as he entered. It occurred to Charles that they had been talking about him moments earlier. The old dog Argos, a lurcher, was lying under the table, and he greeted Charles' arrival in the room with enthusiastic but short-lived barking. Dorcas looked at Charles. She said nothing. The barking subsided. The outside boy, John, who was Coleman's son, stood just inside the back door, but at a seriously meaningful look from Dorcas he went out.

"I say Dorcas, can I have a drink? I have been travelling for hours with nothing to eat or drink, and right now I could manage something."

Dorcas looked from him to a side door and stiffly and silently nodded her head at it, and then turned back to her vegetable preparations. Charles went to the door, and then into what was the still room, and quickly emerged with a bottle of beer which he put on the table, pushing a plate of pears aside for the purpose. The young woman moved. Charles glanced at her and having fetched a glass from the dresser, poured himself a drink. Then, as if actually seeing her for the first time, he looked at her for a longer, but still brief, moment.

"I don't know you," he said, "are you new here?" But even as he said it, he realised from something about her, maybe her clothes, that she was not a servant at all. He saw that she was different, she was very different, she was somehow not right in this kitchen. That this was not her sort of place at all.

"You are Charles, I assume," the girl said, politely, a little doubt-fully, even hesitantly. She had a light lilt to her voice. "I am Francesca, and we, that is my father and I, are staying here for the ball tomorrow. Your mother asked us, you know. I was just getting myself a drink of water."

There was silence in the kitchen. Total silence. Dorcas stopped what she was doing and looked at the young couple, who were just standing there, looking at each other. But their thoughts were not as one. Francesca thought then that Charles was good looking in a careless sort of attractive, if dishevelled, way. It might be all right. He seemed off-hand almost, but he looked at her in a way that she felt uncomfortable with; she felt as if she was being undressed. Charles thought simply that she was very attractive indeed, and when he looked again he could see the curve of her breasts through her thin blouse. What she thought or imagined about him was of no interest to him. For her part, Francesca thought or hoped that with time she could change that look, which she read correctly, using the influence of her future affections. But although she did not like it she knew that she must accept it for now. She hoped there would be enough time for them to get to know each other properly before they became engaged and then married, and she wondered how long that period would be.

Dorcas, who was familiar with Charles' behaviour, was concerned for Francesca. She had seen too many of his young women, some of them called friends, come and go. Some of them were hardly ladies really, not like Francesca, and Dorcas had liked Francesca very much in the short time she had spent with her. She did not want the pattern almost of abuse that she had previously seen repeated. That had started when one of the housemaids, a nice simple farm-worker's daughter called Sally, had left unexpectedly, and that was why Dorcas had always kept an eye ostensibly on them, but really on Charles. She knew Francesca's family, the Trevanions, well by reputation, as everyone did in the county, they were looked up to and respected by all. If there were to be comparisons between the families the Trevanions would be accepted, and the Duffields would only suffer in that comparison.

Sir Marshall had made it clear a long time ago that he wanted the ball and all it entailed to inconvenience him as little as possible. He may have agreed with his wife that he wanted his elder son to be married, but that did not mean he had to be put out in any way, other than by writing cheques. And Lady Eleanor did not want to antagonise him, so for that reason her arrangements for the ball had all to be made unilaterally without consulting him any more than was absolutely necessary. In fact, despite that, the arrangements had come somewhat alarmingly close to perfection, as she had planned.

The following evening, the guests started to arrive by horse-drawn carriages quite early, with the dimming light slanting across the long, tree-lined drive, and they alighted at the entrance to the determinedly imposing house with the aid of liveried servants, who walked swiftly out to help them down. After they had handed their coats to the butler's staff, they were shown to the entrance to the marquee without going into the house itself. The sides of the tall marquee were hung with scarlet pleated drapes slashed with silver, and they were all decorated with long trailing swags of flowers. Around the sides of the timber floor stood dinner tables ready laid with fine napery and gleaming silver, but the marquee was sufficiently large that there was still more than enough room left for the dance floor. The interior of the marquee was lit by torchères sculpted as negro slaves in the fashionable way. The small orchestra, as it proudly called itself, was ensconced at the end of the marquee farthest from the house.

Servants, especially those hired for the occasion, and working under the supervision of Coleman, moved with difficulty among the crowd of guests as they assembled in the marquee. The food was elaborately displayed in a side annex to the main marquee on a series of tables hung with fine white linen, laced with a superfluity of yet more brightly polished silver, and the whole was decorated with swags of colourful flowers. The food itself was placed on a series of raised dishes and stands, and the centrepiece of the rather bold display was a stuffed feathered swan on a wide platter. It did not seem likely that it was to be eaten.

It was obvious to everyone attending and who knew that the ball was in his honour, that Charles was fascinated by Francesca. They stood closely together as guests entered. She was dressed in a long, pure white satin gown and wore her mother's small silver spray-shaped brooch shining with diamonds on her left shoulder. She also, like the other ladies, wore long white gloves, and a programme hung from her left wrist. Her hair shone a very pale straw colour and she wore it coiled on her head almost, thought Charles, like some sort of crown. Her face was pale, and she appeared tense. But she was slim and graceful in her movements, and when the music eventually started she danced with Charles nervously, and not with ease. Charles held her firmly, and wore a look which was not exactly one of love, but was faintly leering, she thought. She knew because her father had told her some time before that she was intended, if all went well between them, to marry Charles. Her father had discussed matters in detail first with Lady Duffield and then when it had been arranged, with Sir Marshall. He had also told her that he could not give her a dowry nor indeed any sort of a settlement, and he had not spared her when he emphasised to her the importance of her marrying someone like Charles, with money, or if not with money at present then with certain prospects of it. And that latter Charles had. Her father told her sadly that was why he had agreed the marriage with the Duffields. She herself was nineteen years old. She thought of herself as having no abilities, and so what would become of her if her father were to die she could hardly bear to think. She was under no illusions. She knew she must marry this man who had made his thoughts about her so plain. Her father was not at all well, and could not reasonably be expected to have a long life ahead of him.

So she danced frequently with Charles, not then with any present feeling of happiness, but almost with a sense of impending fate. She had, she thought, realised from her first meeting with Charles in the kitchen what that fate would be like. She hoped that, if she did the right thing, Charles would in time respect her, and maybe even love her. Perhaps.

For now though, Charles was only a little drunk, and he did not particularly trouble to conceal it from her. He had obviously been drinking before the ball had started. The fact that some of the guests noticed his condition did not matter to him. It embarrassed Francesca, but that was not important to him. He clutched Francesca, and stumbled slightly. A deep voice interrupted them, politely and quietly.

"I say Charles, old man, steady on." The speaker took Charles' arm to help.

"James, leave me alone, will you," said Charles, irritated. He spoke a little too loudly to be unnoticed by the couples who were dancing immediately next to them. One or two glanced at them.

"I am dancing with this lovely lady, you can see that, and I don't need you cutting in on me."

"But that is just what I insist on doing, old boy," said James, and matching the action to his words, he put his hand lightly on Francesca's waist as she stood between them. In a half-hearted attempt to push him away, Charles thrust out a hand against James' chest in a sudden jerky movement. Francesca took advantage of Charles being distracted, moved her hand off Charles' shoulder and transferred her gaze to James. The encounter only lasted a few seconds, but that brief event, which was noticed by others, was enough to cause Francesca thought.

Just at that moment Harry Vardon came up to the three of them, and he moved Charles away from Francesca with practised ease.

The two of them lurched off with Harry apparently talking to Charles, and with his arm around Charles' shoulder, but actually lightly steadying him, in the direction of the sumptuous, if somewhat flamboyantly displayed, food and drink. Almost immediately, they started to resume their usual talk of big game hunting. It was only much later that Charles realised that he had been parted from Francesca, smoothly and efficiently, and with few people noticing.

Lady Duffield was one of those who had noticed, and she took in the little scene and inwardly thanked "that nice Mr Vardon", as she called him to herself. He would not, she reflected sadly, be around much longer, as he had told her only that afternoon that he was off back to the Cape Colony quite soon, she could not remember exactly when, and after that, she thought he was perhaps supposed to be going back to India, as he was only on an extended furlough.

"I am told by Dorcas that you are an artist," said Francesca lightly, and with a small tilt of her head backwards as she looked up at James. James said nothing. There was a pause before Francesca said, "I am sure you don't remember me, but we did meet once, when we were both about sixteen. On the beach at Sidmouth?" James looked a bit blank, she thought sadly. She could see that he didn't remember.

A sudden gust of wind outside the marquee made a slight, brief noise; maybe, thought Lady Eleanor, it was a good thing that Charles had tested the guy ropes, if indeed he really had done. The wind sounded fitful.

"Yes, I do paint a little, but only for my own private satisfaction of course." He paused, a little embarrassed. "And you are right. Sadly, I do not recall any beach, or meeting. I really should, I can see that now, now that I am with you, but I don't. I wish I did. I am very sorry about that."

Francesca thought she should change the subject. "And what, pray, do you paint?"

"Mostly landscapes, a few animals and so on, but I am not really any good. I just enjoy it. They are all painted for myself, no one else. I am a mere amateur, but as I said, I do enjoy it." James felt his talents deserved modesty on his part, although some others did not.

James looked carefully at Francesca, whose earlier uncomfortable passage around the floor he had been following all evening, and found himself at a loss. It had been made clear to him by his mother that Francesca was not for him, she was for Charles, and Sir Marshall had told him somewhat crudely it was true, that he would have to make his own way in the marriage stakes, and in the world, as he put it. But James knew as he danced with Francesca that it was more complicated than that. Yes, he knew she was intended for Charles, and also Charles had made his intentions in that direction quite clear when they had talked about Francesca earlier that evening. But here and now all that was irrelevant. They moved together around the floor, gracefully in tune with each other and apparently happy, and James idly thought that he might be what they call entranced by her, by her looks and grace and the swan-like curve of her neck where a few stray wisps of her fair hair escaped from the arrangement and hung down at the back. For her part, Francesca could see that the physical likeness of the two brothers was only superficial, or at least, that was what she privately already thought.

After their bright conversational opening, they talked almost shyly of nothing, and it seemed to Francesca that she was with a man who was modest and kind. He was, she thought with pleasure and more than a little wistfully, so unlike Charles. This man seemed to her to be gentle and quiet, and he was artistic. She contrasted him in her own mind with Charles, and did so to James' advantage. But above all she was realistic, practical as her mother used to say, and knew and accepted that she was intended to marry Charles. She apparently had no choice.

The couple had no scheme of things, no plan, and after a short while they slowly drifted to a side table towards the back of the marquee, and there they sat and talked. No one else was at the table so they were able to get to know each other a little, and despite the crowd, they felt they were in private, for a while. Engrossed in conversation, it became clear to each of them that they were mutually attracted, she with her lithe grace, her small heart-shaped face and bright intelligence, and he with his soft fair hair and pale complexion, and his self-effacing demeanour. Her vivacity and eloquence. James thought he would have to get to know her better, but to what purpose he could not think, or did not want to think. She was fascinating, and he thought her company was easy and intelligent, but more than that he did not dare to imagine. He remembered only too well what his brother had said about her.

Lady Eleanor, sitting at the far side of the marquee with Sir Marshall and Mr Trevanion, was a little bored with having to listen to what she thought of as their tedious conversation about farming, and where to get hold of good claret (they were largely talking at rather than to each other). But, looking around, she saw James and Francesca with their heads bent close together, perhaps a little too closely, and talking animatedly, even happily, she thought. She could not have that. Not at all.

She got up and crossed the somewhat crowded floor, and without pausing or blushing, interrupted them, saying, "Oh, there you are Francesca. I was just looking for you. I would like you to meet someone if you would." After a short pause, watching the couple exchange a few last brief words, she added, "Mr Penalta is a very old friend of ours, and has always been very fond of Charles. He lives near Lansalos. You may not know, but his estate there is very good hunting country. Please come and meet him, will you?"

Francesca obediently stood and allowed Lady Eleanor to take her away from James. She led Francesca to the table where Sir

Marshall was sitting, and seeing that the mysterious Mr Penalta was not there, as she very well knew, said, "Oh, what a shame, I thought Mr Penalta was here and you could meet him. It will be important for you to know him as his land adjoins ours in some places." She subsided into her chair, pulling Francesca down next to her.

Francesca privately consoled herself by recalling her last few words with James. She was comforted by their mutual, if new as far as James was aware, attraction, even though she knew it could come to nothing. She thought the wind outside which to her had seemed fitful, was definitely dying down. She was certain that he would remember Sidmouth, eventually. It had been such a glorious day, windy and sunny.

3

The Portrait

J AMES HAD VERY DISTURBED THOUGHTS when he retired for the
night after the ball. He had just met, and been entranced by, a
young lady who to him seemed exactly the sort of person he had
hoped he would meet some day. But what had upset him particularly was that, as he crossed the hall to go upstairs, Charles had
called out to him, and they had talked a little. Despite being pretty
much the worse for wear, Charles had told him in detail all about
their parents' plans for him to marry Francesca, and said that he
agreed with them, and he was going to make it official as soon as
he could. James had been very shocked to be told this by Charles,
so briefly and in such a gloating, drunken manner. As he went
upstairs he thought about the problem he now faced. He did not
know a great deal about the Trevanions, except really that they
were an old family, and did not have much money. He did know
that Sir Marshall had once tried to buy some land from Richardson, and had been frustrated and surprised by the rejection of a
very good offer. Apart from that he knew nothing save that
Francesca was perfect in his eyes. He decided that he would not
accept the proposed marriage as a *fait accompli*, and that he would
set about courting her for himself. His mind raced with plans and
ideas, and he found himself quite unable to settle to sleep once he
reached his room. His main problem was that he did not have
enough money on which to base any realistic plans. He had
dreams but plainly he could not compete with Charles who, as the
elder, was going to inherit not just the title but also the estate. Not
the least of his problems was that he still had a year left to

complete his degree at Cambridge, but Charles had already finished his.

After a long time spent lying awake and fretting over what he might or might not do, James decided to go to his studio, as he called it, which had once been a spare room at the end of the bedroom passage. There he sometimes used to retreat when he wanted to be alone and paint. It was a good-sized north-facing room and had good light, and he kept all his artistic materials there. There were also a couple of easy chairs and a sofa which had been in place when he took it over, and these he had kept. That night he sat on the sofa and looked at his latest oil on the easel, and wondered vaguely what was not quite right about it. He was unable to find anything wrong except that it was not what was on his mind just then, so he crossed to his easel, and put fresh clean paper resting on a board in place of the oil, and started a charcoal sketch of Francesca from memory. He wanted to recapture, at least on paper, the beautiful person with whom he had spent much of the evening. Several false starts led to a considerable waste of paper, and he had trouble getting the angle of her head as he wanted. He worked at this for some time, but when it was finished he saw that it was a good likeness, it satisfied him. For him, it captured what he thought of as her free spirit – her head was in mid carefree toss, which seemed, at the angle he had chosen, to enhance her expression of happily smiling beauty. He was very satisfied with it, and, exhausted emotionally, he lay back on the sofa to look at it. He had put his feelings into the portrait, he was drained. He fell asleep as a pale and cloudless dawn started to show: the promise was for a fine day.

After the ball, breakfast was late the next morning, and even Francesca was late. Charles and James were both late as well, but as Lady Eleanor said, Charles had been very tired the night before and needed a lie in. When Francesca was ready to go down to breakfast, not being familiar with the house, she took a wrong turn, and quickly realised she was in a corridor she did not recognise. She tried to find the stairs, but couldn't. Without intending to intrude, embarrassed and concerned, she found herself in front of a half-open door and she simply could not help herself. From where she was standing without even entering the room, she could see the easel across the room with her portrait on it. She went in, and walked up to it to look at it more closely. The sofa was behind the door so she did not see James lying asleep. She gazed at the portrait and saw the gentleness with which it had been drawn, and the care which had been taken with the pose and getting the line right. She thought it was flattering, and she realised that the artist, whom she guessed must be James, had put his heart into it, and she blushed slightly when she realised what it said about his feelings for her. She had not been mistaken in her feelings for him at the ball. She took a step back, to get better distance, and trod on a crumpled-up sheet of paper, and made a small noise. James woke, and saw Francesca looking at her picture.

He stood up, and the sofa creaked as took his weight off it. She heard, turned around and saw him looking at her. She really did blush then, and so did James for that matter.

"I like it. Very much," said Francesca. "But I got lost trying to find the stairs, and did not mean to intrude. And as I was passing, I saw the portrait because the door was open." She glanced at his dressing gown and added, "I assume you will get dressed for breakfast, which I am sure must be ready by now."

"I think it's a good portrait. I think it may be the best likeness I have ever done," said James. Emboldened by her silence, he added, "It was easy, as the subject was someone whose likeness I really wanted to capture, someone whose looks are without blemish, are regular, with vitality, and whose vivacity shone through. I think actually that in the end, when I had the angle of the head right, it was easy, because as I worked I had no trouble picturing you in my mind. I could see you so clearly. I could see your personality and intelligence, and found I could show them in the portrait."

Francesca was very embarrassed by what he said. "You really should not be talking to me like that, you know. Charles would, I hope, be very upset if he heard you. It is nice of you, of course, and kind, but I do not deserve your compliments. I am a simple country girl, quite unused to sophisticated society, and you might turn my head undeservedly. My father has agreed my future with your parents, and I accept what he has decided." Changing the subject, which from her uncomfortable movement seemed to embarrass her, she added, "Your parents will surely want you to come to breakfast, although I see you can hardly come downstairs in your dressing gown, and with your hands all covered in charcoal."

"But Francesca, you must realise that last night after the ball I could not stop thinking about you. I had to draw you, you fill my mind so completely . . ."

"Stop it, you silly boy. I have no choice but to do as my father has agreed with your parents, and no doubt as soon as Charles recovers from last night he will propose, and then I shall accept him. Nor do I wish to do otherwise. I have no alternative at all."

"But you have. When he does, you can ask for time to think about it, and then we would have time. It would give us a chance to persuade your father and my parents that it is we, you and I, who should be married. Not you and Charles."

"We do not have time though. The moment has gone. Once, not so very long ago, I would most certainly have agreed with you. But now my father says it is too urgent, and my marriage should not, must not, wait. His health is failing, rapidly, and as Lewis is away somewhere, God knows where, he wants to get all his affairs, including me, settled while he can."

"We would have no need for plans. I will look after you, and love you."

"You might. You say you will look after me, but you might not be able to. To be practical, I am told you have no money and neither do I, nor does my father if it comes to that. You still have a year to go before you leave university, and you told me last night that you have no plans thereafter, and no calling. I have to say that if my father had not been diagnosed with cancer a year or so ago, I would have listened to you. But Dr Speke is clear that my father has not long to live. He is in great pain you know for much of the day. I spend a lot of time just looking after him. So you are too late. It has all been arranged. In my heart of hearts I might wish it had been otherwise, but things are settled as they are, and I have no choice. It is too late for us. I must obey my father, and do as he has agreed."

"Francesca. You know I love you, you can see it in my picture, you can see it in my eyes." James was devastated by her words. He knew she loved him, but he did not know how to persuade her to believe what he said.

Francesca paused and moved to the window facing towards the moors, and looked out. She said nothing for a while, and then without turning round she said, "I may be inadequate of course, but personally I cannot judge a man's love for me by a picture, however good it may or may not be. There is no time to wait and find out if what he or it says is true. It has all been arranged, and unless Charles finds me completely unacceptable, I shall marry him. Soon. It may not be romantic, but it will be as my father wishes, and it will make him happy. It will be an arranged marriage, just as my parents' marriage was arranged, and they were very happy. There is no reason why Charles and I should not be happy either." Then she turned to face James, and as she ran from the room he saw a tear on her cheek. Her sudden departure, and her words, so hurt him that for a few moments he could not react. Then, dismayed, he started after her, but when he reached the top of the stairs he met Charles coming out of his room, bleary-eyed with sleep, hungover and blocking his way unintentionally. Francesca ran on down the stairs.

"What on earth are you doing chasing Francesca downstairs?" He paused and stared at James, a little blearily, and then looked more closely at him. "I do declare that you are blushing, little brother mine. Blushing. Well I never! Fancy her, do you?"

James was silent but his colouring betrayed him.

"Look here James. You may just be a grubby-handed tick, but she is going to marry me, it is all arranged, and you must just back off, if you know what is good for you." He pointed at James' hands. "Look at you, filthy, just get a grip will you, and leave Francesca alone!"

"You're still drunk," said James. "You were filthy drunk last night, and you still are."

"If you get any braver I will have to give you a black eye, little brother. Just don't you go chasing after Francesca, or we shall fall out." And with that Charles turned and lurched off sideways towards his bedroom. He was very unsteady. Back in his bedroom he fell on his bed, and slept again. Later that morning, he recalled perfectly well what had passed between himself and James, and decided that he must go and see Francesca and sort out their marriage plans as quickly as he could. He simply did not want James interfering. He wanted to get his affairs settled, and settled fast – he needed to get his hands on the marriage settlement, and in turn that meant first making quite sure of Francesca by marrying her. He would go and see her as soon as he could.

James returned to his studio and lay on the sofa, staring at the portrait. The morning passed slowly, and he made no attempt to get dressed or get anything to eat. And no one troubled him, happily enabling him to look at and think about Francesca. His mind raced, but he could decide nothing, no course of action was obvious to him.

Charles slept late, and when he awoke, hungry and strangely thirsty, it was with the fixed idea that he should try and find out why James had been chasing Francesca. He decided that he should see what he could find out, and with this in mind walked along the corridor to the studio, from the direction of which they had both been running. The studio door was slightly open – James was not there, he could see, but like Francesca before him he could see the finished portrait across the room from his position in the corridor. Like Francesca he too recognised what the portrait said about the artist and how he felt about Francesca, quite as much as it portrayed her. James' love shone through his work only too clearly. Charles stood very still and tried to take in the implications of what he was seeing. He had been told he was to marry her, and his mind did not have the ability to accept what he saw. He knew for certain that in order to recover the situation as he saw it, he would have to stamp his authority over the relationship that he imagined he had discovered. But how he might do that he could not think as he stood there. He never gave the slightest consideration to the idea that his reading of their relationship might be wrong. Looking at the picture he decided that it was urgent that he should act firmly and quickly.

It was late afternoon when Charles found Francesca. She was having tea with Lady Eleanor, and her father, on the terrace. Charles suggested to Francesca that she might like to go for a short walk with him, and she stood obediently, with a feeling of slight trepidation, and together they left in the direction of Stoke Coppice. Lady Eleanor remarked sharply to Richardson that she hoped the young couple were going to get along together, and he simply nodded his acquiescence. He said nothing. He was too tired by all the drugs that young Dr Speke kept giving him to relieve the pain. "Perhaps Charles is going to propose to your daughter," said Lady Eleanor.

"Perhaps. I hope they will be happy. Perhaps," he replied.

Lady Eleanor had no misgivings. "They make a lovely couple, I am sure it will all be fine. As you know we are having a dinner party next week, you are staying for it after all, and let us hope that the young couple are going to agree to get married, so it can be announced then. That would be lovely don't you think? So convenient for us all."

When Francesca and Charles returned from their walk, she brushed past Lady Eleanor and ran upstairs to her room. She was crying thought Charles, somewhat conscience-stricken. But it will pass, it usually does. A few moments later Charles saw his father coming along the passage towards him. His father and looked at him interrogatively. Charles paused and said, somewhat apprehensively, "I am sure you will be pleased to hear, father, that Francesca and I have agreed to get married once you and her father have agreed a suitable settlement – if you do, that is." His voice lamely tailed off into emptiness.

Sir Marshall had hoped for this moment, and he twirled his gold watch unthinkingly. He looked at his son briefly. He did not know if he was impressed with his son or not. He did not like Charles' faintly frightened tone, and he wondered what Charles had done to make him use that tone of voice.

"There should be no problem with the settlement," said Sir Marshall calmly. "In anticipation of happy news I have arranged for old Mangold from the local attorneys to come here next week and have in the meantime said to Trevanion that I shall be responsible financially for everything, including what a new wife will need. I shall make you an increase in your allowance as well, of course, so that you can have your own establishment in town. It will all be taken care of, and there will be no call on Trevanion to provide cash for anything. He has agreed that he will make over a few thousand acres adjoining our estate as his contribution to the marriage settlement. He has to do it this way as Lewis has, I think, largely cleaned him out of cash for the time being. As for you, well, all that you have to do is to marry the girl, and then of course," without intended sarcasm, apparently, "have children." Charles looked guiltily at his father, and said nothing.

Sir Marshall turned his back on Charles and quite literally stalked back down the way he had just come, while Charles turned the other way, and then went along to the smoking room. There, he found James smoking a cigarette and reading a rather large book. The smoking room was one of the most comfortable rooms in the house, with four large old leather-covered armchairs, and plenty of room to walk up and down. The men in the house used it this way in bad weather. Beside James was a small Benares table with a bright brass top mounted on four finely turned ebony legs. A cup of hot steaming coffee was beside him. James looked up as Charles entered, and noticed something different about Charles at once. His stance, his manner.

James waited for Charles to speak, as he obviously had something he wanted to say. Charles hesitated, uncharacteristically, slightly nervous of what his brother's reaction would be to his news. He decided that he did not care about that anyway and deliberately loudly and perhaps defensively said, "I say, James, there's no use beating about the bush, I have to tell you my news. I am as proud as punch about this. Francesca ..." he paused, and in that instant James knew what was going to happen. James felt as if his future was decided now, by default really. The girl he had just met and who had so attracted him with her personality and looks and happy chatter, with whom he had spent what he thought of as such a happy, if brief, time, was receding from him. Now, she was about to be declared to be beyond his reach. "Francesca and I are going to be married," continued Charles. Feeling as if he was in some sort of a bad dream James gazed wearily at his brother, and he knew then that this was a turning moment in both their lives. He would not in future be able to be quiet and calm with Francesca as his brother's wife. Dancing with Francesca, and afterwards, he had glimpsed, as he thought, what life, maybe their life together, really might be. Now all that was being taken away from him. He stubbed out his cigarette. He moved uncomfortably in his armchair, and then stood up, very straight.

Although he certainly did not feel happy for himself, he was pleased that his brother was so pleased with his own news. He stretched his hand out, and shook his brother's hand, apparently warmly. "Wonderful news," he lied, and even he thought he was being unconvincing. "Wonderful. What a lady, she will make you a wonderful wife. You lucky dog." His congratulations petered out. He found he hadn't the heart to bluster and say more, but Charles did not notice, so it did not matter anyway. He had lit a cigarette from his silver case and was turning away, almost at once.

"I am off out this afternoon, we are going for a tramp up to top tor, so I will see you when we get back and we can have a real drink and a good talk before dinner tonight. The old man will announce it at dinner next week, I expect. He seemed pretty pleased with the news when I told him."

James pondered this. Silently. He wanted to be alone with his thoughts. He knew inwardly that he had to take the news without showing his feelings, and he wondered what he would or could say to Francesca if they met later. Charles left, and James stared sightlessly, but not thoughtlessly. Sidmouth. He tried so hard, but could not remember.

4

Francesca's Shame

THE NEXT DAY STARTED QUIETLY ENOUGH with all the house party following their chosen pursuits. Charles and Sir Marshall were out "tramping" as Charles had put it, but Richardson Trevanion was feeling very unwell, even sick, and was unable to go with them, so he stayed indoors. Lady Eleanor was ensconced in her private sitting room from which she emerged from time to time to give orders to Dorcas about the food and how she wanted it that night. James decided that he needed to be alone so he went for a solitary walk down to the river, and took with him a set of sketching materials. He always went there when he wanted to be alone and he had found over the years that a good way to find solace was to listen to the sound of the running water, and perhaps sketch. You had to concentrate to do that well, and that would both ease his grave concerns about Charles' news, and wipe out the sense of loss he felt.

From her room, Francesca looked down and saw James leave the house with his sketch book, and she decided to follow him. She wanted to talk to him in private. She dressed carefully and put on stout shoes, and a sensible skirt. She thought it might be cold so she took a cloak with her as well, and she followed James. At first she did not quite know for sure where he was going, so she had to be a bit circumspect in order that James would not know he was being followed, particularly when she was in sight from the house, but she soon realised that it must be the river they were heading for, so she was able to hang back. First James, and then Francesca, were seen by Dorcas on one of her necessary trips to the game larder, and she wondered where they were going so obviously not together.

When Francesca reached the river she found James sitting on a large flat boulder near the water. He was not sketching at all. His sketch book was unnoticed on his lap. He was just looking fixedly at the flow past him of the rather reddish-tinged, fast-swirling water. She did not speak, so as not to startle him, and sat down near him, on the same flat rock. She felt impelled to tell him what Charles had done when they went for that walk. But she did not know how to start. And if she did not tell him, there was no one else she could tell. She could never tell her father. She said nothing. She could not find the right words. She thought she might not even know them.

Unconsciously aware of her arrival, James eventually glanced sideways at her, almost secretively, to see if he could get any idea why she might have apparently followed him to the river. But all he saw was someone who seemed to be struggling both to say something, and with her emotions. He did not in truth know what he saw, but even as he realised that, he knew a disaster of some sort had overtaken Francesca. He gently reached out a hand and very lightly touched the hem of her sleeve. Silently. Almost shyly. That calm and quiet act seemed to break her inability to speak. She visibly steeled herself. The dam burst.

"Oh James. I am desperate, so very desperate. Very foolishly I went for a walk with Charles. In the woods. We were all alone. Charles talked sweetly enough at first, but then he started to make vulgar suggestions, and when I tried to stop him talking that way, he said it was all right as we were going to be married and if he couldn't talk to me like that who could he talk to. I tried to shut him up, but he became very insistent. He was saying he had to make sure of me, as he said he thought you were 'sniffing around' as he put it. He said we were to be married and I would just have to accept it. He was very brutal and coarse in the way he spoke. And then he suggested we sit and have a rest. I did not know what to do, as I knew that his intentions were alarming, so I said the ground was damp, and I didn't want to sit. Then he just grabbed me. He pulled me down onto the ground, and he forced himself onto me. He forced me. Literally." Her croak-laden voice gave out. She was hoarse and only semi coherent. She started to cry. Her shoulders hunched, protectively, and she crouched, bent over forwards, with her small hands tightly clasped together in her lap, sobbing.

"Oh my God!" James jumped up as if shot, his sketch book falling to the ground. His arms automatically reached out gently towards Francesca, but he did not touch her.

"I can't say it. I am ashamed of what he did. He, well, he made love to me physically, against my will. He violated me. I cried and I shouted, really loudly, but he would not stop. It seemed to last forever. I never imagined anything like this. And it hurt, it hurt so much, it was so painful, and no one came when I was shouting. Out loud, and no one helped me. Someone really must have heard, but no one came. Then he said I had agreed to marry him, which I had not, I did not, I really truly did not, and he was so pleased with himself. He said I would never have let him make love to me if I had not agreed to marry him. He said he would never, could never, have forced me to do anything I did not want. That was all untrue. I never agreed to anything, let alone to marry him. He could not see what he had done was so ghastly. He did not seem to see how awful he had been. It was such a mess, and I feel so dirty. Since then I have been washing. I keep on washing myself, but I am dirty. I can't tell you how much I have washed."

She was sobbing as she told her story, great gulping sobs which shook her whole body convulsively. James took a step to her, clutched at her, and somewhat awkwardly put his arms around her. She was sobbing less loudly now, in a dry and harsh gulping sort of way.

"My God, what was he doing? What was he thinking? He told me only yesterday that you had agreed to marry him. That can't be right." But even as he said it, he knew that it was right, that she had been raped, and that despite that, she was going to marry Charles. "He can't love you. If he did he would not have done anything like that. He must be mad. It is madness. You can't marry him after that. It is too awful." He ranted on, he was distraught for her.

"But I have no choice. No choice at all." Her voice cracked. She was crying now. "Papa has agreed to the match, and anyway it will be announced to one and all at the dinner party next week. Oh, dear God."

She released herself from James' half grasp, and moved a little way away along the bank. She dabbed in vain at her eyes. Her breath came in great dry, gulping sobs.

"I have no choice as Papa has agreed, and he says I must marry Charles. He says Charles is a good match, and I will get to love him one day. He says Charles will have money, and the title. I will have none of course. Lewis has spent pretty much all that Papa had. He says I must marry Charles. He said he did not love Mama at first, so I shall be like her, or something, if I do this."

James was completely appalled. He did not know what to do or say. He moved to Francesca and clumsily putting his arms around her again, he clutched her to him, and reaching, stroked the back of her neck. He did not know what to do, or to say. He was lost.

They stayed that way, holding each other for mutual comfort, saying nothing, for a long time. They both knew the dream of possibilities they had half thought of was over before it had even begun. Only a few nights earlier they had talked, and he had thought that Francesca was so perfect, so like the girl he had always imagined, he had almost thought he loved her. For a short time, which in future he would never be able to forget, he had thought that this girl was the person he wanted to spend his life with. The air around them was completely still.

5

The Dinner Party

LADY ELEANOR WENT TO GREAT TROUBLE over the setting for the formal dinner party at which the engagement was to be announced. That is to say, after her husband had told her what she thought was the very best news she had had for a very long time, and indeed the successful culmination of her plans, she had lost no time in ensuring that the dinner party, was to be absolutely perfect. She hoped to herself that she would make her husband proud of her arrangements on such an important night for the family.

Sir Marshall in the meantime was concerned to say a few words to Richardson Trevanion and make sure his after dinner speech struck just the right note. He had a gold signet ring he planned to give to Charles when he was alone with him after the announcement, as a symbol, he thought, of a family tradition. It was a ring that had been in the family for many years, plain gold with the family crest, a sheaf of corn with a motto, on it. Nothing fancy, but special to the family and himself, thought Sir Marshall privately.

In the dining room much heavy large oak furniture was along the walls. In particular behind the chair in which Sir Marshall always sat, there was a sideboard which was so tall it almost reached the cornice, with three mirrors set in the elaborately carved and swirled rear upstand, and in front and below the central mirror was a convex shelf with a large silver cup standing on it. The cup had been awarded to Harry, who had in turn given it to Sir Marshall, as Harry said he did not have a suitable place to display it in his rooms in London. It had been originally given to Harry by the Indian Mercantile Community at Selangor on the occasion when a horse of his called Romano had won a race. Two handsome silver gilt wine coolers bearing Sir Charles' crest sat one to each side in front of their own smaller mirrors, at a lower level. The fireplace matched the sideboard in style and was surmounted by a mantel which had a three-piece garniture of onyx and bronze, the decoration mainly consisting of swirling drapery around half clad angels, and a central clock.

"I would like to make an announcement." Sir Marshall was on his feet at the end of the table. He was a big man, a laughing, smiling red-faced man then in a mood made mellow by good wine and food, with family and friends around him. At his earlier request, the ladies had not withdrawn in view of what he said was his wish to make this very special announcement.

His cigar had a long ash which threatened the table, which bore the remains of the meal and the half-drunk glasses of port and wine. It was a glittering display in the light of the magnificent four-branched silver candelabra (with five brightly burning candles) in the middle of the table.

He paused, modestly. He stuck a thumb in the side pocket of his gold-coloured waistcoat. "I am a very proud man today and I hope you will all agree when you have heard what I have to say that I have good reason to be so. My elder son Charles, who you all know has just left Cambridge, has today confirmed to me that he is ready to come into the family business and to join me as a partner. I am changing the name of the business, and in future it will be called Duffield and Sons. I say that because perhaps there will be another generation along in due course. And maybe when James has completed his degree next year, and got over his present artistic phase, and settled down a bit, we shall all work together." He paused, theatrically.

"The firm is a rich, thriving one, and for the present the firm will manage well enough with the two of us in harness. I know," he continued before anyone could interrupt, "that you will all want to know why I am so sure that Charles is ready for partnership now, and the answer is that he has recently shown me a sound touch of maturity that is, I am sure, fundamental to his nature, and of which I am, I think, justly proud. He has proposed marriage to Francesca, and she, of course, has accepted him."

The guests around the dinner table were silent. The way he had put it was so crass. His friends were surprised, and not a little in doubt as to what they should say, or even how they should react. Someone thumped the table with the palm of his hand, but there was no general outcry.

Francesca looked down at the table in front of her. She, like everyone else, had heard the silence. She understood it. She was concentrating on trying not to show emotion. She knew she could not look up at Charles who was beside her, or James, and certainly not at Sir Marshall, her soon to be father-in-law. Her own father sat across the table from her, and he could see how troubled she was. But he was an old and very sad, lonely widower, and all he could really feel was shame at what he now understood he had done in agreeing to the engagement. He saw it was so very hard for Francesca. He half rose to his feet. But Sir Marshall was not to be interrupted, and so Richardson had no choice but to sit down again. Harry Vardon watched what was happening around the table and he saw sadness and concern where there should have been happiness. He could see that James was far away in his thoughts.

Sir Marshall continued a little hurriedly almost as if he had expected to be interrupted, and had not been. "Yes, yes, as I say, Francesca is a lovely young lady and I have no doubt at all in my mind that she and Charles make a lovely, not to say a handsome, couple, and that they will have a lovely young family soon enough to carry on the family name." He paused.

Harry Vardon stood up suddenly, and said into the silence, "I think the news is wonderful. Come on everyone, we must drink a toast to the happy couple." Another pause. The room was quiet, Sir Marshall was still on his feet and no one made a move to join him or Harry Vardon.

Richardson Trevanion levered himself upright, and raised a hand clutching his glass. "Of course we must. Of course. Francesca and Charles, I give you Francesca and Charles."

Sir Marshall leant forward and picked his glass up. "My friends, I give you Charles and Francesca," he almost shouted, in a rich, slurred voice.

There was then a general chatter and noise. The shock had broken, as the dinner guests all gradually stood, and amid general cries of "Charles and Francesca", and "Francesca and Charles", all celebrated the happy union of the two young and handsome people.

Harry remained on his feet. He tapped his glass, and Sir Marshall and the other guests gradually sat back down. "Friends," said Harry, "I know you are all friends here, and you all know the young couple in your own ways. For my part I think they will make a delightful, happy, and welcome match. Both are talented and intelligent, both are good looking and blessed with grace and charm. And we are all fortunate to have such a good, kind, generous person as Lady Eleanor to host such a magnificent dinner tonight specifically to celebrate such a happy union. As guests, all our thanks are due to her for enabling us to join together to wish the young couple good hunting through the wilds of marriage. The ball was highly notable for the superb organisation Lady Eleanor put into it. And of course the enjoyment of tonight and the ball are only exceeded by the glorious tidings of the match which has just been announced. Sadly for me, I personally will not be here long enough to see the actual marriage as I have a passage booked to take me back to the Cape in a few days' time, but the haste of my departure does not make my good wishes for the young couple, or my thanks and gratitude to Lady Eleanor, which I am sure you all share, any the less sincere."

He sat back down a little quickly, and Lady Eleanor, who had indeed been very gratified by what Harry had said, found her pleasure in those remarks much dimmed by her husband's, as she thought, drunkenness. She hoped that not too many people thought he was drunk. She noticed that Richardson Trevanion was silent, looking rather wistful she thought. And she saw that Francesca still looked down at the table, and realised that strangely she was not talking to Charles, despite having been placed next to him. Indeed now that she came to think of it she realised that Francesca had not talked much, if at all, to him. She hoped that Francesca was not going to be difficult. James too was silent.

As a general murmur of conversation resumed, James got to his feet, standing rather stiffly, nodded to Sir Marshall and turned and left the room, saying nothing. Harry watched his departure and after a few minutes got up, and also with a nod to Sir Marshall, he followed James.

They met up, inevitably as young men do, in the smoking room. "My God," said James. "It's all so awful I do not know if I can bear it. She is so young, and lovely. She is so desperate and so unhappy, and she has told me that Charles has raped her. It was plainly the truth." He continued despite a sharp, strangled outburst from Harry. "I should not have told you that. I know. I know. But you are going away, back to the Cape, and you will not have to endure what is soon to come. How can we sit and watch it all? What can we do?"

"Look, I had not heard of this before. Obviously. And Charles must be mad to have done that. But I cannot help. Really. And you must remember that you and she are not a couple, and you never will be. You have only just met, for goodness sake. I am sad for you, and very sorry indeed for her. But I cannot stay and do anything to help anyone. I have no choice at all but to take the morning train from Exeter up to London, and then I sail to the Cape a few days later. You know I have a very tight timetable. My passage is all paid up in advance so I have no choice about this. I cannot afford not to sail. So, yes, I shall miss the nuptial celebrations, sadly, but I expect you as a man to bear up and to support your parents even if you can't support your brother. I will write to you when I get to the Cape, but I am not coming home. You must bear up. You will certainly not help Francesca if you show how much this proposed marriage hurts you. She, in particular, is going to need your support. She will need sympathy, she will need your strength. I will write to you from the Cape of course and get a letter back by the next ship. I can't say when you will get it, but I will write."

James sat and pondered the chance that had led to him meeting Francesca, the perfect girl, and then finding out that he could not pursue his interest in her. It seemed as if he had had a golden chance, and then ill fortune had taken the cup from his lips. How could he bear to see her marry his own brother?

In all the excitement of the evening, as he thought of it, and in the light of his having drunk too much as lady Eleanor thought of it, Sir Marshall quite forgot to give the ring to Charles. When he realised this to be so, as he went to bed, he thought another night would do just as well.

6

Harry's Invitation

Harry's voyage from London in the Zenobia was very quick, forty-six days to be precise. The barque had been built for speed and not so much for cargo as for the passage of travellers. As a result she was comfortable and well appointed by the standards of the day, and Harry was an experienced traveller. At the Cape the bay was very busy with eight ships anchored, and, knowing as a result that many people would be looking for somewhere to stay, on landing Harry hurriedly made straight for Mrs Parke's Hotel at No. 1 Heerengracht, at the corner with Strand Street. A well-run little hotel, and very English. It was ultra-modern with gas lighting in all public rooms, and even in all the best bedrooms which were reserved for special guests, it had long had hot and cold running water in the kitchen and several other rooms which Mrs Parke called bathrooms, enabling guests to have a bath in private, at any time of the day, rather than having to go to one of the three old bathing establishments in the town. He noted that the road was still very bad, and very muddy, but much better than when it had been little more than a ditch. The canal alongside the road was full of all sorts of foul-smelling effluent. In fact, thought Harry, he would need a room away from the canal because of the all-pervasive foul smell.

Having settled in, he soon learnt from Mrs Parke herself (who was an inveterate gossip) that Cape Town was still, after all this time, in a great state of turmoil, apparently caused by the Anti-Convict Association, and the depression that had followed the successful strike called by the Association against the landing of convicts at the Cape, as ordered by London. This had been wildly unpopular and of course the Boers had, said Mrs Parke, noticed the success of the Association's strike in which they had perforce joined. They had been opposed to the emanciptation of the slaves when it had happened, and having lost their dominance of trade and politics, and having been forced to accept that blacks would probably be allowed to vote if they had enough income, the Boers were in no mood to be at all friendly to the English. They were at serious loggerheads with the new English missionaries who tried to convert and educate the blacks, pointing out that their own preachers were teaching them completely opposed ideas. "Society," opined Mrs Parke, "is very tense, and not likely to heal any time soon. Mynheer and his vrouw are thoroughly alienated from the English and likely to stay that way." The Boers in the north were already a fighting force and very troublesome despite having been worsted at the battle of Boomplaats. "A lot of Boers, particularly in country areas, are moving north, out of the Colony, beyond the control of our Governor, they are," said Mrs Parke, "harassing travellers and robbing them, and the Colonial Government is doing nothing about it." She predicted more trouble, but then she always did.

Harry, being a military man himself, was inclined to take what Mrs Parke told him with a pinch of salt. He had seen for himself as he walked up from the waterfront the thriving nature of the Cape, and no doubt others would have plenty of opportunity to profit from the Boers' departure. Meanwhile, knowing that a good crowd of fellow officers, many of whom he knew, were in the Cape for the sport, he thought to himself that he might well join up with one or more of them and hunt north towards the Great Lake, if it existed. But first he would need to equip himself with all he needed for such a trek of about six or seven months, maybe even longer.

Servants, drivers, trek leaders, cooks, and a whole host of men would have to be hired at the going rate. And then wagons would be needed – perhaps he should have two – with their oxen and spares of course, and Harry knew just where to go to hire and buy all these. In addition, his agents were Hamilton Ross and Co, and he knew young Hunter Hodgson of that company well, and did most of his commercial trading and private banking through them. But of course, for trek equipment and goods he would have to look elsewhere and buy direct for himself, as he usually did, but being inclined to be a touch lazy, Harry thought he would leave it for a day or two.

The critical need was for money first, gold, and plenty of change, and guns and ammunition suitable for trading with natives, should that be required. He would need the coin for payment to the many Boer farmers for food, forage for his stock and occasional accommodation. His mind wandered on about all the things he would need. Before setting out from the hotel, he started to make a list. Trade goods were essential in large quantities, their use ranging from presents for chiefs through whose land he would pass to paying native guides. Everything from spades, whips, casks, thousands of bullets, lead, powder, locks and surveying equipment to a good medicine chest would be essential. He would need a lot of good brass and copper wire; crates and crates of mixed glass beads; chests of tea, and at least three sacks of coffee. The list, when he had finished writing it down, covered two and a half large sheets of paper, and Harry set out as soon as he reasonably could to start on his purchases.

It was while he was at Hamilton Ross' offices dealing with the tricky question of receiving his pay during his already much extended furlough that he first thought of James. Precisely why he did so he could not afterwards recall, maybe it was the guilty realisation that he had promised to write to James, but he suddenly got the idea that he would make a capital companion on a possible hunting trek into the interior, and what was more he was a good artist (Harry had seen some of his work at Highsteignton just before the ball), so James could save him the embarrassment of trying to sketch things for himself. Harry was proposing to travel deep into the interior, which was largely unknown, and he would be travelling by ready reckoning and without any map. He would need to make maps as he made his way. He would see sights previously unseen by anyone, except natives of course, and he would need to record what he saw if his journal was to be any good as a publishable affair. James would be excellent as an artist, a companion and friend, and Harry resolved at once that he would write to James the instant he got back to the hotel.

But it was not to be as easy as that. When Harry got there, he found a party had been started in the parlour, and Mrs Parke had invited a few friends round, as she put it, to celebrate Harry's arrival back in the colony. But they had obviously expected him back quite a lot sooner than he got there, because he saw some of the guests were already pink in the face and enjoying Mrs Parke's hospitality rather well. Among them were Mynheer Adriaan Beck and his vrouw, with their daughter Christina. A very typical Boer couple, thought Harry. He was broad and a bit fat, and she was shorter and fatter. They were well dressed in very fashionable clothes and so must be quite well off, thought Harry. He found himself trapped in a corner with Adriaan Beck, and quickly decided that Adriaan was pretty much a boor, and that his views on politics and religion were not ones that Harry could support. He made a mental note that Adriaan said he was going up to Bloemfontein to stay for a while with some relatives who had already trekked north, but thought no more about it.

When Harry eventually managed to free himself from Adriaan's conversation he caught up with Mrs Parke and asked her why Adriaan was there. Mrs Parke said Adriaan was a general merchant, and that Adriaan's business was likely to be for sale soon as, despite appearances, he seemed to have run out of money; maybe he had lost too much money opposing the

Anti-Convict Association, and his trade had not recovered. And, Mrs Parke said, she wished to be on good terms with Adriaan so as to put herself in the running to buy his business if he did really have to sell in due course.

Harry was distinctly unimpressed with that remark, and having excused himself shortly after, went to his room and composed a letter to James. He had been thinking about James a lot on the voyage out, and he now decided he wanted to try and help his friend, and was now convinced that he should invite James to come to the Cape and join him in his proposed trip north. He knew that James was disturbed by the forthcoming marriage, and it might help him if he was away for that. Harry wrote:

> *Parke's Hotel,*
> *Heerengracht,*
> *Cape Town.*
>
> *My Dear James,*
> *I know that I left you a bit down in the mouth back in Devon, because of you being sweet on that pretty girl, but as you see I am safely arrived back here, and am in the process of starting to get supplies ready for a good long hunting trip north, possibly towards the fabulous Great Lake I told you about. It will take quite some time for everything to be ready, but I do not mind delay as the garrison at the castle is strong, and there are a lot of friends from my old regiment here on furlough like myself. So I have a good crowd of fellows around and there is plenty of amusement I can assure you. Life is very gay. Races and hunting, and plenty of sport, and the social life here is quite delightful. Which brings me to my point.*
>
> *Why do you not come and join me here? I would be highly delighted if you would join my proposed trip. I am starting to get some necessary purchases in hand for the journey, and although it will take about fifty days or so on ship for you to get here, I will*

happily wait for you to arrive. If you did not want to travel inland, you could of course come just for the social life here at the Cape. It is pretty marvellous after all, and I can introduce you to any number of officers, and what with them and their families, you would not want for amusement, I can assure you.

I think I am right in saying that if you look about, you could easily get a passage on a well-found ship like the Lady Flora, or the Agincourt under Captain Hyde. I can personally recommend him to you. You can of course stay here with me at this hotel.

I am, yours affectionately,
Harry

7

The Acceptance

JAMES RECEIVED HARRY'S LETTER, and having gone to his bedroom to read it quietly on his own, decided to take time to think about this suggestion very carefully. He was certainly disturbed by his brother's engagement. The marriage had been officially announced so he knew that it was now definite and would go ahead, apparently soon. He would have to make the best of having Francesca as a sister-in-law, and therefore within close but emotionally difficult distance. But he liked the idea of the life in the colony as he imagined it to be from Harry's letter, better than another year of study at university, and after more than two hours' cogitation went to the library to see if Sir Marshall had any books or papers about the country that would tell him what it was like, and perhaps help with the decision he felt he had to make. Strangely, he came across a bound copy of the *Cape Gazette* which was full of official and semi-official information and news. The volume must have been one of those Sir Marshall had bought as part of a job lot. The book was printed in two languages: English, of course, and another, which James assumed to be Boer. What he read showed him a lively society with exciting goings on and a vibrancy which he thought sounded so different to anything he knew, anywhere, that its very foreignness was attractive.

Charles had been pressing James to join him in a trip to London to try and find a house for the soon to be married couple, but James could think of nothing he would like to do less, and so the idea of being out of the way at the time of the marriage, as he would be if he went to the colony, certainly appealed to him. He knew that he could square his absence with Charles, he assumed Francesca would understand the potential difficulty he was avoiding, for her sake of course, and that meant that he would only need permission from his father to absent himself, particularly as it would mean leaving Cambridge a year early, and so without a degree. If he could, he needed to reach an agreement with his father about an allowance. James had very little money of his own, but he thought he could get a letter of credit if his father would sign to guarantee it. That, thought James, would see him right. And if some of Harry's wilder tales were to be believed he might be able to make some money hunting. Accordingly he decided to accept the invitation, if permitted by his father so to do.

When James, after a hunt around the house, ran Sir Marshall to earth in the smoking room, he was fortunate, for Sir Marshall was in an expansive and happy mood. He listened attentively to what James said, including about giving up university, read the letter from Harry, several times, said he would think about it carefully. He did not tell James of course but he had in truth been on the receiving end of a suggestion from Lady Eleanor that James might be difficult about the wedding, and might even be embarrassing. Although he did not understand that, he did understand that this idea of Harry's for James to go to the Cape might be the answer to his own personal problem of how to deal with Lady Eleanor's request.

So it was that he went and found Lady Eleanor who was standing in front of his desk in the study, idly moving his papers around again, he thought testily. Nevertheless he very happily told her what James had asked. She took it with quite her usual stoicism, and saw at once that this was the way out of what she thought of as her difficulties. Indeed only the poor dear queen, as she put it, had more trouble with her family than she, Lady Eleanor, did. The least of their concerns was that James would be leaving university a year early, and with no degree therefore. They did not even consider this worth discussing.

"I think that we should make a special gesture to James before he goes to the colony," said Lady Eleanor. "Make him a special gift of something or other. We need to make him feel that he will be missed at the wedding. We have to say that we only let him go with a heavy heart and all that sort of thing, but we realise that he must have his freedom. We shall miss him, and greatly so, and that it is a real sacrifice on our part for him to go."

While Sir Marshall appeared to be thinking about this, Lady Eleanor hurried on. "You will have to give him an allowance of course, but not too much. You know how to be generous to just the right level, and make sure you make it clear to him that when he comes back he must repay what he spends."

"I could give him my gold signet ring," suggested Sir Marshall cautiously, deliberately ignoring her last remark, "The one with the crest on it. As you know, I was going to give it to Charles, and I told him so, but in all the excitement of the evening they got engaged, I quite forgot about it. But I imagine that should make it even more valuable to James if I give it to him instead. I could give him my fob of course, but the ring would be better I think. We could get the servants together and make it a special occasion. We could have a glass or two of champagne to celebrate the trip, and I will, as you say, offer him a decent allowance while he is away."

"Do not make that too generous," said Lady Eleanor.

"I was thinking it should be about £500 per annum by two equal half-yearly tranches? For, maybe, two years to start with?"

"That seems rather too much to me, but you be the judge," replied his wife doubtfully. Sir Marshall was standing beside his wife and looked at his desk on which was his silver inkwell, on the ledge of which lay his gold pen which he had had engraved with his name and office address at Clifford's Inn. The pen had his initials carved into the bloodstone seal at the end which he used to press into hot sealing wax on legal deeds when at the office. He wondered how many cheques he had written with that pen to bail Charles out.

As they finished talking Charles came into the room, having carefully knocked first. He looked at them quizzically with raised eyebrows, as if asking them what they were talking about. So they explained to him about James' scheme for a trip to meet Harry at the Cape.

"I wanted him to be my best man," objected Charles. "He can't be best man if he is in South Africa, but I have not told Francesca." He paused. "I suppose I can ask one of the fellows from Cambridge to step in, instead of James – there should not be too much trouble in getting someone else." A small disdainful tone had crept into his voice.

"Well, that's all right then," said Sir Marshall. "I know I said some time ago that you would have the family ring when you got married, but your mother feels, and I agree with her, that we should give something rather special to James as a sort of present before he goes, and I thought the ring would be a good idea, if you do not mind of course."

Charles was silent. Then, "Father, you did promise it to me, and I would be rather disappointed if you gave it to him. Could you not give him something else instead?"

"Well, if you can suggest an alternative then I will consider it, but until you do come up with something else, I think the ring it will have to be."

"Are you going to give him an allowance?" asked Charles.

"Yes, of course. But not as large as yours, and not I think so large as to mean that there is no need for a present as well. The ring is not that valuable, it just has some sentimental value to me. My father gave it to me when we got married years ago. That is all," said Sir Marshall.

Charles looked at them. He was unhappy with the suggestion it was clear, but he realistically assessed the chance of changing their minds as low, so he said, "Well. If that is to be it, then I think the ring is a jolly good idea, and I am sure he will treasure it and keep it very safe. You know how much he respects and admires you both, and he would do nothing that would cause you any grief."

"We thought a presentation, to announce his projected trip, would be a nice idea," said Lady Eleanor. "Of course, you must be with us, it will be a celebration after all. It will have to be soon, as obviously we don't know what his detailed plans are, I mean, with regard to sailing and so on. In due course I will go and talk to Dorcas about the food, and you Marshall, must go and talk to James about likely dates of sailings and so on. We need to get this fixed. You will have to arrange with the London and Westminster Bank about his allowance, and I suggest you go into that telegraph company in Exeter and get them to telegraph the bank." Having announced a course of conduct for everyone for the immediate future, Lady Eleanor decided that she had better get some fresh air and that she would walk to the Home Farm. It was not far, but she thought she ought to blow the cobwebs away. Then she would tackle Dorcas.

Sir Marshall decided he would find James and have a good long talk with him about this trip he wanted to make, and tell him about the plans for a small celebration. The announcement was to be at a low-key affair, not like the dinner party, decided Lady Eleanor, just for family really, although she did of course now include Francesca and her father as family. She decided that they would have it in the hall, just a glass of champagne all round, and a speech by Sir Marshall of course. She thought that what she called simplicity would be the right touch.

Sir Marshall, as he had decided, caught up with James as he was about to go out. He explained that he wanted to talk his request through with him, and they both went into the library. When they were seated Sir Marshall started.

"James, my boy, we shall be very sorry to see you go of course but, not to beat about the bush, we have been thinking a lot about you at this time, what with all that is happening here, and at this stage of your life you must have, if you want it of course, a real chance to spread your wings. So, although it is obviously a terribly hard wrench for your mother and I, we think that in all honesty if you want to go, you should be able to go. It will be a shame not to finish at Cambridge, but never mind that. You would be with Harry of course, and he is a very sound gentleman and will be able to show you the ropes, and all that. I am sure that he will have a lot of good advice as to where to go and what to see and he is so very experienced a traveller. And Sir Roderick Murchison, the President of the Royal Geographical Society, is an old client of mine. I dare say that if you ask him he can give you very valuable advice. He seems a very forthright gentleman, and what he does not know about Africa is not worth knowing."

James inwardly reflected that his father knew very little about Harry in fact, far less than he did, but now all he wanted was to get away, so he decided to keep very quiet while Sir Marshall went on.

"So," continued his father, "we want you to have enough money to travel reasonably comfortably and I shall arrange for funds to be made available to you at the Cape through the agency of Hamilton Ross and Co. They have a branch in Idol Street in London and I will pay in precisely five hundred pounds there, every year, by two equal half-yearly payments in June and December, and you will be able to draw on that from their Cape Town branch when you get there. That should be enough I would think, but if you need more I hope you will get them to let me know and I can send some more. Of course you will not need to repay me when you are back in this country, and there need be no great hurry about coming back either." Sir Marshall, having expounded, leant back in his chair and regarded James with that sort of close look he used to watch clients he did not quite trust. On the receiving end, James felt very uncomfortable.

He realised his father was in effect bribing him handsomely to go away. He knew that whatever his father said they were not going to miss him, and he felt very isolated. Very alone. Why his parents felt like that about him, as they clearly did, he had no idea. His father would in fact want him to pay back every penny, he knew, and make him very uncomfortable if he didn't. He was equally determined that whatever his father said now, he would pay it all back. He just wanted to be gone right now.

"And, before I forget, I want you to have a personal present from me and your mother, to keep by you safely. We want you to have the family signet ring my father gave me. This one." He took the ring off his little finger. He lifted it up, and showed it to James, who did of course know it anyway. He had seen it hundreds of times. "We thought that it would remind you of your family, of your home, and all that. Do not lose it of course, it will be a symbol of our love for you, and it is precious for that reason, if for no other. It has the family crest on it, which is the same as that of the Yorkshire Duffields."

James shifted uncomfortably in his seat. He knew he was expected to show gratitude, and of course he was grateful for the money. But he knew from the past that he had been required to say thank you too many times when he did not really feel grateful, for it now to mean anything. He would look after the ring, of course he would.

"Father, I am so grateful to you and mother for your generosity. I really am. And the ring. I am quite tongue-tied with all this. Thank you. I shall of course repay you on my return, I know you said that I do not need to repay you, but I will, and you can have the ring back on my return as well, if you want it. While I am away I shall treasure it as a memento of you all and keep it very safe, I can assure you." He paused for a long moment, and Sir Marshall waited through the gathering silence with a mild strain on his limited patience. James felt like a small schoolboy.

"Father, there is one other thing I must ask. Coleman knows that I may be going to the Cape. I told him all about it this morning, and he went straight off and told his son John. They both know Harry of course. If I go, as you have now given me permission to do, John wants to come to the Cape with me and act in any way he usefully can. Of course he is employed here by you as an under-gardener, and he would need your permission to leave your employment without giving notice. I hope that you will also be able to agree with this as he has apparently set his heart on it. I heard him telling Dorcas about the possible voyage this morning, and that he was hoping to go with me. So perhaps he may leave, and come with me too?"

Sir Marshall looked at James with some concern. James was apparently trying to enlarge the permission he had just been given, but, pondered Sir Marshall, maybe John going with him might be an advantage as John would surely write home to his father. So even if James did not write, they would still know what was going on. Maybe he should let James take John with him? But he did not let his thoughts appear. Instead he said, "It is up to Coleman of course, if he agrees then I certainly have no objection; in fact, I think it would do the boy good. That boy is too dependent on his father, to my way of thinking, and a good slice of life away from his father could well be beneficial to the boy. Yes, if Coleman agrees, of course he may go with you."

8

Farewell Presentation

THE FAMILY, with Francesca and her father, gathered in the hall before dinner, and the servants were all present as well. Coleman handed round glasses of champagne for everyone including the servants, and they gradually formed a rough circle at the foot of the stairs. John was there shyly towards the back, in a group with McGregor the head gardener and Rowland Philips the boot boy. Dorcas was towards the side near the kitchen door, largely because she wanted to be able to nip back out with her maids of course, as soon as she could, because the dinner which she had left cooking in the range needed watching. There was a low subdued chatter as the well-forecast announcement was discussed.

Coleman struck the big circular bronze gong hanging on the wall against two crimson silken ropes, and gradually the medley of voices fell silent. Sir Marshall moved and stood squarely on the second step from the bottom of the stairs. His black tie emphasised the gleam of his starched and ruffled shirt, and its three gold studs on the front glistened. The evening light was dim and the oil lamps which had long been lit shone brightly on the assembled people who all looked expectantly at Sir Marshall. It was cold despite the log fire burning in the grate under the gilt clock. Argos, the old dog, lay apparently asleep in front of the fire.

James looked around for Francesca and saw her, with a downcast look, standing between her father and Charles. She was wearing a long dark wine-coloured dress, almost black, thought James, as if she was in mourning. She looked extremely pale. He wondered if she had been crying, perhaps. Then he realised that such a thought was intrusive and selfish, and he would have to take care of another now, John, not just himself. He would not have time for his previous cares and passions. He would have no time for that in what lay ahead. He thought his mind was seeing two possible futures. Sadly they were divergent futures. And he knew his feelings for Francesca must not be allowed to rule his life. He understood that they were reducing, not in importance but in immediacy, and instead the future with its dangers and adventures at the Cape was becoming coloured in his mind, and outweighed his former preoccuation, almost obsession, he now realised. She had decided on Charles, despite what Charles had done, and James had no answer to that. He was almost anaesthetised by his thoughts, and only dimly realised that people were looking at him strangely, intrigued by his apparent silent introspection. In particular, Charles was staring at him with a sort of lop-sided grin, but whether that was in triumph, or concern, James did not know. His reverie was interrupted by his father who coughed for everyone's attention.

"Friends!" cried Sir Marshall in a suitably impressive and almost formal tone for such a gathering. "Friends, I am delighted to say that we have very exciting news about James and his plans. He is going off to the Cape Colony, probably quite soon once he has completed his preparations here in England. Once there, he will meet up with Harry Vardon, you all know him of course, and together they will go travelling.

"And James is not the only one of us going. John has asked if he can join James in this exciting trip of a lifetime, and Coleman agrees that he can, and so do we as well. So he is going with James, and the two of them will be off very soon."

As he said this Sir Marshall took his left hand out of his pocket and took off the signet ring. He looked at James, directly.

"James, you are off on a certainly very exciting and maybe even dangerous trip, and I want you to have something to remember us by while you are so far away. My father gave me this gold signet ring which had belonged to his father, and I want you to have it, and take it as a remembrance of us while you are away. Keep it safe now, won't you? Don't go losing it, or selling it just because it is gold, or anything silly like that. It's part of our family history. But most important of all we all want the two of you to come back safe and sound, and thrill us all with your tales of wild travel." Sir Marshall stopped as if he realised that he actually meant what he was saying.

There was a smattering of applause. Charles shouted out that they were to "have a good trip" and one of the two kitchen maids giggled. Charles had long been the favourite with the maids, hence Dorcas' concern.

But James' thoughts were no longer under his own control. His mind raced, and ahead he saw with sudden clarity that his life was being shatteringly divided, as a stone thrown into water divides it. Water, cloudy water, like the river where he had so recently sat with Francesca. He saw that water again in his mind's eye. He relived that brief moment. But she was inevitably receding into the past now, and he thought he might never see her again. He knew he would never feel like that about anyone else, ever. He knew that the almost inescapable outcome of their separation was that his memories of her would fade with time, not out of loss of his feelings, nor because hers would fade either, but because it seemed to him to be inevitable that life would wash over them both, drowning their feelings for each other. He was disassociated from what he was saying. He heard himself speak.

"Thank you, father for the gift of this trip, and for the gift of the ring. I shall keep it safe, do not worry. I shall not sell it or do anything silly. It is very generous of you and mother to agree to our going, and to be so helpful, and to pay for everything. Thank you again.

"I shall miss the wedding of course and that," said James, apparently inconsequentially, "will be a big sadness, but this sudden invitation by Harry Vardon to join him is such a big chance in life that I really must take it. Obviously, I sincerely wish Charles and Francesca every good wishes for their life together. They are such a lovely couple that I can't imagine they will have anything but great happiness."

His family and everyone he had known for so long was there. Around him. He felt the isolation of his undertaking drawing him away even as he looked at them. No one noticed his mood.

"I have to go to London very soon," said James. "There is lots to organise in this country before we can go, equipment to be bought and passages to be booked, and so on. I shall be there for about a week I imagine, and John, you will join me at the docks when all is ready. We shall miss you all, and obviously we will write, but it will all take time. We will both come back eventually, and we will have lots and lots of tales to tell of great adventure."

He paused, and looked round. "Don't go away now, any of you, I want to be able to remember you all while we are away, to be able to see you all in my mind's eye." He was thinking only of Francesca as he said this. "It will be very strange, in a strange land with people we don't know, many speaking a language we don't know, but I shall think of you all, and we will not be doing anything too dangerous, I hope. So we will be safe and well. John will want to bring back some foreign souvenirs I expect, as shall I of course, and we will try not to get ill. We definitely won't be eating any strange food, John will stop that."

There was a quietness in the room as everyone listened and some seemed to read his unspoken thoughts. The dog gave a small snore, and the fire crackled. Normal peaceful home sounds thought James, but my life has now become set on a new path almost without my even making a decision. It all changes; I may never hear these familiar sounds again.

"I can go to London with you," cried Charles, "and help you with the arrangements." James thought this very doubtful at the least and he was startled at the very idea. Besides, he wanted to make a clean break and he could not do that if Charles was at his side to remind him of what he was leaving behind. So James replied, slowly, carefully choosing his words. "But Charles, you would be so bored," he laughed. "You would find it really very boring, with lots of rushing about getting ready, so there won't be much time for fun, you know." He hoped, as he spoke, that Charles would understand, but doubted that.

Crestfallen, Charles understood the unspoken rejection clearly enough, and decided that he would follow James anyway. Not on the same day of course but later, and that they would have a fine old time out together celebrating the impending departure, and ignoring the coming wedding of course. His idea of a fine time would not coincide with James' he knew, but James could be persuaded. James, Charles knew, had no lady friend and he decided that he would make sure James had a night to remember before he set sail for some distant land.

9

Preliminaries in London

JAMES ARRIVED AT PADDINGTON STATION quite early in the morning two days later. His bags were packed in so far as he had items he wanted to take from Devon, but he was travelling lightly. He was intending to collect all the clothes he would need from the house at Clapham, but he would have to make a few extra purchases first.

Once he had got a cab he made straight for the Royal Geographical Society offices. James knew he would need plenty of good advice as to what to get in order to be adequately equipped. He did not know exactly where the Society was based as it was between official offices at the time, so he went to its temporary home at the Horticultural Hall first. That was a decidedly gloomy red brick building with a liveried porter outside who appeared to be rather intimidating to James' way of thinking. Having paid off his cab with what he realised almost at once was too generous a tip, he was stopped from entering the building by this imposing person, who asked him his business. Just at that moment a tall man with perhaps military bearing was entering the building with a grand old lady on his arm. He spoke to James with a slight Scottish accent, and asked what he could do to help. Sir Roderick Murchison, although James did not know it was he of course, seemed brusque but friendly, and on James explaining that he was about to leave for the Cape to join up with Harry Vardon, Murchison said, "But my dear boy, I know Harry well. He has been to the interior several times with this lady's son, William Cotton Oswell, a very great explorer and friend of another Scot,

Dr Livingstone, and we all are looking forward to reading his next letter, and to hearing how they get on with the expedition to find the Great Lake."

"That is why I have come here," explained James. "I am off with a servant as soon as I can get a passage, but before I can go I need some help with purchase of equipment and so on. And I thought I would ask here how I should go about it."

"What do you do, young man?" asked Murchison. He adjusted his monocle so as to peer at James more closely. "And how exactly will you help Vardon and Oswell in their work? Look here young fellow, had we not better go and talk about things inside?"

"Thank you, yes. That would be better. My name is Duffield by the way, James Duffield."

"Yes, yes," the older man replied rather shortly, "and I am Roderick Murchison, the President of this Society. Now, come along inside. We do not want this lady's hat to suffer in the weather, do we?" and suiting the action to the words they all went inside, to the dismay of the porter who had thought that he was going to be interested in the conversation, but realised he would now miss it. Once inside the somewhat cramped hall a small bald man showed them obsequiously to a very small side room fronting the street they had just left, and finding a table with some comfortable armchairs around it they all sat down.

"Well, since you asked what I can do, I can help Vardon by painting, and I can shoot quite well, but I have not shot big game of course. Harry told me that he can't draw or paint, so I may be some help. He is getting the expedition together right now at the Cape and I hope to sail and join him as soon as I can get a passage. He invited me, and I want to go as soon as possible." James spoke excitedly, quickly, the words tumbling out, and Murchison looked at him and smiled thinly.

He was about to speak when Mrs Oswell leant forward. "Can you take a letter for me and give it to my son?" she asked. "Vardon will know where he is staying. I expect they play cards and yarn away till late every night anyway. They certainly used to."

James had never thought about postal services to the Cape and did not know that it was usual for passengers to take mail out with them, and put it in the Cape Town post when they landed, but he was happy to take the letter and he said so.

"And where exactly are you staying before you sail, so I can get the letter to you?" asked Mrs Oswell. James told her the Clapham address, and added that she could leave it for him at Simpsons in the Strand, if Clapham was out of her way, as they knew him well there.

"I see from that you know London," Murchison intervened. "But Mrs Oswell, his name is Duffield, and Clapham as an address tells me that his father is Sir Marshall Duffield, my attorney. I know Sir Marshall well, and he has been to my house on business many times. I would have thought that you might know the family anyway. I do not think that I have met this young man though."

"No. I don't think I do. But as you say, it is acceptable, and as James is going anyway my letter will be quite safe with him I am sure." She smiled encouragingly at James. "I must go now, Roderick," turning to Murchison, "and thank you for a very happy morning talking about all these expeditions and so on. Oh yes, and good luck with your negotiations over the possible royal charter. But perhaps I have said too much?" And with that Mrs Oswell stood, as did James and Murchison, and she left them.

"Now look here, young man," said Murchison when they were seated. "If you are going off into the wilds you will need a bit of advice, and happily we have a little leaflet printed here which I can give you which tells you what you need to take out from London and how to go about exploring. Sounds a little odd I know, but steady advice is in it, which will help you greatly. I know you will be with Vardon, and so maybe with Oswell who will tell you all, but you need to be careful of those pesky Boers. They are a damned nuisance, and quite a few of them have been making serious trouble for travellers. Robbing them and so on. But call on Moffat and then on his son-in-law Livingstone, as you head north. They are good Scots both, and will extend a warm welcome, I am sure. Both are missionaries of course, and you may like to help out at their missions when you are there, for they are all good-hearted people and very generous. They have no or very little money, so you should pay them well for their hospitality when you leave but be quiet about it, as they will be embarrassed otherwise.

"Oswell is aiming to find the mysterious Great Lake, so I should strongly suggest that you take a prefabricated boat with you. Difficult and all that, but very useful when you get there, if you ever do manage to get there, that is. To the Great Lake I mean. If there is one. I know, I know the Kalahari which you must cross first is a great desert with no water and plenty of wild animals, but if Vardon and Oswell find the lake you will need a boat to explore it, and find out its extent. The lake must be fed by a river as well, but we know nothing about it. So take a boat, as I say. Strange but good advice. And try it out first. You can do that on the Serpentine, of course. Handy, and all that. I tell everyone to do that, take a boat I mean. No one does! I suppose you could get a boat built when you are at the Cape. Oh, and make sure you take some good port with you – despite what everyone says, Livingstone is partial to a drop or two. You can get that at the Cape I am told."

He looked at James. "Have you got a good rifle?" he asked suddenly.

"Vardon said I should get the best while I am in town, perhaps at Blisset's in High Holborn, as you can't get one at the Cape," replied James. "I am going there after lunch. In fact, I have several rifles, but I am told that the new rifles he is selling now are much the best. I shall take a few pistols as well."

"Right, well you seem to have all the right ideas, and if you do just as Vardon and Oswell tell you, you will be safe and well, I can assure you. You will need up-to-date maps of course, and I must suggest the new one by John Arrowsmith as the best at the moment. It is a little detailed and he shows farms as if they are towns and villages, so that just looking at it, it may seem as if the place is hugely peopled. Which it isn't. Look, if you ask John nicely I am sure he will let you have a spare proof copy of his latest map to take with you.

"Now to lunch I think. You mentioned Simpsons in the Strand, an excellent place where they do very good beef. So, let us go there together."

With that, the young man and the experienced man of science went to Simpsons, and like a true Scot and trencherman, Murchison made very short work of a large plate of beef, rare with all the trimmings, and let the young man, an Englishman, pay. Afterwards, while still at the table, they played a short game of chess and he did not let the young man win that either. But James did not care, and thought to himself that this was all grand experience. He gave the waiter the usual tip, and looked at his ring, and thought the world was his oyster.

10

Cape Town

THE BARQUE THAT JAMES SAILED IN was called the *Lady Flora*, and arrived at Cape Town after a long, if not an almost interminable, voyage – or so it seemed to an impatient young man, although in truth it had only taken a mere forty-five days. The *Lady Flora* cautiously neared the coast at dawn, the captain having carefully followed the night-time instructions for the approach. When close to shore eventually, using a spyglass, James looked anxiously for the figure of Harry among the large crowd of what seemed like several hundreds of people adjacent to the landing jetty. John was beside him, and he was very conscious of the need to keep an eye out for John's safety.

The *Lady Flora* was the largest ship of nine waiting to discharge her passengers and goods. Among the other ships and nearest to her was a tubby little cargo cutter, and she had a team of men at work on deck. He could read the name on her stern: *The Hamilton Ross*. It was preparing to land grain in large tubs. The rigging of the ships on either side of the *Lady Flora* seemed to him like a giant skein of rope, outlined confusedly against a pale blue sky. Nearby, to the north-west, James could clearly make out an island. It was called Robben Island, he was told, where lepers eked out their lives, and he could just make out smoke rising from the chimneys on their cottages. There was a big fortress right on the shore, or almost so, to the east of the town, with high fortified walls, and James had heard what had sounded to him like bell while his ship was still well out to sea, which bell he could now see was mounted over the gateway into the fort.

On board the waiting and anchored ships all was bustle, noise and hard work. Men were taking down sails and ropes for repair and renewal following the long voyage from their last port. Carpenters were repairing decking, scuppers, bulwarks and all upper deck woodwork, and other sailors were painting hulls and stern decorations. One ship was even re-stepping a new foremast. No ship was still, or without visible, heavy manual labour.

Many small boats, manned by small men in strange conical straw hats, were making their way through the fairly lively waters between the jetty and the waiting anchored ships, like the *Lady Flora*. These boats were moving passengers and goods to and fro between the ships and the jetty. From the frequent shouts of their oarsmen calling for trade and shouting their prices they seemed to be worked by their owners, thought James.

The scene at the landing place was redolent with movement and clamour. There was a colourful, noisy, exceedingly smelly and very excited throng, unlike anything James had ever seen before. One of the most noticeable things about the scene was the smell of fish, even from a distance. Ox and bullock carts moved among the constantly shifting crowd. Gangs of men were hauling at ropes, and pulling and tugging at crates, and all kinds of goods and chattels, and he saw many sheep, horses and oxen. He learnt later that part of the area he was looking at was rightly called the Shambles. Bales of unknowable merchandise of all shapes and sizes and heights lay piled around without any apparent order. But by far the most striking aspect of the crowd to James was the fact that there were so many people of various shades of different colours; in fact he reflected that he had only ever seen one black man before, and that was a few months ago in London. He needed to explore this town.

James was excitedly impatient for his new life, as he thought of it, to begin. The long voyage had been a foretaste of life to come, and he was going to make the most of it. He would not have to always be careful to restrain himself in front of his family any longer. Now he had, or almost had, the money his father had promised him in his hand, he knew he was a young man of independent means. He intended to live life as he had not lived it before. He would be a gentleman of course, but he was going to enjoy himself. He twirled the ring on his little finger, unthinkingly.

John Coleman kept his thoughts to himself among the group of gentlemen's servants on board, but the sights he saw now were beyond his wildest imagination. London had been enough to make him realise that he might have bitten off more than he could chew in wanting to go to the Cape with James, and then the voyage as well. That had been such a strangely novel, almost frightening experience for a landlubber like him, who had never even seen the sea except at a distance. Now he was about to feel dry, firm land under him, the relief of still being alive was almost overwhelming.

James' fellow passengers were disembarking into the waiting small boats, and made a noisy jostling melee of people, some at the rail and some already in the small boats below bobbing up and down alarmingly. On board there had been a few families of immigrants, some with servants as James had, and some labourers, both men and women, journeying and, he assumed, looking for a better life. Ahead for everyone was a brief journey to the real scrum of people at the seemingly fragile little jetty. On the beach were porters and labourers waiting to grasp the people reaching the jetty, and calling for trade. It seemed general chaos. But the apparently disorganised chaos that they now faced as they landed was such that it did not seem as if it had either any possible way of untangling itself, or of passing through it to the town beyond. James, at least, knew of course he had to make for Parke's Hotel, although by what road or how he would get there he did not know, nor did he know how very close it was.

The step he had to make from the landing boat to the jetty was made more perilous by the waves where the boat waited for its passengers to land, but everyone had perforce to make it. The jetty was quite long enough as well as being narrow and slippery. It was ridged so as to make it easier for one's shoes to grip, with a wooden hand rail on one side, but James could see some passengers were still unsteady and as it was wet, some were even slipping slightly as they stepped along. To avoid falling, James moved very carefully, and as he did so he heard his name called. He recognised Harry's voice. James steadied his hand on the rail, and he felt his feet move under him. Tightening his grip, he just managed to save himself from a nasty fall. Harry was there in the middle of the crowd, waiting for him at the landward end of the jetty.

"Welcome to the tavern and the brothel of the two oceans," Harry shouted out very loudly over the heads of the intervening crowd.

James was very relieved to see him, because if Harry could get through that throng so could he, he thought. The smell was absolutely indescribable, and James said so when he reached him. He felt sick and realised he would have to watch where exactly he placed his feet because the ground was so fouled with everything from heaps of rotting fish and the entrails of various beasts, to vomit and cattle dung. James thought he saw human waste as well; he certainly smelt it.

"Good to see you, dear boy," cried Harry over the noisy tumult. "Glad you got here safely." And as James wrinkled his noise at the almost overpowering smell, he added, "It is not just the market making this smell, you know, it is the poor hovels over there in front of you, the absolute dregs of humanity live there. Everyone from poor former slaves, to immigrant Irish labourers who have no work, who have nowhere else to go, runaways and army deserters. In fact the filthy conditions in the lower part of the town near here, and the southern parts near Harrington Street and Primrose Square for example, are absolutely indescribable. The streets are not paved, there is no or almost no running water in many parts, and certainly there are no sewers. You have to walk, almost wade, through it at times to get to the town. It's so bad that even the notoriously indolent Kapenaars, as residents of Cape Town are called, are thinking of doing something about it. Normally that is all they ever do, think about doing something, that is, and they might just do something in a few years' time when they have had enough of a rest. Meantime, you have either clouds of red dust in dry windy weather, or mud at any time else. One day some pretty lady will get so badly stuck in it that she won't be able to free herself. But of course this same area does have certain lovely attractions to a chap. There are a huge number of taverns, and of course an even greater number of brothels.

"That's the name sailors give to the colony you know, Tavern and Brothel, and by heavens it's right too. Actually, the area is pretty lively at night in particular, and any sin you want to indulge in you can find on offer, for a variety of prices of course.

"We can make our way to Parke's together, when your traps have come ashore of course. That may take a little while I am afraid. These boats are very efficient at ferrying things from the off-lying ships, but sometimes the boatmen need a little encouragement."

So saying, he called to the boatman who was still unloading the boat James had landed from, and offered him a shilling to collect James' 'traps' as he called them, and get them ashore with his next load. "And make sure you bring them all up to Parke's Hotel, as well," he added. He turned to John. "You can go to Parke's with the boatman, and get James' things stowed, and perhaps you might tell Mrs Parke herself we shall be along in an hour or two. We are just going to call on a few friends first."

The boatman mumbled something to himself, perhaps intended to be overheard, about gentlemen knowing their places, but agreed. He had been paid in advance after all.

With that, Harry suggested that he and James should step over to the castle to have a drink. It was close at hand, right on the edge of the beach behind outlying bastions. Harry said he had many friends from the regiment staying in the castle, although, he also added, officers liked to, and usually did, take rooms in the town as that meant that they could avoid a lot of the drudgery of garrison life. Sometimes, he said as he winked at James, almost a leer, some of them even had private rooms in the area where the taverns and the brothels were. That was cheaper, and very much more exciting. The main barracks were mostly for the other ranks, and were a short stroll away on the other side of the large parade ground.

It only took them a minute to walk to the castle once they had managed to clear the throng of the market shambles area, and as they approached the main gate James saw close up the old Dutch bell he had heard whilst at sea. The Union flag fluttered above the gateway. A group of smartly dressed officers and less smartly dressed men was marching out of the gateway and passed them as they entered. Harry exchanged shouted greetings with one of the officers and elicited the information that they were obliged to go to the Government House, where they would be on duty as some London dignitary was visiting Sir Harry Smith, the new governor, something to do with a possible new constitution, he thought.

Inside the thick stone walls a small section of maybe a dozen soldiers was marching back and forwards in the courtyard in the heat of the day drilling, with and without rifles, to orders which were barked out by their sergeant who stood stock still to one side. His voice echoed and re-echoed round the walls and although sometimes the men being drilled were some way away they always seemed to hear his command. Harry commented that most of the men would be drilling on the main parade ground which was outside the Castle. Quite a few other soldiers in casual groups, were as far as James could see, simply lounging idly about and taking no notice of what was going on. Some of them were smoking, one was reading a paper – James saw his first copy of the *Gazette* in Cape Town – and some were drinking.

Smoke was rising from the blacksmith's shop, and the smell of newly baked bread indicated the presence of a bakery. There were guns ranged along the inside of the battlements, although what sort of guns James did not know, nor did he ask. Harry led James straight for the officers' mess which was signposted by way of a large red painted notice, and situated in one of the larger buildings inside the walls.

Just beside the door into the rather large well-appointed room, there was a noticeboard on the wall with the Orders of the Day pinned to it, a month old James saw, and he could see another detailing promotions and appointments. It was difficult to read the official notices as there were a large number of scattered handwritten notices on scraps of paper pinned to the board offering goods for sale, horses and goods wanted, rooms to let, servants wanted, and so on. These unofficial notices seemed to be trying to colonise the official noticeboard and certainly overlapped some official notices.

Around the sides of the room were rows of leather armchairs, mostly filled with lounging officers in field uniform, but there were one or two in civilian dress as well. Several officers got to their feet when they saw Harry enter and came forward to greet him. There was a shouted call from one of them for the steward to fetch drinks. "Harry, old boy, is this the friend you told us about?"

"Sorry you weren't with us last night, old chap. We missed you at Rathfelder's, we had a great time!"

"The lovely Anna Maria was looking sad, and asking whatever had become of you! She said she was feeling deserted and unloved. She said she had not seen you for ages."

"She even called round here very late, and asked about you!"

"I went to this amazing Rainbow Ball, you really missed out on that one! I met this gentoo called Hanora who was perfectly adorable. We have arranged to meet again, you know. You should have seen the way they danced."

"I say, steady on there Williamson. I can't talk to you all at once. And the drinks are what?" said Harry. "I would like a good London gin please, steward. One at a time, gentlemen. One at a time, please. Really, I know you are all exceedingly bored, but you must not all speak at the same time. Yes, this young man beside me is James Duffield who has just arrived here at the Cape for a visit, and to have a bit of a good time. He will be staying with me at the nice and to relatively respectable Parke's, and not in a lively brothel like some of you!" His audience groaned amusedly.

The steward handed Harry a large gin, in which floated ice and a slice of lime. He must have readied it when he saw Harry enter the room. He smiled at Harry in recognition of an old friend.

"How could you ignore Anna Maria as you did you after your last visit? She would be devastated if she knew where you were last night. So close but so far away!"

"She knows," said Harry, "that I always stay at Parke's. She could have found me there if she had really wanted to." Harry laughed. "Anyway, to be polite about it and answer you all in turn, to repeat myself, here is my young English friend I told you I hoped was coming out, and he has just arrived, straight from Devon and London, I give you Mr James Duffield.

"Next, last night I was sitting quietly in the parlour at Parke's waiting for James' barque to arrive. And, I am not too happy with all Rathfelder's German talk. And as for your friend Anna Maria, Gervase, you really should look after her better. But do not worry, you know she is not for me. She has no money and that is what I need in a wife. I am only a poorly paid Indian officer on mere furlough pay after all, and so I need a wealthy wife. At least for a short marriage."

"Good Lord, my dear James, we have not offered you a drink. How remiss of us. Steward!"

Later, as they staggered from the castle towards Parke's Hotel James dropped Mrs Oswell's letter off in the General Post Office, as it was in the same street. Needless to say, in the usual way of things, about two minutes later they saw Oswell himself in the distance.

"Now, as to amusements," said Harry as they walked along. "The races and hunting, oh, and cock fighting too, are a basic part of social life here. Everyone here, all classes including both the Dutch and English communities, invariably go to the two race meetings we have here, one in spring and the other in the autumn. During race week nothing else is done and business is pretty much stopped. Everyone goes by whatever means he can get out to the course, and all colours mingle happily from the Governor to the Malay child.

"Foxhunting is based around Wynberg Hill where the regiment keeps its pack, and there are private packs too but they are a bit exclusive. The regimental pack is difficult to maintain due to wars with the natives regularly, or should I say irregularly, taking officers away from the garrison, but I could perhaps introduce you to one of the huntsmen. And Rathfelder has a pack as well at his Diep River Inn, and if you meet him I am sure he would welcome another follower."

James was very happy to receive all this information but rather guiltily aware that all this amusement would bite into his funds, and so his inbred caution suggested that he take things slowly at first until he had become socially accepted.

But Harry had not finished with advice.

"Anyway I thought that one, if not the main, purpose of your coming to the Cape was to join me in a trek of our own into the interior. In the faint hope that that is true, we should set about getting in our supplies. We need to get the wagons first, and we will need two, one for each of us, you see. I think they should be of the cap-tent variety as although they cost more, they are stronger, and we should make sure the axles are all wood, not iron. You can't get iron for repairs when you are out on the veldt you know, nor in the Kalahari. And before we go we shall need a temporary store with a good lock to collect the general stores in, with a room right next to it for a servant to live in so as he can guard them. We can keep the wagons safe by the store and get what is needed gradually, ending up by getting the horses and zuur-veldt oxen at the last minute. We shall need twelve oxen for each wagon, at least, and a good number of spares. I would think that for the sort of length of trek we are looking at, it would take about two or three months to gather everything while we enjoy a social life. It would take less time if we were based in Grahamstown where there are one or two good stores which will likely have everything we need. But that is a long way away, we have to get our general stores here, and anyway I do not know if Andrew Thompson, a Scot from Forres, still has a store in Grahamstown. If he has, he will help us fill in any missing items when we pass."

"Of course I want to travel with you. I want to go to and see the interior, as you called it, I recall. And you once told me about what was needed for a trek. Is trek the right word?" asked James.

"It is a Boer word and everyone uses it, so yes, it is the right word." He paused. "The interior can be dangerous you know," said Harry. "But not if you take care. It's not just animals either, although lions are bad enough. The Boers are frequently very difficult, they have even been known to attack English travellers, and there are frequent native wars, and in the far north are the warriors called the Matabele. You really do not want to meet them. Then there are the deserts you have to cross, and the sand which traps the wheels of the wagons. And mud and dust in abundance.

"Look here, James, we have lots to do getting ready for a trek. It will take us a good time to get ready and it will be quite a lot of hard work. So in the interim while we do that we have to plan our route, recruit the servants we need, and in spare moments we will have, you really must practise your shooting and start to learn some native languages, and then if we have any time left after that, then and only then should we enjoy all that the Cape has to offer. Not before."

Harry said, casually, as they walked, "There is one other fellow staying at Parke's at the moment. I will introduce you when we meet. He is from London, called Thomas Rattray, a young man like you, and also newly arrived in the colony."

11

Good Advice

AFTER A SOMEWHAT LATE BREAKFAST the next morning, James decided that he wanted to write a letter home, it was about time he did, but there was no note-paper in the desk in the parlour. He had just stepped out of the front door to get a breath of fresh air in so far as there was any in that part of the town, and maybe if he felt like it, find a shop selling note-paper, when he was stopped by Harry.

"Whoa there, my young friend. Where are you off to so bright and early?" asked Harry.

"I was going to try and buy some note-paper so I can write home."

"Look here James, I am trying to get our supplies together, and when you have settled in I shall expect some help from you. I could easily have given you some writing paper if you had only asked, I have got lots of it as it will be needed on the trek. And by the way there are shops and shops in this town, you know. Good heavens, look there is Robertson's shop at number 18 right here in the Heerengracht for that, and I might add for artists' materials as well, which I daresay you do need. You can actually see the window from where we are standing!" As if realising he might have sounded a bit sarcastic, he explained, "You could also try Juta, which also publishes books which might be able to help. But they are Dutch and he is married to Louise Marx whose brother you will have heard of from that Communist Manifesto thing he wrote. He publishes some things here as well." Aware that this did not sound very helpful he continued without a break, "Look here. What I mean about all this is that as a person looking to buy in shops in this town you have to be aware of two things. First you do not want to fall foul of the remnants of the dispute over the Anti-Convict Association row, and believe me there are great ongoing rivalries and sore relations which we must all keep clear of. Second you will probably want to buy from the shop with the keenest price. But a Dutchman will sell to a Dutchman for less than he will sell to an Englishman. And you, my young friend, are very definitely English. I mean, look at your clothes, your accent, the way you make assumptions and so on. Just bear that in mind."

"How will I know who is in the remains of the row about the stupid convict thing?" asked James with a slight smile, enough for Harry to notice it.

"That is just the sort of light-hearted attitude that will get you into trouble over the matter in this town. It was, and still is to some, a very serious matter. People have been bankrupted, windows have been broken and shops have been boycotted for less, although I admit that is largely past now. What I will do, when I get back upstairs, is mark the list of shops in my copy of the Cape Almanac which are still, shall I say, problematic, and then you can make your own decisions. After that, just don't blame me if you go wrong in this minefield."

"Sorry, I really am sorry. I did not mean to upset you. I need your help with so much, and it all sounds very difficult. Maybe you can help me fit in a little better. I will try and be patient."

"Look here, James, you have a lot to learn, and what I have to say is very serious. A mistake can easily cost you your life out here. For example, we shall almost certainly be going through the Molopo area and that place is stiff with lions, so you need to make a secure camp, with thorn bushes and so on, and a fire large enough to keep warm and spare brands to help if any lions should approach too close. You have to make sure the oxen are securely either tethered to your trek-touw, or otherwise corralled safely, and are fed and watered suitably, if there is any water. Maybe we will have to dig for water, and that can take hours of back-breaking hard work, my friend. When you get it, it may be foul-smelling and muddy anyway. All of this you must do before you look at the scenery, or for your own comfort. Your personal comfort comes last every time. It will not be some sort of a summer picnic jaunt you know. You will be, on the occasions when I am off for a spot of night hunting or whatever, the leader of the trek and the servants will expect you to know what to do at all times. You will have to control them or else they will get drunk! A native can get drunk absolutely anywhere, I have found in the past. They will be depending on you to show competent and forceful leadership. This you absolutely must do. Failure can sometimes be fatal, especially in a place like Molopo. Lions you know," he ended lamely.

"I am a little at a loss," said James, " to know how to respond to all that. Of course I do not know all these things, but that is for you to teach me. Please. I do know things can be very dangerous, and I will learn, I promise you, but you must tell me what to do and what not to do."

"I accept your inexperience for what it is, but you do have a lot to learn, and you must learn it quickly as I want to go as soon as I think you are ready, providing of course that we have by then got all our impedimenta together.

"I do not know if you have ever used powder or an antimony mix for making a distress signal. If not, you will have to learn how to make rockets as well as everything else. You don't just fire them off for fun, you know. You can't get any more when you run out of supplies and are in the middle of nowhere.

"We will be travelling through tinder-dry country for most of the time. It may look bleak but it is home or part of home to many people in many places even if you cannot see them. They frequently travel long distances on foot, hunting and so on. On those long journeys these deserts often provide their only means of support, even of food and all that they depend on. Even if you can't see any food there, they can. I know that you will find it hard to believe, but some of the most inhospitable places to you and I are home to them; some are very reclusive. So, whatever you do, you do not deliberately set fire to grass or anything like that for your personal amusement. Any fire you build, whenever you build it, must be in a place you can put it out easily and quickly. Even when you may be worn out by hunting or whatever at the end of the day. You choose to travel in their land, you must afford it all due respect. If you do not, it will come back to haunt you, I absolutely promise you.

"I realise I must tell you properly about the Boers," continued Harry. "What upsets and angers me is the casual way the Boer assumes that he can do as he likes with the natives, buying and selling children and others, because he believes he is superior to them. He regards them as savages, and worse than savages. To a Boer a native has no soul, so he has no place in church, indeed for one to enter the same church as a Boer would be monstrous, it would be sacrilege, and the very idea of one of them going to heaven would be absurd. This is why they will not take a native's evidence on oath in one of their courts; they think he does not, and could not, know what it means. The Boers are religious in their way of course, they read the Bible and profess to be governed by its precepts, but they look on native people as the cursed sons of Cain, who are doomed by heaven to perpetual servitude. They consider themselves as performing the will of God, and to be doing him service when they inflict cruel wrong on the natives. They quarrel with any minister who teaches the native differently and as for missionaries who try to convert the natives, they are to be despised and frustrated if at all possible. The term they use to describe a missionary is 'zendeling'. It is a term of reproach, and signifies to them a most dangerous man.

"I have made several trips through Boer country, and have had many young children as young as nine or ten years of age offered me by the Boers as payment for a horse, or for a small purchase, of coffee even. They buy and sell these people quite freely in their own country beyond the colony, and their slavery is as bad as anything anywhere in the world. And God knows there is enough slavery around. Slavery has long been legally abolished by London, but it abounds here in the far reaches of the colony, and beyond, out of the reach of the government here in Cape Town, and the Arabs on the east coast take no notice anyway. But slavery is not the only, or even the main problem. The main problem is the firm belief the Boers have that the natives are an inferior race because God made them so, and that they are therefore to be suppressed in every way as part of God's work.

"All I can imagine is that one day some long time ahead, there will be a reckoning. There have been one or two small attempts by individuals to rebel against the Boers, but they have always failed, and they have all been killed for their troubles. But on the day when they do not fail, I really do not want to be here. And nor should you be, my friend. It will happen and I pray that it will be soon. It cannot be soon enough. Their ghastly repression of the natives is one of the main reasons why the Boers do not like the English. We always take the side of the native, the oppressed, and the problem for the Boers is that they do not understand why that is what we do. They think it is unnatural, almost un-godly for us to do that. We try to educate the natives and tell them about God, and the Boers hate that."

James was disbelieving during this talk, and obviously impatient. He looked around, as if he was still thinking of going shopping. He shuffled around a bit, almost like a schoolboy. Harry was concerned at this as he did not think that James was taking it in properly. All the same what he had told James was true, and while he wanted to make his point to James he did not want to completely deflate his high spirits.

James was embarrassed by the way that Harry spoke to him. He thought of himself as an independent young man. He did not have to be told everything or talked down to at his age. Much of it, but not that about the boers attitude to the natives, sounded like commonsense to him. He just had to be sensible. He was almost bored.

Harry could see his thoughts clearly. "You may not want to be home in Devon for your brother's wedding to the woman you are sweet on. Oh yes, I saw you looking at her you know, so I know your secret. You may be running away from your home in that respect, if not any others, but home I will send you if I must. Look, I understand that Charles' engagement was a shock to you, and I realise that you are hurting underneath that innocent expression. But when your affections are engaged in a lost cause, as yours were my friend, you have to learn that, as the well-known saying goes, it is not as bad in daylight, and you simply have to get over it as best you can."

Harry could see that he had hurt James and realised there was a need to try and divert him, to try and mend the fence that his diatribe, as he thought of it, had caused. Somewhat stiltedly and cautiously he said, "There is probably a party on somewhere tonight. I can ask around in the officers' mess at the castle, and someone there will know. We could go together and try and see what it is like. You never know where this may lead. Let us give it a go and see if we can blow your problems away. Come on now, be a sport and say yes, if I can find a decent party of course, and that you will come with me."

James understood that this idea was attempted pacification, almost an apology by Harry, and as he was in his opinion in the right, he decided to try and smooth troubled waters, and that it would be best not to be too hard on Harry over this.

"I am sorry. Yes of course I will go with you. And yes, I must confess that I was rather just a little fascinated by Francesca. Not really, you know. But I am over all that now. It's now all in the past I can assure you. Long forgotten. Honestly." As he said that James was acutely aware with a stab of remorse that it was the first time he had said her name to anyone since he left Devon. He was also more than a little ashamed of what he said, of denying her. He did not know how he could have said that. But he could not take the words back. Worse, it felt like some sort of betrayal of her for him to even think of going out to a party. Now. When he was so far away from her, even if she would not know. She might think if she knew what he had half agreed to, that he had forgotten her. But he had not. He felt very guilty.

"In the meantime," asked James, "how do I go about getting money here? I have an account with Hamilton Ross and Co in London, and they tell me that their office here will make my allowance available to me here whenever I call on them. So can you tell me how to go about it please, and where they are?"

So Harry told James the facts of financial life, and how to avail himself of his agent's financial services.

12

The Meeting

WHEN HARRY RETURNED FROM THE CASTLE, he was with a friend, a captain Bladen Shelley, also on furlough, just like him. So many people seemed to be on furlough, thought James, that the East India Company must surely employ many more men than he had dreamed of, and probably more than it needed. Bladen himself was a very tall, thin, and dark-skinned man who looked as though he needed to shave twice a day. He was young, maybe thirty years old or a little more, had dark rings under his eyes and a tired, louche look about him. His lips were very full, and rather dark coloured. He introduced himself to James as being from Yorkshire, and claimed to know the Duffield family name from his village where he said the local school had been founded by someone he thought was one of James' forebears. As Bladen told it, apparently that ancestor had left his crested helm in the village church. This made James feel rather awkward as he had never heard of this person, and so claimed quietly, and justly therefore, to have no knowledge of him. He thought briefly that his father might be pleased to know that his proud boast about belonging to an old Yorkshire family might after all have some basis in fact. James had never thought there could be anything in it until then.

Bladen had an invitation to an evening at the house of a local businessman, although he was uncertain what trade this man followed. He thought the man was a general dealer or something like that. But Bladen also seemed to think that this man kept a sort of open house on occasion, such as that day, and he was sure James and Harry would both be welcome. As he rather tactlessly put it, any new face in

Cape Town was worth an invitation if only to relieve the monotony of having to see the same old faces all the time. He advised that they should meet up later at Parke's at about six thirty and strengthen themselves with a little tipple for an evening with Mynheer van Zyl and his vrouw, Aletta. Then they would go on foot to the house which was but five minutes' stroll from the hotel.

Bladen then left to go, as he put it, to his bankers for a quiet word, being a touch embarrassed about money at the time as his last draft from home had not arrived.

The three of them, together with Thomas Rattray, met up at the appointed time in the hotel parlour, and Bladen ordered "a nice bottle" as he put it, of the local champagne. The men chatted about the day they had spent, sightseeing and in calling at Hamilton Ross and Co's offices to obtain an advance on his allowance in James' case, and making other purchases for the trek in Harry's.

The conversation moved happily and excitedly on, and Bladen talked about army desertions, which he said were regular occurrences. The latest he said was a poor Irish immigrant who had only joined up in the hope of a square meal after he had landed anyway. He would not apparently be missed, and would be soon caught as he could not travel far, and then he would be flogged. But James was more interested in Harry's preparations for their travels. Harry had been to a variety of stores and was, he said, making a list of their expenses. But so far the biggest bill he had had to pay was for the first wagon, one with a cap-tent, which had cost seventy-one pounds. It had a trocheameter which was important. They also needed all the fittings for the wagons, like water casks, which were all additional expense. Horses and oxen would maybe be the next biggest single expenditure. He envisioned spending at least eight or nine hundred pounds apart from personal firearms for them all, and it could well be more.

James nonchalantly called Mrs Parke for a second bottle, and privately wondered how far his money would stretch.

"I say young man," said Bladen, "you're pushing the boat out a bit, aren't you? Jaco is a very generous host and you may be sure there will be plenty to drink there, even by Boer standards. Don't go too fast."

"We are walking, aren't we?" asked Thomas, who added that he wanted some fresh air.

"Yes, we are, and you had all better drink up, there's still another glass each in this one," said Bladen, lifting the second bottle up and looking at it against the light.

When they all got to the van Zyls' house it was about half past seven, and guests were flooding in. They joined those waiting to be introduced to their hosts, and as they waited James looked at the somewhat motley crowd. He was used to a more formal atmosphere, with people more formally dressed, and being announced by a butler. But here it was very informal, you just waited with a few guests, in no sort of real order as far as he could see, and after introducing yourself to your host you simply went into the room and helped yourself to whatever you wanted to eat or drink.

The large room had three tall windows opening onto a verandah, or stoep, as James learned to call it, and the bareness of the floor was matched by the bareness of the walls. Bladen whispered that van Zyl had sold a lot of his business stock for what he could, as the compensation he had been due for his slaves had never come, and as a result he was not all that well off. Bladen also said that it was even rumoured that Mrs van Zyl, Aletta, was looking for a rich husband for her daughter, and that one should steer clear of her as a result. Harry and Bladen gravitated, as was to be expected, to the drinks table, but James and Thomas stood together to one side, as newcomers who knew no one, in order to survey the room. Quite a few men were smoking, and one or two women as well noted Thomas, and the room needed some fresh air, despite the windows being open.

It was then that James heard the somewhat distinctive deep voice of Aletta at his shoulder. "Now, you two young men, you must surely need a little female company, mustn't you? I can join you but of course what you really want is to meet a young woman, or two even," she said a little archly. "I am Aletta van Zyl, your hostess."

Turning to James and apparently departing from the subject which had been said to be dearest to her heart she said to James, "Mrs Parke tells me that you have not been long in the colony."

"That's right. Just a couple of days, Ma'am."

"And pray, what do you and your father do by way of profession in England? And what is your family?" she asked, now directly on her subject.

"Well, my father is an attorney, and I left Cambridge early, so I could join Harry here at the Cape. I have one brother and no sisters. My mother Lady Duffield is very much taken up with looking after us all."

"Lady Duffield? She is titled then?"

"My father is a baronet but of course I shall not inherit the title, my elder brother Charles will have that when my father dies."

Aletta could scarcely conceal her interest. Her breast heaved with her thoughts. "And what are you doing here at the Cape?"

"I am looking at travelling into the interior with Harry Vardon. Maybe we might find the fabled Great Lake."

"My word, you must be very brave, or rather rash. And of course, travelling is so expensive nowadays. As well as being dangerous, a long expedition like that will cost a fortune," she said. "Even with an experienced man to show you the ropes so you do not spend cash unnecessarily, it will cost you a great deal."

"Oh, I can afford it, I hope. I have my allowance and so on, and I shall fetch back some ivory no doubt as well." James instantly regretted being so expansive in this reply. Maybe the alcohol he had drunk at Parke's had already loosened his tounge too much.

"But will not your mother and family be concerned at you going on such a long and dangerous journey?"

"Oh no," said James, who was not fully aware that his naive replies were of increasing interest to Aletta. "I do not think anyone will miss me too much while I am away. Obviously my mother does not want me to come to harm, but on the other hand I have no one to please but myself, and how I spend my life is only a matter for me to decide, so it hardly matters, does it, as to how dangerous the journey may be."

"Oh that is so sad. You have no young lady then?" she pried, very directly.

"Oh no, not really," said James denying Francesca a second time, to his increased personal but unspoken angst.

Having obtained all the information she wanted from James, Aletta moved on to Thomas and subjected him to the same blunt examination as to his personal circumstances. Thomas was rather fuller in his replies, but even so it was clear his background was less attractive than his appearance would indicate. He was well turned out in what was no doubt his best suit, and looked every inch a dandy. James by comparison was still in the suit he had worn the day before.

Aletta moved away through the crowd right across the room and James heaved a sigh of relief to himself. He was a private person, and he had not liked giving away as much about himself as he had, to someone who was a perfect stranger to him – indeed it was only the politeness that a guest owes to a host which had lead him to reply at all. He relaxed slightly and looked around a little. As far as he could see most people seemed to know each other and were conversing freely and animatedly. The drinks and food were laid out on a couple of tables along the wall facing the windows, and people having helped themselves to whatever they wanted were holding glasses and small plates of food as they moved around and talked. The conversation was general and quite loud. It was against this background that a few moments later James heard Aletta's voice, in one of those brief moments of silence which sometimes happen in crowded rooms.

She was calling, "Claudina, Claudina." Her voice did not sound loud at all, it was a call intended not to be heard except by the person to whom she called. But James heard it. "Claudina, Christina, come here. Listen. I have just met two young men I think you both should meet. Let me tell you all about them first, before I introduce you." And this she did.

She made her way back energetically towards James and Thomas, bustling importantly through the throng. In her wake came two pretty young women, both slim, and dressed in long gowns of the latest fashion, which looked extremely expensive. And, thought James, from her determined look it would seem likely that Aletta wanted Claudina, whichever she was, to make a good impression.

"James, Thomas, may I introduce my daughter Claudina to you both. Claudina, this is James and this is Thomas. They are both newly arrived from England and at the moment they only know Harry and Bladen. So, as they are a bit alone and do not know anybody else here tonight, perhaps you could entertain them while I look after some of our other guests." Aletta did not trouble to introduce the second girl who simply stood there. Obviously a little embarrassed by the oversight, she shifted her feet uncomfortably. Aletta moved off quickly without a backward glance. She knew what she hoped she had done. Both girls were about twenty years of age, James guessed, and roughly the same sort of height. Claudina had dark shiny hair which was elegantly piled up in a series of coils dressed with small pearls.

Claudina turned to Thomas and said, "This is my friend Christina Beck. Her family are friends of ours. They live next door." To James she said, "Mama says you will be travelling into the interior. Is that right?" He nodded assent. "And your family do not mind? That is very good of them, I should certainly be concerned if I was them. They are all in England of course, so I suppose that you are out of their sight, and out of mind. I should not be so uncaring if I were a member of your family."

"Oh, don't worry about me," said James somewhat more confidently than was justified by his private worries about the journey he was to make. "I have no one especially to be concerned about me."

"No one?" asked the other girl, slightly blushing, whom until then James had not really noticed. She was standing a little behind Claudina. But he did notice her as she said that. And he thought to himself, that is thrice I have denied Francesca, and this time when he made that denial he saw that he was faced with this girl Christina, and all he could think was that this girl, as he put it to himself, was simply entrancing. She took his breath away. Her small heart-shaped face, the glowing skin and pale gold hair, and her eyes, above all her eyes, a dark brown colour, absolutely took him and held him. Her figure showed to perfection in a long pale green coloured gown, which had a deep turquoise sash. He could see nothing else but her. He felt he could say nothing. He felt as if he had met someone, just as he had always imagined he would, someone who would dream the same dreams as him. Rightly or wrongly, he simply assumed from the look that she directed at him that she felt the same.

"No. There is no one," he eventually managed, lightly. "No one at all."

Thomas was speaking to Claudina. "It was very kind of your mother to welcome us to this very grand gathering. In case I do not get the chance later please will you make sure to let her know how much we are enjoying it."

"Of course I will. It is nice of you to call it a grand gathering. My mother quite frequently welcomes large numbers to the house. We never know in advance how many gentlemen will be coming. The servants find preparation of the food difficult as they never know how much is going to be needed."

"That must be difficult indeed," said Thomas, "and I can see that your mother sets a very high standard of hospitality." He looked around again, as if seeing it for the first time, at the large room which seemed to be full of people, many of whom were apparently enjoying a free drink at someone else's expense. A few people were smoking, cheroots mainly he saw, and Thomas could see thin wreaths of blue smoke rising vertically in the air and then layering themselves in small level clouds, as there was no draught despite the windows being open.

Claudina changed tack, and looked at James, who had been standing silently. "But James here seems very quiet, and perhaps he is not enjoying it as you are." James looked down, a little uncertainly, almost shyly.

He answered Claudina by speaking entirely to Christina. "Indeed I am. I am just a little overwhelmed at the way people here at the Cape are so hospitable. I have only been here for a few days, and already I feel very welcome." After a short pause he continued, still looking at Christina, "It was polite of you to ask about my proposed trek to the interior, but Harry is in charge of getting supplies. As yet I have not found myself in a position to help him. But we are looking forward to going as far north as we can."

"No, Claudina was asking about your trek, but personally, I was wondering why you were going on your own, so alone. I mean …" she said haltingly, "I mean, I suppose, that I do not understand why you are going to set out on such a dangerous trek. There must be a reason, and forgive me, I wondered what it was. I know I did not say that very well, but that is what I meant," she ended a little lamely.

James decided that he was not going to tell her why he had decided to come. Instead he said, "I had no ties in England, and Harry invited me to join him, as I am an artist, and a good shot. It was that simple really." James instantly regretted his deception of Christina, and told himself that he would tell her the truth about Francesca as soon as he could talk to her in private. Not here with all these people around, including Thomas. And anyway, he could see that Christina had immediately doubted what he had said.

"Last year," she said, "we met a young man called Peter Robinson, very nice and polite he was, and so gentle, and so brave too. Quite the gentleman in fact. But he died somewhere north in the interior, we don't know where, and ever since his death was reported back here, his family have been trying to find out what happened to him. No one seems to know. But he was apparently greatly missed by his family. If anything was to happen to you, of course your family would miss you."

"Naturally, they would. But no one else would, I can assure you." And then feeling rather brave about what he was about to say, and possibly impolite too, he added bravely, "But I would hope that our very newest friends here in the Cape would miss me as well." He was looking directly at Christina as he said it, and the remark was unmistakably addressed to her. He had been looking at her steadily for a long time. Christina was unembarrassed by James' very direct look.

Claudina of course had seen that look and understood James' remark and what it portended. She clutched at her friend's arm as if to protect her. Christina kept very calm and did not in any way show what she thought about that reply, or why. But she did think to herself that she must verify what she already knew about this young man standing in front of her, somewhat awkwardly.

James was at a loss, the silence in the little group was palpable, so he felt he just had to break it. "Perhaps I can be a help, and get you a drink, or some food?" he asked Christina directly. She shook her head, and said nothing. The other two, Thomas and Claudina, aware of the fragility of the atmosphere among the group, at last started to talk. Trying no doubt to move off uncertain ground, they chose to talk about the news that Sir Harry Smith had announced in one of his numerous official proclamations in the *Gazette*, regarding exhibits of colonial goods and manufactures for the Great Exhibition in London which was being organised by Prince Albert.

James and Christina did not join in this small talk, and as a result gradually the group of four split into two, with Thomas and Claudina drifting over to the buffet still chatting together, although not animatedly, while James and Christina were left alone in midst of the crowd of people. Standing still and mostly silently.

Christina hesitated, apparently shy. She seemed to blush, and visibly almost to gather her courage. "I would like to see you somewhere a little less crowded. I have no wish to be forward of course, and that does sound forward I know, but it is so difficult to talk here with all these people and the noise they are making. I can hardly hear what you say." She coloured a little more, as James still said nothing.

"That," he agreed with a start, "would be perfect."

"I should tell you that my father, who is away in Bloemfontein staying with relatives, is very strict, and insists on my going absolutely nowhere unaccompanied, as I am sure you will understand." She smiled, sweetly. "He would say that being here in this room is very safe with all these people, and Aletta and Claudina of course. I would have to have a companion when we meet. But it would not be anyone here." She chose her words carefully as she spoke.

James did not know what to say. He knew of nowhere suitable they might meet. "I am very newly arrived here so I have no suggestions, but I have just made one new friend called Bladen who might be able to suggest somewhere suitable. He seems to know everyone, everything, and everywhere. I can perhaps send you a note with an idea? But will it be private enough for me to do that? I mean that at home the post is not secure in that sense, so will a note be all right?"

"Good heavens, young man, what on earth do you think you are doing not circulating?" boomed Aletta in his ear, appearing out of nowhere. She put her arm around Christina, and clutching her, turned her away towards the window. And as she was almost dragged away Christina turned to one side, and nodded her silent agreement to James. Aletta, who was intent on their joint forward progress, did not notice. James dragged his eyes away from the retreating Christina and saw Claudina looking back at him across the room.

Claudina came back to James, without Thomas. "I saw you ogling Christina," she accused. James did not reply. "I saw you. Do not try to deny it. Christina is my friend, my inseparable companion, we go everywhere together, and if you want to see her again, despite Mama whisking her away from under your steadfast gaze, I can arrange something. Only if you like, of course," she added disingenuously.

He could see that Claudina was serious but what he did not know was whether her offer was treacherous or not. Bearing in mind her mother's suspected desire to marry off her daughter, James doubted Claudina. It could even be a sort of a trap, he thought. How much of a friend was she really? Christina had apparently not wanted her as a chaperone.

"No, I am sorry, was I dreaming? I was just thinking about my proposed trek. Do not worry about me, I assure you."

James took Claudina at her word and moved away, leaving her with a tall man who happened to be standing next to them, who was not best pleased at that happening. He went in search of Bladen. Bladen was with a group of military men, and it was with some difficulty that James detached him and tentatively broached the subject of how to meet a young lady in appropriate circumstances in Cape Town.

"Got your eye on Claudina have you, you young scamp?" How little he knows, thought James. "I really can't say. Indeed, it would be most ungentlemanly for me to do so," responded James. "Is there somewhere we could go for a nice excursion into the country perhaps, which might be suitable for me to take a young lady? I mean nothing too grand and nothing too public, we would like to talk, and so on."

"Talk? You might forgive me for doubting that. You are a fast one, you really are. Shall I tell Aletta your intentions are honourable or dishonourable? Good heavens man, you have only met her for a few minutes and now you want to take her off somewhere! You will have to watch your step out here, my friend. Out here too many vrouws want to get their daughters hitched to wealthy young Englishmen like you. Beware marriage bait and hooks is my advice. It is not like London where you know the rules. It is a very much smaller society here and everyone knows what you are doing, or what you want to do, as soon as you do yourself. It's a very small place with a lot of gossips. So, my advice is for you to take great care."

James made his excuses and moved away, leaving Bladen slightly irritated. James had asked for advice, and now was apparently not interested in what he was saying.

13

Getting Acquainted

THE NEXT DAY JAMES, after spending quite some time mentally composing what he had to say, sat in the privacy of his room, and after many false starts, wrote a carefully worded note to Christina. He had no experience in writing notes to young ladies he realised, and this particular young lady was already very special to him. After sealing the envelope, and addressing it, he shouted downstairs for John, and when he came up gave John instructions to take it round to the house next to the van Zyls' house, and deliver it there. But he must be careful to whom he handed it, and James particularly directed him to only hand it to the addressee. He was to bring back a verbal reply if asked. John left as instructed, and on his return about thirty minutes later he told James that he had delivered it to the young lady. He said he had asked her if there was any reply, and she had said not.

They met at the museum in Long Street that same day. James had said in his note that he would be there every day at three o'clock until she came. She came promptly, at three, that same day. She was accompanied by a native girl whom she said was one of the family servants. Christina wore a long pale blue-grey dress which had a layered skirt and a sash of a dark crimson, and carried a pale cream-coloured bonnet and a frilled parasol. The servant who accompanied her was a poorly dressed native girl, pretty with short hair and her skin was a glowing copper colour. The happiness in Christina's eyes when she saw James was very evident, and despite their apparent eagerness to be together they demurely walked up and down the museum between the display cases, with the servant girl, who it turned out was called Foolata, following dutifully a pace or two behind them. They talked in low tones in case anyone, including the servant girl, might hear. They were both more than a little wary of being seen together in public, despite the servant girl being with them, and so they did not so much as even touch. James felt that the distance between them was electric. That day there were very few members of the public in the museum, and Christina knew none of the few they did see. They talked to no one anyway, as a precaution. James was fascinated by this very presentable young lady, as he thought of her: her accent, her looks, her strange way of speaking all seemed to him deeply and utterly fascinating. She seemed so fragile and so delicate. The way the stray strands of hair escaping at the back of her neck danced as she walked. The graceful-ness of her walk. The solemn tilt of her head. And her cautious smile, her high cheekbones lifting her eyes, and to crown her, her hair shining and as it seemed to him, glowing.

It was not until almost an hour had passed that, coming to a step, James took her hand to assist her. She gravely looked at him as he helped her, and did not withdraw it when she had mounted, nor did James seek to withdraw his from her. James felt himself come alive, heart-rendingly alive, he thought he had never experienced such a feeling, such a touch before. It seemed from her expression that Christina had felt the same. They both stood motionless and looked at each other wonderingly, saying nothing.

The servant girl behind them stopped too, and she saw what had happened. After a little while with nothing happening, she coughed quietly, a pretend cough, thought James.

"I must go soon," said Christina. "I told Mama that I was only going out for an hour, so I have to go back now. I am very sorry but I truly must go home now or I shall be late, and then I shall be in real trouble."

"I have made enquiries," said James, "of the people at Parkes, and I am told there is a daily passenger omnibus to Wynberg which leaves from outside Robertson's Bookshop in Adderley Street. I am told that Wynberg is a very nice little place, but I am sure you know that. Perhaps we could go there tomorrow."

"Let us meet on the Wynberg omnibus at eleven o'clock in the morning then," said Christina decisively. "I will not be late, so you must not be late either. Do not talk to anyone as you wait to get in the omnibus, will you? Do not acknowledge me or say anything to me. If you do, someone will see, and it is bound to get back to Mama if you do. Oh dear. I shall have to tell another lie to my mama! The girl Foolata will be with me again."

"I shall never be late for you, never, and that is no lie," said James. Christina did not reply to that.

Vrouw Beck was on her way home later that afternoon when she met Claudina at the top of Adderley Street. "I thought Christina said you two were going shopping this afternoon," she said. "What have you two been buying?"

Vrouw Beck saw immediately that Claudina had not been coached by Christina as to what she was going to do, and assumed the worst. Claudina hurried on, and even by the time she had passed Vrouw Beck she was still unable to think of a reply. So, Vrouw Beck knew for certain that Christina had been doing something behind her back. It was not that she automatically disapproved, but that she wanted to know what her daughter had been doing. She could ignore it if Christina had been seeing someone she approved of. So she decided to see what happened if she did not let Christina know that she knew. Claudina, for her part, thought that Christina deserved what she got if she did not even tell her best friend what she was going to do. She was, she thought, off with that young Englishman.

The next day, the omnibus was nearly full when James boarded it. He had seen Christina waiting across the street as he approached the halting place, and she was already aboard when he mounted.

Luckily for them, as the omnibus was so small and fairly crowded James was able with perfect propriety to sit in the only vacant seat, which by chance was next to Christina. To the casual onlooker they might have appeared to be strangers as they sat down. But they sat very closely as there was limited space, and actually there was more space than their propinquity justified if you really looked.

"Where is your servant? I have not seen her," whispered James.

"On the roof I hope, looking after our picnic," replied Christina very quietly.

"I did not see her get on, how many are outside then? Will she have room?"

"She will be fine," said Christina, "don't worry about her, she is used to it. It is her job." James reached his hand out and took Christina's in his. No one else took any notice. James was completely elated.

The journey to Wynberg took the four horse-drawn omnibus around the northern and then eastern slopes of Table Mount, by what seemed to James not to be too bad a road if at times the horses had trouble with the gradients. Table Mount towered barren and somewhat bleakly on their right, and as they passed it the view to the left opened out. In fact it was very beautiful, a verdant extensive green. Christina pointed out False Bay to the front, where she said the sharks were claimed to be very terrible.

Wynberg, when the omnibus reached it, James found to be a very pretty little place, just as he had been told. It was a glorious sunny day, the air was still and very warm, and not a breath of wind disturbed the trees as they looked around them. Distantly they could see a number of small villages, and beyond that a range of mountains. Behind them was Constantia, Table Mount which they had passed and Wynberg Mountain. The village itself was quite small, with a scattering of cottages, some in the Dutch style and some typically English, and a small church. There were many trees in the village, providing welcome shelter from the sun. Sloping down away from the village was a shaded grassy area, altogether a delightful place for a picnic.

There were quite a few people strolling along the paths, taking the air. Some were sitting on benches or the grass, and James and Christina decided to join them. They walked to a cool spot with the servant girl carrying the basket behind them. Foolata spread a blanket on the ground and put her rather large basket down to one side. Saying something inaudible to Christina, Foolata then moved a few paces slightly behind them and sat down too. Christina opened the basket and began to lay out the picnic. She passed a plate and a glass to James and he helped himself to salad and a piece of pie.

"What about a plate for your servant?" he asked Christina. "Doesn't she want something to eat?"

"There is no need for her to eat right now. She would have had a large breakfast this morning so it will be perfectly acceptable for her to wait until evening." James thought this strange, but when, despite what Christina said, he turned and tried to offer the girl a piece of pie. Christina slapped his hand away, and the servant girl looked blankly at him, almost as if unused to any consideration.

As they ate the rather elaborate picnic Christina poured James a glass of white wine from a bottle. It was a bit warm. "I must not give you too much now or you will fall asleep this afternoon, I expect, just like my father always does after lunch."

"If I did that I would miss the whole point of my being here with you. I just want to be with you, and look at you. I have never met anyone like you, to me you are the ideal person I have always wanted to meet. When we touched in the museum I knew then, as I do even more now, that I never want to leave you."

Christina said contentedly, "You do not know me at all really. For all you know, I could just be after a rich English husband. We have only just met, you do not know what I am like at all. It is all pretend. You are just being silly."

James was too young to realise that he was really being asked to deny this, was almost being encouraged to do so.

"Christina, I have always had the image of someone like you in my mind, and now here you are, and now I know what the reality of my dream is, it is you, and I never want to let it go."

"We only met the day before yesterday, you can't possibly be serious about me. You do not know me, or my family. You know nothing about me properly."

"I know all that I want to know at this stage. We shall get to know each other better as time passes, and I want to pass that time with you, I really do."

James was to remember that afternoon and their conversation, much later, when he talked to his lawyer. And to regret it. Meantime, he basked in the warm sun on this lovely and completely windless afternoon.

Later that afternoon as the sun started to set behind the mountain the three of them re-boarded the return coach for the town. It was not as full, but they still sat as they had before, with James and Christina too closely, and Foolata outside. Vrouw Beck was waiting at the stand outside Robertsons when they alighted. She looked rather grim.

"And just what do you two think you have been doing?" she accused. With their happy looks, and Foolata with her basket, it was obvious, thought James.

"Mrs Beck, I am afraid I took the very great liberty of taking your daughter Christina on the coach to Wynberg, with the servant girl of course, and we had a picnic there, in the park. We were always in public, and always were a party of three. It was all very proper, I can assure you."

"You can't just go doing things like that here in Cape Town, whatever you may do in London. Here we have standards. We may be old-fashioned, not like modern people in London, but a lady's reputation is very important, and young gentlemen who do not tell the whole truth are not very welcome around here. Yesterday you took my daughter to the museum. You did not have my permission for that any more than you did for today's jaunt."

"Mrs Beck, I assure you my intentions are completely honourable."

"Honourable, indeed. If they were, you would never have compromised her as you have just done. You do not know what you are talking about. A young man like you who flouts society deserves nothing but contempt. My husband, when he gets back, will be enraged that an Englishman has done this to his daughter's reputation."

"But, madam, I can assure you, we have done nothing but talk. Christina will tell you. It has all been perfectly proper." Looking at Christina, he added a little lamely, "We just want to get to know each other, that is all."

"In the absence as I say of my husband, I must think about this," said Vrouw Beck, "so you come round tomorrow at about six in the evening and we will talk again. Do not think I am going to allow anything. I am not. We must just have a few words, in private. Before then, I shall take advice from the minister." So saying she led Christina and Foolata away down the street.

Precisely at six o'clock the next evening James presented himself at Vrouw Beck's door. Foolata answered his knock. She looked doubtfully at James as she showed him in to the front parlour. It was a rather dark, dingy room, and furnished with far too much large, old-fashioned furniture for James' taste. Vrouw Beck was seated to one side of the fireplace when he entered, and she did not ask James to sit. Seated the opposite her was a thin, ascetic-looking, bearded man in a black and somewhat dirty suit, with a very dirty waistcoat.

"This is our minister, Mynheer Coetzee, and he has been giving me advice about you, which I am inclined to take." She breathed deeply, and with a deep sigh, continued. "You may call on

Christina, here at this house, and meet her here in this room. Not alone of course. Under the supervision of myself or another lady, and under no other circumstances whatsoever will you meet her. You will not write to her or otherwise contact her. All this is, needless to say, on the advice of the minister here." She waved a hand towards him.

"In addition, Christina will not be allowed out to any social event while you are in Cape Town. I do not know exactly how long you will be in the town before you leave on the trek which she tells me you are to undertake, but I do not expect it will be too long. These are the rules. If you wish ever to see Christina again you must abide by them." So saying, she breathed very deeply, and looked aggressively at James, as he thought.

"Mrs Beck, I have to apologise most humbly and sincerely for my thoughtlessness in anticipating your permission to call on Christina. It was very wrong of me. You are extremely kind to make such a generous offer to me in the circumstances, and of course I have absolutely no hesitation in agreeing to anything you require in this respect. My father, Sir Marshall, would be most gratified if he knew of your generosity. I shall make sure to tell him when we next meet."

Vrouw Beck's eyes narrowed. The minister shifted quite uncomfortably in his chair.

"I have no interest in that. My interest is solely in my daughter and in her maintaining her position here in this town." But as she said this James could see her thoughts as clearly as he had hoped he would. The incidental mention of his father's title had clearly had a mellowing effect on her and the minister, as it was designed to do.

14

Lewis Trevanion

GERVASE WAS STANDING in the middle of the mess holding forth to his fellow officers in stentorian tones. He commanded the floor, standing four square, arms akimbo, red faced, talking loudly and forcibly. He had been talking for some time, it would seem, from the somewhat mutinous reaction of his auditors. The top two buttons on his mess tunic were undone. "I say you fellows, come on, let me finish. I had it from Baines, the painter fellow. It must be true. This chap Robinson was a capital swimmer, swam like a fish. The boat was sheltering in Angra Pequena, you know, come on, where Bartholomew Diaz came ashore. There was a very bad storm to the west, and they decided to try and land there instead of here at the colony, as they mistakenly thought that was less dangerous. Then their landing boat capsized and they all ended up in the surf. This chap, despite being absolutely terrified to death, swam like a fish, with sharks alongside him, and collected the oars and rudder and got the boat steady. He saved all of them. The master, by the name of Merriman, can verify all of this apparently. It must be true. The thing is, Robinson swore he would never do anything as dangerous or as silly as that ever again. Said he was terrified and all that. Lots of chaps heard him say that. How we all laughed at him for being so foolish."

"And all this about Robinson has something to do with Trevanion has it?" shouted out a voice from the recesses of the mess.

"Yes it does, my dear fellow! Because the real point of my story is what happened when Robinson was with Trevanion somewhere up north at a stretch of some river or other. That place was infested with large crocs, and for some unknown reason Robinson decided to go for a swim there. He would have had to be absolutely mad to have tried that. He dived in and of course a large croc got him. He gave out what Trevanion later said was an anguished cry, and disappeared from sight in the muddy waters. The point is not that he was a fool to try and swim there, despite having previously sworn an oath that he would never do anything as stupid as that, but that Trevanion was at the campsite, and not with Robinson, so he never saw what actually happened, so he could not have heard anything. It is just his story. It sounds plausible, but consider this. Each time that Trevanion tells it, it is slightly different. The real point is that no one can contradict him on any version of events because no one else was there. Just those two, and maybe their servants I suppose. No, Trevanion was not there, he was at the campsite by his own account so he could not have known what actually happened and so the story must be doubtful, as there is no way it can be corroborated. So we only have Trevanion's word for it as to what did happen, and as to how poor Robinson died."

"And do you mean to say," shouted Spellman, "that this chap Trevanion is the chap we have to go and help?"

"It is. My orders are simply to get Trevanion to somewhere safe. To make it more difficult, we don't really know exactly where he is. No, come on. Be sensible chaps, it's just a simple little extraction mission, and the reason we have to do it, is because ever since the Boers closed the eastern route northwards to the interior, they have been trying to close down the western route we English would normally use as well. They want all the land, from west to east across the continent, and I say that can't be allowed. Only a few weeks or months ago, apparently, they beat up an English farmer chap called McCabe who had travelled the western route, and then published a pretty detailed description of that route in the Grensblad newspaper. They have put him on trial for treason, and by so doing they are claiming sovereignty over all the land where the western route is. If they can find Trevanion before we do, and then step in and arrest him for something, anything, maybe killing a native, whatever, we have a political problem. We can never allow that to happen, and in my opinion that is what all the fuss is really about. We have to get him out of that place, wherever it is, fast, as the Boers are now claiming the whole area as sovereign. If we can do that, we will avoid a diplomatic incident. It is only sad that Trevanion has a bad reputation stemming from a couple of doubtful episodes in his recent past, one of which is very recent indeed. Anyway, as if all that were not bad enough, the Boers are rumoured to have sent a commando north of some unspecified number of troops, maybe about nine hundred or so, to take possession of the land. That is another reason why troops have to go now, ostensibly just to help Trevanion, but really to prevent any acts being carried out which might lead to a formal claim to sovereignty being made to that land. What has to be done is to demonstrate to the Boers that they are not allowed to deal with anyone as if they had the legal right based on sovereignty to do so. Trevanion and McCabe are all part of that."

Lewis was waiting for rescue, and recovering from a severe beating he had been given by some natives, which had left him badly shaken. He was now marooned in the Kalahari with no wagon or oxen, and no native servants at all, as all of them had melted away, as natives sometimes did. Unable to move himself, he had sent a desperate message for help by the last of his men, called Dedderich, but now he was just waiting. His other servants had said, most unreasonably he thought, that they were frightened of him after he had that argument with that thin, straggly looking servant. Lewis did not know his name. The man said he had not stolen from Lewis, and he was quite obviously lying, Lewis had thought. Lewis had to punish him for theft, and he had done so, and taught the man a good hard lesson with a jambok. The servant had been fine when Lewis had left him, it was not his fault if the man's wife had taken so long to get help for him that the man had died. He could not help that. That was not his fault, it was the woman's fault. And then the assault by the servant's chief's men, said to have been in retribution for the beating he had given to the thief. That had been the last straw. He thought he had a few cracked ribs, anyway they were very painful and the cuts on his back from the whipping were still very sore. Those men had rousted him, which was an appalling affront, thought Lewis, and then had driven off all his oxen, in reparation, they said, for the death of the servant. They said they were going to give Lewis' wagon to their chief, and all but one or two oxen to the dead man's family in accordance with their custom. Lewis thought the custom was just an excuse for the theft of the wagon and oxen.

This last South African trip of his had been the final throw of the dice for him. He had long ago been told by his father Richardson that he was no longer able to let his son have any more money. Richardson had told him, in clear and unmistakable terms, that the formerly wealthy estate was now almost bankrupt as a result of his spending, and could not make any more payments. He said it pained him to have to write to his only son like this. In response, as far as he could remember, Lewis had asked why the rents could not be raised, and was told the cottages and other properties were not in a fit state of repair to justify more rent. Apparently they had all been let go, and all the money saved on repairs which should have been made, had been sent to him instead. There had been a lot more that his father had said about having to live within his means and so on, none of which touched Lewis at all, and he did not remember it anyway.

Lewis had been quite desperate at this and had explored as far as he was able the chance of acquiring land from the government of the colony. In order to avoid having to ask at Sir Harry Smith's office where he well knew he would be refused, he had made detailed enquires in London of the Secretary of the Colonies, Earl Grey no less, and all quite fruitlessly. No land and no mineral rights could be freely granted him. That was the gist of the reply. Lewis had even invented a cock and bull story about having cotton seeds which he said he had obtained from America and which he claimed would do well in the climate at the Cape if planted there. But even this had met with a polite refusal by Earl Grey's secretary on his behalf, to the effect that no land could be made available to him for mineral exploitation without payment of two or three years' rent in advance, or in the case of the cotton scheme, without a sale at the standard price charged. And he had not the money for anything like that.

So Lewis, who had been away for about three years now, realised he would certainly have to go home, back to Devon, and eat humble pie. He really hated the idea of meeting his father again and having to admit that his adventures had all been in vain. But he had made no fortune, so it would seem that he had no choice. The ivory he had stolen from Robinson's wagon after Robinson's death had sold well, it was true, but it had only fetched what to Lewis was a small sum, and anyway there was not much of it after he had paid a few of, but not all, his debts, and the poor remainder had all been spent on this latest misadventure anyway. If Robinson had only agreed to share the cost and profits of that trip, and had not insisted that as he was paying for it the profits should all be his. If only he had agreed, Lewis would not have pushed him. There had been no one around except a native, the one who later stole from him, and so it had been easy. It had been completely necessary and to Lewis it had been justified, in a way, by the fact that he was the one with all the experience and had showed Robinson how to trek and hunt, and so on. He had done all the hard work and Robinson was going to take all the profit. It had been totally unfair, on this basis, for Robinson not to help out financially. He had deserved what had happened. Lewis reflected that if he only had enough money for another try he might not have to go home at all. He needed to fund another trip to shoot some ivory, if only he could. Maybe he could meet someone with money, like Robinson, but more open-handed. He had no particular wish to explore anywhere, he had done that, he just needed money to keep going, and that was all.

15

The Railway

CHARLES HAD BEEN ENGAGED TO FRANCESCA for almost three months and he enjoyed the status that it gave him, as an almost-married man. It gave him, he felt, a certain cachet among his friends to be semi-settled. Of course it was a little inhibiting at first, but he thought that no doubt that feeling would pass. After James had left, Charles had taken what he thought of as a rather nice little house in Chelsea, suitably far enough away from Clapham he thought, and found that town life really suited his tastes. Shortly after Charles had taken it, Francesca went up to town on the train with him. They both still enjoyed the novelty of the train, and Exeter was so convenient for this. The trains were exceedingly fast, almost dangerously so you might say, and very clean with new carriages, and there were never many passengers either.

On her first visit to the house in Chelsea, Francesca expressed her surprise at the delightful way Charles had had the same decorated and furnished, and thought she might have misjudged him a little. As he showed her around, Charles had to confess to her that he had engaged the services of Harrod who was now operating at a new store in nearby Brompton, and Charles Harrod himself had, with his son of course, looked after everything splendidly. All Charles had done was pay, it was that simple. Harrod had even arranged for the hiring of staff for the house, and that, in particular, made Francesca realise how easy it was to live with money. Her father was always having to make do and mend on the estate, and she somewhat relished the idea of the freedom from such straightened circumstances that would be hers after marriage. Charles would be spending the night at the new house, but as, sadly, Mrs Griggs would not move from Clapham to help out as a chaperone, for decorum's sake Francesca would stay at the rather nice hotel in the next street. It was expensive, but Charles was paying.

Charles had arranged for the nearby restaurant, called Jepsons, to send staff in and prepare and serve a splendid welcome dinner that first evening she passed at the house. The very fine meal of fish and game with a wonderful German Hock was just to her taste. And afterwards she realised too late what the price of the meal was. Sadly, Charles had taken too much to drink and perhaps because of that, at the end of the meal when Francesca said she had to leave for the hotel, Charles stopped her, physically. He grabbed her by the wrist and pulled her back into the hall as, encumbered by her valise, she tried to open the front door. It was in vain she struggled. He was far too strong for her. And ignoring her resistance, he kept saying that he knew she had enjoyed herself the first time they had made love. She would enjoy it again. He pulled her back into the dining room and locked the door behind them. She was not strong enough to prevent him. He pushed at her and knocked her, largely accidentally she had to admit, onto the floor near the fireplace. Her back hurt where she had hit the edge of a chair as she fell. To resist was obviously hopeless. She knew very well that she should never have gone to London with Charles. What was happening was her own fault, and she was suffering for being wilfully short-sighted. Why had she even gone to see the new decorations in what was soon to be their new house? She had sort of half guessed in advance how Charles would want it to end. So as she had half known in advance how it would end, why was she there at all, she asked herself? Was it that she wanted to please her widowed father by marrying a rich and maybe soon to be titled man, or even worse was it to please herself? She did not love or even like Charles. Not at all. But she could not ignore her own part in creating the situation she was in. The immediate problem was that Charles was drunk, and he was demanding she make love, or let him make what he called love to her. Her feeling of self-guilt was overwhelming.

At this point Francesca rather sadly decided that because what was going to happen was so inevitable, she would not resist, which would be futile, but would remain totally passive and unresponsive, and give no indication of enjoyment. She could not do anything else. She would have to accept his unwanted and selfish act for what it was, she should never have let herself be in this position in the first place. In that sense, it really was entirely her fault; her thoughts about her father wanting her to marry this man she saw for what they were – an attempt to blame another for her own stupidity.

Charles held her closely, but briefly for a moment, glancing down, she could see with dread fascination, from his trousers tightly strained across his crutch, how aroused he was. She did not know how she would ever manage to accept the act she was about to perform, but they were going to get married anyway. He unbuttoned his fly very rapidly, and she saw that his penis was very stiff. She thought it looked enormous and she felt it press between her thighs. It was throbbing she could feel. She wondered how such a large penis could ever fit inside her. The act did not last long. She felt no thrill, no pleasure. When it was over, and he had poured his sperm into her with a series of violent pushes which seemed to go on interminably, Charles lay on the floor beside her, and gasped. His penis was flaccid now and wet – how could it have changed so much, she wondered as she looked at it, just as a last pale drop came out. He said how wonderful she was, and how much he wanted children. His remarks petered out after a while. He never said he loved her. He fell asleep on the floor. She said nothing. She left the house without his waking.

The next day Francesca caught the early train back down to Exeter and was met at the station by her father with a new brougham. He said he was afraid that she would get wet if he had come in the trap, and anyway it was too far for the old horse on his own. When

Francesca queried the expense of a new brougham, he denied it was unnecessary. They went home together, and on the way Francesca told her father all about the house where she and Charles were to live after the marriage. She managed to enthuse about it. It was lovely after all. And Francesca thought to herself how strange sex was. She felt bruised.

Paddington, when Charles reached it much later the same day, was very crowded. Steam billowed noisily over the moving, pressing throng. He had wanted to travel back separately from Francesca because he wanted to fit in a quick visit to his club (the Oxford and Cambridge) for lunch, and a friendly drink at what turned out to be quite a convivial bar, before he left town. He managed to find the four o'clock train to Exeter quite easily, but only after being directed by a porter who helped him along the platform, and settled him into one of the new first-class carriages at the front of the train. It was quiet and very clean with new upholstery on the bench seat, and Charles relaxed drowsily, and tried to recall Francesca, and what they had just done, again. They passed Reading, and the train picked up speed.

Richardson decided that he would also fetch young Charles, as he thought of him, from the train, and he got to the station at Exeter a little early to be on the safe side. But the late train from London which was due in that evening did not come. Charles did not appear, so Richardson went to the station master's office to make enquiries. The station master was someone he had known distantly from the days before railways; he thought the man was called Henry Turner. Although Richardson had never had much to do with him, Turner usually came to see Richardson off when he took the train to London. For an occasion like that he wore his top hat of office very proudly. Not many people went to London, but even so, Richardson did not quite understand why Turner did that.

Richardson explained to Turner that he was waiting for Charles to arrive on the late London train, and asked why it was delayed. Turner did not know the answer, and looked at Richardson, concerned. He told Richardson he did not know what had happened, but they had a new electric telegraph in the office, so he could find out. However, he confessed that he himself was not familiar with the code he had to use to receive or transmit messages. So he called his assistant and in turn explained the problem to him.

The assistant, a young round-shouldered grey-haired clerk named Felix Smith, sat at the side desk in the snug and still warm office, even though the coal fire had almost died down. He tapped at the key to one side of the machine. The gas lamp gave a dull glow to the office where they were. It was raining, and the windows were too wet and sooty to see outside into the dark gloom at all adequately. When he had finished sending his coded message Felix remained sitting, perfectly still, and there was silence while the other two stood awkwardly together and waited for the reply. The machine lay silent for a period. Richardson could not afterwards say how long it was, but no one said a word while they waited. The big clock on the wall ticked on noisily. There was no sound outside so when the machine clattered into life, everyone started involuntarily. Felix peered at the tape when it had ended, and then stood and looked at Richardson.

"I am very sorry, sir, the message simply says there has been an accident and the line is blocked. No more than that. I am not able to get details about what has happened. In a case like this I am afraid we have to wait for the next train to bring us a message, or even for the newspapers to tell us what occurred when we get them in the morning."

Turner was very embarrassed at not being able to help Richardson and pointed out that there was no point in his waiting for the next train, which certainly would bring information, because they had not the slightest idea when it might arrive. He asked Richardson to go home and said he would ride out with the news when he had some. That would likely be from the newspapers the next day. Unconvinced that he was doing the right thing, Richardson left and went back home and when he told Francesca on his return that he had no news beyond the fact of an accident, he thought that she took it very calmly. But then she said something about it all being her fault, and fled upstairs. Richardson thought she was crying as she ran.

The next morning, Turner went to the station much earlier than usual and met the train bringing the newspapers down from London, and he deliberately but surreptitiously purloined one copy to see what it said about the accident. The very detailed *Times* report about the crash, with bland eye-witness accounts thrown in for good measure, confirmed the numbers of people who had been injured and killed. The report said there had been a signalling failure and explained that a goods train coming out of a branch line, fortunately at a relatively slow speed, had struck the express train's leading first-class carriage at an angle, to one side. The only fatalities had been in that carriage, and seated at that side of it. Two people had died, and Charles was named as one of them, and six people were said to have been injured. Turner, although he would never have admitted it to anyone, was a little in awe of Richardson and the Trevanion family. So, in view of Richardson's concern the previous night, that fact coupled with the fact that he knew from the local press that young Mr Duffield was engaged to Richardson's daughter, Turner thought that he should make an effort to help. So he went to the stables and took the railway messenger's horse, and rode out to the Trevanion family home. He had never been there before and he did not know the way, so the journey took him longer than he thought it would. But when he got there, the imposing external appearance of the old mansion decided him quite firmly that he had done the right thing in going. Because he was not quite brave enough to go to the front door, he went instead to the back door, which was unlocked. He entered and left *The Times* on a table in what, he was surprised to see, was a rather untidy kitchen, and then left the house without seeing anyone.

When he came down, Richardson had no idea who had brought the newspaper, but nevertheless he read it with increasing concern. When Francesca came down, later than usual, he was sitting at the table still reading the report, and he gave it to her, wordlessly. She read it, horrified at the detail. But she did not cry. She knew her father's hopes for the estate depended on her making a good marriage, and while she regretted her part in what had happened only the day before, and now the loss of her fiancé but she could not stop herself thinking that that would leave James free to marry her when he returned to the country, as she hoped he would soon do.

As the result of a long discussion after she had finished reading the newspaper, Francesca and her father settled that she should write to James to give him the news once that course of action had been agreed with the Duffields. So that same morning she went over in the trap, alone, to the Duffields, unannounced, taking the newspaper with her of course. In fact when Coleman met her at the door, he immediately offered his very sincere sympathies, from which she knew that their newspaper had been delivered. Secretly she was glad that the Duffields would already know the terrible news about their elder son, and that therefore she would not be breaking it to them. Ushered into the morning room by Coleman, she had a very painful meeting with Lady Eleanor. Lady Eleanor was quite untypically distraught, and in that state readily agreed that Francesca should be the one to write to James. Francesca was herself upset by Sir Marshall who said that he was sure she would not mind writing as she and Charles were not married yet, so she would be perfectly calm, as he put it, when writing. She also thought that she must write to John as he would be sure to be upset. But Francesca was already thinking about James far too much to be rational. His return to her side would surely follow swiftly on from his receipt of her letter.

16

The Engagement

MUCH TO HARRY'S IRRITATION, James' frequent visits to see Christina soon established a pattern. Harry repeatedly, and to James' guilty annoyance, said he was not pulling his weight in the preparations for the trek, and that was perfectly true. James would usually call at the Becks' house in the middle of the morning, and be met at the door by the girl, Foolata, who would show him into the parlour where Christina sat with her mother. He usually took a small posy or other small gift, one for each of them, and they would sit and talk while her mother would sew while seated a little apart in the window seat. After a few such visits Vrouw Beck took to sitting on the stoep, just outside the window, and so they were able to talk relatively privately. James could not imagine his attraction to Christina getting any stronger, and he fretted at the restrictions they had to accept for seeing each other. Christina all the while calmly accepted the homage that James paid her, and it seemed very obvious to James that their feelings were entirely mutual.

In order to prosecute his case with Christina, James felt he had to leave Harry with some help from John to deal with the boring business, as James now thought of it, of getting their purchases together for the forthcoming trek. James made excuse after excuse for not helping, and Harry gradually became increasingly upset at James' indolence in this respect. Thomas, who was still at Parke's, made jokes about James always going off on his own. One day when Harry came across James in Long Street, he had a small parcel under his arm, and Harry guessed that it was likely to be a gift for a young lady, but he said nothing. He felt responsible to Sir Marshall for James, so that evening back at Parke's, he tackled James about it, head on.

"There is nothing underhand about it all," protested James. A little pompously, he said, "I am courting Christina Beck, and doing so with the permission of her mother and her minister. I have a very strong attachment to her, and she returns my feelings. The relationship is all very proper, and I may well make it more permanent. I have known her for almost three weeks now, we have been seeing each other almost daily, and I am certain of how we are placed towards each other. I intend to ask her to marry me, probably tomorrow. Then, assuming there is no objection from her mother, which I do not think there will be, I shall write home, and give them the good news."

"But, my dear boy, she is a Boer. Do you understand what you are doing? The Boers are not like us you know. What do you know about her family, for example?"

"My God, you sound like my father! And you are not he. If it is any concern of yours, which it is not, I must tell you her father is away in Bloemfontein. I have not met him. Her mother, whom I have met many times, is in full agreement. I mean, she seems positively to approve of me, in her way."

"But of course she would!" cried Harry. "Look, like many such vrouws, they are on the lookout for young Englishmen with a fortune, and will do anything to ensnare them for their daughters."

"It's not like that at all. Christina really loves me, I know she does," said James.

"My God, what have I done? I should never have let you out of my sight. What will your father say? He thinks I am taking you off on a trek, and here you are making love to a Boer behind my back. This is just terrible. I must stop it. You must stop seeing her right now. You must. I insist."

"If that is all you have to say, I shall definitely ask her to marry me tomorrow."

"It is no good without her father's permission, and he is away in Bloemfontein, you said. It will not be lawful without that."

"But Christina was twenty-one last month," said James, "and anyway her mother and her minister both say they accept me. She does not need any permission from her father. So they are perfectly happy for us to marry. There is nothing to stop us now. We shall get engaged tomorrow, and in due course we shall marry."

"Your father will kill me for this. This is stupid. You are just a young fool. You know nothing about the Becks, nor the Boers. You have hardly met this girl. You can't know her. Beck is a small tradesman, and not a very successful one at that I am told, and also everyone knows that he has a fearfully violent streak. In the past, about a twelve month ago, he was put in court for beating Mynheer Dreyer up. He beat Dreyer so badly he had to go to the hospital. It will be a disaster from the start."

James replied calmly, "But I am not marrying him, I intend to ask his daughter to marry me."

"I say. Look here. I am sure you think you love this girl, but you may well end up paying the devil for that privilege. My God, it's impossible for you to marry her. I am certain also that Beck will be strongly opposed to the idea when he gets to hear of it. Don't forget that he can be violent, will you."

"But I do not want to marry him. I want to marry her."

"That's facile, old chap. How can you take that man anywhere? You could not go to any society reception, you would be socially ostracized, and you would suffer for it. What would happen if he turned up at Clapham? Good God, what would your father, or your mother say? It is just unthinkable." He paused and seemed to relax, but it was only to change his line of attack on James' proposed course of conduct.

"I suppose Vrouw Beck knows about your father's title." James reddened, guiltily. "I see you told her about that. Well, that is it. The old vrouw will never let you escape now, I can swear to that. You have made your own bed, and even if you wanted to get off it you might well find it hard to do so now."

So, after he had been round to Hamilton Ross' office the next morning to see if his allowance had arrived, which it hadn't, James went round to the Becks', this time with no present for either Christina or her mother. He had sent a note ahead by John to let them know that he would be calling at eleven o'clock precisely. Foolata met him at the door as usual. Vrouw Beck was there, of course, and his beloved Christina. After that he did not really look around but he heard a cough and saw Minister Coetzee sitting near the door to the kitchen, wearing a grim expression. He stood up.

"I think it is high time we called an end to these meetings. You have been coming here with permission for some weeks now, and plainly have no intention of doing anything other than enjoying the generous hospitality of Vrouw Beck in her own home. There is no purpose or result to these meetings except to upset Vrouw Beck. They must stop. Visits like this may be all the rage in your Godless society in London, but here, and in the absence of Mynheer Beck, they are an affront to common decency, Vrouw Beck, and our society."

"Minister, I have come here against the better judgement of my companion Harry Vardon …" At that the minister jumped in, interrupting. "You see, Vrouw Beck, this young Englishman has been deceiving us all along. He never had any good intention towards this house. He was always intending to dishonour us. He thinks that just because he is the son of an English nobleman he can do as he likes with us."

"Nothing can be farther from the truth," cried James. "I came here today with the express intention of asking permission to propose marriage to Christina, against, as I say, Harry's advice, but I do not care about them. I care for Christina. Indeed I love her. Very much. I have always loved her from the moment I first saw her."

The room was silent. Christina took a deep breath, looked down at her lap, and clasped her hands. Foolata, inexplicably still in the room, stared at James. The minister looked at Vrouw Beck, and she at him. James looked at Christina, hoping for a sign of encouragement.

"Well that is a surprise. Are you asking for my permission to marry her, or are you not?" said Vrouw Beck.

"Mrs Beck. May I have permission to marry your daughter Christina? She and I both feel the same about each other and we want your permission to marry. Please. I know that I may not be the sort of person you thought should marry your daughter, I am not a Boer for example, and I quite understand you would have preferred her to marry a Boer, or a Dutchman. But whatever you thought, I know that I will make her happy. I do that already, as I am sure she will have told you. And whatever else, I will never do anything to hurt her in any way. I love her far too much to do anything at all that she does not want," James protested. "I have a ring to mark the engagement".

"Let me see it, now, this instant," said Vrouw Beck.

James took off the signet ring his father had given him, and passed it to her.

"What is this marking on it?" she asked, peering closely.

"The family crest, and our motto, in Latin, of course," he replied.

James saw a cupiditous gleam flicker across her face briefly, but did not recognise it for what it was. Belying her look she said, "Young man, your father has a title I know. But you are the younger son, so you will never inherit it will you? So what does it matter if he has a title or not? A title is unimportant to me or Christina. The ring is the important matter. Is this what you intend to give her if I agree to the idea of your proposing to her?"

"It is."

Vrouw Beck looked across to Minister Coetzee, who nodded back to her. "Well, I suppose you had better give it to her if that is what you want to do, and if she really wants it. You must understand that Mynheer Beck is still away for the time being, and this permission is only given to you because of the approval of the minister in his place." Brusquely, she then said, "Go on, ask the girl." She handed the ring back to James, who took it in his hand.

James moved across the room to Christina. They looked at each other. James saw, as he thought, love in her eyes, and he knew that he was then at the most critical moment in his life so far. He knelt on one knee in front of her.

"Christina Beck, you are the most important person in the world to me, and I love you more than my own life. I have never loved anyone else, and I never will. I want to spend my life with you, and I shall never tire of you. Whatever happens, I will always be faithful and true to you. You will always be able to depend on me, I shall always honour you and make you the most important person in my life. Will you do me the honour of marrying me? Please."

James held the signet ring out to Christina, and she took it. She put it on her engagement finger, but it was a little too large, so did not fit properly. She did not seem to care, and smiled happily, very happily. For that instant, the air in the room seemed to stand completely still.

Back at Parke's later that afternoon, James came face to face with Harry. He told Harry everything that had happened, and confirmed that he was now therefore engaged officially to Christina. He told Harry about the ring.

"But do not you see, my dear James, that Vrouw Beck and the minister always wanted you to get engaged? They set you up. You are a real catch to them, and they would have wanted you to get engaged to Christina whether you and she loved each other or not. My God, when I think how they would have behaved if they had thought you were the older son of, how did she say it, an English nobleman, well it hardly bears thinking about. They only put up nominal resistance to conceal what they really wanted, which was an engagement."

James, who had thought that it was his polite and loving terms which had led to the permission and hence to the engagement, protested. But he did recall one or two things Mrs Beck, as he called her, had said, which might give that impression.

"And do not deceive yourself. Even if you call her Mrs Beck she is Vrouw Beck as a fact, and do not forget what that means. She will do what her minister or her husband orders her to do, and nothing else. She is not some nice English lady who you can take tea with, and then come home full of her polite conversation.

"And now you must face the unpleasant task of telling your father," said Harry. "You will have to tell him, not write to him! It is serious news and telling him personally face to face is the best, I can assure you. Indeed it is the only thing to do. You will need to take passage home immediately, and go and see him, and tell him what you have done. Look, James old boy, Charles has got engaged to a young lady of great respectability, more or less at his mama's request. And here are you, running off and getting engaged after just a few weeks, without their approval, to a foreign woman they have never met. If they ever find out what her family is like they would die a thousand deaths."

James' protests were ignored. Harry went on, "You have said to me many a time, that you resent your parents preferring Charles to you. But your behaviour over this will merely confirm to them that they have always been right about you. You are an impetuous, immature young man."

"I thought you were meant to be my friend, but listen to you now."

"But I am a friend of your parents, as well as you. You must go back to them now, and make your peace with them, quickly. Do and say whatever is necessary to that end. You must expect that they will stop your allowance of course."

A silence developed which neither seemed to want to break.

"Yes," said James. "Perhaps I should have spoken or written to them first. I must of course go home as quickly as I can, to explain things face to face. That is obviously best.

"I say, I have just thought. I must tell Christina that I am going back, to tell my parents I mean. I can do that tomorrow. She will not mind. John can stay here with you while I am gone, and look after things for me here. With your help, of course."

That night James sat up late in his room and, in a mental turmoil, wrote to Christina, explaining that he would be sailing home as soon as he could to tell his parents personally that they had become engaged, as it would not be right to break the news by letter. He also told her he loved her. The next morning he tore the letter up, went round to the Becks' to see Christina, and with many pauses, told her he had to go back home and tell his parents of the engagement. If he did not do that he feared for his allowance, and without that they could not marry. Christina said she quite understood he must go home, and only asked (or as James later reported to Harry "pleaded") for him to be as quick as he could.

Later that morning as James walked to Hamilton Ross' office to try and find out about booking a berth he met Bladen, and he was a little blunt when James gave him the exciting news, as he thought of it, of his engagement.

"My dear fellow, what a thing to do! Your mama will be a little surprised I'll wager, and what they will say at your club in London I cannot imagine. You will not be able to take her about, you know. But you can live here reasonably happily I dare say if you only mix with the Boers. She is very lovely and all that, and I hope she will make you a good wife, but her old man is well known as a bit of a tyrant and I suggest that you watch out for him, if you do not mind my saying so."

When James arrived at Hamilton Ross' offices he saw Hunter Hodgson and told him about his engagement. James was elated and wanted to tell everybody. Hunter expressed very quiet and polite surprise at the news, and undertook to book James a passage to England on the first halfway decent ship he could find. James' allowance had still not come through, said Hunter. Although he was far too polite to say anything critical, Hunter's raised eyebrows showed what he really thought. "I am sure your parents will be very happy for you," he lied.

On her return home, Francesca wrote the two letters as she had undertaken to Lady Eleanor that she would, and in them she tried as gently as possible to let James and John both know what had happened. Her letters went by ship and by the time they eventually arrived at Parke's Hotel some two months later, James had sailed for home long before. His letter was left for him to receive in due course, and Mrs Parke took it into safe custody for that purpose. John of course received his own letter, and when he opened it was shocked and suitably worried. Not just because he assumed James would now have to stay in England for quite a spell, perhaps even permanently, but John also wondered how he would be expected to return home or even if that was what was to happen.

His first thought was to speak to Mr Vardon, as he called him still, and this he did at once. Harry pointed out that in view of the engagement John should go at once and tell Christina. That morning therefore John walked round to Long Street and called on her. Foolata opened the front door as usual. She had a purple bruise on her cheek. John only noticed it as he passed her when she held the door into the parlour open for him. It did not show clearly because of her copper-toned colouring, but John saw it nevertheless.

Vrouw Beck and Christina he knew of course, and sitting in the parlour with them was a stout middle-aged man, bald but with a rim of pale reddish hair around his pate, very small eyes which were pale blue, and a pudgy, ruddy face.

Vrouw Beck said, "Ach, John, this is Mynheer Beck, my husband. It is nice to see you now that James has left us temporarily, but why have you come? What is your news? Not bad news I hope?"

So John told them all what had happened, and as he had it with him, he read Francesca's letter out loud. Then, under questioning from Christina, he had to explain who Francesca, the author of the letter was and what her relationship with Charles was. He was sure, he said, that Francesca would be devastated by Charles' death.

Mynheer Beck questioned him closely about this and then asked, "I suppose this also means that when Sir Marshall, the old nobleman, dies, the title will pass to James now as he is the only son?"

John said he thought that was so. He said he was not too sure however, being only a junior servant, but he thought that was probably right.

"So it also means that James will inherit the estate, does it not?"

"Yes, I suppose it does," agreed John.

"Yes, Aletta, you did well by Christina. No mistake about that. She will be a titled lady one day, and married to a rich man with a big country estate. That is good work. You did very well indeed. The English here at the Cape will have to be very nice to us now. We really ought to let them know all about this. That is, about the engagement and about the death of Mr Charles." He puffed his cheeks, stood up and started to stride around the room. He was smiling and pleased with himself at the thought of his own enhanced position in society.

John said nothing. He did not understand these things too well, but he did not like Mynheer's tone as much as anything. He knew it was not right. It was "foreign" to him and his nature.

After he left the Becks' house John thought he ought to check with Hunter Hodgson and see if he was aware of the likely length of time James' ship would take. When he told Hunter the news, that gentleman was silent at first and then said, "Well if the Becks know about Charles' death, they will have their claws into James forever now." John privately pondered whether, when he met up eventually again with James, he should tell James about his conversation with Mynheer Beck, which on reflection he did not like. He decided that he must admit to it as soon as he could.

17

Return to England

THE RUN FROM THE COLONY had been fast and comfortable, and James' ship docked in London after a voyage of some seven weeks, on a miserable dawn, dark, with a grey fog and unpleasant drizzle which matched the cold, and James' mood, precisely. He quickly got a cab from the docks to the house at Clapham, and was surprised to be greeted on his arrival there by a tearful Mrs Griggs the housekeeper. She wore black bombazine, as she always did, but James noticed at once that she had additionally sewn a black armband made of a very slightly different material onto her right sleeve.

James did not know that his brother had died, and the sight of him at the door sent Mrs Griggs into a veritable storm of tears. James realised that she was not mourning one of her numerous sisters or brothers, and when he was at last able to get a word in edgeways he asked the reason, because until then her tears had made her words completely incomprehensible. She then told James all about the dreadful accident at the railway, some seven weeks or so earlier, which she blamed firmly on the company, and the modern need for speed and all this rushing about. She told him she had saved all sorts of newspaper clippings for him. She hoped she had not missed a single report in any newspaper. She apologised for the papers being a bit crumpled, but as she explained, she read and re-read them often, because she wanted to remember it properly.

After her initial outpouring of grief for Master Charles, as she called him, she was so busy telling James how she sympathised with poor Lady Eleanor in her sore loss that she exclaimed dramatically that she had almost forgotten that she had a letter for him from that nice Miss Francesca. As she gave it to him, she said that Miss Francesca had been in London for some reason and had called and left it for James to await his return, whenever that may be. Her message was that he must read it before he did anything else. Certainly whatever happened he must read it, Miss Francesca had stressed, before he went down to Devon.

As soon as he decently could, James escaped from Mrs Griggs' explosive grief, and retired to his bedroom to open Francesca's letter. In it Francesca was insistent that he should arrange to go to her house before he went to Highsteignton. She was very clear that she had something most particular she had to tell him, and most important of all, she had to tell him before he spoke to either Sir Marshall or Lady Eleanor. James was mystified at this. He was not really able to take that in however, as he was too consumed by distress at his brother's death to notice much else. He worried about Francesca and what was to become of her. But the interview with his parents, which was yet to come, hung over him like a black cloud.

When he got up, James, having had a good bath and a sound breakfast, as he put it, packed a suitcase of fresh clothes with Mrs Griggs' invaluable and inescapable help, and went across town to Paddington Station to catch the midday train to Exeter. Charles' death, as explained to him by Mrs Griggs and the newspaper cuttings which she had thrust into his hands as he left, occupied him for a good length of time, and then he spent much of the rest of the journey trying to think why Francesca would want to see him so urgently. He had news for her of course. His engagement. Of course, he knew she would be pleased that he had found such a wonderful fiancée. He was sure she would help him with the conversation when he had to tell Sir Marshall of the engagement, who depressingly, he saw, would not be too delighted. He reflected that his life had changed so much since he had gone to the Cape. He saw in retrospect how, before he went, he had been unformed in many ways, how his feelings for Francesca had been perhaps simple youthful enthusiasm. That, he thought carelessly, was all behind him now. Christina occupied his thoughts. She was his future.

When he arrived at Exeter in the evening, he hired a coach to take him to the Trevanions' house. It was a fair journey but it was all there was for hire. The rain had got steadily worse as the train had progressed, and it was raining quite hard when he reached their house.

Richardson opened the door to him; he had no butler as the Duffields had. The old grey stone mansion his family had lived in for centuries was cold and draughty, and even the roaring log fire in the dim candlelit hall did not help much. The room was very high ceilinged, and along one wall facing the black glass of the oriel window, which had no curtains, were three suits of armour off which the firelight flickered. The floor was old, bare planking, and the only furniture was a wooden settle to one side and an old comfortable-looking armchair facing the fire. A rather tatty tapestry with very faded colouring covered one wall. James heard footsteps approaching along a passage outside, and then Francesca came into the hall. Dressed in a long and thick black mourning gown, she was holding a small handkerchief, with which she dabbed at her eyes. But she brightened when she saw James, and moved across the hall towards him. James moved slightly back to avoid an embrace, and as he did so saw a hurt look flit across her face.

"Please sit down by the fire, James," said Richardson. "Francesca has been so looking forward to your returning, you can have no idea. She has asked about you every day for months now. Of course we would all wish the circumstances were different, and the loss of Charles has been a very great shock to us all. And of course to you. And the way he died. It must have been awful for him. The points were not switched back as they should have been and his train was hit sideways on by a goods train. Two people died, and all the company can do is say sorry! You have heard all about it I expect. The newspapers were full of it. Trains are so dangerous. Francesca wrote to you all about it but maybe you did not receive the letter?"

"Mrs Griggs gave me an armful of cuttings, so yes, I have read all about the terrible railway crash. And no, when I left the Cape about seven weeks ago, no letter had come from anyone, and certainly not one from you, Francesca. I came back to give you my news, that is all."

The old man sat down next to James. "Well now, James, tell us that news first. That would be a start. How was the Cape, what was it like and did you do much travelling?"

James started to speak.

"Father. I must interrupt, I am sorry." Francesca looked at James, and paused, hesitated almost. "I hear you say you did not get my letter?" She paused, questioningly, and James nodded his agreement that he had not. She continued "Well. After you went away, I had a lot of trouble with Charles." She stopped speaking for a while, apparently trying to master strong feelings.

"You will recall what we spoke about at the river just before you went away. About Charles and how he had behaved to me earlier." With a sudden surge of memory James could see the scene by the river in his mind's eye, all the details of it. He nodded. He could hear every word she had said then. "Well, he repeated that behaviour to me again, several times, and I was unable to stop him. I tried. God knows how I tried, but there was nothing I could do. I know how much this news will hurt you in view of your feelings towards me as you showed them then, and I really do not want to hurt you. But I need to think about what I am to do in this situation now. I am bereaved, unmarried, and with his child."

"Great heavens, Francesca, what do you mean?" asked Richardson. His voice was quiet, and he sounded very old and tired. He sat back in the armchair, with his eyes closed, as if to blot the world out of sight. There was silence for a moment.

"I mean father, that Charles has made me with child and that is all there is to it. My, and as a consequence, your disgrace will now follow without me or you doing anything. We shall be complete social outcasts as soon as people see my condition, in my unmarried state. Society will be ruthless. I have not told anyone but you two, as you are the two who are dearest to me, and I shall need the help of both of you when I tell Lady Eleanor and Sir Marshall face to face, as I really must do very shortly. I half expect them not to believe that it was their beloved Charles who did this. Heaven only knows who they will think of instead. It is some time now since Charles was killed in that crash. I cannot go on sitting around just getting larger and larger without people noticing my condition." Francesca felt humiliated to have to talk about these things with, and in front of, her father. She grieved silently for her mother, and over what had happened to her. The silence lengthened. The old dark room was hearing more family secrets, and seemed to absorb them by the dim light of the candles.

James kept quiet. He did not know how he could now tell her and her father about Christina. After what she had just said he felt it was impossible to tell them. This was clearly not the moment to do that. Maybe later, much later, would be better. And he recognised from the way she was looking at him and what she had said, that it sounded as though Francesca thought he loved her, even after all this time.

"James, dear James, you are very quiet. Can you say something, please?" begged Francesca. "James, before you left you had feelings toward me, I know you did. I even thought, foolishly perhaps, that you loved me. That picture you drew of me, that was itself a declaration. I have not changed my feelings towards you. Although I never said anything directly, I loved you then, and I still love you now, despite my condition. Perhaps I should have spoken out. It was my idea, conceited as it now sounds, that you only went to the Cape because of me. To get away from me and my engagement, and because you did not want to be around when Charles and I got married. That you did not leave because of the invitation from Harry at all."

"This is all news to me," said Richardson. "I cannot keep up with all this. Do you mean," he said to Francesca, "that James was, or for that matter still is, in love with you? That's not right. Charles loved you. I know. You two were engaged to be married. What are you talking about James for now?"

"Father, I never loved Charles. I have always loved James. And with all my heart I am deeply sorry for bringing this disgrace on you. But I did not mean to. Charles insisted on forcefully having his way with me, more than once because, as he said, we were going to be married anyway, as indeed we were, so what did it matter if he anticipated that happy event. But he is dead now, and I am with his child as a result. I tried to resist him, I did really, but I was just not strong enough physically. I only became engaged to Charles because of his prospects, and, although perhaps I should not say this, maybe you wanted me to marry him, father. But I loved another. James. I always have."

James stood. "Richardson, what Francesca means is that she and I thought we might be in love, once, one evening, and then Charles proposed and that was that. It was all over before it had even begun. It had been decided between you and my father that they would be married. My father blessed that engagement, as you know. You were there that awful evening. Francesca and I could do nothing about it. So I left to get out of everybody's way, as to stay would have been far too painful for both of us."

Richardson sat with his eyes closed, as if in pain at what he was hearing. He was silent for some moments, and then said, in a sad old tone, "I have been very selfish, or very blind, or both, is what you both mean. I never knew. Just an old fool with no understanding of young people. One or other of you should have said something."

132

"No father, you only did what you thought was for the best at the time. You did not know about James, and how we felt, because we did not tell you, and even if you had known it would have made no difference."

"But you are still with child, and unmarried. That does not change."

The three of them did not speak for a while. James was silent. He felt he was trapped between two women. He was facing the awful moment that he had realised was nearing ever since Francesca had started to tell her story. The next moment or two were going to be, he felt, deciding moments in his life. It seemed he had no choice. He was going to inherit the title in due course, and of course, the estate. And it was true, he thought that he might once have loved Francesca, in a youthful way. But it had been a very inexperienced love, he thought to himself, the love of a young man on a summer evening. But he was more mature now, and he loved Christina. She and she alone was everything to him, even if they were not married. And of course they had not anticipated their marriage in the way Charles and Francesca had. But he knew Francesca was a lady who for the sake of personal honour had to be protected from certain and very public obloquy and shame, as also did his own family's honour, and his brother's good name. He realised even as he under-stood, that if all that was to be avoided, and that if Francesca was indeed to be protected from scandal and social ostracism, he had no choice but to marry her, and that meant he would have to give up Christina. To end the love of which he was certain. Perhaps most important of all, if he did not marry her, both his parents and her father would be socially ostracised, and none of them would be able to hold their heads up in any company. But he could only protect Francesca and them by ignoring his heart, where he felt his true, mature, feelings now were.

He knew they both were certain he would do the right thing. He felt they were both looking at him with great intensity. He wanted to do the right thing. Neither Francesca nor her father had any idea at all of even Christina's existence, let alone the engagement. They of course assumed that James would behave like any unmarried gentleman in his situation would. They both thought he was a carefree single gentleman, and naturally expected him to behave like one. It was his brother after all who had created the problem. They looked at him expectantly, waiting for him to speak. The longer the wait continued, the more difficult it became for him to say what he knew he had to say. The silence was intolerable. James broke it. Eventually.

"I will marry you, Francesca. If you would have me of course. It is not the sort of proposal I had ever thought I might make to you, but I hope it will be enough." He was looking at the floor as he spoke, downcast, and realised sadly that his voice had no joyful tone about it. But just then he could not bring himself to say that he loved her. He knew she expected him to say that, but that was simply not possible. He loved Christina, and although he knew he was doing something very terrible to her, he silently vowed to himself that he would never openly deny her, as he grimly recognised he had denied Francesca. But that was all in the past. He was sadly aware how stilted and dishonourable his unspoken thoughts were.

Francesca was plainly disappointed at the way he expressed the proposal. She did not understand why he had put it that way or why he had not said that he loved her, as she was sure he used to. He seemed so reticent, and she fretted that he was in his way impliedly criticising her for the fact that she had, against her will it is true, let Charles ravish her.

"James, of course I love you and I am so happy and pleased to be free and able to marry you. It was what I always wanted to do anyway. As I thought you always knew. I shall do my best to be a good and suitable wife to you. I am only sorry that we shall have to get married in a rush now in view of my condition. I would have so loved the perfect wedding with you. Church bells, flowers and the whole wide world to see our happiness." She paused. "You do still love me don't you, James? You have not said so."

"Do not press the man," her father said to Francesca. "Can you not see he has had a terrible shock, what with first his brother's terrible death, and now your dreadful, and very shameful news too. We have all had a shock, and I am not at all sure I understand it all myself."

And so James was spared, at least temporarily, the personal embarrassment of saying the words he could not then mean, might never be able to mean. Of course, the next hurdle would be calling on his parents and telling them he was engaged to Francesca. He would not tell them about Christina, and Francesca would have to be the one to tell Lady Eleanor that she wanted the marriage to happen quickly.

Richardson insisted on driving Francesca and James over to the Duffields in the brougham the next morning. It looked as if it might be a nice day, with high fluffy white clouds fast scudding overhead. The air was sharp in the way the last few days of summer can sometimes be, and a few leaves in the hedgerows were starting to change colour. Had he not been sunk almost in despair about meeting his parents and what he had done to Christina, about which he could tell nobody, the artist in James would have enjoyed the journey.

Coleman was at the door for their arrival, as he always was. Despite what had happened, he was respectfully delighted to see James, and he obviously wanted to talk about John and how the trip had gone. James said he would seek him out later to give him all the news about John, but in the meantime he must speak to his parents first, and he led the other two into the drawing room.

"Oh, James. We did not know you were coming home. What a lovely surprise. We did not know you knew about Charles. We did not think you could have. Surely there hasn't been time for

Francesca's letter to reach you at the Cape." Lady Eleanor paused expectantly. "And you Francesca dear, how are you bearing up today? It is all so awful."

"I am very well today, thank you," said Francesca, lightly. "And I hope you are both managing to get by."

James interrupted the proprieties. "No, mother, father, I have not had any letter, and I did not know about Charles' accident. At least, not until I reached Clapham yesterday morning when Mrs Griggs told me in huge detail, and gave me all her newspaper cuttings about the accident. She must have bought up a newsagent's entire establishment. I came down last night and rather than disturb you so late, I called on Richardson and Francesca en route, and spent the night there."

"That was kind of them, and very thoughtful of you too, my boy," said Sir Marshall. "Very thoughtful indeed." He smiled, a little thinly.

"Mother, father. Francesca and I have some happy news for you, which I hope will take your mind away from sad thoughts about Charles, even if only for a while. I know it is something you will not have dreamed of but the short truth is that Francesca and I are engaged to be married. It is a shock I know, so soon after Charles' death. There has been no mourning yet. But the fact is that I always loved Francesca, and when it was arranged for her to marry Charles I was so upset that I could think of nothing better to do than to go abroad for an extended period. That is why I went to the Cape to stay with Harry, not because of his invitation. But I did not get over her, as I thought, so I came home, and then I heard the news about Charles, and realised she was free. She took a lot of persuading, of course, but late last night she agreed to marry me, with Richardson's approval, and so here we are to break the happy news. We are to be married."

Sir Marshall looked silently to his wife for inspiration, but even if he had wanted to do so he could not have prevented her from taking the lead in replying. The news which she had only lately received about Charles' dreadful death was completely lost in this latest news of a new wedding. So any worries that Francesca might have had about her reception were dispelled at once. Lady Eleanor was delighted, absolutely enthusiastically, volubly and very loudly delighted. She rushed across the room and, flushed with excitement, embraced her, and then held her at arm's length and admired her. She kissed Francesca's cheek, and embraced her again. Francesca was very relieved at that, and inwardly she was very happy that she was going to marry the brother she loved.

"But, Lady Eleanor, there is one way our very happy news will upset you, I know," Francesca continued lightly. "We have decided that in view of the very sad, tragic, circumstances about Charles, and because we are all in mourning, and do not want to cause you any unnecessary trouble or embarrassment, James and I are to be married quickly and quietly, without too much fuss at all. It will all be very difficult I know, because of the mourning of course."

"But my dear," boomed Sir Marshall, "I shall be paying, so there is no need to be so reticent about it."

"No, we are not being reticent. We just want to respect your mourning, and the memory of Charles. And that is how we both want it to be," said Francesca.

Richardson said, "I am quite happy with a quiet wedding as well. It is what they both want, and it seems fitting to me that in these terrible times, that should be the deciding factor in the how and the when of it all. I am sure they only want it this way out of respect for the delicacy of your feelings."

And so the matter was settled as simply and as easily as could be. Lady Eleanor fetched Coleman in and told him the good news as she put it, and he on Sir Marshall's instructions fetched two bottles of champagne, and they drank numerous toasts until it was all gone. Conversation flowed as well, and James was able to tell Coleman about John and how he was making out. He explained that John was busy helping Harry in getting the stores ready for a trip, but he did not say where they were going, and Coleman did not know to ask. He told Sir Marshall about his new friends at the castle and life in the colony, and kept him as entertained as he could. Francesca and Lady Eleanor were busy talking about clothes, and the strangeness of the unusual and informal low-key wedding they wanted, and how it would all work out, and where they would live. Lady Eleanor suggested Charles' new Chelsea house might be a suitable place for them, but Francesca made a very strong objection to that.

Sir Marshall almost inevitably noticed that James was not wearing the signet ring. James said it had been stolen from his room when he had been downstairs in the dining room. The moment passed without more questions, to James' relief. Sir Marshall just looked up at the ceiling and sighed. Later that evening as James sat on his own with his father, James thought they might be going to have the sort of talk that a father and son should have in these circumstances. But it was not to be. And all the while they were talking, James was thinking about Christina. He could see her in his mind's eye. He would have to tell her what he had done. But he could not yet leave Francesca in order to do that.

18

The Wedding

THE MARRIAGE WAS TO BE, as Lady Eleanor put it, "a hole and corner affair". True, it was in Exeter Cathedral with Bishop Philpotts officiating, with a choir of thirty, and with the bells ringing out over the city. But to her it was rushed, "an early morning do", and not at all what she had wanted by way of ceremony. She had wanted something in the City of London with a lot of City pomp and circumstance, and the Lord Mayor, and the Freemen of the Guild of Attorneys in their robes. But Francesca held out that it was to be as simple as may be allowed, and Lady Eleanor had to give way eventually. In fact did she but know it, Francesca was so happy that it mattered not to her where the marriage took place. She just wanted to be married, and to be married to James. She and James had led a chaste period of engagement lasting five weeks, and she wanted the wedding night with James to be as happy as her experiences with Charles had been awful.

The wedding luncheon was at Highsteignton, and although no expense or frippery was omitted, Francesca was only too keen for it to be over. The speeches to the surprisingly small number of guests were, she thought, quite dreadful, and Sir Charles was as bombastic and as tight as he had ever been.

Lady Eleanor had been utterly appalled when she heard that the young couple were going to spend the wedding night in a fisherman's cottage in the Cornish fishing village of Fowey, of all places. Francesca thought James' choice was perfectly romantic but then James spoilt her dream of the place for her by telling her that the former fisherman's cottage nowadays belonged to an artist friend of his who used it as a studio, and he had gone off to Brittany on a painting holiday. Apparently Quimperle, where he had gone, was the up and coming place for artists, and he would not be returning for about three months. So they could have the place rent free.

James of course had other thoughts than romance on his mind. His guilt at what he knew he had done to Christina by marrying Francesca was all consuming. That first evening together as a married couple when Francesca rose after their supper in the tiny, and in truth rather depressing, little whitewashed cottage, she assumed that James would quickly follow her – she liked to think he would be in unseemly haste – upstairs to bed. She undressed and put on her new satin nightgown, which she had especially chosen as she knew eau de nil was James' favourite colour. When after a discreet period he did not come upstairs, she called him.

He came to her much later, when she had almost fallen asleep. He looked so serious that she knew immediately that something was grievously wrong. But she had no idea what it might be or what she had done. He spoke in low-pitched, staccato sentences. His voice was a little hoarse at times. He would not look at her as he spoke.

"Francesca, I must talk to you. I have to tell you something very serious. I know you are pregnant, and we are married now, but there is something dreadful I should have told you before now, well before, long ago, before we got married. I am very deeply ashamed I didn't. It was wrong of me, very wrong of me not to have done so. You will not be able to forgive me when I do tell you, but that can't be helped. I am very sorry about it all. It is far too late now.

"No, no, please do not interrupt. It is hard enough to tell you anyway, but tell you I must. You will have wondered why I came home from the Cape when I did. After all I had not received the letter you wrote about Charles' terrible railway accident, and so you must have wondered why I did come home. Well. The reason was that I had news of my own for you and all the family that I wanted to tell you in person and not by letter. While I was out there I met a young lady called Christina Beck. We fell in love, and with the approval of her mother and her minister, we became engaged to be married. I gave her my signet ring as an engagement ring. It wasn't stolen, I gave it to her. We are, or we were, very happy. So, I came home to tell everyone about this."

"And I stopped you doing that, by telling you I was with Charles' child. Is that right?"

"Yes it is. And when you told me about your problem, I knew I had to marry you because you are pregnant, and it was his baby, so I had to give both you and the child a name. And that would let you keep your honour as well, and both families would be protected from scandal. You would not be disgraced, and neither would Charles, or the baby for that matter. So we got married and all the time I was thinking of Christina, and how we are, or perhaps I should say were, engaged. 'Impediment.' Good God, when that word was said during the ceremony I half expected someone to shout that the wedding should, must, stop. I could think of nothing else. Indeed, I still can't. I can't stop thinking about it and I do not know even now if I have done the right thing by you, the baby or the family. I know for certain I have done the wrong thing as far as Christina is concerned."

"Is that why you would never say you loved me James? Because you love someone else? You used to love me, I am quite sure you did. In fact I know you did, once. That portrait. I rather vainly thought that was why you left and went to the Cape."

"Yes, of course that was why I went to the Cape. I loved you then, or at least I thought I might be starting to fall in love. But then I met Christina. And I knew the difference between what I felt for you then and the way I felt about her, and I still feel now. Oh, it is all my fault. I should have told you all this well before the wedding, I know. I should have written from the Cape, I suppose. But the longer it went on without my telling you anything about Christina, the harder and harder it somehow was to tell you, that I do not love you, and that I love Christina."

"But surely you would never have married me if you did not love me a little. Just a little?"

"I am so sorry. I really am. I don't know how I can say it differently. I know I should have trusted you and told you everything much, so very much earlier, but I didn't. I have no excuses. It is her I love, as I say."

"James. Oh James, you have been so much for me, and have been so kind and generous, and now I have separated you from her, and you will never be able to marry her because we are married. But you must go back and tell her we are married. At once. If she loves you as I do, I hope she will understand the reason for our marriage, and while she may not forgive you, in fact I am quite sure she will not, I hope she will at least understand that you did what you did in marrying me out of kindness and respect for me and the baby, and in obedience to society's dictates."

Francesca had known since they got engaged that things were not right between her and James, but she had placed all her hopes on this one night and it all coming right then, but now it was clear that that had been a very insecure and very false hope. She had hoped that this their wedding night would lead to James understanding at last how much she loved him, and he would in turn love her, as she was sure he had in the past. Now she knew that her hope was completely impossible. She was emotionally shattered.

James did not feel he had to reply directly to her last remarks. He felt anything he said was likely to be wildly wrong. He had a presentiment that all would not go well when he told Christina what he had done. So he changed his thinking and said, "I am very happy for you to have Charles' baby, and I am very happy for it to have my name, and for us to bring it up as mine. All the world will think it is mine. I will never do anything, ever, to make people think otherwise. I know I cannot marry Christina now, and that that engagement is broken by what you and I have done. I will never repeat to a soul what I have said tonight, and all the world shall think we are just an ordinary, happy married couple."

James' words, intended by him to be calming, were not. Francesca's calmness broke. She had been very still up to that point. A violent storm had raged within her, and she was very angry and tearful. She started crying now, and almost shouting with despair.

"Ordinary. Happy? My God! Ordinary did you say? If what you say is true, and I must accept that it is I suppose, you had absolutely no right to marry me. You should have left me to rot in my own sin, and said good riddance to me. You did not do that, and I suppose all credit to you for that, but it would seem that you only married me so as to be able to be cruel, to both of us. You have made an unhappy trap, a horrible trap for both of us. We can never be happy. You married me out of pity, and not because you loved me."

Francesca was sobbing violently now, and out of bed, pacing the small bare-boarded little room. She clutched her nightgown tightly around her shoulders and turned to face James. "But for whatever reason you married me, I have to tell you that I still love you James, I always have ever since I first met you. I treasure the happy memory of that glorious sunny day at Sidmouth, and I thought you did too. We were both paddling in the shallow water, you built a sandcastle, I can see it now. My father met your parents by pure chance that day. Oh God, if only we could go back in time."

She paused for some time, lost apparently in thought. She seemed to calm, a calm of desperate decision. Then, determinedly and after a deep breath, she continued, "But whatever you do now, and whysoever you do it, I will go on loving you. I should have said outright how I felt about you long ago I know, and I did not. That silence. That is my fault, not yours. If I had told you all how I felt, none of this would ever have happened. It is all my fault for being silent when I should have told you. But I cannot undo the past, and nor can you. It is all too late. So now I just have to try to win your heart over time. I will be a good wife. I can do that at least. I will make you a home to love, and I will love, honour and obey you in all things. I must be punished for my sin, I know, but that is not for you to do. I will most certainly do that for myself. My child will never hear of any father but you. He will love you as I do. I can say nothing more."

James stood absolutely still. He too could say nothing. He had trapped both of them in a hopeless marriage, and he knew he must pay for doing that. Ignoring him, Francesca lay down on the bed, and put out her candle. Her body was wracked by quiet sobbing. Later, much later, when she seemed to have dropped off to sleep, James very quietly got in the hard little bed beside her. He could feel the warmth of her body, and thought of the new life stirring inside it, but could not respond. They lay together for a long time. Woken, Francesca sobbed again, quietly at first, and then they gently held each other closely in their individual sadness, and when she had almost given up any thoughts of lovemaking Francesca found that she and James were making soft and tender love of the sort she had never known. James was silent as they made love, but as he climaxed, he called out, aloud. Francesca could not hear it clearly, and ever after hoped that it was her name he had called. She never knew.

Most days James went out fishing for mackerel with a fisherman called Harold Martin who lived in the village, and when successful he brought home what he had caught. He even asked Harold if he could go out with the cellar members in a seine boat if the pilchards came, but when Harold asked the other members of the cellar they said no. During these fishing trips Francesca was left on her own, and as the cottage was so small, and so sparsely furnished, she was much at a loss as to what to do. As a result, to fill her time she spent many hours walking by herself around the harbour, and gradually came to know a few of the fishermen's wives who stood and chatted as they knitted, and waited for their men. They made it plain to her they thought it strange and sad that a newlywed should be so left alone by her husband. They seemed to feel sorry for her, and as a gesture of friendship they tried to show her how to use knit sticks, but she could never manage them, and anyway it made her back ache. The women said that was because she had no need of money, and had she needed it she would have learnt like them. But they gave her a pair to practise with, and an old widow called Mrs Clark who lived down by the quay said knowingly that they sometimes used them for dealing with other problems as well.

After they had been at Fowey for ten days James suggested a bit shamefacedly that they should return to her father's house. There seemed, he said, very sadly, to be no point in their staying on. Francesca agreed, regretfully, because she still hoped that one night more James would come upstairs instead of sleeping downstairs on the cottage floor, as he did after that first night. Part of Francesca's unhappiness was caused by the fact that James was a kind and considerate man and behaved so well to her that she was devastated. His unfailing kindness made it all even worse she thought. So she made it plain in every little thing she did or tried to do that she loved James, and he for his part was gentle and helpful to her. But when they were alone together he would not hold her, and sometimes she thought he flinched when she kissed him in greeting, and he would not say he loved her. Above all he would not say that, the one thing above everything that Francesca craved. But he had made love to her, that once, and she longed for him to do so again.

Even as they caught the coach to leave Fowey, with the fisherman's wife from next door looking at them slyly, anyone who did not know the true state of affairs would have thought from seeing them together that they were a devoted, loving couple. The old woman from the quay merely smiled at Francesca, and wished her luck with the knit sticks.

*

James had known for some time that he would have to go back to the Cape to face Christina with his news. But what he did not know was how to tell Richardson or his parents that he was leaving. A newly married man leaving his wife before they had even settled down! It was not to be borne. He was too ashamed. It was not what a gentleman did.

After a spell of some two weeks at Trevanion's house, they went by train to Clapham for a visit to see some of James' friends, as Francesca thought, because James had told her it was so. Mrs Griggs was delighted to see them of course, but soon became concerned at the way James, as a newly married man, always slept on the bed in his dressing room while they were there. It was not her place to say anything so she kept her peace, but she knew that something was wrong between them. It was not really comprehensible to her as Francesca was so loving towards James, and he was so kind to her, considerate and gentle.

The fragile peace Francesca thought she was constructing for their marriage was shattered by James one morning at breakfast. He opened his newspaper, and sat pale-faced, pretending to read it. Looking up from it he said, very abruptly, "I have written a letter to my parents telling them I have to go to the Cape in order to fetch John and bring him safely back home." He did not look at Francesca as he said it. The newspaper was a pretence, thought Francesca.

"Please do not leave me. I love you. I want you to stay."

He looked down and tried to pretend he was reading the paper, and said, "I have absolutely no choice in the matter. I have left it far too long already. I should have gone weeks ago. It would most definitely not be suitable for you to come, and I am sure it would be most unwise for you to undertake the journey in your condition anyway. And I have to bring John back with me."

"Why cannot John find his own passage back? He does not need any help, he is practically a grown man now, and if he does need help, then Harry is at hand. You do not need to go for John."

"No, I agree, but I need to go to Christina for my own reasons, which of course you know only too well. She will be worrying about me and why I am not there, and I cannot permit that."

"Well, if I am not allowed to go with you, then I will wait here for you, so at least I will be near you when you land on your return."

"What you do or do not do is for you to decide. I must go to Christina. You are your own mistress now and you can live wherever you choose. You do not have to wait here for me. I have been to my bankers, Martins Bank, and arranged an allowance for you. It will not be very large I am afraid, but it will be dependable, and enough for you. If you need more, I am afraid I must ask you to rely on my father's generosity. I may be away a long time, it all depends, and your baby will certainly be born while I am away."

"You will be away that long?" gasped Francesca.

"I cannot say how long I shall be away. You said in the marriage service that you would always obey me, and this is what I ask you to do now."

"How shall I explain it to my father, or to your parents? They will think it very peculiar that you have gone to the Cape again. What on earth do I tell them?"

"You must tell them that I have gone to fetch John. Don't forget that I do not want them to know about Christina, and nor do you want that either, I imagine. Tell them that I shall bring John back safe with me. Tell them that you do not know how long I shall be away. That will all be the truth. Just not the whole truth."

And so he made Francesca lie, as well as cry.

19

Return to the Cape

J AMES SAILED FOR THE CAPE on the *Agincourt* under Captain Hyde on 19th July 1850. Shipboard, he made an agreement to meet again with his fellow travellers with whom he shared what was a happy and social passage. The little group called themselves "The Agincourt Club", and engaged to dine at Simpsons in the Strand the day after the Derby, some ten years ahead. James noted it down in a spare notebook he had. They had a fast run south of about two months, and anchored in Table Bay safely, the wind being very light at that time. The ferry boatmen were soon hard at work taking passengers and crew ashore with their baggage and goods, and James scanned the large waiting crowd on the beach to see if he could see anyone he knew. James was familiar with the scene, but it struck him afresh as being chaotic and highly mephitic, and also it was certainly a great deal busier than he remembered. The day was as hot as any he had experienced at the Cape and he was therefore delighted to hire a Malay (one of many who offered) to take his luggage up to Parke's, in return for a small payment. For himself, James decided to stroll around slowly on his own and enjoy the sights. But this was not to be.

"You young scamp!" cried Bladen on spotting him on the corner of the Town House on Green Market Square. "We wondered if we would see you again. What have you been doing with yourself back in the old country? The place is all aswirl with rumours about you, apparently there was something in *The Times*, which I did not see myself, but apparently it was an announcement of your marriage to someone. I forget who. So am I to assume that you will not be calling on the Becks any time soon?"

(Engaged to dine at "Simpson's", Strand, the day after the Derby, 1860, with the members of the "Agincourt Club." —

This note about a future dining engagement was found in a discarded notebook in the back of James Duffield's wagon and was among the loose papers not included in the inventory that was taken of its contents after his death. It is in James' handwriting.

James inwardly cursed his mother's desire for all things to be done with due formality. She would have been responsible for placing the announcement in the paper. He and Francesca had not seen it, but that was because there was nowhere that sold newspapers in Fowey. And it was his own fault, guilt he supposed, at what he had done, that had then made him delay in setting out for the Cape.

"Mynheer Beck is back from another of his protracted visits to Bloemfontein, and apparently very keen to meet you. He is telling everyone that your being married will all be found to be a great mistake, and that his beloved daughter is going to marry a rich nobleman. I thought I ought to warn you. He knows you are planning on a good long trek, and says he wants you to marry the girl before you go. He is showing everyone the ring you gave the girl as proof of the engagement. You may," he concluded in a rather sweeping understatement, "have a few problems there." He smiled rather bleakly at James.

James mumbled an embarrassed reply which said nothing, and tried to pass off lightly what he had just been told. But he had to admit to himself that perhaps he had not been too wise to return. Of course he did have to fetch John back safely, and he groaned as he inwardly admitted that John could have managed that without any help.

A little while later he met Hunter and Gervase who said they were on their way to the printers for something. Hunter politely congratulated him on his marriage. But Gervase asked if it were the case that he really was married, what he was going to do about Christina and his alleged engagement to her. James could not really answer properly. He did not know, and trying to pass it off wittily as a youthful indiscretion which was what he had half thought he might do – actually it was his only plan as to what he could do – did not seem such a good idea.

Hunter took him slightly aside as Gervase moved ahead a little, and asked, "Have you heard from Harry yet?"

"What do you mean? I have only just landed, and have not had time to talk to anyone yet, except you of course, and Bladen. I met him in the street just now."

"Well I think you ought to know that Harry was unable to get another extension of his furlough, and has been recalled by his regiment, and left about a fortnight ago to return to Madras. But there is a serious problem now. There is a bill that is outstanding with us that he ran up as we ended up, being his and your agents, paying various traders for the supplies he acquired for your trek, and he just left without paying us. Your allowance did arrive just after you had left, but it is rather less than you had led me to expect, and this is rather embarrassing. So the account looks pretty black, or should I say red, at the moment. But the real point is as you know that the account is in your name, not his. You will recall setting the account up on your first visit I am sure."

"Yes of course I remember, I know it is all my debt. But how much is owing?" asked James anxiously.

"Well over one thousand pounds sterling. But that is not the worst thing. He had to leave Coleman in charge of looking after the supplies already bought. John did the best he could after Harry left, but he has had to sell one or two things to pay his own way while you have been away, and plainly he is not experienced in these things. So he has lost a little money, not much, but a little.

"On the other hand, the good news is that I have found a young Englishman who can take Harry's place on the proposed trek. He is a nice chap, very experienced, and wants to crack on with things as soon as he can. He tells me that his family come from Devon. His name is Lewis. Or at least his Christian name is Lewis. I am not sure I know his surname. He only went to a local school, not like you of course, and he seems a bit of a rough diamond. He tells me he has been near to the sort of area that you aim to try and reach, and he is as I am told very experienced. I think he may make a good trek companion for you."

James did not note the cautious terms Hunter used, although he recalled them well enough later on.

"That is good news. But Harry, going back to Madras? I know he did not want to go. He still had about twelve months' furlough left, did he not?"

"Harry said there was some sort of military crisis, I did not really listen, you know. But anyway, I think the real problem was that he ran out of money, furlough pay is so low, and so he had no choice but to answer the call to return. Others, such as Bladen for example, who seem to have plenty of the ready stuff, just ignored the call. In fact it was Harry who found this chap Lewis and sent him to me. Harry said you and this chap Lewis are well matched and you will find him very good on trek. 'A veritable treasure,' Harry called him, and 'one you deserve.'"

James wandered on in a deep reverie. He was staggered at what he had just been told, and assumed there would be a letter from Harry waiting for him at Parke's when he got there. He was not really looking where he was going. He was also worrying about Christina and trying once more to work out what he would say to her. Something which he had been trying to think about for some time now, for months in fact, without success.

Loud and repeated shouts of "swart skepsel", meaning black creature, intermingled with other shouting, broke into his thoughts. A little way up the street ahead he could see a small crowd of people, and amidst them a big burly white man armed with a jambok slashing fiercely at a native girl, who was cowering on the ground under blows which were raining down on her. She was trying to protect herself by curling up, with her arms over her head. James knew instantly that she must be protected from this furious assault. Whatever had led to the beating it must be stopped, and at once. The melee was just outside a Boer church or chapel, and the small crowd of people had presumably emerged from that building and were standing watching what was going on. But they were making no attempt to interfere with what was happening. Indeed the encouragement the white man was getting from the crowd determined James on decisive action to halt the attack. No one at all was trying to help the girl. Possibly this native had tried to go into the church and had just been driven out. James knew that a black man even entering a church is considered sacrilege by a Boer, but even so the beating was completely intolerable for any reason, it was far too violent, and the non-interference by the people standing by was just as bad, if not worse, in James' eyes.

James gave no thought for himself or what he was about to do. He instinctively quickened his pace and, coming up to the crowd, pushed in. He seized the man's right wrist with a firm grip and snatched the jambok out of his hand, before he was aware of what he was doing. James instantly threw it down, swung his fist at the man, and hit him squarely on the cheek. The man staggered and turned to face his unexpected assailant. He stepped back a half pace and threw a haymaker at James, who swayed away from that, and again hit the man, this time full on the jaw, with a strong uppercut. The man staggered, and James hit him again, this time in the belly. Hard. The man went down winded, and sat on the ground speechless, gasping for breath. The onlookers had not moved, but there were shouts at James that it was the will of God that she should be beaten, and others encouraging the man to get up and fight, and other shouts cursing the girl as a daughter of Cain. James was afraid the man might well get up, so he grabbed the girl by the arm and, pulling her to her feet, dragged her away. He pulled her along as fast as he could because he did not want to be pursued, so they were almost running. The girl said nothing, but then she was in no real state to say much. She was bleeding from where the jambok had cut her arms, hands and shoulder, and she was snivelling.

They rounded the corner, and James only saw then with great relief that they were almost at Parke's, so with only a pace or two more he was able to pull her in through the door. As he sat her down on a hall chair she said, "Oh Mister James, oh, Mister James. Thank you. Thank you." It was Foolata. James had not realised who the girl was. It had all happened so quickly he had not had time to look and see whom he was helping, but now he saw it was Foolata, and that she was in very great distress. She could hardly speak. Her breath came in great gulping sobs, and she was trying to stop her face from bleeding with a rag from her pocket.

Mrs Parke came bustling up to see who had burst in her front door, and saw her and James. James explained very briefly what had happened and how he had stopped the man from beating Foolata. As she shushed James and Foolata through the hall and into a back scullery, Mrs Parke called out for one of the hotel maids called Maureen to fetch a bowl and some warm water, and when it arrived Maureen started to bathe the cuts, which she could see were pretty deep. Impatiently, James took the cloth from the girl, and as gently as he could he washed the wounds clean. Meanwhile Mrs Parke had been and brought some bandaging, so James was able to put a dressing on the shoulder. Foolata winced but made no sound, she simply watched James intently.

When he had finished, and was safely in her office, Mrs Parke and James talked the incident over much more fully, and James asked Mrs Parke if she could find a place for Foolata to stay for the night, in view of her sorry condition. He offered to pay for what she needed. Mrs Parke asked how the girl had known James' name, she had said it and Mrs Parke had heard her say it, so James explained that she worked for the Becks, and was their servant. Mrs Parke, of course, was friendly with the Becks but she said that so long as James was paying of course Foolata could stay the night, provided she shared a room with Maureen. She said Maureen was the daughter of a poor Irish immigrant but she was a good worker, and that she missed having all her sisters around her, so sharing a room with another girl would make her very happy. She could help Maureen stoke the boilers for the hot water.

Foolata said nothing as Maureen helped her up, and then supported her away to the servants' quarters at the rear of the hotel. As she went, she looked back at James.

Still in a state almost of shock at what he had done, James asked Mrs Parke about Harry, and was told that there was no letter from Harry waiting for him. He had more than half expected there would be, but there was none. Mrs Parke also pointed out that Harry had not paid for his room and lodging because he had told Mrs Parke that James would pay. So although Mrs Parke said she was sorry that Harry had left, it was always sad when a regular like Harry left, she hoped that James would not mind letting her have a bit of money on account as it was really mounting up for the three of them. John had a cheaper room of course, but they all cost money, and his had been kept empty ready for his return. At first James had been so shaken up by what he had done to stop the attack on the girl, that the cheek of Mrs Parke, as he thought of it, in asking for money had quite driven the incident out of his mind. But when he was able to sit quietly in his room a little later, he realised he had given no thought to what he had been doing when he attacked the attacker. He then realised that acting out of instinct instead of after rational thought had been foolish, maybe, but he knew he had simply reacted to what he had seen in the only way he could.

The next day James asked after Foolata, as he did not see her. But he thought that as a servant that was understandable. Mrs Parke told him that Foolata had left, she did not know for where, but presumably she had family somewhere, and sadly she had apparently helped herself to a silver jug kept on the sideboard when she left.

"And how much do I owe you, all told, for all of us, including the jug of course?" asked James with a sense of being about to be told an unrealistic figure.

"About one hundred and seventy pounds in all, including one night for Foolata, and the jug is extra."

When Mrs Parke later found the jug, which had fallen down the back of the sideboard, she did not mention it to anyone. She just put it back in its place.

20

Accounting

ON TOP OF EVERYTHING ELSE, James was now worried about money. He had already spent more than his father had said would be his allowance, and anyway he had not even fully received the whole of the promised sum. His main worry however was Christina. James was only too well aware that he could no longer delay seeing her and her family. With a heavy heart he knew that he was going to have to tell the person he loved most in all the world that he could not marry her, as he once wanted to do so much. He thought he must tell her bluntly; he was quite sure he would not be able to bear giving a long explanation.

But the next morning before he could do anything else, John came to find him, and recounted his whole conversation with Mynheer Beck. James did not fully take in all that was said to him, but he did not like the tone of what he was told. With those concerns ringing in his head, James set off to see Christina, without any feeling of happiness or joy. He would probably not, he reflected despondently, ever see her again once she knew what he had done. When he knocked at the Becks' door there was a long wait and then it was opened by Christina herself.

James was taken aback, but then he recalled that of course Foolata was somewhere else, he did not know where exactly, but after the beating he had interrupted, he assumed Foolata would not return to the Becks again. Christina stepped towards him and reached out her arms expecting an embrace. He flinched as she held him tightly. She was physically more beautiful in reality than he remembered, and he could feel her warm body pressing against his.

She kissed him passionately. James was as unresponsive as he felt a married man like himself should be.

"Come inside this instant. We cannot be shamed by two young people standing kissing in public. You cannot just go doing that," boomed out a smiling Vrouw Beck who suddenly appeared, who loomed almost, thought James, behind Christina. She led the way into the parlour. James and Christina sat next to each other on the sofa and held hands, and Vrouw Beck sat opposite them and not in her usual chair by the window.

"Well, James. Have you come back to marry my beloved little girl, and make her a noblewoman?" she asked.

"There is a problem," said James slowly, with a feeling of dread, as if the ground beneath him was about to open up. "The problem is that I cannot marry her ... you I mean," he said, turning to Christina. He put Christina's hand down gently and laid his hand on top of hers. "The thing is, when I returned to England I got married to my dead brother Charles' fiancée. So I cannot marry you. It was a family arrangement. I had no choice, I was required to do it."

"But we are engaged to be married. You cannot just not marry me. You love me, and I love you."

"Of course I love you," said James. "You know I do. But when I returned I had to marry Francesca, she was my dead brother's fiancée, and so I am married to her and I cannot marry you, however much we both want to be married."

"Why did you have to marry her?" demanded Vrouw Beck, peering at James grimly through narrowed eyes. She rose very threateningly to her feet. "No one can make someone marry them against their will. Why did you have to? What on earth do you mean?"

"I just did. I cannot tell you more. There is no more to tell you, anyway, it is all too shameful. It was a matter of family honour, and I had absolutely no choice about it."

While James was saying this, the door next to him slowly opened and a big, somewhat overweight man stepped in. He was bald save for a thin rim of reddish brown hair around his head, and a very pudgy face, and on his right cheek was a nasty red bruise mark. James recognised him instantly. He was the man who had been thrashing Foolata with a jambok in the street the day before. The man peered at James. He leant forward, and then out of nowhere, as James later thought of it, a fist appeared and crashed into James' left eye, and then another on his chin. James fell on the floor. He was stunned and he felt, rather than saw, a boot crash into his ribs. Christina and Vrouw Beck were screaming. Then in a half stunned state he felt himself being dragged along the hall, and next minute he was picked bodily up, thrown out of the front door, and hurled into the street. He heard, felt almost, such was the force of it, the front door slammed behind him. James had met Adriaan Beck.

When James had picked himself up, he found his eye was swelling fast, and his ribs were hurting. He lurched a few steps and sat down again, in the street. A passer-by shouted at him, and a woman said something about drunks so early in the morning. James was thoroughly ashamed of himself, and when he had got his senses a bit more together he got up again, and a little wobbly as he was, with difficulty and feeling great shame, he staggered rather than walked back to Parke's. At the hotel Mrs Parke was very surprised to see James in that state but made no real comment other than to say that everyone knew Adriaan Beck was a rough, tough man you did not cross. James' eye was closing very rapidly, and Mrs Parke fetched some red meat from her kitchen which she gave to James with instructions to put it on his eye.

"I say old chap, you look a bit the worse for wear. Not a very good state for a chap to find his brother-in-law in, you know," said a voice from the parlour. "My name's Lewis, and I gather you have married my sister Francesca. Fancy that! I had heard that she was engaged to someone else, but lo and behold, it is you, I am told. You are now an old married man, and here you are going about getting beaten up by that Adriaan Beck. People do not tangle with him, I can tell you. He is a nasty brute. But he would have had a reason, and that is what might be tasty gossip. So tell me, what have you done that might make him thrash you?"

So James told him about Adriaan beating Foolata in the street with a jambok, and then he saw Lewis did not believe that was the whole story. "There must," as Lewis put it, "be a bit more to it than that, old boy." James then admitted, in grudging and protracted stages, that he had got engaged to Adriaan's daughter (he did not name her) and had just broken it off. On account of his marriage. To Francesca. "It is always best to put these things behind you when you get married," said Lewis. "I, for example, when I take a sable dam up country always let her think I would like to marry her, but cannot as I have a wife already, and that is a good defence mechanism. Saves all sorts of trouble don't you know? You just did it the wrong way round.

"Look I don't care what you have, or have not done. I really don't. Harry told me that you are the man who is wanting to go up country," said Lewis. "I am looking to join someone doing that and as I have done that all before and have experience, perhaps as we are so closely related and all that, it would be nice if we could travel together. I mean, I know the route, or part of it, and so on, and know how to manage the natives, I even speak a few words of some of their languages, and you are part kitted up ready, if what Harry said is right. Which I am sure it must be. He said you could shoot and were an artist, all of which sounds good to me. What do you say?"

"I think that sounds quite a good idea but we will need to sort out a few things before we can go," replied James.

"That is good enough for me. No great objection then," agreed Lewis. "Mrs Parke" he shouted loudly, turning round toward the kitchen, suddenly happily boisterous. "Fetch this man a bottle of champagne will you, we both need a drink right now. He needs it for being beaten up, and I need it as I am so deeply shocked at meeting my brother-in-law for the first time, and finding out he is as big a rascal as me, don't you know. And we are going into the interior together you know."

James, clutching the steak to his face, drank the champagne with Lewis, and talked about women and their problems with them. The pain in his eye lessened, and James felt less of anything as time passed. At some stage later in the day, he could not recall exactly when, he knew he had talked to Lewis about the trip again and said that they should go together. He dimly sort of remembered later calling for at least several other bottles, and for cigars, and then all he remembered was being put to bed by John who appeared unannounced like a genie at his side. John brought some coffee for him, and cleaned his vomit up, and then he disappeared, and James slept.

21

In Court

Two weeks later a letter arrived addressed to James and written by Messrs J and H Reid, attorneys at law, on behalf of Adriaan Beck as the natural guardian of Christina, described as a minor, enclosing a summons which had been issued in the Supreme Court. It claimed that James had promised to marry Christina when he returned from England, and said that now he had returned, but refused to do so. As a result the claim was for damages amounting to two thousand pounds, and for costs of course. Adriaan was suing him on Christina's behalf for breach of promise of marriage.

James had known that there would be severe retribution for jilting Christina, but it was very fast. Much faster than he had thought it would be. And what he had wanted above all was to avoid having to tell his family about Christina. He had had to tell Francesca about Christina in the end, but he could never tell her or his family about these court proceedings. That would be impossible. And Adriaan had as yet done nothing about being knocked down in the street by James. That was presumably still to happen.

He decided to talk it over with Lewis, whom he first swore to total secrecy of course. To his surprise Lewis was not too sympathetic. "You can afford it old boy, why don't you just pay up and have done with it? You have plenty of money, it is not a problem for you." But James did not have that sort of money although he had no intention of telling Lewis that. He would be bankrupted if he had to pay up.

So, James like a true lawyer's son, decided that he needed legal advice before he did anything, and so, on Mrs Parke's wise suggestion, he consulted Charlie Fairbridge, a partner in the firm of attorneys at law called Merrington, Fairbridge and Hull. They apparently had offices near to Parke's at 65 Longmarket Street. Charlie, as he asked James to call him when first they met, was a pleasant fellow, not very tall, with bushy grey-coloured lamb chop whiskers, and a bright gleam in his alert eyes. His office, when James was eventually ushered in, was full to overflowing with bundles of papers, many tied with red tape: some on tables, under the table, on the floor, on the window sill, on the mantelpiece, and on his desk above all. In fact there was no spare open space on his desk at all and he had to scrape some space on it in order to put a clean sheet of paper down ready for note-taking. James, who had never been in his father's office, assumed that all lawyers' offices looked like this.

"My partners," started Charlie, " all say that I must have a tidy-up, and one day I will. They are all very neat and tidy themselves." James muttered an indistinct reply.

"I am very sorry, I see you have dirt on your boots. Longmarket Street is very bad right now, I know. I do apologise. Some lady will get stuck in the mud one day, and all our clerks will run out of the office in droves to help her, I have no doubt. You would not have a pinch of snuff about you, would you?" pleaded Charlie.

Charlie sounded very English. James regretted that he did not have any snuff. He never used it. He was, however, prompt and ready to tell Charlie all, but Charlie would not let him, and wanted to know about James personally first, and was fascinated to hear that James was a lawyer's son, even though his father was only a Palace Court Lawyer, and he made James tell him all about how that had come about. He said he had heard that there might be a possibility of there being new law courts built in London, and said how he envied that, if in fact a decision was ever made, especially compared to their position at the Cape.

And then when Charlie was good and ready in "listening to the client's problem" mode, James told him all about Francesca, and of his brother's death in a dreadful train crash, and how he had had no choice but to marry her. He did not say that Francesca was with child. And then he told Charlie about Christina, and his giving her the ring, and then he handed Charlie the summons he had received. Charlie spread it out and read it. He said, thoughtfully, almost immediately, "You really can't defend this can you?"

"Could I not say that we were not engaged at all? That we never got engaged?"

"If you risked a defence like that and you had to admit on oath in court that you had given her your signet ring and had the blessing of her mother in whose presence you gave her the ring; that you went down on bended knee to offer it to her, and that she took it from you in the presence of two witnesses, one of whom was a minister, I suspect that you would be laughed out of court. And worse, you would almost certainly be condemned in costs. Chief Justice Wylde is a very fair man, and he would not like to see that sort of defence made only for it to fail. And when it did fail, you would almost certainly have to pay the full damages claimed, plus costs of course. You could well end up bankrupt unless you are careful. Worse still, you would be a laughing stock, and then even worse still, a complete social outcast as well. So you really have no choice but to settle. I have no idea how much it will cost you to settle but, in the end, settle you must, in my considered opinion. But," he added in a typically lawyer-like way, "it's your decision of course. I only give advice. The damages claimed of two thousand pounds, are of course a make weight, and will be settled for a very much smaller sum, I have no doubt. The object of the proceedings is of course the vindication of the girls feelings of rejection." Charlie shrugged his shoulders, silently eloquent of the damage he saw James could suffer.

James was shocked at the brevity and forcefulness of that advice but he understood that Charlie was right, and that he must settle. But his ability to do that would depend on Adriaan and how much money he wanted. Another thought occurred to him.

"Can you get the ring back for me?" he asked Charlie. "It was really my father's ring, and he has asked where it is, and I said it had been stolen. But can you retrieve it for me? It matters."

"That is very doubtful indeed. The jilted woman is not usually deprived of her gifts from her lover," said Charlie. "In fact it might make it worse if we try to get it back at the start. It might antagonise the Becks badly. The best we can hope is that she agrees that you can have it back when all the dust from the case has finally settled. But it would have to be voluntary. No court would ever at any stage of the proceedings order her to return the ring, I can assure you. Look here. I may not be related to you, but I feel that you should have some personal advice, as well as legal advice. From a personal point of view I can tell you that there are many Vrouws who are looking out for wealthy young Englishmen to catch for their daughters. And from all you have told me it sounds as though you have fallen into that trap, like others before you, and no doubt others will in future. Just learn from your mistake, and get this sorted as quickly and as cheaply as you can."

Charlie continued. "From a legal point of view, the very best and indeed the only legal thing we can do, is to engage the services of Mr Watermeyer of counsel, and let him see what he can do for you by way of negotiation or mitigation to prevent this from becoming a contested case, which I can promise you, you will lose. Watermeyer is the best there is at the Bar here in Cape Town, and I have no doubt he will soon be a judge. But we must not lose sight of the prime objective, which must be for us to keep the damages as low as possible, and then if we can, to get the ring back. Do you know him, by the way? His full name is Egidius Benedictus Watermeyer, what a name, my goodness. He was called as a barrister in London where you come from, at the Inner

Temple, a couple of years ago, so you might know him. Did you say you had no snuff about you?"

James, ignoring the snuff question, offered a bit doubtfully that he might perhaps have met Watermeyer at Simpsons where lots of lawyers went for refreshment. James wondered to himself if Watermeyer's fees would be too high. He was already beginning to face bills which he might not be able to pay.

On his return to the hotel Lewis was waiting for him, and asked his news. "Look here," said James stuffily, "It is no business of yours, but I have left it all in the hands of the attorneys, and it is all up to them to do the best they can. But I have no choice now. Mynheer Beck will do what he wants and there is nothing else to it. I must wait to know how much I must pay for the pleasure of loving a girl. I will have to pay what I have to pay." I am leaving all money worries from the court proceedings and so on with Charlie Fairbridge, and he will settle for me whatever it is I have to pay." He paused, looked at Lewis and said, "What I want now, is for us to start on the trek. I think that I need to shoot some ivory to recoup a little of my present and likely future exceptional expenditure. Can we make a quick start, now?"

"No. Not yet. There is still a lot for us to do first before we can leave," objected Lewis. "For example we have to engage servants and preferably they should be experienced and be able to speak English and Boer plus a native language or two. We also have to buy food for immediate needs, those things are always left to the last minute, and to pick up trading stock as we set out. Not least we have to make sure that the oxen we get are zuur-oxen as they last longest without water and can eat more or less anything.

"We also have got to get a gunpowder license before we can set out. I don't know if Harry had even applied for that before he left. That can take an age. That is something we absolutely have to have before we can take gunpowder across the border of the colony. This dammed government we have here has decided it is all right to take any quantity of gunpowder if we want to go to Boer country, not aparently understanding that the Boers are hostile to the English. But if we want to go anywhere west of that in tribal country, as we do, we must submit all sorts of details to them, like precisely where we are going, how many wagons we are taking, and so on. In other words with the ineffable wisdom always given to all legislators everywhere, we are not to sell gunpowder to the natives, who on the whole welcome us, but we can sell any amount to the Boers, who generally hate us. Typical."

22

Francesca

STILL AT CLAPHAM IN LONDON, just over four months after James had returned to the Cape, Francesca received a letter from him telling her that he had decided to go on his long-planned trip to the interior. He said he thought he would be away for most of a year, but could not be certain. That was the bad news as he put it, but he also told her that he had met up with her brother Lewis, whom he liked, and they got on well together. He explained that Harry had been recalled to India by his regiment as a last-minute request to extend his furlough had been refused. Lewis, however, had volunteered to take Harry's place on the trek, as he claimed to have experience of parts of the interior. James continued by saying he regretted therefore that he would definitely not be at home when she was delivered of her child, but he expected she would understand his reluctance to attend on her at such a time.

Francesca had no one she could talk to about this. She read the letter as a considerate action on James' part, but she doubted that was the real reason for his writing. Inwardly she was saddened that she had no one with whom she could discuss it. Her mother-in-law was not the sort of person to encourage confidences, and must never know the secret at the heart of her marriage, so Francesca could not confide in her. Her father was ageing rapidly and found all sorts of difficulty remembering what had happened even the day before, and she never talked much about personal matters with him anyway. She was alone and unsupported at this time. She was on her own, except for Mrs Griggs, and heavily pregnant.

In her heart, Francesca still did not really understand why James had been so unwilling to make love to her, apart from the wedding night, nor why he would not say he loved her. She did not believe all he said about Christina. She was sure in her own mind that something new, other than his breaking it all off with Christina, had now happened and that was why he was going to travel into the interior, but she had no idea what it was. She loved him, and she did not understand what the reason was.

And she worried about her brother Lewis, whom she knew from her childhood had always been a wild and very untrustworthy companion. His participation in the trek filled her with concern for James', her husband's, future. She did not know what could go wrong but she knew for certain that things would not go well if Lewis was involved. The Trevanion Estate was still maintaining a labourer from years ago whom Lewis had beaten up so badly that he was unable to work, with the result that the estate had been morally obliged to keep him and his family ever since. Things went wrong when Lewis was around. That was a real threat, she thought.

She slept badly, worrying and fretting about James and Lewis, and the proposed trip. On going to bed, Mrs Griggs had made her a glass of hot milk, and she had taken a small tincture of laudanum as well, so she hoped that sleep would overcome her. But sadly, her tired worries only seemed to make her the more wakeful. At about one in the morning she decided that she would try and calm herself by reading her Bible. It was in her bedroom on top of the chest of drawers by the fireplace. The fire was almost out, but she thought it gave out enough light still for her to see what she was doing, so she got out of bed to cross the room, but in doing so her foot caught in the rug in front of the ottoman at the end of her bed. It tripped her up, and she fell heavily against the brass fender, which hit her in her lower stomach. Almost at once she found that she could not move without real pain, so she called out for Mrs Griggs who slept along the corridor. But Mrs Griggs did not hear, being rather elderly and slightly deaf, and did not come. Francesca found that what with the pain from the fall and being the weight she was, and so ungainly with it, she could not get up. It hurt her when she tried. She thought at first that she might have broken something. She lay there for a few moments and then she found that she was wet, her waters had broken, and she was bleeding between her legs, slowly at first. She feared for her baby. In just a few minutes the pain in her stomach sharpened, then it quickly became intense, pulsing and insistent, rhythmic waves of pain, and she knew she was about to give birth prematurely. She was having a series of contractions, and they became more and more violent, and came faster and more strongly each time. Despite the difficulty in so doing, she tried calling for help again, but still no Mrs Griggs. She felt a very deep sharp and pulsing contraction, she felt awful pain, she felt she was being split in two, and then there was just blood and mess. She shouted aloud again, but more in anguish and despair than pain. No one came.

When Mrs Griggs came in the next morning with her early morning tray, she found Francesca lying on the floor in a mess of blood, and with a stillborn child beside her. She had tried to crawl towards the door, but then apparently passed out. Mrs Griggs tried to help the still only half-conscious Francesca up, but could not. The doctor was called, a nice enough young man called Fergus Brown, and he picked Francesca up and put her to bed. He told the now distraught young woman that she had lost her baby, but she must have known that already. He wrapped the dead and bloody child's body in a towel and put it in a box. Doctor Brown said that he was sorry for both parents, but he feared that after something as bad as this and the length of time she had been without medical help, she might well not be able to bear another child. He gave her a bottle of sedative from his bag, with instructions to Mrs Griggs about dosage. Mrs Griggs washed Francesca and cleaned up the blood on the floor. She also gave Francesca a cup of hot sweet tea, and sat and kept her company for most of the next day. Francesca was hysterical for much of the time, and not to be comforted. She wanted James to be there, she just wanted James.

23

Last-minute Preparations

A T LEWIS' SUGGESTION, James had rented a run-down farm at the far western end of Roeland Street, and there they accumulated their joint stores in readiness for the trek. James paid the rent to Lewis who in turn paid it on to the owner, or so he said. James was worried, and fretted because he was doubtful that Lewis was in fact passing all the money on to the old farmer. He did not want to check up on this as it would show Lewis, if it was found out that he had done that, that James did not trust him. He thought that was not a good idea so early on in their relationship. Looking back many months later, he thought he should have satisfied his doubts when he had them first.

John was in charge of looking after the stores before they set off, and at the farm all was safely under lock and key in the barns save for the two wagons, and of course the livestock. The horses were housed in a range of loose boxes and stables, and the oxen were all crammed into the fold yard. The various dogs were kennelled at the farm in disused sheds. It was not going to be long of course before they actually set off, but James was worried about the cost of keeping all the livestock fed and watered until then. This hard labour was done by the servants he had engaged, under Lewis' supervision, and John oversaw generally what he could. That was more in his line.

In addition to helping get in the stores, James had been busy settling his legal case, which is to say he had sat through numerous interminable meetings with Watermeyer the barrister, and had agreed eventually that he would pay whatever sum was negotiated.

That sum, when it was finally settled and rubber-stamped by the court, had been more than he had bargained for, but a great deal less than he had feared from the summons, and then in addition to that, he had paid Charlie Fairbridge's bill as well. Chief Justice Wylde, when he heard the case, made a remark about young gentlemen having to pay for their pleasure, which upset everyone, including Mynheer Beck. He had also paid his last bill to Hamilton Ross as Hunter had been difficult about that as well. The latest tranche of his allowance had arrived from his father which fortuitously had bailed James out, but he felt that he was well out of his depth financially.

At the farm, the base for their operations as James thought of it, James sat on a broken chair that he had dragged out of the almost ruinous house, and placed in a sheltered corner where two walls met, in a patch of morning sun. His position gave a direct view down the road towards the town. He was depressed, and the thought of having to write to his father again, as he realised he should, must actually, do soon, and for money, pained and irked him. It was a nagging dead weight on his mind. Even the strengthening warmth of the sun did not lift his spirits. As these thoughts pressed down on him, he watched the rough dirt road into town, and saw the wind stir the dust in small pale brown spirals which seemed almost to dance. At first he did not give this much notice, but the wind seemed to increase ever so slightly, and started to swirl the small spirals upwards, very prettily, so that the little twists of air were prancing lightly just above the surface of the track. James idly thought that he should try and catch the scene in watercolours. He could just see though the sparkling dust that someone was walking along the road towards him. Only partly visible at first, the figure gradually became more distinct as the person neared. It was a woman, he could see. She was a slim native girl, copper skinned, with short hair. The dusty breeze was in her face, and she shaded her eyes from it. Her short light green skirt was being twitched by the wind. She was barefoot, and walking very slowly. She walked as if tired. But when she gradually got near, and he could make her out better, he saw she was smiling at him. It was Foolata.

Although she had not been asked to help, Foolata, once she had arrived, thereafter started to come to the farm on an almost daily basis. She said she had run away from the Becks, and could not think of where she might find shelter or help, other than from Mister James who had helped her when that "bad man Mynheer Beck" had attacked her. After she had appeared, Foolata, without being asked to do so by either James or Lewis, made the farmhouse, which had been long deserted and was dirty and ruinous, clean enough for herself and the native servants to sleep in for the last few nights before they were to leave. James and Lewis did not discuss her reappearance either with her, or with each other. They just accepted her work, and let her come and go as she pleased. Meanwhile they rode to and fro between Parke's and the farm on a daily basis and overnight they stabled their horses near Parke's well enough. Foolata cooked a few stews and soups for the others while she was at the farmhouse, and tidied up as best as she could. It was too ruinous to make much of an impression on it however, nor was there a need to do so.

James said he wanted to pay Foolata for what she did, but she would not take money, she said because he had helped her in the street. What she was doing, she explained, was her way of repaying James for his great kindness to her as she saw, and felt it. As she was a former house servant James eventually agreed that she could come with them on the trek, but only if she had specifically allocated tasks, such as washing and darning, sewing, mending, and of course, cooking. They would give her some status with the other servants, and make her position seem more "appropriate" as he put it. This she very happily, and quietly, agreed to. And James did finally manage to persuade her to accept payment at the same rate as the driver Martinus Alexander he had engaged, on the now departed Harry's recommendation. He said this would make her position with the party seem more regular.

The final evening before they set off Lewis and James spent talking at Parke's, with John and Martinus with Lewis' wagon driver, a surly man named Dedderich Hattingh, a Bastard Hottentot whom Lewis said he had employed before. Dedderich, said Lewis, had travelled part of the route they were to travel in the past, and so would be useful.

Lewis set out his very detailed plans for the route. The route, as he had said earlier, was to be what was generally known as 'the missionary route'. For the first part they would travel eastwards along the coastal plain as far as a village, or small town as the local people thought of it, called George. This was to be, said Lewis, the simplest part of the journey, and it would give them all ample time to learn how the trek would actually work physically. How the wagons were worked and how the oxen handled. They must learn the good habits of out-spanning like tying the oxen to the trek-touw, and getting enough firewood in for the night. The country they were to travel through first on this stretch was relatively easy, although they would have to cross a number of rivers. Game supplies were adequate, and although there were no great herds to be found there any more, he still expected they would be able to feed themselves off the land without too much difficulty. When they out-spanned at the end of the day it would usually be at a farm, maybe Boer, maybe English. They would need to get permission from the farmer before actually out-spanning, and of course could not expect to be welcomed if there was only a very little water or forage, barely enough for the farmer to manage with for himself.

Many Boers, said Lewis, were very hostile to the English, and some few farmers would turn them away. This hostility had become much more noticeable since the battle of Boomplats a few years previously when the Boers had been routed by a small force of regular troops sent out from the colony for that purpose. They held hard grudges. Lewis explained that the English were more numerous nearer the coast, and Boers were more numerous inland and to the east of the town of Graaf Reinet, and north from there. The further from the coast the less the English influence, and the greater the problem with Boers could, maybe would, be. The Boers wanted to cut off the English from getting to the north from and beyond the colony, and the main obstacles preventing the Boers from cutting that route northwards were the mission stations along their proposed road, at Kuruman and Kolobeng.

When at a farm, any farm, he and James would normally stay in the farmhouse if there was room, which would not always be the case. He suggested that John should sleep in or under the wagon, or around the camp fire if the weather allowed, or in a tent of which they had a good number if he preferred. The natives would sleep where they could around the wagons. They would not expect a roof over their heads: they would usually lie beside the camp fire, keeping it going as required, and anyway they would have their karosses to keep them warm. They all had these animal skin blankets or cloaks. If it rained, they would shelter under the wagon or in the tents. Lack of water was not expected to be too great a problem on this first section of the trip but they must learn to keep the water barrels topped up as and when they came to clean water. They would also learn the taste of bad water, and to bear it. There would be plenty of places further along their route which would have very little water.

The Boer farmers were prodigious drinkers in Lewis' experience, and merely a single little soopje, or sip of Cape brandy, would not be enough. At farms, after eating, and often before, they would smoke a pipe and drink soopjes. The vrouws would always have coffee on the go, and with their menfolk away most of every day they were all without exception in his experience eager to chat, and would happily do so for hours on end. The party would buy what they could from farmers, if anything, and coffee, without milk or sugar, would be their usual drink. They would often barter with their own trade goods, and this was a good way for the party to get little luxuries from farmers like flour for bread making and so on. If such things were sold they would usually be at high prices. Forage was always expensive and they would always have to pay for that. He thought that he and James, and perhaps John, might be asked to go hunting by Boer farmers. Mostly they had old-fashioned roer guns of prodigious weight and length, and James would find out their strange method of ambushing game in due course.

After George, the next part of the journey was away northwards over a number of mountain ranges. Precipitous sometimes, and extremely rough almost always, they would have to use the chain rheims frequently, to put a brake on downhill speeds, and Lewis said he expected most damage to the wagons to happen on this part of the trek. North of George, they would cross Mitchells Pass over the Outeniqua Range, thus avoiding the dangerous Craddock Pass which was said to be the worst in the colony, and then through the Lange Kloof, "a very dreary valley", and then, very simply "over a few more mountains", as Lewis put it, and the Great Karoo desert, to the village of Graaf Reinet.

"A few more mountains," asked James. "What does that mean?"

"Van Roy's Poorte. This is a really frightful pass, almost in a complete state of nature leading over the Kamanassie Hills. It is likely we shall get stuck there, but you never know your luck." Then there would be the Zwart Berg chain, and a long way past that the Great Karoo itself, after which would be the Candeboo and then Graaf Reinet. "The Karoo gets very cold, especially at nights," said Lewis. "It is high land, about three thousand feet and the air gets really nippy up there, so although in the daytime the temperature is acceptable at times, at night be prepared for cold. Travelling on the Karroo itself is relatively easy work, and it is pretty flat. But game can be difficult to get, especially if we do not hit the great herds on migration.

"Oh, and one last thing before we set off. I do not want to put you off our very excellent drivers here, but most Hottentots are given to two things, namely thieving and drunkenness. Anything not nailed down, secured without a lock of some sort, and not in your pocket, is liable to be stolen. So when we get to a native village or kraal as they called, you must watch them all the time. Drunkenness you will see for yourself is one of their chiefest occupations, and "tapping the admiral" as they call it is a real skill. What they do in that escapade is to lift a hoop off a barrel and drill into it through the hoop mark, draw off what they want, and then slide the hoop back on. When you find there is less in the barrel than you think, they blame the person who sold you the barrel. Otherwise it's tobacco they are after, and they will beg remorselessly for it, but will be satisfied with a mere pipeful at a time, and as you will see, their pipes are pitifully small."

After they had finished their meeting, Lewis asked James privately for payment of his share of the cost of equipping the expedition, and confessed that it had cost them more than he had estimated, and he had no money to pay for it himself. Although silently astonished, James had paid him straight away, thus further depleting his already diminished resources. Partly by way of explanation, Lewis pointed out that one of the objectives of the expedition as far as he was concerned was to get up into good elephant country, if they could, so as to be able to shoot some ivory. If he was successful in that he would be able to repay James his own half share of the costs when he sold the ivory. He was planning, he made it clear, to make a good profit from the trek by selling all the ivory he had shot on their return.

There might well be a little difficulty with some natives Lewis said, and he just hoped that it would not interfere with their sport. Personally, he said he had been having a bit of trouble with one eye, and so he hoped he would be shooting well. James suspected that might be an excuse. Before they started out James had been practising his shooting at the castle and now thought of himself as a good shot at targets, but Bladen had said that that was totally different to shooting moving, and sometimes hostile, game. He was right. Lewis said they would leave before dawn the next day.

Lewis could not say how long their trek might take, as they would have to stop and shoot game as they went, and stay on two nights here and there, for example at George and similar places, and in any case time was not critical to them. The trek would take as long as it took.

24

The Trek Begins

TRUE TO HIS WORD, and as James had imagined it might be, more than a little chaotically the two wagons set out next day, in the cold very early dawn. James was just thankful that they had started. He wanted to put the past behind him, and like Lewis, he wanted to recoup the outlay of the trek, and to be able to repay his father when he got back to England. Leaving all the ills and worries of Cape Town behind him was important: it was an exciting and very new venture he was starting on, and he meant to make the most of it. He had to, financially. But as the party assembled that first morning, a native arrived with a letter from Charlie Fairbridge, and in it he said he had managed to get hold of the ring. That ring. The one James had given to Christina. In the letter, Charlie said James could pay him for getting the ring back on his return. The ring was enclosed with the letter, and James put it on thankfully. He realised with a shock that Christina could not have had it altered to fit, as it still fitted his finger. It seemed to James that as he started on this journey he was also starting on a new path in life at the same time, finally free from the shackles of the old, and the ring was a symbol of that release.

James had one wagon, and sat, when he was not riding, on the large fore chest at the front of his wagon, next to Martinus Alexander and John. The fore-clap hung down behind them, and inside was his cardell or bunk for when he was to sleep in the wagon, rather than underneath or in one of the four tents he was taking. Such very few clothes as James took with him were mostly in the fore and after chests, but his shaving kit and all his personal effects, such as the hairbrushes his mother had given him when he went up to Cambridge, were in interior side pockets. He kept his maps there also, including the map proof given to him and signed by young John Arrowsmith, the son of the great man. He wore a wide-brimmed hat for protection from the sun, and carried a flask of water at his side.

Inside the wagon were several layers of large padlocked chests in which were guns, ammunition, the medicine chest and a large supply of a wide variety of trade goods. The outside boxes hung from the long narrow outer sides of the wagon and were bolted on to it, and in them, handily positioned for everyday use on Lewis' advice, were tools such as spades, pickaxes and suchlike. At the back of the wagon, suspended underneath, was a strong wooden frame on which were kept all the pots, gridirons and similar utensils. At the back were also the tar barrels, and two long powerful rheim-chains, and of course inside were the two water barrels called fagie, and a few ankers of brandy, plus other assorted luxuries James decided he absolutely had to have. He had added writing paper for his journal, artists' materials and his pipe as essentials, which he did not think of as luxuries, but these he kept safe inside.

James' wagon was pulled by twelve oxen which Martinus had assured him were called by various names, and that he knew them all of course. Blauberg was the strongest oxen, but Creishman, although strange looking, was not far behind. They were all fastened along the trek-touw rope which was itself attached to the diesel-boom. Martinus in his capacity as driver wielded a whip of prodigious length: it was about twenty-five feet in length and attached to the end of a bamboo which was itself about twenty feet. At the end of the main length of the whip was the after- and then the fore-slock. These were what he lashed the oxen with, very precisely, when he wanted to. When cracked it made a noise like a gun shot, and Martinus could touch each individual ox in the team with it. He also wielded a vicious-looking jambok made from rhinoceros hide for closer work alongside the team.

The in-spanning of the oxen to the trek-touw was a noisy affair with a great deal of shouting and swearing, and to James it looked in that first experience to be chaotic as well. But despite the noise and the length of time it took, Martinus had it all under control so far at least as James' wagon was concerned, along with the help of Edward Wolhuter, another Hottentot who was a herdsman, and Jessa Cramer, a young Malay helper. James had recruited all these servants as a result of recommendations from Bladen, who knew them all personally. The lead pair of oxen, he was assured by Lewis, who knew about these things, were experienced oxen and even in the desert they could easily follow the track of a single wagon or spoor which had passed that way up to six months earlier. They were started into movement by the lead ox, after the most terrific swipe round his ribs by Martinus with his fore-slock, and then gradually the heavy wagon started in motion, the fore-slock sending a cloud of blue hair flying and a thin red streak of blood appearing on Blauberg's flank.

The lead wagon was to be Lewis', because as he put it, he knew "roughly" where they were aiming to go. Accompanying the wagons was a large strange taggle of hangers-on, about eighty in number thought James, some of them female, and many of them were drunk as they set out. They were driving a motley collection of sheep and a large number of spare oxen. Many of the women followers carried babies on their backs. There were also their own dogs, maybe about a dozen or more bounding excitedly around – all good hunting dogs, assured Lewis, who had largely been responsible for buying them. James missed Argos as he looked at them, and decided, too late now that they were leaving, that he must get his own dog when the chance arose. The horses were for that day tied to the wagons or led with the assorted livestock. James had three horses, as did Lewis. John had two. Lewis told James that they would be eating much of the following stock as they travelled along, and trading, and he expected the hangers-on and stragglers to drop off quite quickly as they got away from any form of civilisation, as he put it.

Lewis was absolutely right that the crowd of followers would disperse in the course of the next few days. A lot of them got drunk that first evening, and so, sleeping it off the next day, pretty well all of them missed the second in-spanning just before dawn.

The trek moved very slowly, to James' way of thinking. Travelling in the second wagon, he found that he had to stay a good distance behind Lewis' because of the clouds of dust the lead wagon made, and anyway the oxen only seemed to have one speed (and he thought that was very slow) when they were drawing the wagon. He was soon to learn that oxen could run very fast when they felt they were threatened in any way, and for many other reasons, such as when you wanted them to be patient like in-spanning, and on such occasions, which were numerous, he often thought how slowly he would like them to move. On the first couple of occasions however, the in-spanning had gone very easily, maybe because they were all fresh and the oxen were well fed.

After the first day, Lewis and James both rode on horseback alongside their wagons, as Lewis said an eye needed to be kept on both wagons. Foolata usually sat on the after-chest at the back of James' wagon, on her own.

The village of George (the first place of any worth they reached after starting out) was what James described in a sulky complaining voice to Lewis, as "a dull hole" the day after they got there. He said he was bored, and felt like having a bit of fun. Lewis pointed out that after all the excitement of Cape Town, it was probably a good thing for him that George really was dull. But it was indeed dull, he had to confess to himself in private agreement with James. Instead he said, "Look here James, if you don't stop grumbling about this place I shall write this instant to my sister, your dear wife, and tell her all about you, and that little legal matter in Cape Town."

Then, as a new idea, to cheer himself up, Lewis suggested they

Crossing a drift, Natal (1874).

Oil painting by Thomas Baines now in the South African National Gallery collection. This picture gives an idea of the slow nature of wagon travelling

visit a place he knew where one might find a willing gentoo, at a large house in Meade Street.

"Not for me thank you," said James. "And I doubt you will write. You never do write letters as far as I can see, and I can think of no reason why you should start doing so now. After your old man finally cut your money off a few weeks back while we were at Parke's, I have not seen you put pen to paper except to write me bills or IOUs. And I have never known you do anything 'this instant' as you say."

"You are just too good for this world," said Lewis. "You always pay. Happily for me."

"There is no need to be rude because I do not want to go to Meade Street with you. All you wanted me there for anyway is just to pay the bill," said James. "And if I did go, I imagine you would have been quite happy to write to Francesca then, to give her news of how I got on. I have little doubt about that."

"Oh, come on. Don't let us disagree about this. George is a boring old place to be sure, but we will be on our way soon. Meantime we can drink the wine, and the brandy, and relax for the rest of the day. But don't let us get too riotous will you, as there are too many police and churches here in George for the good people to tolerate anything other than religious singing, I am sure. That house in Meade Street was an exception. Strange that, come to think of it."

The passes to the north of George were far worse than Lewis had described them, thought James. People in George had boasted to them how much they had improved the local roads of late, and James thought privately that there ought to be some sort of legal redress for such deliberate deception. At one place they had to descend into what looked to James like an alpine ravine along a track which only existed, James thought, in the imagination. Lewis said that heavy timber wagons must have managed it, upwards of course, so if they

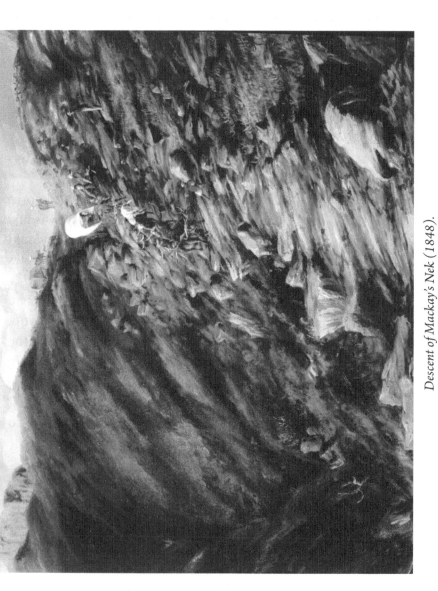

Descent of Mackay's Nek (1848).

Oil painting by Thomas Baines now in the MuseumAfrica collection. This was called a road by the locals.

could manage it upwards then their trek party could manage it downwards. James thought it completely impassable but Lewis insisted vigorously it was manageable. So having rheimed, or secured the two hind wheels by means of drag chains, they commenced the descent. Jolting furiously along, the wagon crashed and jumped from rock to rock, at one moment the hind wheel resting on a projecting ledge of rock several feet in height, and the front wheel on the same side buried in a deep hollow, and the next moment the larboard wheels suddenly both elevated by a corresponding mass of rock on the opposite side. The wagon tottered from side to side and seemed as if it must overturn, and James was ecstatic when both his and Lewis' wagons made it safely down. Martinus of course put their safe descent down to his inestimable skill, and was heartily and volubly delighted with his own prowess. James thought of all the road improvements he had been told about.

Other problems occurred at several river crossings. At one, the river was flanked by a steep wall of deep and slimy mud, and an immense amount of hard manual labour was required to cut a pathway down one side and then up the other. Pickaxes, shovels and spades were wielded by men stripped to their shirts, toiling while half wading and half swimming, and most of one day later the two wagonways, one on each side of the river, were ready for them to attempt the crossing. It was a fearful pull for the poor oxen, and James' wagon stuck fast three times, and was within a hair's breadth of being upset. The water came up to the bottom of the floor boards but fortunately did not wet any of the cargo.

After crossing that particular river the road continued good for about three miles but then it had been washed away, and the wagon stuck fast. They had to dig it out by hand, and they broke the trek-touw three times in extricating it. In such cases it was often not possible to say where the road was at all, and they had to make do with ready reckoning and hope that their drivers had an idea where they were going.

Shooting game for the larder was a daily task, the difficulty of which lay in finding it, hitting the target, then butchering the beast and lastly carting the meat back to the wagon. James and Lewis nearly always rode off together to shoot, but sometimes John went with them as he could be a help in trying to drive the game towards the two guns. When game was relatively scarce such a device was needed to get a shot in, but when there were quite literally thousands and thousands of animals, for example springbok, it was simpler just to fire at the mass of animals and then follow any trail of blood. Sometimes they managed to reach a wounded animal this way, but a surprising number seemed to get away. And if they shot one and wanted to chase after another, the dead animal had first to be hidden under thorns or whatever scrub was to hand, because on the occasions when they did not do that the vultures came down and picked the carcass clean. The vultures were foul with insects in their feathers, and they fouled any water they splashed in, as they sometimes did, so badly in fact as to make the water undrinkable, even by thirsty oxen.

Amazing as it might seem, they were overflown toward the end of this initial part of the journey, by a single enormous swarm of locusts. They were standing in the middle of a plain about five miles across when James saw them first, coming like a vast storm, flying low and steadily. The air was darkened with them, and the ground below was densely shadowed. For as far as they could see in all directions the swarm stretched in one long unbroken brown cloud. It took about an hour to pass them by. Later, farther north when he saw other swarms, James would see natives gathering them up in crude baskets to take back to their huts to dry or roast and then eat them. They said the locusts were very good eating.

Lack of water was a problem that James had not realised was going to be quite as bad as it sometimes was. On the Karoo and to the immediate north, they frequently went without any water for two or three days at a time, but later when they got up beyond

Kolobeng, James would look back fondly on those times when by comparison water had been so easily found. At one river which was almost dry, they were trying to get some water for the oxen which had been without water for too long when a veldt-cornet, a mounted country policeman, rode up. He was seemingly unaware that slavery had long been abolished, and was on his way, as he told them, to apprehend an escaped "apprentice", which is what the Boers then called slaves. It took all Lewis' powers of persuasion to convince the veldt-cornet that they were not planning to set up a farm, plus a long session of soopjes, which made them all sleepy. After that, the veldt-cornet rode away happy, and in the distance he was seen to fall off his horse, then remount, and disappear. James complimented his friend Lewis on the way he had persuaded the veldt-cornet that they were mere innocent travellers and not would-be settlers, nor helping a runaway. Lewis responded by saying that he doubted his sister would be so charitable to him. Later James would think to himself that that was one of the few times he had thought of his wife Francesca since he had left Cape Town.

James soon learnt some of the tricks of trekking. For example if they wanted to make an early start they did not allow the oxen to graze free overnight, but always tied them to the trek-touw; that way they knew where they were when they wanted them at dawn, and so did not have to waste long, sometimes hours, trying to find them. Lewis always said that they would always have to do this when they reached serious lion country. In the meantime it was easier to let them roam free, and he was, he said, all for the easier life.

Lewis chaffed James as, unlike Lewis, James kept a detailed daily journal of what they had done and what had happened as they travelled. Lewis constantly said that he did not want his lack of skill in shooting game to be recorded for posterity. Sometimes he became quite upset when James read him a brief passage and protested that it was all a waste of good smoking time. That was because after their evening meal, prepared by Foolata, they would often sit and lie around the fire as a group, and it was usually then that James wrote up his journal, while Lewis yarned to John and the boys about times past. Foolata would usually sit a trifle apart and darn and try to repair the tears in shirts caused by thorn bushes during the day's hunting. James, with scant experience of these things, thought the scene almost picturesque, this little group of people in the middle of nowhere, lit by the flickering camp fire, resting after a day's hunting and trekking. He tried to sketch it often, with poor results he thought.

Several times when he went back to his journal to write up that day's events and so on, James found that his papers, including the journal, had been disturbed. But why that should be so when none of the servants except Foolata could read, he did not know. He was saddened at his own laziness, as he thought of it, in not trying to draw or paint some of the wilder scenes through which they passed.

25

Graaf Reinet

FTER THE HARDSHIP OF THEIR CROSSING OF THE KAROO, the town of Graaf Reinet was welcoming and surprising in equal measure. Lewis and James got dressed in their best, and wandered about the town for an hour in quest of a hotel, a bank and a house to let where they could stow their baggage. They also needed somewhere to repair their wagons, both of which had suffered on the passes. They stopped at Stewart's Hotel where the prices, thought James, were very reasonable, as he noticed when he later paid the bill for the two of them. The talk with another traveller at the hotel was about the old battle with the Boers at Boomplaats, when the Boers had been "soundly thrashed" as he put it. One result of that, and he emphasised Lewis' earlier message in this respect, was that they were still, even after a couple of years, very hostile towards the English. The message was to be wary of them.

Graaf Reinet was a pretty village of about two thousand people. The streets were lined with orange and lemon trees. Mynheer Graaf and his vrouw Reinet had planned it well. Many people had well-kept fruit and vegetable gardens, and against the mountains which surrounded it on three sides the village presented, thought James, a very soft and gently rural appearance. People seemed to be mostly Boer, but there were quite a few kaffirs wandering around, wearing karosses and many ornaments of beads. James was secretly glad they had brought so many hundredweight of beads with them, as he had not understood beforehand how many could be worn by a single person. James bought three more hunting dogs at the village for sixteen pounds, a bargain he thought, even though Lewis said they were very costly. James privately thought that a cheek, as he was paying for them, not Lewis. One of the dogs was a light grey-coloured lurcher, and James really liked it. It was friendly, and attached itself to him. James had missed his old dog Argos back at Highsteignton, and so he called this new dog Argos. They were to become inseparable, and the new Argos would follow James more or less everywhere, when James would let him. James came to think that Argos obeyed every word he uttered.

The last evening before they set off from Graaf Reinet, Lewis discussed with James the route they would be following for the next part of the journey. The objective, he said, was the mission station at Kuruman, under the Rev. Moffat, and then on to Livingstone's station at Kolobeng. After Kuruman they would need to hire guides on a regular basis, if, of course, they could get them, as the country to the north of that was not on any reliable map, not even on the draft Arrowsmith. From his scanty description of the route north from Kuruman, it was very clear to James that they would then be travelling across country that was not well known. In fact they would be travelling through unknown lands as they went even farther north beyond Livingstone's mission station. Lewis had had some trouble with missionaries, in the past he said, and he did not much fancy having to go to church when they were at the Rev. Moffat's station, so he would be spending a lot of time with David Hume who was the trader there. James thought privately that Lewis would not be doing much socialising with the Rev. Moffat and his wife if that was the case, and that that might not be an altogether bad thing. That was indeed to prove to be so.

The trek was resumed after a week's rest, and also after some wagon repairs which were ably carried out by a local Boer carpenter. There was a heavy hoar frost as they left the village, and their journey north was marked by the notable barrenness of the landscape. They climbed the steep Old Berg Pass, a long pull and a very bad road, and camped on the Sneuberg mountain at five thousand feet. At that height there was a surprising amount of grass, and they were making unusually good daily distances of up to twenty-five miles a day now that they were fully settled into a routine and the going was so easy, if cold. At the most inhospitable spot on the plateau they came upon a bushman and his family in a small hut of rushes. James thought them miserable, poor-looking objects, almost destitute of clothes. But the man had killed a gnu with a poisoned arrow and having cut away the part pierced by the arrow, they had cooked it and were feasting gluttonously on it, without ill effect.

A few days later they out-spanned as usual, this time at a farm called Drie Fontein, with excellent water. Their experience at this farm was typical of many they visited along their trek. Mynheer Kamfoor was the owner and invited the three white men to eat with him and his family. Their servants ate outside with his Hottentot "apprentices". The house resembled a large barn divided into three. One part was the kitchen, the others being for living and sleeping. There was no ceiling, the whole house being open to the thatch, with the rafters hung with a variety of leaves including tobacco, dagga, which was a local name for cannabis, and of course that staple, biltong. All of them were drying. On the walls were his whip and jambok, plus the skin of a lion, and his two old roer guns rested on wooden brackets on the walls. A Bible was on a side table, and Vrouw Kamfoor presided over a perpetually ready coffee urn at the eating table. A big old, brightly polished brass Dutch clock in a wooden case stood in a corner. They ate a meat stew, which was a typical dish, as James came to learn, with maize, peppers and pickles and pumpkin, and very excellent bread. Coffee was taken, as was always the case, without milk or sugar. Later, prayers were said and sung, and then the men sat around and drank soopjes, or Cape brandy. Lots of soopjes. And smoked.

The family was up early and before they in-spanned and left, James and Lewis had to pay for the forage and water for their oxen and horses, and the hospitality of the house for their party. Prices for this sort of accommodation and supplies varied at every farm, and they found that generally English farmers charged about the same as the Boers, but prices could always be negotiated. The only gradation in the hospitality available was to do with the poverty of the farmer who gave it. This was not because of any lack of willingness, except in some few Boer cases, but due to lack of anything at all to offer. Indeed, on several occasions the party gave hospitality to farmers who had not enough for themselves. Very often even the wealthiest vrouw would come to their wagons to see what they had that she could buy, maybe cottons, buttons, some foods such as coffee, or sugar which was a luxury, and so on.

Three days out from Graaf Reinet they came to a river which was very low and excessively muddy, and in this the wagons stuck fast in mid-stream. This time they managed to divert the miserable flow after a hard day's digging, during which time a Boer passed on after stopping to stare, but without speaking and without offering to help. The next farm they visited was that of Mynheer Van Sail and his vrouw, both of portly dimensions, and thriving on their almost alpine farm.

By this time the party had reached the turn-off towards Colesberg, a town which they had been warned was full of hostile Boers, so they took the north fork in the track to avoid it. They were well clear of the Sneuberg by now, but the oxen were much reduced and one was moving badly. They met immense herds of gnus and springboks, so many indeed that it was very difficult to get a shot in. In fact they killed nothing, despite firing at random into the crowds of beasts, and the larder was pretty bare. The weather was still bitterly cold at night, so that on more than one occasion James found the coffee frozen solid in the morning.

A bit farther on, at Papkuils Farm, if that is not too descriptive a word, thought James, the place had the reputation of being infested with lions, so that night they fastened all the oxen up to the trek-touw and some to the wagon wheels as well. A large steel trap was set by Lewis for any nocturnal intruder such as hyenas or jackals, but nothing was caught. The next day James got lost in thick bush while away from the wagon trying to shoot some meat. Luckily he heard a gunshot from the wagon and made it back again, but that was the lesson they all needed, and so Lewis, using a receipt for making rockets he found in James' notebook, prepared some rockets for possible future use in emergencies. But that night, Lewis got excited after a few too many soopjes and fired them off, much to the delight of the natives. So much so, that more and more natives emerged from out of the darkness to marvel and laugh, and to beg tobacco and snuff. They then all stayed by the camp fire for that night.

When they moved on again the game was still everywhere, but by now James had found his touch with his rifle, and brought home a couple of springboks which he cut up and brought back to the camp on the back of his horse. The country was alive with game, as Lewis put it, and he too had his successes, but even so, the problem was that unless James or Lewis cut up the beast immediately when shot, or hid it under thorn bushes, the vultures would take it. They would eat it so voraciously that they became too engorged to fly. James shot one but could not bring himself to pick it up it was so vilely infested with vermin. He later saw a hyena approach the carcase, sniff it, and walk away.

The next afternoon, James left his wagon, and walked out shooting on his own. Lewis had advised against that because of the number of lions about. But James wanted to walk for a change as they normally went on horseback. This time he wanted to get a buck for they badly needed meat for themselves and the dogs, who were half starving. He only had Argos with him for company. While he was walking along a dry watercourse a young lion trotted across his path without seeing him, not thirty yards ahead. On James' whisper, Argos stood silent and still. James levelled his gun at the lion but did not fire because of bush intervening in the line of fire, and merely to wound a lion when so close and alone would not have been sensible. He walked on therefore.

A week later they reached Dwaal Farm, and were invited to dine by the owner, Mr Dickson. He farmed 26,000 acres under a quit rent, and had ten thousand sheep plus horses and horned cattle. Mrs Dickson complained about how dreary the countryside and the inhabitants were, and she was right. Mrs Dickson took pity on Foolata in her ragged skirt and sadly much-worn blouse, and gave her one of her old dresses, saying that the ragged skirts she usually wore were "inappropriate". The landscape consisted of masses of stone as far as the eye could see, and scrubby bushes, but there were thousands of springboks on migration. Farmer Dickson complained long and emphatically of the damage they did to his farm on migration, by eating every blade of grass.

A few days farther on they met quite a crowd of natives. In this case Korannas and Totties, as James came to call them. Korannas were an outcast tribe of Hottentot beggars. What became more and more common with natives they met, was the use they made of fat and red ochres with which they smeared their bodies, and onto which they stuck shiny silica-type gravel called sibilo. They also wore necklaces and bangles of bones, and sometimes of foul and even rotting entrails. Many also wore strings of beads, and pretty pebbles they picked up off the ground. They jabbered away with their clicking language, and made numerous, not to say repeated, attempts to steal anything they could. The Hottentots were often nearly destitute of clothing, having just a kaross over the shoulder and a tsecha encircling (or nearly doing so) their loins as modesty clothing.

The country to the west was very different to the dry naked deserts they had just crossed: it was an extensive and boundless landscape, enlivened with multitudes of large game. But they were now almost at Rama. Rama was an abandoned mission station and was, as James saw, a wretched Griqua village of a few mud huts with roofs, poorly thatched with grass after a fashion. Perhaps because of its name the place seemed dispiriting, James thought. Lewis explained that the Griqua were people of mixed Hottentot and European blood who until recently had been known as Bastards. Their present chief was one Cornelius Kok who actually lived some way off at Campbell's Dorp, and as they had a few old guns, they were to be respected as a tribe. They made alliances with other tribes as they needed, and had their slaves like any tribe, and made war to suit their needs, such as to acquire cattle, or as defence required. But Kok protected them and that was what mattered. The government had realigned the frontier of the Orange River Sovereignty recently, and by so doing had deprived Kok of fifteen hundred acres of his land, and left Rama on the wrong side of the frontier. The Griquas at Rama gladly traded with James and Lewis, milk for handkerchiefs, and they begged tobacco, and tried to steal.

The party passed on to the north over a grassy country much burnt from want of rain, for about twenty-one miles according to the trocheameter. They found water a little off the track and filled every keg and bottle and cask they could find, because according to the guides they had hired at Rama, they now faced a much drier country. And it was three days' dry hard work before they reached the Vaal River, and the frontier. The river crossing was easy as the river was low, had a stony bed, and was only about one hundred and fifty yards wide instead of its more usual seven hundred. The banks were thickly lined with willows and acacias, and looked to James very much like parts of Suffolk. Lewis said he had never been there. After they crossed the river they immediately out-spanned, as it was always sensible to be near water if you could.

Many Bechuanas came to their camp bringing milk, skins, ostrich feathers and karosses. Trade was brisk with knives, beads and buttons in some demand, the buttons being for necklaces, as worn by Foolata who with her strange clothing, and her familiarity with the white men, was the subject of much envy on the part of the natives. James showed them his gold watch which excited much surprise: they could not comprehend the movement of the hands or the ticking, and seemed afraid to touch it. Foolata's bravery, not to say foolhardiness, in handling the watch excited much admiring comment. Lewis complained about the smell the natives had and said, with justification, thought James, that it was foul. More enormous swarms of locusts were passing overhead (they had seen four by now claimed James) and he saw natives picking them up by the armful. This latest swarm had been overhead for three days in all. Lewis said the natives preferred to roast them, but sometimes ate them raw. Apparently oxen ate them too, as did dogs, and all sorts of animals from gemsbok and antelope to hyenas.

Locusts were still overhead at the next village called Campbell's Dorp, where James and Lewis were welcomed by Mr Bartlett, the missionary of more than twenty-six years' standing. Foolata in particular welcomed the vegetables and bread which Mrs Bartlett gave them, and Mr Bartlett was delighted with the packets of seeds which James gave him in return. James was visited that evening by Cornelius Kok, the Griqua Chief himself, who gave them useful information about the road ahead. Kok was happy to accept two oxen which could go no further, and Lewis said they would pick them up on the way back. In return, Kok gave them a pair of replacement oxen, and told them that only the week before three lions had been shot out of a party of eight, which had raided their cattle kraal.

The next few days of hard travelling were notable for the intense cold at night and in the early mornings. The country was on the whole barren and desolate, hardly a tree in sight, and not enough grass for pasturage for the poor oxen, but it was easy enough to draw the wagons. Lewis, mounted on his best horse, chased some springboks, but shot none. Game was again very scarce. At the next native village, called Daniels Kuil, most inhabitants were away on an expedition to try and find game somewhere. That night they were visited by the old Griqua General David Berghover who was one of the few to survive from the Griqua attack on Mosilikatse, the Matabele chief. The attack, he said, had been beaten off with heavy Griqua loss of life, and so would certainly not be repeated. Old and infirm, all he could talk about, mumble really, was the ferocity of the Matabele. James made him up a laudanum mixture which gave him some relief from the pains in his ears. He wore what he said was his old soldier's kaross.

At Kramers Fontein James exchanged a fancy waistcoat in which he had cut such a swell at Simpsons at his last luncheon there, for a fine kaross, and the new owner of the waistcoat put it on at once and danced around very happily. He wore no tsecha, or loin cloth, so the sight was unattractive.

Sadly, however, the country all around was still very dry (so that forage was accordingly very scarce) until night fell, when there was a ghastly storm and rain fell in torrents and the tents were nearly washed away. Foolata, who was sleeping under the wagon, had the driest spot, and had to share it with James and John. The natives at the next village were eager to trade karosses for beads, but small blue and red beads only. Such fashions were very changeable, said Lewis, and last year, he had been told, white and green beads had been all the rage. Foolata's clear colourless beads in her necklace were much admired, and fingered, but they had no clear beads to trade.

26

Kuruman and Moffat

FOOLATA WAS NERVOUS as they approached Kuruman that morning. James' wagon was leading the way as Lewis' had slowed down for some reason. She did her best to make herself tidy. She could not wash for lack of water of course, but she spangled her hair with some very tiny and bright, shiny quartz and crystal pebbles she had picked up along the way. She wore the dress she had been given by Mrs Dickson – she felt it gave her status. She was shy as well as highly excited at the same time, because Kuruman, the mission station of maybe seven or eight hundred souls, was certainly one of the larger, or perhaps the largest, mainly native inhabited place they had been to on the journey. Because there would be so many people, she wanted to make a good impression, most particularly on the Moffats.

The Rev. Robert Moffat had two missionaries working at the station with him, Messrs Hamilton and Ashton and they and Mrs Mary Moffat (Ma-Mary as Robert always called her after the native style), all came out of the house and very warmly greeted the new arrivals. Robert, as he insisted on being called, was a tall man whose principal feature was his beard, really more an eco-system than a beard, thought James. Robert, and Ma-Mary both had slight northern accents (which James could not quite place) even after all the years they had been at Kuruman. Behind them, James could see that their house was stone built and thatched, like all the mission buildings at the station, and later learnt that they had all been built by Robert himself, with help from Hume, a strange man called Arend or Arends, who was a runaway slave made good, and the natives. James said how nice it was to see a proper house for once. Ma-Mary swept him and John indoors and immediately offered them food and a bath, and asked them which they wanted first. They both chose a bath.

Lewis, who was a little way behind James just then, said something about seeing his friend Hume the trader, who had a general store at the station, and he unobtrusively drifted off in that direction and so did not then come into the house with them. James did not know what had happened about the servants and where they had got to, but assumed that no doubt they had also made for the store.

Ma-Mary prepared a special lunch for the party, and after grace was said, they sat down to the best meal, exclaimed James, that he had seen since he left Cape Town. Robert explained that they had a very good vegetable garden, as James later saw for himself, and that they grew everything for the meal which was vegetable, and he had shot everything which was animal. Ma-Mary wondered where Lewis had got to, and Robert said, with a grimace, that Lewis must be with Hume, and would presumably eat something there. Robert and Ma-Mary were fluent in Sechuana, which was the language of the local tribe – indeed Ma-Mary told James that Robert was the first person who had reduced it to a written language. Until then it had only ever been spoken. Most tribes locally spoke Sechuana, or were familiar with it. Robert said that where James was going to travel he would need to speak the language, so he must learn it quickly. He thought that would be quite easy, he himself had learnt it without help, and James would have help no doubt from the guides they would be taking. Then everyone fell on the meal, and silence reigned. Robert, once he had eaten his large fill, told what to James seemed several very detailed and interesting anecdotes about life at the station, and amused the assembled party for almost an hour.

Ma-Mary interrupted Robert's exposition of his achievements. "The natives at the mission much admire my husband, but sometimes I have to admit that I think that is because he has such a bushy beard, and a good white head of hair, while many of them are bald, which they seem to consider a sad defect."

Robert stroked his beard, slowly and thoughtfully, amusedly. "I would much prefer," he said, "to be thought of as an Old Testament prophet, but there you are, that is married life for you." James kept silent. Ma-Mary said, "You ought to see Robert when he is at the forge, with his beard tied behind his back to keep it out of the way." "Oh please stop", said Robert – "you know I do that for safety reasons, and in order to amuse you, of course."

Robert resumed his instruction. "The nearest local chief," he said, "whose village is near Kolobeng to the north, and whose tribe is called the Bakwain, is Sechele. He is a good man and a baptised Christian, but the chief whose trust in me I badly need to rely on as real, is the very warlike Mosilikatse. He is chief of the dread Matabele. This man is no Christian, but he does trust me implicitly. He generally calls me "Matchuabi", meaning father, and once he called me that, according to tribal custom I could demand from him anything I could see within his dominions. Among Mosilikatse's slaves is a Griqua girl called Truey whom he stole from her parents some time ago while she was still a child. Actually she is the child of Peter Davids who was chief of the Lithuani Bastards, and successor to Barend Barends, and she was stolen following the defeat of her father in battle. I want Mosilikatse to restore the girl to her parents, and so when I visited him in his kraal I tried everything I could think of to persuade him to either give her to me, or to give her back. But she was studiously hidden away from my sight, so I could not demand her by right of my title as Matchuabi, because I could not actually see her in the flesh. I am told that she is a very real Griqua beauty, whatever that is. I suppose that was why she was being kept hidden from me. I was later told by one of Mosilikatse's slaves that she had cried when she was told about the incident. It is all very sad. Apparently, I could have anything, or anyone else, but not Truey."

Ma-Mary said, "I think you are dreaming about that girl you have never seen. That Mosilikatse has great affection and respect for you, for whatever reason, and that is something very remarkable in a savage. Don't you forget it, and don't jeopardise it either."

Robert agreed. "The unwavering kindness and affection of Mosilikatse towards me, keeps astonishing me. When we are travelling together in my wagon, he will insist on sitting next to me, and rubbing my feet or stroking my beard. Why he does this I am not completely sure. I do not like to stop him doing this, but I do find it embarrassing and inconvenient."

Ma-Mary broke in again to the monologue and told James about the first time, quite long ago, that Mosilikatse had sent two very daring ambassadors to Robert. "They were dressed as usual for Matabele, in other words they wore no clothes at all, save for a kaross over their shoulders. When the men very bravely, as they had never been in a house before, came into my hall stark naked, I showed one of them his reflection in a large mirror which I handed to him to look at. The man was obviously frightened, and peered behind the mirror, to see the man who was hiding there, and then waved his hand behind it. He then pulled a face in it, and finally he smiled. They gave me quite a shock, and when our natives here at the station saw them, they were horrified, and offered them clothes, which the men happily wore." Ma-Mary laughed as she described how these Matabele, dressed in their new clothes, went to church one Sunday. "They sat very patiently, not understanding a word, through an hour-long service, including the sermon, and afterwards asked if the hymns were war songs. I said the songs were in honour of God, and that God was God of peace, not war. The men said they were, and apparently they really were, deeply impressed with the orderliness of the way the service was conducted. They said they wanted their chief to know everything that Robert was doing. I was completely amazed, but very pleased, of course."

Following the lively talk at lunch, James and John were given a guided tour of the station, but Lewis was still not to be seen anywhere. They inspected the very fruitful gardens, which were the Moffats' pride and joy, and where peaches, nectarines, vines, apples, oranges, lemons, corn and vegetables all grew in the very greatest liberal profusion. They were well watered of course as the Kuruman River gave them plentiful clean and pure water for irrigation. James saw the printing establishment, and Robert said he had just received a spare set of type from his supporter Miss Lee of Grosvenor Street Chapel in Manchester. He gave James a copy of *Pilgrims Progress* which he had himself translated into Sechuana, printed and bound, and he signed it for James. Robert also gave him a catechism (which he forgot to sign) and explained how he had converted many of the local population to Christianity, and he hoped James and John, "at least", a sideways reference to Lewis thought James, would attend church the next day.

The church was a fine building with a bell-cote atop, and when they went inside to have a look at it, James saw it was large enough for four or five hundred people, maybe more. It was filled with rough backless benches, a reading desk pulpit, tallow lit chandeliers and an hour glass beside the candle snuffers in the pulpit. There was a harmonium as well. The church was plain and simple just like, James imagined, a non-conformist chapel would be. When he mentioned this however, Ma-Mary told him that she and Robert had both been brought up in the non-conformist tradition, she in the Albion Independent Church in Ashton-in-Makerfield. She said, their communion service had been a gift from Mrs Greaves of Sheffield. Ma-Mary told James that they had celebrated a Christian marriage a few days ago, with the ceremony conducted after the English fashion. She said a large number of people attended and they were decently dressed in European clothes, with, of course, she laughed, a kaross over their shoulders.

They saw the school rooms where Ma-Mary said she taught, both inside and out of doors, which were also lofty and well built. In addition, she ran a sewing school of about thirty persons, which had also been greatly helped by the generosity of Miss Lee. The main street was about a quarter of a mile long, lined with syringa trees, and at the western end was David Hume's store with his house. The native houses beyond, in an area which Robert's assistant the Rev. Hamilton mysteriously called New Hackney, were of course much smaller, and less permanent looking structures, being built in native style, again with trees in front. They too had neat productive gardens, and their owners were almost all neatly dressed in decent, if old, European working clothing.

James had looked without success for a sight of Lewis as they walked around, and after the tour was finished he made a considerable effort to find him. Lewis had made himself very scarce, and when James eventually found him he was at the private room at the back of Hume's store. He and Hume had had a few soopjes, one or two too many, thought James, who although he was no prude was a bit concerned at Lewis' rudeness, as he privately thought of it, in not so far meeting up with the Moffats. Lewis was in an argument with Hume and said he wanted to buy some guns for the purposes of trading for ivory with some of the remoter tribes they were about to encounter when they renewed the journey northwards. Hume was saying that he did not have any guns for trade, and Lewis did not believe him. Hume explained that Robert did not want any of that sort of trade in this store, so he complied with that wish.

David Hume had been picked by Robert as a suitable person to be based as a trader at the mission. Hume was patient with Lewis. He explained carefully to Lewis that there was an Act of Parliament which made the 25th Parallel the northern limit of the colonial laws. South of but up to that line, he explained, offences had been rendered capitally cognisable. So Lewis might take it that the intended object was to curb the excesses of the Boers below that line. So Hume was afraid that if he sold guns to people who took them north of the line as indeed they would be at Kolobeng and beyond, and there killed someone, he as well as the offender would be in trouble with the law. Maybe not immediately, but perhaps when he went back below the line, for example when he went to Cape Town as he did every eighteen months or so. And there would be problems with Robert.

This conversation was almost over by the time James entered the room. When he did so he saw Foolata standing just inside the back door, but as soon as she saw him she moved outside. James told Lewis he would have to be sober in time for supper, and that he absolutely had to have it in the house with Robert and Ma-Mary and their family. Lewis grimaced, and acquiesced, ungracefully. He would need to be clean and tidy, warned James. As James left the room, Lewis pulled a face behind James' back.

Foolata was waiting for James at the front of the store. "Oh Baas," she started.

James stopped her. "Don't call me that. You know you must call me James. I have told you this many times."

"Yes, Baas, I know that. But here we are with white people and they will not think it right for me to do that, so I was trying to be polite is all."

"Well, whatever, what did you want Foolata?" asked James.

"Baas, Baas Lewis keeps grabbing me, and trying to do things to me, and I am a good girl, and I do not want it. What can I do?"

"Well, I shall speak to Lewis, and see if I can persuade him not to do this grabbing, as you put it, but you know he is not married, as I am. It has been a long time since he saw any woman except you, so be careful and do not encourage him in any way."

"I would not mind if it was you grabbing me. You have always been kind to me, ever since you saved me from that bad man Mynheer Beck who was beating me. You are kind, Baas Lewis is not. Look at his driver. I think he had something to with the scar on his driver Dedderich, maybe he was beating him with a litupa, and that is why he has that scar. You would never do anything like that, I know."

"Foolata, you really must not gossip, and of course I would not do anything like that. But I will do what I can to stop Lewis from behaving as he does to you, and you must leave it to me, and not tell tales."

Supper that night started with grace being said, as always in that household, and Lewis, who had forgotten about grace, had to stand up for it as he had sat down too early. He apologised for his absence on the tour of the mission but said he had been to see Hume about some purchases he wanted to make. Lewis then said how much he want to make money on this trip by taking ivory back to the Cape for sale. Robert told him, "You will have to go much farther north to find elephants – you will have to go a long way past the Molopo country and its lions and other game first. The best place, I am told, is beyond Sekomi's country. But I do not think that the pursuit and slaying of God's creatures for profit is acceptable in the eyes of God: food yes, profit no. But I will let you have guides as far as Molopo and then you will have to hire more guides beyond there, but that would be up to Sechele or Sekomi, who is the lesser chief. Do not tell him that. Both are Bechuanas, but Sechele is Chief of the Bakwains and Sekome is Chief of the Bamangwato. Everyone speaks Sechuana, and many speak a smattering of Boer, and some even a little English, although not many can do that."

Ma-Mary had been very patient during this exposition, and afterwards she adjourned the meal to the parlour for coffee. It was a spacious room and there were seats for all of them. Like everyone in the interior Ma-Mary loved coffee, but she and the rest of her family drank it with milk, because unlike most people they had cows to provide it, and sugar. She said that they sometimes obtained that latter by barter with passing travellers or as gifts from visiting ministers. Also, Hume sometimes brought it up from the Cape when he went down there. She knew it was a luxury. On the floor by the fireplace she had a collection of ostrich eggs, but when James looked more closely he could see that holes had been made in them so that they could be used as water containers. When he enquired about them, Ma-Mary said the Bakalahari did that, and some of them had given the containers to her.

James noticed the strange colour of the floor, and Ma-Mary explained that they were all the same throughout the house. They were made of the soil from levelled anthills, which were dead of course, with the earth being rammed down very hard and polished, and she got them that fine clear green colour by spreading fresh cow-dung mixed with water on it, as thinly as possible. This was done every Saturday. "It lays the dust better than anything, kills the fleas, and I love the colour," Ma-Mary said. "I now look upon my floor smeared with cow dung with as much complacency as I used to do upon our best rooms when well scoured."

The pleasant chatter around the room was called to order by Ma-Mary at ten o'clock as school before breakfast was early the next day, as it was Sunday. "You will hear the early church bell," she said, "and Robert will be ringing it. Your breakfast will be after that, and then morning service. How many of you are coming to morning service tomorrow?" she asked. "I want to know as I have to make arrangements for chairs with backs to be taken since the forms are backless, so I need to know the numbers going." The numbers settled, with Lewis, John and James all saying they would be at church, an evening prayer was then said together, everyone standing for that, and they all dispersed to their rooms for the night.

As he lay down, James heard Lewis tip-toeing down the passage and out of the house, and sleepily wondered where he was going.

On Sunday morning James was woken by the bell as Ma-Mary had said he would be, but he lay in bed for a while and luxuriated in its softness. The clean white sheets had almost become a forgotten memory. He washed and shaved in clean water, a really magnificent change thought James, and dressed himself in clothes which had been washed and pressed overnight and placed outside his door while he was asleep. When he reached the dining room the family was already there, and had started their breakfast. Lewis was not around.

Morning service was every bit as enthralling as Ma-Mary and Robert had both said it would be. Outside, beforehand, there was a crowd of natives standing talking to each other quietly, waiting for the service to start in the shade of the syringa trees. Some were carrying chairs with backs to make the length of the sermon less of an endurance test. The service itself was in Sechuana, and the congregation, James thought, behaved as properly as if they were in an Anglican cathedral. The enthusiastic singing to the harmonium was very tuneful and not just in unison, but also on occasion in parts. The congregation wore decent clothing in the European style and some ladies patronised hats, but of those who did James saw there was a division of opinion, and some among them wore them on their bare heads, and some had an intervening handkerchief. Lewis cut the service, and there was a spare chair as a result.

In the afternoon Robert took James for a walk on their own to a cavern nearby. It was the place where there had been an enormous serpent according to native legend, but if it ever had been, was no longer. It was the source of the considerable river Kuruman and they penetrated the cave itself for about thirty feet. Robert said the water which issued felt cold in summer, but warm in winter. He could not explain that. They then went for a long walk, and had a talk that James found engrossing. He realised with surprise that since he and Harry had last seen each other he had not had any major conversation with Lewis which did not in some way or other include the subject of money. That was why this talk with Robert was so different. They had been able to talk freely about life and art, but mostly about native politics, and not once did James feel he was being pressed to talk about Lewis' money problems, as he usually was by Lewis. But then later as the walk progressed the topics changed, and James became introspective and thought about the others who had featured so much in his life.

James felt that Robert was a kind and good man, gentle with underlying moral strength, which he kept hidden. They talked freely as they walked, and James found himself wanting to confide in this man of God, and tell him about what he had done. As they walked, his need to talk became almost like a compulsion. Telling Robert would be like going to confession he imagined, although as an Anglican he had never confessed. So as they walked, he unburdened himself of what he now regarded as, and once during that walk even called, his sins. He wondered guiltily if he would feel, or indeed be, better as a person if he did confess as he felt he should. He was dimly aware that in telling Robert all about himself he was imposing a burden on someone who had not expressed a wish to receive such a burden. James had, he said, felt he had made a dreadful fool of himself over Christina. He should never have got engaged to her, because he realised now he did not love her, and never had. It had been a youthful infatuation and no more. He was merely blinded by her youth and looks, by her family and friends, by the novelty of life at the Cape, and by freedom from his family. He had not seen that they had nothing at all in common. All her family had ever wanted was his money and his title, potentially. What Christina herself had wanted, he did not know. But he had treated her badly, breaking it off so suddenly and gracelessly like that. He was deeply ashamed of what he had done. He had been very ungentlemanlike in his behaviour to her, and he had no excuse for the way he had treated her. None at all. They were from two different worlds, and here he thought of but did not mention her father's behaviour. His only excuse, as he put it to Robert, was that he had been overcome by the new experiences and sensations of the new world he was then finding at the Cape. But James knew very well in his mind that what he had just said were mere excuses, and that in truth his unacceptable actions could not be covered by a deceitful and self-serving confession designed for sympathy and possibly forgiveness. He apologised to Robert for burdening him with what he had said. He tried to explain that he was sorry for his behaviour, which he admitted he did not express very well, but Robert just walked on silently, looking straight ahead.

What James silently realised for himself was that his confession to someone who had not asked for or encouraged it, was an act itself of great selfishness. He had been trying to shed some of his guilt by way of a semi-public confession to another, and he finally realised that he could not rid himself of guilt by simply telling his confessor what he had done.

So James made no more spoken confession. But as they walked on in silence James understood that what he had done to Francesca was far worse than how he had behaved towards Christina. When he had returned, he had treated her as if her feelings were to be ignored. Indeed he had not just ignored them, he had treated them as if they were not worth the slightest consideration, almost as if she did not have any feelings. To describe the way he had behaved as selfish, inconsiderate, even as cruel, was not enough. Without intentionally doing so, he had originally, knowingly let her believe that he loved her. Then later, when he had shown how apparently empty, even contemptuous of her, his feelings for her were at that time, she had offered him her undying and faithful love. In return, he had failed to understand that what she was doing was making a desperate last sacrifice, of herself, in the hope that he would under-stand how much she loved him, and in the hope he might respond to her. But he had done worse than be contemptuous of her, he had rejected that last overture in the most unfeeling way he could have done. And he hoped he had done so because he had thought that that would be the kindest way he could think of to let her down gently, but he knew he had not thought like that. In fact, all he had done was to show her what a worthless and unthinking and shallow man he was, and by that, he knew then how worthless he was of her, or indeed anyone's, love. And James understood that in confessing how badly he had treated Christina, he was avoiding telling Robert how much more badly he had treated his real wife, Francesca. Maybe that was his ultimate self-betrayal.

Perhaps the worst aspect of his own character, thought James, was that he could not emotionally respond to Francesca when he could see her need, indeed he had not even felt any reason to do so, and now he could not respond feelingly to Christina either, and had no wish to.

James, emotionally drained by his spoken and unspoken confessions, stopped walking. He stood still. Robert walked on, saying nothing, so James never knew what he thought. They were not to talk about such matters again. James wrote all this in his journal later that night.

27

Onwards

OVER THE NEXT FEW DAYS James and Lewis prepared for the next stage of their journey. They did not know where they were going exactly, but Robert told them they would have to go north to Kolobeng where his son-in-law was minister. His name was David Livingstone, and his wife was their daughter Mary. He had proposed to her under the almond tree in the garden at Kuruman, and Robert pointed to it happily. To get to Kolobeng he said they would have to cross the Molopo area, where there were dry sand rivers, and water would be hard to come by. James and Lewis needed guides to get to Kolobeng, and engaged two of the men from the station whom Robert said were good men, and as one of them claimed that he knew the way, all seemed set fair.

They made a few last-minute purchases at Hume's, mainly more brass wire and beads, and then after Robert himself had completed repairs to the wagon at the carpenter's workshop, they prepared to leave. Robert and Ma-Mary filled their wagons with fruit and vegetables. Ma-Mary had looked out some of her old dresses and gave them to Foolata, to try and make her look more decent she said. The two of them waived the party goodbye, and Robert said, "Take care, and may God go with you, and forgive you your sins."

Game was very scarce for the first few days of the journey, and on about the third evening at out-spanning they were joined by a small party of armed natives for the night, because they were worried about the lions, or so they said. Their bodies were well smeared with fat and red ochre, and their heads sparkled with sibilo mixed with the grease. Others had shorn heads leaving only a ring on top which they had greased and adorned with feathers, coloured stones and anything in fact they wanted, and they were all well decorated more or less everywhere with beads and brass wire. Once James had given them each some tobacco, they happily traded a few spare arrows and two fine karosses for more beads. What the natives were really calling for as soon as they saw them were gaudy handker-chiefs, of which James realised they had brought far too few. Money was of no use to them, handkerchiefs and beads were the real currency. The next morning as James was boiling the karosses because they were filthy with vermin, a group of Balalas passed them. These very low-caste nomadic outcast tribesmen were friendly, and were mightily impressed with the boiling of the karosses, seeming to think of it as some kind of magic. They peered and grimaced and crouched down out of fear at the clouds of steam.

The going from Kuruman had so far been reasonable, the ground being chiefly sand, but the march was a very hot one indeed under a burning and persistently fierce sun. Despite that, the dawns were freezing, piercingly cold. The landscape was barren and boundless, with only a few anthills to break the monotony. There was the occa-sional tree and stunted bushes among which James saw ostriches, their heads peeping over the top of them. He found he could also see the clouds of dust enveloping them when they were busy dusting themselves down in large semi-circular bowl-like scrapes in the ground. Martinus said that once their nests had been robbed of even as few as one or two eggs out of the clutches, which could be large, they would abandon the rest entirely. James felt guilty about taking one egg, but he did, for his collection of curios. He admired the pattern of the shell and blew it for preservation purposes when the wagons halted that night, and before he wrote up his journal. He tried a pen and ink wash drawing of ostriches, but did not think it successful.

James had been collecting specimens of native arts and weapons as they had gone along, and so he also added the previous day's acquisitions to the pile in the back of his wagon. Lewis had not bothered to trade as he said he was saving his trade goods for farther north where the trade would be for ivory, "And that is money in the bank, old boy. Your souvenirs won't be worth anything like ivory, and why you spend so much time curing trophy heads and skins and so on, I really can't think." Farther on, at Loharon, with the scenery changing to a coarse grass land, with just a few trees, straggling clumps of mimosas mostly, game was very plentiful, and there was a vast herd of maybe five hundred brindled gnus, hartebeests, zebras and quaggas. James and Lewis were able to refresh the larder by shooting three antelopes which, as Foolata pointed out, was just as well because otherwise all they had left was poor biltong. Dried meat, she complained, so often became contaminated in the wagon for one reason or another, that she wanted to cook a meal of clean fresh meat for once.

A native who approached them begging for tobacco said that they had reached Kosi Fontein, which belied its name, as the ground was bare again at this site and there was only dry sandy dust. There were no trees to be seen, only some very small bushy scrub and thorn, and there was no pasturage for the poor oxen who had been without water for two days. At this point James walked for many miles beside the wagon because he wanted to take in the beauty of the landscape, its colour and form, and it was while he was doing this just a little off the track made by Lewis' wagon that he came on some drawings made by bushmen on rocks. He literally ran back to his wagon and fetched his sketchbook and drawing materials into which he diligently, and he hoped accurately, copied these drawings. The drawings had been made by chipping at the rocks with a harder rock or stone, so the mark was basically an indent. Martinus had come with him to look at the marks, and said he knew of many more, back beyond Kuruman.

The trek-touw on Lewis' wagon had for some days been showing signs of strain, and a few days later it snapped. Dedderich, his driver, had obviously been asleep and the wagon had run into a great mass of rock. That had thrown the wagon onto its side, hence the break. Two oxen were hurt in the collapse and when the trek-touw was repaired the two oxen had to be taken off it and tethered at the back of the wagon. He decided to put the time while the trek-touw was being repaired to good use, so he picked up his sketch book, and took an artist's look at what was in front of him. It was still quite early in the day, and the light was clean and fresh. The tints in the sky faded and merged into each other, and ranged from a brown dusty white to a pale blue. As he watched all the colours were being washed into a faded tone by the increasing brightness of the sun. James had on occasion tried to capture the transient nature of the colouring, but had not up until then succeeded to his own satisfaction. At this particular time he was standing on the fore-chest, and from there he commanded a considerable view. He saw the way the grasses bent in curving movements from side to side in the breeze, and was reminded of breezes skimming the surface of the sea when calm, like cats' paws. The movement of the grass fasci-nated him, and Martinus, noticing James' preoccupation with it, said that the height of the grass made grass-eating animals fear, as it meant they could not see approaching predators while eating. He said that at his village they had used to burn off the tall grasses and small shrubs once a year, to make the landscape more attractive to the springbok. On the other hand, he pointed out that areas of taller grassland like this were ideal for hunter animals like lions, hyenas and leopards.

They were only a week or so beyond Kuruman, and Kolobeng was still a long way ahead, when their head guide now appeared to be, or said he was, lost. Lewis said this was not really likely, he was probably angling for more pay, and so what was necessary was for them to make sure he did not lead the wagons astray. His complaint might also mean that he wanted to go back home, thought James.

He had been trying to learn Sechuana from one of the guides, and had been doing quite well. James was better than Lewis at the language, as he had made a systematic attempt at learning, unlike Lewis who did not bother enough. Lewis said that when guides did something like this, pretending to be lost, it usually meant trouble, and that they should keep their eyes open for whatever might happen. But the going gradually became easier and the landscape changed for the softer too, with glades of mokaala trees everywhere. Their shade was very welcome but water still remained a serious problem.

That night, long after they had out-spanned, a troop of about fifty or sixty natives materialised out of the surrounding trees, gradually surrounded the wagons, and started to demand tobacco, innocently enough at first. But their demands increased fairly rapidly, certainly in terms of volume and the numbers of natives. At first they had been a little dispersed, but they soon began to crowd together rather too closely around the wagons, thought James, and they shouted at Martinus, who was in a blue funk. Neither Lewis nor James gave them any tobacco despite the increasing demands. Martinus said to James that he did not understand everything that they were saying. He said much of it was some language he did not know. James noticed, as if in a bad dream, that quite a few of the natives were carrying spears, and one or two he could see had clubs and axes, battle-axes. By the flickering light of the camp fire, their bodies glistened with the red fat and ochre they had smeared on themselves and sprinkled with mica and sibilo. The stones reflected light, and sparkled as they jumped around, and made their fierce warlike appearance very impressive and frightening. Their posturing and threatening increased rapidly and, to James' way of thinking, alarmingly. Assegais were now brandished and pointed at them in a jabbing, stabbing motion. Their cries and shouting increased. They did not want tobacco now, they wanted more, much more. Foolata, who was behind James in his wagon, gasped over his shoulder that they were all going to be killed. James knew that Lewis always kept his rifle ready loaded, as indeed did he, and when the shouting seemed to Lewis to have reached a threatening, physically threatening, pitch and James was really starting to inwardly panic, Lewis picked it up and raised it – as he hoped – menacingly. The crowd seemed poised to attack at any minute, and the sight of the gun had no noticeable effect on them at all. One of them pushed James in the leg, and then clutched at his boot. James felt them start to rock his wagon, Lewis' was rocking already.

"Get your rifle to hand," shouted Lewis. James heard him, just, above the uproar. "Ready!" cried James snatching his up as well. "Watch out now, when I fire." With that, Lewis fired into the air above the heads of the natives. James fired as well, almost simultaneously, above the crowd, towards the surrounding mokaala trees. Instantly there was complete and utter silence from the natives who, shocked, stood absolutely rigid and totally quiet. Seconds later they were all in flight. The oxen who had all been fastened to the trek-touw moved uncomfortably at the gunshots, and one, more troubled by the gunshot than the others, bellowed. Another beast, therefore fearing something unseen, bellowed as well. Within seconds, or so it seemed, the entire team was straining at the trek-touw trying to get away from some non-existent threat to them. James' wagon rocked from side to side as they strained, and for a moment or two it seemed as if it must be pulled over. Passing his rifle to Martinus, James jumped down and, pushing the last of the fleeing natives aside, ran to the lead ox, Blauberg, and took the animal's head in his arms, pressing his cheek against the ox's cheek. The ox strained against him and flashed his head up and down trying to break free, and James thinking, certain almost, that he would be gored at any minute, held on for dear life. But the ox gradually calmed, and as he did so, the others calmed too. James well knew he had been extremely foolish to try to calm Blauberg, but he knew that if he had not, there would have been a stampede, and another broken trek-touw. He was just pleased he had managed to calm the beast, and that the natives had stopped their shouting.

James was sweating profusely with both fear and exhilaration, and when he looked up from what he was doing, he saw that the natives had left, and not even the backs of a few stragglers were visible. The darkness had swallowed them. James was left very shaken, standing among the oxen, stroking one of them.

Their main guide was cowering in the bottom of Lewis' wagon when they eventually found him, and nothing would persuade him to emerge, not even snuff. He lay there snivelling and calling on his gods to have mercy. Lewis predicted, quite correctly as it turned out, that he would slope off in the morning. Foolata and Martinus were full of praise for both Lewis' and James' bravery, which to them was heroic. In his turn Lewis' driver Dedderich was fulsome in his praise for Lewis' bravery and kept saying that he owed his life to his baas. Wolhuter and Jessa said nothing, but John looked at James with something like hero worship.

Lewis was very thoughtful after it was all over, and the following morning as they ate fried biltong and drank coffee for breakfast as usual, he said to the assembled party, "You realise of course, that first lot of natives we saw, and did a bit of trade with, or at least you did a bit of trade with James, a few days ago now, were doing nothing more than trying to see how strong we were in numbers and weaponry. I think they also wanted to see what we had that was worth robbing and killing us for. I assume they liked what they saw, and so they went away to get reinforcements against the macooas, which is what they call us white men. After they left us they must have left some of their number to follow our spoor. That is how they found us yesterday. They only attacked us, or prepared to attack us, because they did not immediately see we were armed. My view is that they would happily have overpowered us and almost certainly have killed us if they had thought they could." Martinus was equally certain, as was Foolata, that they had all been about to be killed, and it was decided that for the foreseeable future guards would be kept at night to prevent a surprise attack.

The going had now become fearfully difficult as the ground was sandy and the wagon wheels dug into it deeply, sometimes by as much as eighteen inches. There was no trail to follow any more, and Lewis and James were not at all certain where they were going. James had taken a bearing at Kuruman which he had thankfully written down on a scrap of paper and a hunt was now made for it. When found, with much rejoicing at the impending knowledge of where they might be, the trocheameter on the rear nearside wheel of James' wagon was consulted. From this they knew exactly how far they had gone, and when they had taken their sextant reading for the day at noon, according to James' watch, James was able to tell Lewis more or less exactly where they were, if, of course his mathematics was right. But the real problem was not knowing where they were, but that their water supplies were very low, and the route ahead, although liable to be no more daunting physically than what they had passed already, might or might not have adequate water as they proceeded. The oxen were very thin, and had been without water for two days, having been on very short rations before then as well.

Later the next day, James went out on foot hunting with John, trying to see if they could find any water or game, or anything they could eat; their horses were too spent to bear another day as they were. They did not take Argos with them: Foolata wanted him to stay at the wagon, as a companion she said, and perhaps, thought James to himself, as a guard against Lewis' attentions. James and John followed what they thought was the recent spoor of some brindled gnus, but after they had been moving along for about two hours they lost the spoor. During this tracking they had fleeting glimpses of some hartebeests and made wild shots at them, but without success.

Neither of them could recall the precise route they had taken to the point where they had lost the track of the gnus, and trying to walk back the way they had come along the very dusty track was extremely hard as the wind was blowing sandy dust into their faces. That was not the main problem though. The immediate and serious problem was that the light wind-blown sand had largely obliterated their earlier tracks. They had back-tracked successfully many times during hunting while on the trek, but on this occasion they completely failed to find their way back to the wagons. So they stopped trying to find their way, they just stood and tried to take stock of their situation. They had lost themselves miserably, and had no idea of where they had got to in the completely novel landscape. The mokaala trees, while very beautiful to James' artistic eye, even if their leaves were shrivelled up and a pale fragile brown for want of water, effectively obscured any long-distance views on the sandy plain where they were. James idly wondered if he could climb one of them to see if he could get a view from the top, but as John pointed out, even if he did manage to do that, because of the intervening trees he would not be able to see the wagons, which were at ground level. "No," asserted John, "we will have to wait for the evening camp fire to be lit, and then we might see the smoke spiralling upwards."

"They might fire a gun, we might hear gunshots," added John, doubtfully.

"That would depend on how close we are to the wagons, and we might be too far away to hear the shots. Unless we are reasonably close, in this country I doubt the sound would carry to us."

"I do not agree about the sound not carrying in this country," said John. "But that does not matter as they would not be worried enough to sound a recall shot until evening anyway. Well we can't wait here or we will die of thirst or hunger." He paused ruminatively. "I have no water in my flask now, I only had a little when we started, and nor I suspect do you?"

"No. I have been out of water for some time. I very stupidly

forgot to top up my flask before we set out on our wild goose chase."
John refrained from saying that James had, as he himself said, been
very stupid. It was normally an everyday task to fill one's water flask
before setting out, in case of just such an eventuality as had in fact
occurred. It was routine, as routine as making sure you had enough
ammunition for the day.

John said, "Well the practical thing is not to get even more lost
than we already are. Of course I will share what water I have with
you. I thought you were drinking very little, and now you say you
have no water at all. I think that to conserve what little water I have
left, we should stay here and wait for the evening, and see if Lewis
or Martinus fire off a rocket, or something like that. We would see
that and then find our way back, I am sure. Sound carries better at
night as well."

James thought about that for a moment. He was silent as he was
studying the ground where they were. "I can see lions' spoor, I
think," he said. "I am not at all sure that being in open country like
this near Molopo, and at night, is such a good thing. The Molopo
area is famous not just for being a river allegedly with fabulous
amounts of water, but for lions as well, as everybody has been
telling us, and so perhaps we had better check what we have left in
the way of ammunition before we decide what to do."

A hurried check of what ammunition they had left was reassuring.
"Look, I have no desire to be hereabouts wherever we are, at night,"
said James. "Everyone tells us that the general area abounds with
lions and night-time is their favourite hunting time as we know. So
we have to be prepared, if we are indeed going to wait. Is your rifle
fully loaded, and have you spare ammunition actually to hand?
Waiting here in the hope that someone would send up a rocket to
help us could be quite exciting you know."

They both sat down on the ground leaning their backs against a
tree, and prepared for a long wait until evening. James regretted that
they had not brought Argos along. His senses would have helped

them if an animal approached. Their rifles were on the ground beside them, and John passed his flask to James who took one sip, and passed it back again. James' mouth was sticky dry, and he found talking quite difficult physically: his lips kept sticking, and his throat was sore from the light sandy dust in the air. They sat quietly for a while, simply waiting, because not talking was easier. John had a small book in his knapsack and he took it out and started to look at it. But he was obviously very tired and it was not long before his head nodded, and he dozed off. James was left alone with his thoughts.

For several days now he had been troubled by thoughts of Devon, home and more particularly of Francesca. He thought now, as he sat alone in the African bush, lost and without water, that he had had a privileged youth, and that he had not repaid what he had accepted so freely. So did he perhaps deserve this? He dreamed back to Cambridge, and seemed to see the Backs and punting, college dinners in the dim candlelight of the college hall with dark oil paintings of famous men above, the green manicured sward of the college lawn, and bright sunlit garden parties. Boaters, berib-boned blazers, parasols, shy, smiling girls with swirling long dresses in bright colours, champagne and fresh cucumber sandwiches. Youth and happiness. Always laughter. He thought he glimpsed Francesca.

"Baas, Baas," said a voice next to him, waking James from his pleasant reverie. "Baas, Baas." Standing in front of James was a tall native, wearing, as far as James could see, a kaross and nothing much else save for the usual fatty ochre smeared all over. Around his neck hung three necklaces of beads interspersed with large ivory-coloured claws that looked like lions' claws to James, and he carried three spears, two of the throwing kind and a shorter one of the stabbing kind. Over one shoulder he had a ragged sack out of which he pulled a handful of locusts, and stooping, he offered them to James and then to John. James took some, but John, who had also woken, shook his head violently. The native stood back and looked at them.

"Kuil," he said. "Kuil." And he pointed over his shoulder with a spear.

"What does that mean?" asked John.

"It is the bushman word for a water hole. Perhaps he is trying to show us how to find some water," said James. "I think we should go in the direction he is pointing and see if we find a kuil, and if we do at least we will have water."

"I think I remember a man with necklaces like that from the attack the other night. I think he might be trying to trap us and lead us into their hands," said John.

"How certain of that are you?"

"Not terribly certain I admit, but certain enough to be worried. I don't think we should go where he is pointing his assegai."

The native was following what they were saying and looking from one to the other of them as they spoke. He was observing them closely. James ate a locust, and the man smiled. It tasted sweet, crunchy and perhaps a little salty, but maybe that was just his sweat. James smacked his lips to show appreciation, which he did not feel really, but thought he ought to show. The man grinned. He was very dark coloured, with perfect white teeth evenly set, and his lips were very protuberant. James stood up, followed by John, and they both looked at where the man had pointed. James hesitated. The man stabbed with his spear in the same direction several more times. James looked at the sky. There were no vultures or other birds to be seen anywhere, and certainly not in that direction, just the almost blinding white light of the sun. There was no wind now, and not a sound to be heard except their breathing.

"He is definitely trying to lead us somewhere," said John.

"Yes of course he is. But sadly he is pointing west, judging from the sun, and to our west is the Kalahari, so I don't think heading west is really a very good idea."

James turned to the man and, pointing in the direction the native had pointed, said "Mi-Kalahari. Mi-Kalahari."

The man shook his head violently and said "Kuil. Kuil. Kuil," and kept on jabbing his spear in a westerly direction.

"Well, we have a choice now, don't we? Do we follow him and hope he is telling us the truth, and that there is water in the direction he says, or do we stay here and wait for nightfall?"

"Do you think Lewis will try and follow our spoor here?" asked John. "I mean, maybe if we go with this native we might get even more lost than we are, and Lewis or whoever tries to follow us, if anyone, would not have a chance of finding us at all."

"Come on," said James. "Let's go, and see what happens. There are two of us after all, and as long as we stick together and keep our rifles handy we can't go too wrong surely? We need the water, and to be somewhere safe at night, so let's go."

James turned to the native, and said, "Kuil. Kuil."

28

Hendrick Brewis

Lewis and the rest of the party stayed with the wagons, and waited for James and John to return. Lewis slept most of the day, to conserve energy he said to himself. Their servants sat around the remains of the previous night's fire, and talked in their click language in low tones as they knew better than to wake Baas Lewis when he was asleep. Presently Martinus, Jessa and Edward got up and started to collect branches and bushes for the next night's fire. The oxen had been released from the trek-touw that morning and had wandered off slowly, as they usually did, trying to find some sustenance in the arid landscape around the camp. They would need to be fetched back before nightfall. Foolata sat on James' fore-chest, and watched and waited. The air was very still and she worked fitfully at some sewing that was needed on a dress Ma-Mary had given her, but she soon laid it aside as she was too distracted by the delay in James' and John's return to concentrate.

When the boys had collected enough firewood, they sat down again beside James' wagon, but Foolata pointed out to them that the oxen were way out of sight somewhere and they had better hurry up and find them before nightfall as they had to be fastened to the trek-touw by then. With much grumbling they started to their feet as they knew that what she said was right, but then she was only a woman, and not the baas, even if she rode in his wagon. Clicking away to themselves they moved off and were soon lost to sight. They followed the oxen's spoor which was an easy trail to follow, as the oxen usually kept together, and to Foolata's relief they were all safely back after about two hours – two hours which

Foolata passed with increasing nervousness. She did not want to be left alone with Lewis and Dedderich. She thought that they were not to be trusted. Not thinking that she spoke Boer fluently, as she did from her employment with the Becks, Lewis, who did speak Boer fluently, sometimes used that language to talk privately with Dedderich. Foolata had heard them talking about James behind his back, and what they said made her very worried. Lewis had been saying that James still owed him money, but Foolata knew that to be untrue, as she had heard James talking to Lewis when he made the final payment for the full costs of the trek, including Lewis' share. That payment had meant that James owed nothing, and that Lewis would have to pay his half share of the cost back to James at the end of the trek. Lewis had then said he would indeed repay James when he sold his ivory. That was back at the farmhouse. She had heard Lewis now say that James had not paid enough, he wanted more money from James to take account of all the work he had had to do organising the trek, and that James had not paid as much as Lewis wanted. He had said that James would come to regret not paying what he was rightfully owed.

About five o'clock Lewis woke and stumbled half asleep out of his wagon, and came round to the back of James' wagon. He relieved himself against the rear wheel, and opening the after-clap reached in and helped himself to a mug of James' water from the back barrel. Lewis looked around, and seeing that James and John were not there he came to the front where Foolata was with Argos beside her, and asked her how long they had been away. She told him they had left at dawn and now they had been away all day. Grunting, Lewis returned to his wagon and, picking his gun up, after taking out the bullets, he fired three blank shots into the sky, and then stood still to listen for return fire. Hearing none, after a short while he fired another three shots, and again waited, but still there was no responding fire. He then hauled out a large crate from the back, and sorting some small boxes out he started to mix the ingredients for a number of rockets. When they were complete, he returned to the back of James' wagon and again reaching in, this time he helped himself to a small cup of James' brandy. Foolata observed all this; she said nothing, she just sat and watched silently.

The native led James and John in total silence though a rapidly thinning forest of tall mokaala trees. As they walked, they conversed quietly together. They were both worried about where they were being led, but having once started to follow this native it seemed a bit pointless to stop doing so. The ground seemed to be getting drier and drier, thought James, and on one occasion they passed across a completely dried-up river bed. James wanted to stop there and see if they could scrape a hollow, where they might find a little dampness or even water. But they had no spades with them for digging properly as they usually did, so they just kept walking onwards. After they had been walking for about two hours, the light began to fade, and the evening noises of the country started. They had been walking for what was a worrying distance, and length of time, and James felt that about now they should be making camp for the night, with a brush fence for security. The air was absolutely still, and cooling rapidly. James was sure he heard a quiet purring sound, but even as he did the native held his right hand up in a silent signal for them to stop. About fifty or so yards ahead they could see a full-grown male lion, standing with his back to them on a raised mound, which looked like an old termite nest. Its mane was laid back, and that emphasised its enormous size. All three people stood absolutely still and silent. The lion was looking directly away from them, and was intently watching something or someone they could not see, with great, and luckily for all of them, fixed, attention. Its tail flicked from side to side, then it lowered its body so that it was crouching, and after inching forward very slowly for a few short paces the lion sprang, away from them. They heard a frightful, agonised, high-pitched, human cry and James instinctively ran forwards as fast as he could. Rounding the mound, he saw the lion had sprung upon a man, a native. The impetus of the spring had knocked the man down, then in the attack the lion had obviously bitten his shoulder and was now crouched over him and holding him firmly down with a large paw while it looked around. The man appeared to be unconscious, at least he was not moving. James gave a great shout and the lion turned and faced him. The lion crouched on its prey and snarled angrily at James, who was now running towards him, and seeing him attacking, as the lion thought, it reared up and faced James, roaring very aggressively. James dropped to one knee, and sighting the lion's shoulder for a heart shot, very carefully let fly with two shots. They both hit as intended, but they did not stop the lion, which charged at James who now did not have another shot ready. At the same instant it sprang at James, John fired at the lion from close behind him, and this third shot also hit the lion. The momentum of its forward charge carried it on, and as it died it fell partly on top of James. The lion was hot, very heavy, and smelt foul, thought James, and the hot blood oozing from it soaked into James' shirt. It also seemed to James, lying partly under it, that it was an enormous weight. Petrified as he was by the appalling charge the beast had made at him, in a moment of almost psychic calm, James could clearly see minute vermin in the lion's mane trying to escape the bloodflow.

The native who had been leading them to the kuil ran up to the lion's hot and dead body, and pulling it off, he jabbed at it repeatedly with one of his assegais. He was shouting something triumphant all the while, but James did not know what. His language skills were nowhere near good enough. The native stopped the stabbing, and ran over to the unconscious man on the ground, who had not moved. The native knelt and said something to the wounded man, in Bakalahari perhaps thought James, that he did not understand. He was crying out, and crouching down and held the man in his arms. John helped James to his feet, and they both stood and marvelled at the size of the lion, which was the largest they had seen, and at the narrowness of James' escape. In fact they were both seriously in shock from the closeness of the encounter, and were half awakened from their stasis by the native who started to sing something: a weird sort of keening song, that had all sorts of dissonances in it.

They stood where they were, immobile, for what seemed a long time to James. He was shivering now, and not from cold. John put his arm around him and then threw his jacket onto James' shoulders. James' shirt was sticky with the lion's blood, and he looked at it and felt both interested and slightly sick. He had been very foolish, and had been so lucky to survive that charge. The group did not move, the moment seemed to be one of those silent moments that never end. James' teeth chattered.

There was a soft popping sound somewhere, and looking up startled, James saw a rocket in the sky. It started to fall almost before any of them could react to it. "Look!" he cried. "That's a rocket from our wagon. That's them. It is Lewis trying to guide us back. All we have to do is walk in that direction. Try and remember where the base of the rocket trail is John." He was slightly hysterical with relief, both because of his escape from the lion, and now because of the rocket.

As he said this, the native looked up in fear at the light from the, to him, magical rocket, and hid his face in his kaross. But after a short while when the light had died down, he peered out and then stooped and picked up the wounded man in his arms. He carried the man to James, and James could see that he was a shrunken, wrinkled old man, filthy dirty and with numerous scars all over. He was just the faintest scrap of skin and bone, with not an ounce of spare flesh on him. He had the usual sort of kaross around his shoulders, and wore nothing else, apart from a lambele, or gastric belt, fastened very tightly around his waist, and he had what might be a ring on his left hand. James could not see it properly because of the dirt which was encrusted on the man. The old man's minor abrasions were festering scabs really, thought James. Some looked dirty and infected, smelt and were leaking a yellow-coloured pus. James took the old man from the native, and set him down on his feet very gently, but he was very unsteady and could not stand on his own unaided. His shoulder with its teeth and claw marks was bleeding, although not copiously. With John's help, James and the old man started off at a very slow pace in the direction they had seen the rocket. The old man must have been in serious pain from his shoulder, but he made no sound as he was half carried, half walked along. He seemed to be making a grimly determined effort to keep going. His spirit was amazing, thought James, and while something must have been driving him on, now, with the attack from the lion wounding him so badly, plainly he was near the end of his struggle for survival. Wounds inflicted by lions were very liable to become grossly infected quickly, James knew, and that would likely be the case here.

The small group staggered on as best and as fast as it could, and after about fifteen minutes another rocket went up, showing them they were walking along the right alignment. They eventually reached the wagons, and were met by Lewis and the others crowding round, who were all full of questions of course, not many of which James or John could answer. James told how they had found the old man, and about the lion's charge, and Lewis said bluntly but truthfully and accurately, that he thought James had been a bloody fool. "You have done two things wrong today. You failed to take proper mental note of where you were going as you both hunted – if you had done you would have been quite able to get back to the wagons. Secondly, and even more stupidly, you charged a lion. That was incredibly stupid. Let me tell you this. Any experienced hunter can always find his way back to his wagon from a day's hunting. He always takes very careful note of his route as he sets out. In my opinion you are extremely lucky to have come through unscathed." James silently reflected to himself that Lewis was absolutely right. "You have got to take much more care of yourselves next time," said an angry Lewis.

Foolata took charge of the old man who was laid down on a clean kaross from James' wagon, and she did her best to clean the wound in his shoulder, and then bound it with cloth. The old man watched her attentively all the while, but said nothing, he never made a sound. She gave him some water and then a little broth, which she warmed for him over the camp fire, and sat him up against a bundle of wood, and put another clean kaross over him to keep him warm. The old man smiled thinly at her.

He extended a skinny arm out of the kaross towards James, and uncertainly beckoned him over. James and the others who were all crowded round sat in a small circle as the old man told his story in a faltering voice, deep and throaty. He spoke in heavily accented, broken Boer, with a little English added occasionally, to their complete astonishment, but what he had to say was even more astonishing. He spoke with frequent pauses as he waited for the next sentence to come to mind, and then to gather his strength to say it.

He said his name was Hendrick Brewis. But he was a full-blooded Bakwain. When he was born, as was normal Bakwain custom when twins were born the smaller and weaker of the two, was going to be left out in the veldt to die, or be killed by animals. That had been his fate, but just then his village was being visited by a Boer couple, and the vrouw had helped in his birth. The couple were both so distressed by this custom and what was going to be done with the baby, that they said they wanted to have him, and bring him up as their own child, and they took him away. The villagers and the chief had all agreed to this. The couple were, he said, childless, and they had indeed, against all the odds, brought him up as their son, despite their different colour. They gave him their name, and they loved him. "I think the man's name was Hendrick, like mine, but I can't remember mutti's," he said, sadly. "They were very kind to me, and never beat me." But they were very poor nomadic farming people, and they did not have a settled farm, and first the vrouw died of some poor wasting illness, and then when the old man died of grief for his wife not long after, as he was dying he gave Hendrick his ring, as he had nothing else. He had buried them both at the site where his father, as he thought of Mynheer Brewis, had last camped, and a few days later a passing Dutch minister had said a prayer at his request. They had always said prayers together like a family all his life.

After that, for many years Hendrick said he had worked for various farmers as a labourer. It had been a hard life and he had often been whipped by them. One farmer had even sold him to the last man he worked for, and he got a good price for Hendrick, since because he could speak Boer he could be very useful. When Hendrick had felt he could bear it no more, he had run away. That last Boer had sent the veldt-cornet after him, but he had managed to avoid being caught by travelling deep into the Kalahari, and now he was trying to make his way home, to the tribe where he was born. But he did not know where that village was, and he was lost and had been lost for some time, maybe months. He did not know how long he had been lost. He only wanted to get back to the village of his birth in order to die among his own people. He was not sure where that was, he did not even know the name of the village, but he was sure he would know it when he found it. He had been helped by some poor bushmen, who had tried to show him how to find food and be safe in the Kalahari, and he had lived with them for a year or maybe more, he did not know. But then they had just abandoned him, and now he had no one. James and John were the first people he had seen for a long time. He did not know who the native was when they found him. He was very hungry – he had had no food or water for days and that was why he wore the lambele. James took his hand gently and looked at the ring, and rubbed the dusty dirt off with his handkerchief. It was a simple gold ring, with the barely visible emblem of a sword on it. The old man smiled weakly at James, and said thinly, "Batavia, Batavia."

The party gathered around the old man had listened intently to his story, and when he had finished there was complete silence. Even Lewis, who was generally pretty unemotional, was silent. Foolata took Hendrick in her arms and tried to comfort him. As she did so she gave a small exclamation, and partly lifted the kaross from Hendrick's back. His skin was ridged and rough from the top of his shoulders to below the waist. They were the rough, old scars from many beatings by jamboks or litupas.

During the night Foolata sat up with Hendrick, and occasionally gave him a sip of brandy with water. The little stimulus this gave him may have helped ease him a little, but sadly it was not enough. His wound received from the lion, and his open sores, had not stopped weeping blood or pus throughout the night. Poor Hendrick died in the cold early dawn the next morning. They dug a narrow grave for him, James made a small cross and painted it white and placed it at his head. They covered the mound with stones. Then every member of the party gathered round and James read the burial service from his prayer book. Foolata found a branch with a little greenery on it and placed it on the grave. They stood in silent respect for a while, and then prepared to move on.

29

A Detour

THE AREA WHERE THEY WERE LAY to the south of some dried-up rivers, rivers they had hoped would provide them with plentiful water, but that was not to be. There was none. The native whom they met at Siklagole had agreed to lead them to Kolobeng, but James felt that the only reason he had said that was because he wanted to be with a party who had rifles, and hence might have food and would have tobacco and snuff. That night as the camp was sleeping, or dozing by the fire, a lion purred. Lions prefer hunting at night, and James was to come to know that sound well. It prowled around very close to where he lay in his tent, and he could "distinctly", as he put it to Lewis, hear its breathing. The lion had prowled around their camp and fearfully upset the oxen which were safely tied to the trek-touw, but thankfully departed without molesting them. Within two days however, game had become plentiful, but it was all very wild and required hard riding to come up with it. Fires abounded on all sides caused by the Balalas who used them to burn the locusts which were then everywhere, and James saw them later with sacks harvesting large quantities of roasted locusts for later consumption. Later James was trailed by a hyena which seemed to think he was likely to shoot him a good supper.

The Molopo when they reached it was then no river, it was nothing but a wide dried-up ditch, and the guide told them no rain had fallen there for two years. Lewis rightly grumbled that he could have told them that before, instead of saying he would lead them to water. To make matters worse all the grass here had also been burnt to catch locusts; forage for the oxen was therefore non-existent. They had no choice but to dig a pit in the dry river bed to try and find life-sustaining water. It was five feet before they got any dampness even, and then they had to dig on down until they met the hard base ground, and then wait for the water to filter into the bottom of the hole. All the while they were restraining the oxen who were trying to charge at the mere smell of water. What water there eventually was had to be bailed up for the oxen which were desperate by the time it was given to them. It tasted tangy and was very dirty anyway, but better, thought James, than not having any at all. The larder was bare again so James and Lewis went out hunting the next day, but six hours' hunting through thorny country was no fun, and their legs and arms were cut severely. And they shot nothing.

The day after that, Martinus woke James with the cry that a herd of brindled gnus was coming to the smell of their water. "What water?" thought James, as he rode after them, but when he got up to the gnus he found the cold of the morning was so intense his hands would not work to pull the trigger. He ordered a ration of meal to be cooked in the most palatable way, as they had no meat at all. Two days later, after trekking through plain and forest, they came across a Balala village. There was no water there either, the natives said. What they usually did when strangers came, said Lewis, was to bury their most treasured possessions, namely ostrich shell containers full of water, and then put a fire over the spot, just a small enough fire to hide them, nothing more. He was convinced they had water even though it was not to be seen. The parched and tired oxen were harnessed up again next day and they continued on northward through dense forests of thorn trees

As they moved slowly on, James tried to stalk a giraffe. He was at least eighteen feet tall and a magnificent fellow, but all James' endeavours were to no avail as a few strides of the giraffe's long legs soon took him out of range, beyond any shot. Later they saw a dark shining surface in a hollow, and thinking it to be water, rushed to it, only to find it to be thick mud. James saw the spoors of rhinoceros and jackals among others which had trampled what water it once had far too much to leave anything liquid enough to be drinkable. Now there was only mud. A little farther on they found a deep pit, dug by Balalas for hunting and trapping, and this contained a little water. The pit was fourteen feet deep. James wondered how they had dug it without spades, and their guide, who stayed with them in the hope of food other than locusts, said they had used shells. Pots and tubs were filled as fast as the water could be bailed up, and the oxen pushed and fought to get to it, but as they could only water two or three oxen at a time, the scrum was fearful. When it was all used up, a small supply being reserved for themselves, the guide found another water pit. But there was a brindled gnu lying with its head in the stagnant water, dead and decomposing. They dragged its body out and cleared the hole, but no more water flowed into it that night. In the morning they set to again, and dug for water, and after a little while they saw a trickle coming in, and so they waited and rested the oxen that day, and used the time saved from hard labour to try hunting on foot again. Herds of animals were seen – some of them were worn to shadows from the intense drought – and all were heading eastwards, and that was because the worst desert of all, the Kalahari, was to the west. James and John walked for miles through dense stunted forests of thorn three and mimosas and came to some salt pans which game liked to lick for the mineral content, and he shot at a hartebeest, but only wounded it, and lost it in the bush. On their return to the camp empty-handed, as Lewis and Dedderich had been, they found that there was only a little thick clayey water at the bottom of the pit. But it tasted delicious thought James.

The guide and his companion were now mutinous, and from somewhere they had acquired another fellow, to help with the apparently onerous task of not knowing where they were. The three natives did not take part in the digging with pick and shovel, which was five hours' hard labour, well into the evening. Then they struck some flat stones, but they managed to drill through and opened up a small spring just enough to satisfy the wants of the oxen for the night. Looking round the next day James could see the evidence all around of water having been very abundant once, dried stream and river beds, and massive layers of rock that looked very much as if they had been subject to the action of flowing water. Lewis pointed out that the small water pit they had opened up would attract game, and suggested they rest up and watch. But James and John, and Dedderich, wanted to press on to Kolobeng, and so they moved off in a northerly direction. The input of their guide on the route was practically nothing. He and his companions were simply more mouths to feed.

They were now travelling through dense forests of mimosas and mokaalas and all traces of any track had long gone. Their pioneering skills were in use much of the time and the felling axes were hard at work cutting branches hanging in their way, and chopping away any offending stumps. Ordinary bushes of eight or ten feet they just drove straight through, and no notice was taken of them. Spoor of the elephant and rhinoceros became more numerous, and they saw trees of considerable size pulled down by them so that they could browse on the young shoots otherwise out of reach. In the evening they fell in with Mahura, a young Batalapee chief, who was with a large party of natives on a hunting expedition. He was very civil and gave them a quantity of rhinoceros and giraffe flesh, in return for which James gave him many little presents of beads, ammunition, and a few gaudy handkerchiefs, and undertook to repair a broken gun stock that Mahura owned. As soon as he did this he was sent another gun to repair but this time nothing was broken: the problem was simply that a bullet was stuck in the barrel, and James was soon able to withdraw it. The third and last request for a gun repair was however beyond what James could do: the barrel had been split somehow and the rifle was worthless. The following morning Mahura's party assembled around the wagons and Lewis said they had very decent guns. They were begging of course, but James explained as well as he could, not having a skilled interpreter and his Sechuana not being all that fluent yet despite all his recent practice, that his cattle were in a forlorn state, nearly skin and bone. So he said he was quite willing to barter anything in the wagon in exchange for fresh oxen. Mahura would not agree to this, but he was very anxious to obtain ammunition, and so Lewis and James went to his camp to see what they could see. It was a wonderful spectacle, with the flesh of nine rhinoceroses, six giraffes and five elands cut into long strips and left to dry in the sun. Every tree and bush for a hundred yards around was festooned with great flaps of meat, and there were heaps of muck and guts in all directions. Greasy savages, as James thought of them, gorged to the mouth, lay at full length on the ground, lazily sucking marrow from bones. Others were busy repairing their weapons for future use, or cutting the hides of dead animals into portable pieces with their assegais. Failing to trade despite happy protestations all round, the party continued onwards in the direction in which, Mahura assured them, lay a village with water, as in fact there was. It was not flowing, but in detached pools along the line of what had once been a river. Game seemed to be abundant judging by the number of spoors, but the village's human smells meant that large animals would not stop there. And so they came eventually to Kolobeng. Lewis had assured them that David Livingstone, the missionary in charge, would welcome them.

30

Kolobeng and Livingstone

IN FACT, KOLOBENG, when at length they reached it, was a serious disappointment by comparison with Kuruman. Livingstone, who sounded very depressed, and explained his croaky voice by saying his throat was badly infected, met them. He said, "Kolobeng has had no rain for two years and the river here is dried up to such a degree that the irrigation channels that I dug in the hope of growing food for the natives, and for myself and family, has been an awful wasted effort. Very little food can be grown. Food has to be sent up from Kuruman by infrequent and chancy wagons, three hundred miles or so by the best route or roughly two hundred and seventy by the more difficult, and this is no way to live." James knew from the trocheameter that they had travelled three hundred and fifty or so miles since Kuruman, and that the guides therefore really had been lost. Livingstone grumbled that fetching supplies up cost time and money which, as a poor missionary, he simply did not have. He seemed particularly upset when he looked at his dried-up vegetables, and muttered something James did not hear properly about other people having his garden now.

"How I can be expected to do everything, and to live on a very meagre salary and run a mission station at the same time I do not know. I built this house, personally, every bit of it. No help from anyone except Mary. It is the third I have had to build, and it has cost me physically. For example, I cut myself severely with an axe, and when I worked on the roof I got such extreme sunburn I was very ill. My shoulder, where a lion bit me is still very painful, so it was all very difficult." He complained bitterly that the *London*

Missionary Society should have paid him enough money so he could pay workers to build for him, thus giving him time for preaching. "But we have the happiness of God's love, even here in the wilderness," he said. In the meantime he was travelling constantly around trying to win converts, but sadly he had only made one, namely the local chief, Sechele. "I am dispirited by this general lack of success and dispirited also by the fact that although I have a young and blooming family being brought up by Mary, my wife, I cannot spend much time with them, as any time with them would mean that much less chance of making converts.

"The Boers who live to the east are," he continued, "very hostile to me, and want me to disarm Sechele who is living comparatively nearby, to whom they say I have given or sold guns, and they claim, falsely, a cannon. I did give him an iron cooking cauldron, but no cannon. Sechele would and should have no guns at all they say, were it not for me and any passing missionary." Livingstone was adamant that he was not responsible for the old guns that Sechele did have, and that Sechele did not have a cannon. He continued, "Sechele has been baptised, and he has put away all forty-seven wives save one, much against the wishes of his tribe. He has learnt to read the Bible, and to write, all in two months, and he is a really important convert. So I will not do or say anything to him which might stop him from being a good Christian influence on his people. I will certainly not disarm him, or attempt to persuade him to render himself defenceless against the Boers, as they demand. The main problem is that the Boers think that the natives only live in their own country by sufferance, and the price of that sufferance is that they should supply 'free labour', as the Boers call it, to Boers. They want native children as house servants, and grown men and women for field work, which is simply slavery by another name. I intend to try and stop that happening."

He was sadly afraid, he admitted, "that Sechele may have lapsed a little from Christianity because I suspect that he is having sexual relations with one of the wives he told me he had put away."

Livingstone said he had gone to see the Boer Commandant called Krieger and prevailed on him not to attack Sechele, but "I refused point blank to act as a spy on the Bakwains as Krieger wanted. On one occasion, I was told face to face by a leading Boer called Potgeiter that they would attack any native village which received a preacher. I am afraid, very afraid, that it is inevitable that the Boers will attack Kolobeng some time soon. When they do, they are certain to try and destroy Sechele as well. I am concerned that if they attack Kolobeng while I am away on a round of preaching at native villages, that all my valuable specimens and my diaries will be lost. I have put great effort into my collection of mineral and plant specimens. They are important scientifically, and not just to me."

Although Livingstone spoke Sechuana, he had such a heavy Scots brogue that James found him very hard to understand, even when he was speaking English. He thought that a Scots Sechuana brogue would be altogether too hard for natives to follow, and maybe, he said to himself, that was why Livingstone had no converts – they simply could not understand him! Livingstone said to them that he was trying to start writing a Sechuana grammar, but it did not seem likely to James that he would succeed as he would not have enough time since he was travelling and preaching, albeit unsuccessfully, to the natives in different places so much. And, plainly, if the river Kolobeng remained as dry as it was for very much longer he would have to move anyway, and that would be another time- consuming block to the writing of his grammar.

Livingstone opined, "The fabled Great Lake is over five or six hundred miles away. Its existence has been known for many centuries, and it was on Portuguese maps from as far back as 1508. Obviously, I do not know where it is precisely as I have never been there, although I desperately want to try to go. I will very definitely go with my friend Oswell one day. But the real trouble with the distance, whatever it is, wherever the lake is, is the nature of the country which has to be crossed to get to wherever it is, and who would provide guides. You would be leaving Sechele's country, and he might or might not be willing to let you pass him. He might, if you had traded with him satisfactorily from his point of view, provide you with guides to take you on to Sekomi's country. If Sechele does provide you with guides, all well and good. Then you should go north-east to Bamangwato country, where the chief is Sekomi. His is a populous tribe called the Bamangwato, and the mountains around the place where they live helps protect them from the Boers. After that the route is all guesswork."

Livingstone continued, "As to the journey itself, from here north it is strong lion country and rhinoceroses abound," he said. "Then at some unspecified distance into the trek after you leave the western part of the Bamangwato mountains, the country becomes desert, and if you miss the correct road and are too far west you end up in the Kalahari. Many people have tried to cross that and many have failed. That is the last mistake they make. I have heard that an Englishman called McCabe tried to cross it but failed. The Bakalahari people, and a few even more primitive people than them called the Katea live there. I am told they live on melons. So, perhaps it may be possible to cross it if you only knew how. But so far it has been the death of many people, and you must avoid it if at all possible."

Lewis asked, "Would Sechele have ivory and would he trade for it?"

Livingstone said he would. "What you have to trade for it is a matter of conscience. Guns I do not want to know about. But there is much more ivory to be had at and beyond Bamangwato which is far better elephant country. I myself have almost none, and what I have, I have not traded for, that is not what a missionary does."

OUTWARD
TREK

LECHLULATEBE'S
TOWN

BOTLETLI (ZOUGA)
RIVER

LAKE
NGAMI
APPROX EXTENT (1850)

N'CHOKOTSA

SALT PANS
MOKOKONYANI

MOKOLANI

KALAHARI DESERT

SEROTLI

BAMANGWATO

KOLOBENG

25°   25°

LOHARON

KURUMAN

VAAL RIVER

DANIEL'S
KUIL

ORANGE RIVER

CAMPBELL'SDORP

RAMAH

GRAAF
REINET

CAPE
TOWN

GEORGE

ALGOA
BAY

Lewis had done complicated sums regarding the value of a load of ivory and how much weight his wagon would take in terms of ivory, to make him rich. James was more concerned with whether his wagon would hold up for the rest of the long trek which lay ahead to be too much worried about ivory, but he was a better shot than Lewis, and expected that he would have much more when it all came to be sold at the end.

Livingstone began a long rambling story about lions. "They are really dangerous," he kept saying. And he then gave them a blow by blow account of how he had been attacked on one occasion and had his shoulder badly wounded by a lion. "In biting me the lion had to bite through my tartan jacket, and to that tartan I owe the fact that I did not get an infection from the lion's teeth. As the lion bit through it, the tartan must have taken all the germs off the lion's teeth. But the damage to my shoulder still haunts me and has left me weak in my right shoulder.

"You would not happen to have a bottle of port on that wagon of yours, would you?" he asked James. James (forewarned by Murchison) had.

31

North from Kolobeng

SECHELE HAD HEARD OF JAMES' party's arrival at Kolobeng and had sent two men there to greet them, and to act as guides for the journey from there to his current town. Lewis promised the men fair wages for the journey but asked if Sechele had elephants' teeth for trading. The men vehemently assured Lewis that Sechele had many such teeth, and so when supplies had been obtained from the village at Kolobeng, the party set off. Hardly had James' wagon travelled three miles when, going through a wooded area, they were startled by the sudden appearance of an incredibly large white Quababa rhinoceros. The senior of the guides, who was called Shoshe, later explained that the white rhinoceros was one of the fiercest beasts in Africa, and certainly it was not afraid of the wagons, or of horses. As James first saw it, it was enormous and armour-plated, with a long forward-pointing horn. Seeing intruders in his domain, the furious beast charged at what it saw as a crowd of enemies, and although Shoshe dodged the charge, it managed to drive its long horn into his companion's stomach. The man died very quickly, almost instantaneously. He made no sound, and the giant rhinoceros, hurling his body violently to one side, continued his charge and was quickly lost to sight in the wood. The charge, and the death, were over in an instant.

Foolata made James stop the wagons, and grabbing their guns, James and Lewis took off on horseback with their dogs in hot pursuit of the animal. The rhinoceros' sudden rushed attack of course meant that it was unwounded. Not a shot had been fired at it in the heat of the moment when it killed the native. It was not until

A pen and ink drawing by James Duffield of rhinoceros types found on the floor of his wagon after his death.

the dogs, including Argos, cornered it in a thicket of tall grasses after an hour's hard ride, that it was brought to bay. James sent the dogs in after it and the loud barking of the dogs who had found it angered it and brought it out into the open. It caught one of Lewis' dogs called Rufus, and tossed him and then trampled him. It turned and ran at James' horse, which promptly took fright, and James could do nothing to stop it fleeing with all speed. But the Quabaoba was not as quick as many species, and James' horse was able to keep ahead of it without too much difficulty.

When he could no longer hear the rhinoceros' pursuit, James eventually wheeled his horse about, and looking back over his left shoulder saw the rhinoceros standing, and it appeared to be trying to recover from its chase of him. Its eyes were small and sparkling fiercely. James brought his rifle up to his shoulder and sent a bullet low down, into the shoulder, aiming for the heart. That enraged the rhinoceros, and it instantly found its strength reinvigorated and charged directly at James' horse. This time James managed to keep his horse steadier, and he let fly with a second shot, but missed completely. Lewis, who had been following, also let fly and he also hit the rhinoceros in the shoulder. Blood spurted from this second new wound, but its speed did not seem to slacken. Its charge caught James' horse a glancing blow on the flank as it passed, and James was thrown to the ground. He was reloading as the rhinoceros' charge slowed to a halt, and it wheeled round to look at its foe. It saw James standing on the ground in front of it. This time, James was about twenty-five yards away when it started to charge, and this time the charge was head-on at him. To miss the shoulder shot this time was probable death. James took careful aim, and fired. This time the bullet found its home correctly, and the violent beast's charge was brought to a stumbling halt mere feet from where James was standing, shaking.

Lewis came up, on horse, and descending put another bullet into the beast behind its ear, and the animal lay very still. About ten minutes later the native servants caught up and literally danced around the body of the dead creature. They had armed themselves with spears out of James' collection in his wagon, and stabbed at it, for no purpose and wholly ineffectually anyway, as it was clearly dead. As they danced, they sang an old warriors' song of triumph, although they had taken no part in the killing. James instructed Jessa to ride back to the wagons and fetch a very sharp knife as he wanted to keep the horn for his collection. Accordingly, when Jessa returned he set to with the knife, and managed to free the horn, which was twenty-three inches long. The servants told James and Lewis that this sort of rhinoceros was very good eating, quite unlike the smaller black varieties. By then it was very dark, so only stopping to cut off the tail, which was another popular trophy, they all rode back to the wagons, leaving the remains for the night-loving hyenas and jackals. They would be enticed by the smell of blood and it was not likely that there would be much trace of the beast left by the morning.

Back at the wagon, Foolata had made the dead guide look a little respectable. She had covered him with two karosses, winding them round him, and binding them on with a rheim or thong of antelope skin. She had started to dig a grave but the ground was too hard for her. Moreover she was worried about lions as there was no fire prepared for the night. She was sure she could hear a purring noise, just like lions make at night when they are most active. She had got one of James' guns with her and loaded it, like she had seen James do, and was prepared as she dug to sell her life dearly. Her relief was considerable at the return of the party with the trophies, and she was even more appreciative of their safety when she saw the length of the horn, and heard all about the dangers of the kill.

Lewis was incandescent with anger when he realised that both wagons had been left unattended by the servants, save for Foolata. It was, he said, a desperately stupid thing to have done, and he slashed at Dedderich with his jambok. James tried to pretend he had not seen this, but he couldn't. He moved to Lewis, with what intention he did not know, but that slight movement was enough for Lewis to see he should not have done that. He stood hesitantly, and faced up square to James. But Foolata stepped forward and asked James if he would come to the wagon as she had something to show him. Fortunately her intervention stopped a stand-off from developing, and took the wind out of Lewis' sails. James followed Foolata to his wagon, and she showed him what she had been doing that day while he was out hunting. She had taken all his clothes and darned all the tears and rips, and patched them up as best as her poor sewing equipment would let her. James muttered a thank you to her. "You should not have bothered," he said, shortly. "They will only get torn again tomorrow." Which was as true as it was ungracious.

That night the camp fire was not as large as usual because not enough fuel had been gathered in advance, and lions' visited. "Night time is the lions favourite hunting time", warned Martinus, yet again, "and luckily it is a still night because lions are at their most active on dark stormy nights." But that night was moonless and comparatively still, and a pride roared, loud, deep-toned, five, six or more times. Then the roaring died slowly away into a muffled sound resembling thunder. The oxen were terrified at the trek-touw, and tugged and strained at it, but thankfully it held. But two of the dogs broke free and rushed off into the darkness. They could be heard barking furiously, only a short distance away. Then one dog literally screamed, and the other came rushing back whimpering and with blood streaming from a long gaping gash in its shoulder. In the morning they went to look for the remains of the missing dog and all they found was the site where it had died, marked as it was by a small amount of blood. The lion had eaten it on the spot, maybe twenty yards away from the nearer wagon. James was all for following the spoor and taking revenge if he could, but Lewis told him to save the effort.

They in-spanned late that day, but even so they had hardly gone more than a mile when two natives approached the wagons and said they were from Sechele, and that he was anxious for them to get to his kraal. After a short discussion with Lewis, James sent one of the men back to Sechele with the message that they would be there very shortly, and would be bringing him presents, and wanted to trade with him. Lewis said that this opportunity to trade with Sechele was what he had been waiting for. He wanted to trade for ivory. Dedderich had apparently told him that Sechele had plenty of ivory. James did not want to trade for ivory, as he said they could do that on their return journey; he wanted to collect curiosities.

But when they out-spanned that evening apparently the wagons were still short of his village. Lewis said that stopping short of Sechele's like that would make him keener to trade with them, and the keener he was to trade the better the prices they could haggle. It would likely take several days to haggle as much as Sechele would like. What he wanted from them was guns and ammunition, as well as trinkets. But Livingstone had warned them not to trade guns with Sechele. The Boers already thought that he had too many guns. "Tempt," him was the word Lewis used. "We must tempt him to trade with us." In the event that was the last thing they needed to do.

After Sechele's men had left, James spent several hours that evening drawing a pencil picture of the rhinoceros they had killed. His daily journal was getting more and more detailed, spangled, as he put it to himself, with small sketches, and Lewis said he really should publish it when they got back. But James thought to himself that he had written down a lot of his private thoughts, and maybe publication would be a bit embarrassing.

James had been completely entranced by the colours and shapes of the country through which they travelled. He had stopped on many occasions to draw a scene, the landscape, the animals, roughly sketching at any stop during the day, and often filling it in with light and colour (later on when the wagon was halted). One evening, he tried hard to capture their little party seated around a camp fire, with the space and the openness of the country around, and of the completely star-filled sky at night above, with its brilliant cobalt blue and darker colouring. The colours of the sky at the brief moment night fell, were unlike anything James had tried to paint before. He thought his sketch of Foolata's likeness by firelight was quite good, in fact he quite he liked it. It was better than his sketch of Francesca, but James made no such comparison.

While he was working at his sketches and paintings in the evening, Lewis would often come to James' wagon, and discuss the latest scene he was drawing or painting, or what he had written in his journal. James had already filled several sketch books by the time they had reached Kolobeng, and had seven or eight more still to be used. Lewis said he particularly liked the sketch of Parkes' hotel which James had done in an idle moment a long time ago, and was in the first sketch book. James wondered if he had brought enough books with him.

The next day while hunting a large troop of elands, James fell heavily on rocky ground, and his horse rolled over him. Luckily he received no other injury than a good shaking, though his right foot was much pinched, and his favourite rifle was much damaged, particularly the stock. So he, and John who was with him, lost the elands, which, said John, was not the worst thing about the accident. It made him realise how far they were from proper medical support. There was none for maybe one thousand five hundred miles. But just after midday they saw a great cavalcade coming over the a slight rise in the otherwise generally flat terrain. It proved to be Sechele himself with a multitude of counsellors and attendants, followed by a train of pack-bullocks loaded with ivory, horns and curiosities.

32

Sechele

IN DUE TIME the chief himself approached the camp. He was surrounded by numerous counsellors, and a page bearing a three-legged stool. A levee was held at the entrance of James' tent, and conversation commenced largely through an interpreter, although not wholly, as James was much better at Sechuana now. Sechele informed them that the news of their coming had preceded them by many days, and he was very anxious to know when they would be visiting his town. James replied to that by saying that almost all the waters having been dried up on their route north, the oxen were so exhausted that it was impossible to go any faster right at that time. But they would be very happy to pay the desired visit if his majesty would sell them fresh cattle. Sechele avoided a reply, and ordered a sheep and a large bowl of milk to be set before them, which they acknowledged to be very acceptable. In return, James offered a large and long belt with a very showy brass buckle, with an eagle pictured on it. Sechele was a tall man, well-made, and was dressed in European clothes, strange and incomplete even if they were a little dirty, but his top hat set the outfit off nicely. The belt would perfect his appearance. He had a fair understanding of good manners and eschewed the national custom of greasing and daubing his body with red ochre. He gave every sign of being very crafty, and James had to do quite a lot of explaining as to why they could not visit his town that very day. But he did promise that that evening they would set off many coloured rockets, and burn blue lights, which, when it was done, caused the watching Bakwains to be literally open-mouthed with astonishment. They roared and yelled with ecstasy as each rocket whizzed into the air. Their wild, excited shouts outdid anything heard before on the trek.

The very next day, quite early on in the morning, Sechele came to the wagons again and now it appeared that he no longer wanted a state visit to his town. Instead he opened up a large market at the wagons, his retinue bringing up several wagons which were full of goods they wished to trade. He had ivory, horns and curiosities aplenty, and Lewis traded for the ivory. James, although he acquired two elephants' teeth as the natives called them, traded for curiosities such as karosses, utensils and weapons of which there were a wide variety, ranging from war clubs and assegais to poisoned arrows with quivers, daggers, bowls, calabashes and beakers. He also managed to acquire two ostrich egg water containers, the same as he had seen at Kuruman. He was given a live tarantula spider, which having suffocated, he later mounted in a small blue cardboard box to take back to Devon. In the afternoon, Sechele, contrary to Lewis' expectations, said he had to move on as he wanted to set up a new camp to the west, so as to be that much further from the Boers. So after a last mutual exchange of gifts Sechele gave them two guides to take them forwards to the Bamangwato Mountains, where Sekomi was Chief of the Bamangwato. He said he was on good terms with this tribe, and he was sure that the party would be warmly welcomed there by Chief Sekomi. The guides were members of the Bamangwato tribe and he assured James and Lewis that they knew the way, and would find them plenty of water.

A few days later the promise of a good water supply was proved wrong, in the sense that they came across a dirty water pit, and after three hours' digging were able to obtain only a small supply, but not nearly enough for the wants of the oxen. The poor brutes had then been thirty-six hours without water, and crowded round the pit watching their efforts to dig it out with eager eyes. Each got barely enough to keep life going, but no more. The next day the cattle, dragging under a burning sun, were so desperately thirsty that they pushed and tumbled over each other in their eagerness to get at water in a shallow pool they stumbled across. The chief guide was triumphant, and kept saying that he had always said there was good water on this route and was now proved right. James had to restrain Lewis from striking the man. The casks were all filled, and the party rested hopefully and contentedly.

That night they set gun traps up by the pool and camped a little distance away from it. Game would, they knew, visit the pool because they could smell the water, and they wanted the chance to shoot something. Lewis set a rifle up with almost their last piece of meat used as a bait and tied to the trigger with a length of rheim. The rifle was loaded. At ten o'clock that night a dull report was heard, so each taking a spare rifle, James and Lewis sallied forth in the direction of the trap. They found the rifle lying on its side, besmeared all over with white foam, the bubbles of which were still bursting, and the marks of some animal's teeth deeply indented along the rifle barrel, and in the stock. Nearby were footprints of some large animal. They were too indistinct to say what it was.

A perfect silence prevailed and they were at a loss to know what to do, but Lewis whistled up the dogs, and they quickly hit upon a scent and followed it up for two dozen yards to a large bush. The dogs halted a short distance from the bush, and Lewis walked the dog at the front, which was called Sall, up to it. James held on to Argos tightly. Sall was looking over her shoulder as if afraid, and Lewis took one more step towards her. At that very moment as Lewis stepped forward, a lion sprang upon the dog, and "crunched her up in a flash," as James put it. They heard the crack of her bones and her death howl was anguished and shrill. Just at that moment a second lion sprang out of the same bush startling James, who could not help letting go of Argos. The lion ran right past James, within touching distance, not at him but at the other dogs. It chased all of them including Argos back to camp, but pulled up at the sight of the fire. Foolata had left the camp with a lantern and was looking for James and Lewis, and in chasing the dogs this second lion also passed her within three yards. She quickly met James and Lewis and they at once extinguished her lamp so as to make their night-time vision better. All three were now in a very perilous position, with lions between them and the camp, and also somewhere between them and the water. His favourite and faithful dog, Argos, had stayed with James, and as carefully as they could in the pitch dark they retraced their steps towards the pool. It felt safer going in that direction than going back towards the camp. When they reached the pool they went about a hundred yards to the south, and only then tried to make their way back to the camp. Hardly had they left the pool when the impatient hollow roar of a lion was heard close at their heels. Lewis whispered it was all up with them as the lions were so close.

They crept forward slowly, and then Martinus suddenly appeared in front of them, seemingly out of nowhere. He had left the camp with a large burning brand of bush, and he accompanied them back to the camp waving the brand above him as they walked. At the camp there was a big fire, well stoked and burning strongly. As they reached it, the lions, and there were four full-grown lions in all, set up a fearful screeching and roaring of rage and disappoint-ment. They prowled round and round the camp making the oxen, who were all safely fastened to the trek-touw, tremble dreadfully, and the party fully expected an attack any minute. All spare rifles were very quickly loaded and made ready for immediate use. The guides were in a blue funk and came up to James with their mouths wide open, and implored him not to fire as they said they could hear young lion cubs crying, and indeed every few minutes James and Lewis could hear a strange whistling noise, which the guides said were made by kleinje, or little lions. The older lions sometimes approached very close, howling with apparently frustrated rage, and it seemed that any minute they would attack the oxen which were absolutely terrified, and bellowing with fear. At that moment Lewis had the idea of firing off some rockets, which he did, and the bright lights arching through the night sky somewhat calmed the oxen down, because they also quietened the lions. But the party had to wait for dawn before they could really assess what had happened.

Poor Sall, who had rushed into the bush so boldly to seize the lion and thereby met with such a miserable end, was doubtless a great means in their preservation, by drawing the attention of the brutes to herself. One of the lions had received a shot in a leg or foot, and this, with their cubs being with them, had rendered them very savage. As daylight came the lions took themselves off and the party heard their bass voices growing fainter and fainter as they left. A wounded lion, presumably that which had set the trap-gun off, had lain under the same bush all night, as they could see from the collection of blood at that spot. However, not one vestige of Sall remained, every trace of her was gone. The lions had again visited the trap after James and Lewis had left it, and had pulled up the stakes it was fastened to, and carried them off together with the lines attached to the bait. They had also tried to walk off with the rifle itself, but presumably finding it too heavy or hard, had dropped it about one hundred yards away. There were numerous paw prints all around the camp, some of them far too close for comfort.

33

Sekomi

O N JAMES' RETURN TO CAMP WITH LEWIS and John they found
that Martinus had led the others in fetching water from the
pool, watered the oxen properly, and filled the barrels in both
wagons, and so they set off in relatively good spirits for Sekomi's
town. The guide assured the party that they would reach it in two
days at the most. But three days later they had still not got that far,
although they could see the Bamangwato Mountains ahead quite
clearly, highlighted against a very pale blue almost white sky. As
they approached from the south, the range stood about seven or
eight hundred feet above the plains at their feet, and was composed
of a mass of basaltic rock. There existed a curious cup-shaped
hollow at the eastern end, which suggested the idea of craters or
volcanic vents to James. Old lava streams could be clearly seen and
the basaltic columnar pillars in hexagonal form were reminiscent of
Fingall's Cave, he thought. The rocks had many caves among them,
and Sekomi himself lived in among a group of caves. A besmeared
emissary from Sekomi lead them the last few miles up into the hills.
Chief Sekomi did not present himself immediately, but his message
was that the wagons were to halt when they reached a flat area
within a wood but clear of trees, half way up to the ridge, and he
sent gifts of milk and honey for the party. James and Lewis sent him
in return, through the medium of one of their guides, fulsome
thanks, and a tail coat encrusted with gold braid on the sleeves.

The next morning they were awoken by the morning leina. This
was a loudly half-shouted and half-sung oration praising Chief
Sekomi, the words of which Sekomi was said to have composed at

his own boguera, or initiation to manhood. This oration was, the party was later told, so pleasing to Sekomi that he always sent a present to the man who cried it out. The voice echoed up the well-wooded and rocky ravines, and died slowly away with a wild cry. Apparently that last cry was meant to be that of a dying enemy.

At mid-morning Chief Sekomi appeared at the camp with a large and servile group of nobles as company. He looked around fifty years of age, and was of middling stature, but his most notable feature was a wall-eye which gave him a roguish look that did not belie the cunning and deceitful nature of the man. James privately described him as the cock-eyed king of the Bamangwato. He was wearing the coat that James had sent him, and kept stroking the gold braid on the sleeves. James (who was fairly confident of his Sechuana now) and Lewis walked forward to greet him, and invited him to have coffee with them. Sekomi talked at a very rapid pace and assumed a rather dictatorial manner, turning round and cracking jokes with his cringing nobility nearby. He was very anxious to hear what the contents of the wagons were, as he wished to trade, or so he said, and would give one large bull elephant's tooth for each gun they had. This was a fishing exercise on his part as he just wanted to hear what James or Lewis would offer for the teeth. Lewis told him that the guns, which he assured James he had bought quite legally, had cost him many teeth in his own country, and that they had not been stolen. Lewis gave him a present of beads, snuff and ammunition, which pleased him greatly as the beads were apparently the right colour. Lewis smiled when Sekomi said that.

It amused James to see the timid cringing manner of the noblemen when seated in the presence of their chief. Approaching him with the utmost humility, they saluted him by stretching out their hands, clapping, and crying out "Rumela cosi", which means "Hail chief". His majesty graciously acknowledged this by squinting at them with his cock-eye, and saying "Eh", which was the usual

acknowledgment of a greeting in Sechuana. After the usual prelimi-
naries Sekomi ordered boyalwa, which is native beer, to be brought,
and all the party drank deeply. Trading had stopped, if indeed it had
ever started, and Sekomi, after long and deep conversation with
Lewis and James, left for the night with his noblemen, promising to
come and visit early the next day. Sekomi, fearing that the party
would trade with anyone whilst he was away, left an uncle behind to
make sure that they did not do any such dastardly thing.

Early the next day a procession appeared with Sekomi at its head,
attended again by a large number of his warriors, this time all
carrying their battle gear. Presently James, who was still in his bunk,
peering out from the fore-clap, saw a savage coming up the glen
with an extremely large bull elephant's tooth on his shoulder. It had
a very good pale clean colour and was only very slightly curved, and
was undoubtedly the best that James had seen on the trek. Lewis
watched it with close attention, and saw it deposited under James'
wagon as a gift. The native bearer explained to James that it was a
gift for him as the leader of the expedition.

James and Lewis had decided to be as careful as possible and to
give Sekomi no encouragement about wanting to trade, an indis-
pensable tactic they had mutually agreed if you wanted to trade at
all profitably with the natives, and so they waited for him to make
the first move. Trading always proceeded slowly, even more slowly
if you showed that you wanted to trade, and so it was after they had
all had coffee as usual, without milk or sugar, that Sekomi said he
had some more elephants' teeth to trade, but he said the party had
better start to trade as there was an armed group of Matabele
coming up who would be likely to attack if they saw them trading
with Sekomi. This too, James realised, was a usual tactic to try and
rush trading ahead, so he laughed scornfully at the threat. (Two
days later the Matabele were there, James discovered, but only after
they had safely left the area, and he then realised that Sekomi had
more or less been telling the truth.) James told Sekomi that they

were planning to go north and asked if guides could be hired. Sekomi agreed he would make guides available but only if they did in fact trade satisfactorily. James said he did not want to take a whole load of ivory north as they would later have to carry it back past his town as he called it, and that seemed to him to be a heavy-weight task and pointless. But Lewis said he was willing to trade there and then for ivory, which James thought was bad tactics. So he said that he was not interested in taking any ivory at all away with them, except for the tooth under his wagon which he had accepted as a gracious present; he only wanted curiosities.

During a lull in this exchange, which was conducted by both sides with the lack of urgency which was typical of the way negotiations were usually conducted when trading, James sat in his wagon with Lewis and took the opportunity to write up his journal. Sekomi, apparently thinking that maybe the party really was (despite what they had just said) indifferent to trading, came forward and said he had a present for everyone. Actually what he meant was that he wanted to give them items he did not value, in exchange for items which he did value. The main thing he wanted was a small mirror, which James was happy to give him, along with the usual mug or two of coffee beans. The present to James was a necklace of lions' teeth, which James put in his box of curiosities. It was interesting but not unusual in any way – the teeth were blunt and mildly discoloured.

After the long dragging day's excitement of not trading had ended, and Sekomi had left, James and Lewis sat up late, next to Lewis' wagon, refreshing themselves with a soopje, and talked the day over. James wrote his journal up as usual, with the result that he was not really paying great attention to what Lewis was saying. But he suddenly realised that Lewis had said he, and not James, should be the person who had the enormous elephant's tooth which the native had laid under James' wagon. This was because, as he said, the tooth was intended by Sekomi for the leader of the expedition, and he was the leader, not James. James pointed out that he was paying for the expedition, so he was the leader and he was going to keep the tooth. Lewis grew angry, and having earlier had some boyalwa which James did not know about, as well as more soopjes than James, got to his feet and offered to fight James for the tooth. Martinus and Foolata, who were seated nearby, became anxious that there would be a fight, and talking together in low tones expressed their fear for James, as Lewis was the bigger and stronger man, so if they did fight, Lewis might harm James. But the argument blew over as quickly as it had started, and with even less reason. When James simply stood up and said he would fight Lewis then if that was what he wanted, Lewis sat down ungraciously and far from promptly. James put Lewis' aggressive posturing down to the drink and thought no more about it. He had seen many men who had drunk too much and then behaved like that in his college days, and he was not in the least alarmed by the hostility, enmity almost, of the words used by Lewis.

The next day very early Sekomi came again to the wagons, and this time it was a different story again. If they did not want to trade then they could have no guides for their onwards trip north. Sekomi knew, he said, that there was no water to the north, and no game there either, so they would die of thirst and hunger in the desert land ahead of them if they went that way. But if they did manage to come back he would trade ivory with them, but not on the same terms as he was offering now. Sekomi was very angry and his accompanying nobles and pages were in evident terror of his rage. So in order to calm him down, James presented him with a gun as a present – it was one of James' better spare guns. And the gift did indeed calm Sekomi down with quite miraculous speed. Sekomi changed his tune now, and said that he hoped they would have a safe return from the desert ahead, and he said he was very sad they were about to leave but he still did not know where any water or game was to the north. He still could provide no guides as, he alleged very untruthfully, none of his followers ever went north. They had good hunting land where they were, and so had no need to risk death in the desert.

This remark about the quality of the country they were about to cross caused James to look around the site where the wagons were halted and make a fresh appraisal of their situation. The wagons had been halted about half-way up the hills, on a level patch of clear grassy ground surrounded by good-sized trees of maybe thirty or forty feet in height. The slopes of the hills up to that site were covered with green trees, so welcome after the dry country they had been passing through earlier, and James could see that the forest continued right up to the very top of the hills, or at least all those he could see from where he was. The rocky outcrops featured as dark, almost blackly brooding interruptions in the canopy. The smoothly contoured slopes of the valleys between the hills were a verdant shade of green. The trees could be seen to grow smaller as one looked downhill from whence they had travelled, as of course the land became flatter; in fact the plain to the south gradually lost its green appearance, and after quite short distance was a dun, almost yellow, colour.

Sekomi had told them that to go north they had to cross the mountains, as he called them, by way of a pass called Manaka-longwe, or the Unicorn's Pass. The creature after which the pass had been named was a large edible caterpillar, which looked pretty unappetising thought James when shown one, and certainly he would never try to eat it. It had an erect horn-like tail from which it took its name. The pass was also called Porapora or "the gurgling of the water", and the stream which gave it that name was indeed running through the glade where the wagons were halted. Sekomi advised that they absolutely had to fill every water container they could before they set off over the pass which lay ahead. James at once assumed command and ordered that every barrel and every water bottle be filled in both wagons. The oxen were much improved by the few days' rest and the horses also looked so much stronger. James thanked Sekomi for his wise advice before they left and said he wished to express his gratitude to him for his hospitality, and so on the spur of the moment, he gave him a deuced good dinner shirt which he had with him. He had bought it from old Mel Meredith in his new shop at 17 Piccadilly because he knew the old man's very junior partner James Gieve and his friend Joseph Galt, and had been recommended to go to them as tailors many times. Sekomi did not apparently understand the grand sacrifice James felt he was making, but Foolata, who had kept the shirt in almost pristine condition throughout the trek, although of course she said nothing about it, was horrified at the generosity of the gift.

34

Francesca at Highsteignton

LADY ELEANOR WAS EXTREMELY WORRIED about Francesca's health. Ever since her very late miscarriage she had been unwell, ill really, with a high temperature for long periods, and the village doctor, Dr Speke, who also treated her father, could make no headway with her condition. Although he had written to Dr Brown to get any suggestions that he could from that gentleman, even then he had not been able to effect any improvement. Francesca found it physically very hard to look after herself and her father – she seemed to have little strength and was easily tired. Richardson was increasingly infirm now and he walked with considerable difficulty as his hip was so painful. Distressingly for Francesca, he was getting to be very untidy in his dress and personal habits. They had no help at all inside the house, and Francesca had to do everything for the two of them. Dr Speke tried to help and sent a girl in from the village on occasion, but she almost drove Francesca and her father mad with her lack of common sense, so it seemed easier to Francesca to manage without her. She would not use James' allowance, which was still being paid to her, to pay for staff to help herself and her father. She needed the money for food. Although Lady Eleanor had frequently expostulated about all the housework that Francesca did personally, and offered her the loan of staff from Highsteignton, Francesca would accept no help at all from that direction. She thought she would be under an obligation if she did so.

At length, more or less as a result of desperation at her own inability to manage, Francesca gave in to the repeated invitations from Lady Eleanor and decided to go and stay at Highsteignton for a break, as she put it, or as Lady Eleanor put it, to give her "a break from looking after her father". This last invitation this time, however, had been different to those that had previously been put forward, as Lady Eleanor said she had agreed with Coleman that he and his wife would go and live with Richardson and look after him while Francesca went to stay with them at Highsteignton and rested. Francesca liked both the Colemans, and thought with relief that she could trust her father to their care.

One of the reasons, out of many, that had caused Francesca to refuse these generous invitations in the post was that she knew that if she went to Highsteignton she would be quizzed remorselessly by the Duffields about James. Why had he really gone back to the Cape, what had he said about returning, and had she received another letter from him, or indeed from Harry? It had been very bad when she had to tell them "no" the first time, but after all this time, and with no letter at all from James, she feared Lady Eleanor would be even more pressing and direct. In any case, she was privately a little ashamed of the fact that James had gone back so soon after they got to London, and she found it easier to evade the questions by not accepting any hospitality from the Duffields. They were kindness itself, sending fruit and vegetables by McGregor when they could, and she appreciated this greatly, but she felt that she ought to be able to manage without all these gifts. But of course she could not. In the end it was because she was gradually weakening physically, she was so tired, that she had capitulated and accepted the invitation, to her personal private chagrin. One morning, therefore, when Coleman and his wife arrived in Sir Marshall's carriage, after introducing them to her father, and showing Mrs Coleman around and where things were, she was returned to Highsteignton in the carriage.

On her arrival at Highsteignton Francesca was greeted by a volubly talking Lady Eleanor who was still dressed in black even after all this time. She had not of course worn mourning during the week of the wedding festivities, but she had now not only resumed it, but also gone further by adopting the whole system, from black-edged cards to mourning rings and the like. Daguerrotypes of Charles in silver frames draped in black were everywhere, and his old bedroom was decorated with his personal possessions. The oar which he had displayed so proudly in his college rooms had been reduced in length to just the decorated blade, and was on the wall, along with his rugby fez, team pictures, his college scarf and similar ephemera. A squeeze box he had played and a pile of books, novels mostly, were on the bedside table, and Lady Eleanor said that she herself laid out clean nightwear once a week. The water in the carafe was also changed regularly. Francesca was appalled at the display.

Lady Eleanor greeted Francesca very sympathetically, and suggested that she might like to go straight to her room to freshen up. Catherine, Lady Eleanor's maid, whom Francesca knew, went with her and carried her valise. When the door opened, for the first time since the event, Francesca saw again the room she had been staying in when Charles had raped her. Afterwards, her fruitless attempts to wash and clean herself had all been in this room. The room brought back the most awful memories, vividly. It had not changed. She sat numbly on the bed, while Catherine fussed around unpacking and setting out her few toiletries on the dressing table. She was unable to think clearly, it was so long since she had been in that room. All the memories flooded back: she remembered the beach at Sidmouth, that was the first day she had seen James, the cottage at Fowey and their wedding night, and their love-making. She lay on the bed and let exhaustion overcome her.

Mercifully, she found the relief that Sadak sought.

35

Into the Unknown

J AMES KNEW THEY HAD TO MAKE A LAST PUSH NOW, or fail, and so early the next morning as the sun was starting to lighten the sky to the east and the sights on the plain below were still darkly shrouded, the party set off up the last short incline to the head of the pass. On reaching it James could see that the land below and ahead was flat as far as the eye could see in all directions. To the north, where they were heading, it appeared forested for the first few miles only, but the trees when they reached them were sufficiently far apart that they could with care pass the wagons between them. They saw occasional game in the form of elands and a few gemsbok, but Lewis and James both failed to kill any. This meant they would have to rely on the provisions they had bought from Sekomi.

On the plain, the tough grass, where it existed, looked a faint dry grey-brown colour and appeared in tufts. The bare ground between the tufts was really not soil at all but a darker coloured soft sand, but even so pulling the wagons was not too hard. In fact contrary to what Sekomi had said, they found an adequate supply of water after about twenty-five miles on at a place that the lone native who was there called Serotli. That first day's travel had been gruelling for the oxen and they were glad to out-span that evening with comparative ease and to give the oxen enough water. They were on the very edge of the Kalahari and where they were journeying was nearly bare of vegetation, and James could see that it grew more sparsely up ahead as well. They opened up a further pit to get more water and refreshed the barrels of water as they had already used large amounts.

So, just as Sekomi had said, beyond Serotli the land became gradually more and more desolate. The sand became softer, and the oxen had a harder time of it. They came across an isolated well, a sort of wide and open pit, a short distance on, around which were a group of Bakalahari people who had carefully hedged it in to prevent it from being filled in by blown sand. The party moved on without stopping, and thence for four days across about sixty miles of countryside without any water being found at all. There were now no trees and hardly any bushes at all, and the ground became softer and softer, and the going harder and harder. Occasionally they had to stop to dig a wheel out and sometimes they were as deeply embedded as the axle. This meant heavy manual labour for everyone, Foolata included. The temptation to slake one's thirst after an hour's digging under the strong burning sun was overpowering, but not knowing exactly what lay ahead, Lewis wisely ordered that they should use their water sparingly and put the whole party on half rations. There was no forage for the oxen or horses.

Much of the ground which they now covered had large expanses of bushes and short wiry grass, and they very rarely saw a completely treeless horizon. Lewis saw plenty of ostriches and wanted to try and shoot one, but they were generally to be seen feeding quietly on some spot where Lewis and James could not approach without being seen themselves. But the ostrich is a silly bird with very little brain as Lewis soon discovered, and they sometimes tried to avoid being outflanked by the passing wagons by running parallel to them. But once they started to run they usually, Lewis found, only ran in a straight line, and thus by moving across their line diagonally he was able to get in a shot at one, but missed it. As the birds' heads were held so high, they had a very good field of vision and were hard to take by surprise, but on the other hand they did not find concealment easy as their plumage of black and white feathers contrasted so strongly with the natural palette of colours around it. James put some feathers that he found lying on the ground in his curiosity collection.

Jessa, who claimed a knowledge of the Kalahari, which he had not mentioned before, although he did say something under his breath about a Bakalahari native girl he said he knew, pointed out that sometimes the stray tufts of weed-like grass seemed to form a ridged line across the otherwise flat sandy plain at somewhat above the surrounding level. And if you applied a little imagination to that line, thought James, and knew that the Bakalahari women often dug for water on such a ridged but sparse line of grass, that might mean that the grasses had originally grown along what was once a water course. He thought the encroaching sand had piled against the grasses which grew there so as to create the ridge, and the advancing sand eventually had almost buried the grasses from sight. By experiment, they found that was right, and that if they dug a trench at a right angle across a ridged line of half dried-up grass, the trench might indeed provide something in the way of water. But of course their spades meant they could and did dig a very great deal deeper than the poor Bakalahari women ever could.

They came across a place that both Martinus and Jessa described as a "sucking place", where there was a small group of Bakalahari women with ostrich eggshell containers with long hollow reeds. They had scooped the sand away as deeply as they could using only their hands, and after shading the small pits they had dug with cloth, they waited for many hours until the sand at the bottom shaded darker. Next, they poked their reeds down as far as they could get them to go, and then they hoped to siphon water up through their hollow reeds which they then let flow into their ostrich eggshells with great care. Martinus assured James it could take over an hour to fill a single egg with water in this way.

The party had a weary four days trekking north-west now, a direction they took because they sighted a flight of birds heading in that direction, and as birds often fly towards water Lewis suggested that they veer slightly in that direction. The weather had been fearfully hot: ninety-five degrees in the shade and even hotter about six inches below the surface of the sandy ground. Clouds of sand from the oxen's hooves were blowing directly into the faces of the wagon drivers, which smothered them and made them as dirty, if not as black, as chimney sweeps. Every particle of food was impregnated with sand and tasted of sand. There was no game or water. Plainly, thought James, they were trying to get wherever they were heading at the wrong time of year. The dry season was upon them, and their lack of care over timing could be dangerous. He realised too late that they should have started out across this land shortly after the end of the wet season when the country had more life in it.

Even taking the precaution of only moving the wagons at night in order to save the oxen as best as he could, James wondered how long they could go on. The mythical Great Lake the natives talked about, and which some claimed to have visited, and which so many Boers and other white people had tried to find, was no more than a fable, he thought. The land seemed to be an almost never-ending undulating plain, with occasional rank grass, thorn bushes as dry as tinder, and a very few sparse trees. The trek seemed endless.

Suddenly, out of nowhere as it seemed, James spotted a tiny crook-backed little native woman running in a crouching fashion across the rough ground. She ducked down into a slight dip in the earth to hide, and was plainly running from the wagons in fear. She carried two ostrich eggs in a string sling over her shoulder, which might or might not have been full of water, and another which held something else less weighty, all of which meant of course that she probably knew where there was water. Lewis thought he could catch her and ran off after her. But despite the obvious difference in their ages he was quite unable to do so. She could cover the ground easily, taking the dips and rises lightly, and Lewis soon found it too hard to catch her. So James mounted his horse, and set off after her. He could not always see her in the uneven ground, and when he eventually came across her, more by good luck than anything else, she was crouched down in a very shallow gully behind a tuft of withered grass. He dismounted and walked up to her. She cowered in fear and was plainly terrified by James' approach. She opened the second, smaller sling she had over shoulder, reached in and took out a small scorpion which she put on the ground between her and James. She said something in a high-pitched and terrified voice: it sounded like "Kagn". James had no idea what she meant or if he had heard it right as it did not sound like Sechuana to him, but he stopped a few paces short of her. He squatted down so as to be level with her, and reaching inside his waistcoat pulled out his snuff box, opened it and slowly held it out to her. But she did not take it. She did not, thought James, know what it was. She seemed about to run away again, and so James moved forward and caught her by the arm, and pulled her to her feet, and then the two of them, followed by James' horse, walked back to the wagons where the party awaited them.

Foolata came forward and held out some biltong towards the woman, who hesitatingly crept forward and took it from Foolata and bit it. Then, after she had tasted it, she quickly ate the rest as if famished. James held out some more biltong and again she took and ate it, this time without the least hesitation. The old woman spoke some more but no one understood what she was saying. She was about four feet tall, and was pitch black in colour, quite unlike anyone the party had seen before, and totally naked, save for a necklace of bones round her neck. James thought that the bones looked like human finger bones, but was not sure. Jessa said he thought she might be Katea, but as no one could speak that tongue, or apart from him had even heard of the Katea people, his remark was of no help. As the party was still in dire need of finding water they all tried to tell her, with gestures, what the problem was. The old crone cackled when she eventually understood, and Jessa, on James' instructions, made her understand that she would be well rewarded if she helped the party. Jessa thought that she was saying that she had relatives nearby, which seemed unlikely to say the least. But on being lifted onto the fore-chest of Lewis' wagon, she screeched out a shrill call, and as the wagon moved on, every few minutes she repeated the noise. After about fifteen minutes of this procedure Lewis' doubts as to the truthfulness of the woman's claims, which he expressed volubly, were quelled when a short distance ahead two very short and very black men, very dirty and sandy, and also totally naked, appeared to rise up out of a sunken hollow in the ground. They came forward, cautiously, and talked to the old crone when the wagon reached them. Jessa tried to talk to them as well, but he failed to make himself understood. Then one of them started to speak in Sechuana – he asked for food and a small portion of biltong was given to each, along with some tobacco, and he said they would be happy to guide the wagons to metse, meaning water, which he said was nearby.

He also told the party that it would suffer no more from thirst, and true to his word after a hard day's work for the poor oxen dragging the heavy wagons, and for the men digging them out of the sand, the two guides pointed out a place in the distance which they called Mokalani. It was shaded by camel-thorn trees. This sight gave the whole party great comfort, but when they reached it, there was still no water.

They were certain, said the man, who along with his companion was now acting as a guide, that there was water at Mokokonyani, which was somewhere close ahead, but how far it was to that place they could not explain. The party had left Serotli on Wednesday at first light, and by now it was Saturday. The place where they were was in an area with scattered stunted thorn trees, and leading from there was, the two men then pointed out, a dry river bed, or at least that is what they said it was, although to the unpractised eye that was not visible. The party nevertheless followed this alleged river bed and it was true that with considerable labour digging enough water could be found in some places. The main problem seemed to be trying to find the overland course of this dry river. There was even a small spring a few miles further on, and at this place the guides, as they now described themselves officially, left the alleged river bed and found a large lagoon-like marsh which was dry and dying. They had been two full days without enough water at this point, and suddenly the old crone cackled (she had stayed with the wagons in a most determined fashion), and then led them through a surprising belt of scrub with some trees. Trees meant there was water here once, thought James, but they had already found that trying to dig out the roots in order to find water was a waste of effort, as they could never reach the end of any root. When they tried, the roots simply disappeared farther and deeper than they could dig. The old crone found no water.

Occasionally James mounted his horse and rode on ahead to see if he could see water, but all he saw was the horizon literally bubbling with a dry heat. The distant view always looked as if they were coming to water, but they never reached it. It was never there as the mirage receded in front of him at his pace. Gradually the shimmering mirage morphed into a horizon marbled brown in various shades, and white tinted with blue and then shading to a definite but feeble and pale yellow colour. The wind blew a light powder which irritated everyone's eyes. The ground changed as they approached the seeming end of the mirage, and it became covered with a thick white salty substance. James saw a grey and unusually shaped stone on the ground, and dismounting, he picked it up. It was, he was astonished to find after he had cleaned off the dirty encrustations, and was able to see it closely, an arrow head, but it had been fashioned from a flint. The only flint he had seen on their journey was at Kuruman. How it might have travelled from Kuruman to this place he could not imagine, nor who could have fashioned it so perfectly. He climbed up into his wagon and put it with his other curiosities.

They had reached, as James was soon to learn, a group of salt pans, a place which was a series of dried-out lakes, at one side of which was a very small muddy pool with foul-smelling and undrinkable water. But the mirage on the horizon changed and it looked as if there was a fringe of trees, which as they neared, the men said were real and not a mirage. The trees were in fact a thick belt of mopane trees. The party had arrived at Nchokotsa as the self-appointed guides called it, which turned out to be a particularly large salt pan about twenty miles in circumference. It must once have held a good body of water, but that was clearly some time long ago. The setting sun from the west shaded the colour of the incrustation on the pan and gave it a beautiful blue haze, cruelly making it look exactly like the shining surface of a lake. The mirage effect was perfect, and they could even see waves dancing on supposed water in the distance and false trees at the far edge of the pan reflected on its false surface.

Eventually they found a muddy place on the western edge of one side, but the brackish salty-tasting water was to no one's taste and not even the oxen would drink it. James still saw birds flying northwest, and Lewis said they were guinea fowl, which gave hope of still distant but possibly better water. The guides cried out "metse, metse", and joyfully pointed after the rapidly receding birds. When they moved onwards, after some hard hours the ground became gradually greener in appearance, if not in fact, and with more and more signs of having had the benefit of water recently. For some time after they had left the mud hole, they had seen what might have been trees on the horizon in increasing number, and at first they had thought they were looking at yet another mirage as their forms shimmered in the glare of the sun. But when they firmed in view and did not recede on being approached, the party knew that they were real, and in James' private thoughts at least, that they were saved.

With this rapidly improving hope they reached, almost as a

surprise, save for the increase in the number of birds and elands around, a good sized river flowing through a well-treed Eden. A river with live, flowing water. The guides waved their arms around happily. Martinus said he thought they knew all about the river, and had always known that was where they were going. Sadly, he could not account for the trouble that they had finding the river however, and James thought that they were simply being wise after the event. A few minutes' checking with the trocheameter showed they had come about 350, maybe 400 miles if you included detours and mistakes of the route, from Kolobeng.

36

The River

THE OXEN HAD BEEN SO WILDLY EXCITED when they first smelt the water that their pace had quickened. Once the oxen could not only smell but also see it, it was all Martinus and Dedderich could do to prevent them from dragging the wagons straight into it. That out-spanning was exceedingly difficult. When the half-crazed oxen were released from the trek-touw, lead by Blauberg who was released first, they rushed down through the reed-encrusted bank into the water, and stood in it up to their shoulders soaking and drinking. They drank so much that when they left the water their flanks were seriously distended. It looked as if they would all be ill, but none were. They moved off a short distance and almost immediately found good forage grass nearby, and settled under the trees to the long luxurious slow feed of which they were so desperately in need. The dogs and horses stayed beside the river, the dogs barking as if bewitched, and the horses, saddle-free at last, after they too had drunk their fill, just stood looking at the shallows resting and doing nothing. Argos was the leader of the dogs and he seemed afraid of the water. Maybe, thought James, there was too much water and he had never seen so much. He never went in the river.

James was so relieved that they had found a good supply of very clear water safely after all they had been through, that he offered a short silent prayer of thanksgiving. Lewis simply said that James must have been mad to even try to lead them across or round, he knew not which, the edge of the Kalahari, and he only hoped to God that now they would stay by the river.

The best site for their camp was in a small clearing sloping down to the water. They cleared away a large circle of dry grass so as to prevent a camp fire spreading, and set up camp beside it. The site was fifty yards south of a little reach of the river, the banks both sides of which were, except where the oxen and horses had trampled them, thick with reeds. The river itself seemed full of translucent brown water, and James, from where he was standing, could see thousands of pale yellow-coloured lilies on the upstream surface. The camp site was under a tall graceful, even noble kameel-thorn tree, the spread of which was considerable. Beyond, a little farther from the river, James could see a number of tall baobab trees of prodigious size and enormous girth. James could see something that looked like a box on the trunk of one of them, but that would not be possible, and he thought to himself that he would go and look to see what it really was the next day. He was too tired right then.

James and Martinus studied the ground all around the camp site and could not see any lion tracks. There were plenty of tracks of all sorts of animals, such as elands, gemsbuck and elephants, but no lion tracks. When they had satisfied themselves as to this James called Lewis over and he agreed with the assessment that the oxen could be left loose that night.

Ducks and guinea fowl were flying along the river, and Lewis saw a goose. But they had no shot gun to try shooting supper, and to use a rifle which would only fire one bullet at a time would be a waste in all probability, so they missed out. When setting up was complete, Lewis took his horse and started off after some elands he saw in the distance, and returned surprisingly quickly with three which he had shot, slung across his saddle, all of which were immediately prepared for the pot. Even as they did that, from out of nowhere, a small party of natives came up and by gestures asked if they could have some food as they were, they indicated, starving. Lewis said they must have been watching him shooting the elands. So elated was the party at their escape from the desert, and the discovery of the river, that the newcomers were welcomed and joined in the feast. There was plenty of firewood around, so a good fire was quickly built for the night, which was just as well because as the light faded mosquitoes came down in thick clouds, and only those who were seated or lying in the lee of but close to the fire had any respite from their bites.

Foolata sat quietly on her own, apparently exhausted and relieved in equal measure, like everyone else, and then she crept away under the wagon preparatory to sleeping. Lewis, who was watching her closely as she moved, called quietly to her.

"Come here Foolata, I would like a word please." She crawled out, went to him and stood obediently in front of him, with her hands to her sides.

"Yes Baas, what do you want?" she asked softly, uncertainly.

"Why are you being so anti-social, my girl?" Lewis replied with a laugh. "Why don't you come with me and we could have a bit of fun?" And so saying, he stood up and put his hand on her left shoulder, and roughly pulled her closer. Then he took her forearm in his right hand and started to tug her towards his wagon. She politely and calmly said she did not want to go with him to his wagon, but Lewis simply ignored her and pulled her along more firmly. She held back as best she could, dragging against his clutch, raised her voice a little and said, still firmly and reasonably, "Stop it, Baas, you are hurting me. Stop it. I do not want to go in your wagon."

Lewis ignored her and pulled her towards his wagon. The two of them were now a little way away from James' wagon and the other natives including Martinus, who thus could not see or hear precisely all of what was happening. Their voices were too low at that point to reach the camp fire. Lewis bent, swept a strong arm around Foolata's waist, and lifted her up and onto his wagon's fore-chest, leaping up behind. Then he pushed her roughly inside, and she, tripping on a shovel which had been left lying loose, fell heavily. Lewis stepped to her, grabbed at her, pulled her up, and then pushed her down onto his palliasse. Putting a hand on her shoulder he held her down. He pulled hard at the belt to her skirt, but it held fast although the skirt itself did not and that was torn from the waist to the hem.

"Please let me go, Baas," she pleaded.

Lewis raised his voice a little. "No, my girl. Oh no. I have been waiting for this. I have been watching you for months now, and I can see you are ready for a bit of fun with a real man. Come here."

"But I do not want to do this," she pleaded desperately, the fear audible in her raised voice.

"That is what they all say, but when they have done it, they all enjoy it," Lewis boasted. "You will enjoy it my girl, that is a promise. Look here, a girl like you needs someone like me, and now I think I want to see you properly." So saying, he tugged hard at her blouse and clumsily tore it from her shoulders. The blouse ripped as it fell away from her so that both her breasts were fully exposed, and in the poor half light inside the wagon Lewis could see, as he already knew of course, that she wore nothing under her blouse. Foolata seemed at first to be almost transfixed with fear, and then tried to crawl to one side away from Lewis. But he caught her round the ankle, and twisting her leg, pulled her back towards him. She was crying now, a low moaning sound, and she was saying "no" repeatedly, her tears coming in great noisy gulping sobs. She was twisting violently to and fro, trying to escape from Lewis' grip as best as she could, but he held her ankle fast. Lewis undid his belt and tossed it to one side, and the buckle gleamed briefly as it clattered to the floor. Lewis knelt over the girl, pushing her legs apart with his knees. He started to drag his trousers down to his knees with his free hand. At that point, as he did that, Foolata went limp with fright, and seemed almost to acquiesce in what was about to happen. She was breathing rapidly, gulping air and breathily tried desperately to protest. "Please stop it Baas, please. No Baas. Please, no." She was gasping now, great gulping breaths.

"Lewis, are you absolutely mad?" As he shouted, James climbed into the body of the wagon and striding forward, leapt at Lewis. Grabbing him by the collar of his shirt with one hand and the hair by the other, he pulled his head hard back and upwards. "Lewis, for God's sake, stop it. Get off her. Leave her alone," he shouted.

Lewis looked up stupidly at James. He seemed stupefied by James' sudden onslaught. "What do you mean?" he said in a thick, aggressive tone.

"Get off her. Get off her, you stupid fool." James jerked at Lewis' hair again. "For Christ's sake Lewis, stop this, now. Leave her alone."

"Come here, Foolata. Get away from him. Now. Get behind me," said James. He was frightened by what he was doing, and his voice was almost a croak. Foolata wriggled out from under Lewis and off the palliasse, grasped her torn clothes to herself, and stepped away from Lewis. She was crying, for shame.

"Well, well. Look here, see who has come to your rescue, Foolata! I did not know, I never dreamed that my brother-in-law was so bloody keen on you. I thought he loved my sister, his beautiful wife, he married her after all. My mistake, and it was a big mistake. After Christina I should have guessed he would have his eyes on you. I expect he wants a bit on the side and you are to give it to him. Is that it, James? Is that right, Foolata? Sweet on you, is he?" Lewis, who seemed to have recovered some bravado, was braying loudly now, jeering even, and looked round his wagon, but his rifle was nowhere he could reach, or even see. He was trying to pull his trousers up as he jeered.

James stood steady, and passed Foolata behind him, to the front of the wagon. He replied, "Listen up, my friend, I am not going to quarrel with you, Lewis. Not now, nor in the future. Foolata is coming away with me, now, and no, I do not want her for myself. I am, as you say, married, and all I want is for Foolata to be free of what to her are your obviously very unwelcome advances. You and I have spoken about this several times before, and you absolutely have got to leave the poor girl alone. She told you no, as she has told you before, and you must learn to take no for an answer."

Lewis, who seemed to be enraged at the interruption, said roughly, aggressively, "If you persist in continuing to take this slut's side you must expect to take the consequences. I have warned you. My sister will learn of your vile relations with this girl as soon as I can make them known to her."

"But Foolata is innocent, it was you trying to assault her that was the problem. She told you no, and she is entitled to say no if she wishes. She so wished, and so you have no choice in the matter. I can always tell Francesca the truth about what you tried to do. Go on, Foolata, get out of here, you are leaving, now."

Foolata picked her way through the debris on the floor of the wagon and then through the fore-clap, and onto the front of the wagon, and she then jumped to the ground. James backed out of the wagon carefully, facing Lewis all the while, and after he had let the fore-clap fall, he too jumped down. Then he led the almost naked Foolata back to his wagon, past the startled natives by the camp fire, and he handed her up into the relative privacy of his wagon. After she had climbed into James' wagon, and the fore-clap had fallen behind her, James, who did not get into the wagon with her, went over to the camp fire and sat down between Martinus and John. He suddenly felt very weary. He was shaking.

Martinus and John, who had both seen Foolata's return in tattered scanty clothes, realised what had happened. Martinus said, "Baas. I don't think that was a good idea. I am sorry Baas, I know it's not for me to say, but we are a long way away from home, and it is not good to be making quarrels with anyone. Certainly not Baas Lewis. We both heard the shouting in Baas Lewis' wagon, and we know what he was doing and what you did, and what you did was right, but you should not have. I am very sorry, you should not have done that."

James snapped at Martinus. "Shut up, you have no idea, it's not for you to say."

"Martinus is right, James," said John.

James looked at both of them, and then quietly, looking at the ground as if ashamed said, "I know. But I had to. He had gone too far."

The camp fire was burning low. Jessa silently fetched some more branches from the reserve pile of wood and the flames flared up at once. The four of them sat still and silent, and silently and individually considered how they would all get on together as a party after all that had happened.

Next morning over breakfast James decided that he had to clear the air with Lewis. He was ready for Lewis to be aggressive and antagonistic, as he could be at times, but instead, and much to James' surprise, Lewis was apologetic. Not that he apologised to Foolata. James started to say something, but Lewis interrupted him. "James, dear boy. I have to say how sorry I am for our little fracas last night. I did not know what I was doing. I must have had a few too many soopjes or something. It was very stupid of me to do that in front of you like that, I cannot imagine what came over me. In my experience as a hunter and trader, particularly when one is so far from base, one has to keep the party on an even keel, or there is trouble. Look, I am willing to forget the whole thing, and will say no more about it, if you agree."

James thought that these few words were wholly unacceptable, almost Boer-like in their lack of consideration for a native, and failed grossly to recognise the seriousness of what Lewis had attempted. The problem that James wrestled with inwardly was whether he should accept what Lewis had said on the basis of "least said, soonest mended", or take him fully to task for his attack on Foolata. That would mean the end of their joint expedition, and James was loath to break their little party up. There was a certain security in numbers he thought, even if one of that number was Lewis. That was what Martinus had meant the night before, and he could see now that was right. But he also knew that it would be wrong to just ignore the attempted rape, to pretend it had never happened. Foolata and the others in the party depended on him in all sorts of ways, such as protection, and he had to take that into account. If he said nothing he would be letting them down. That decided him in the end. He thought back to the river in Devon, and Francesca, and what his brother had done, and only with difficulty returned his thoughts to this river and their camp in the here and now.

"Lewis, you know full well that what you tried to do last night was completely unacceptable. You are a civilised man, and you have absolutely no excuse at all for what happened. But, having said that, we have got to stick together as a party for this expedition, and I do not want us to split the wagons up, as that would put everyone in possible danger. So we must stay together, and for that to be the case you must stay away from Foolata completely from now on. I already warned you about your relationship with her back at Kuruman, and I repeat that now. This is deadly serious for all of us, and you must change, or there could be dreadful consequences for everyone which we cannot foresee."

Lewis sat silently. James thought he was accepting the rebuke, but it was not so. "James, you really are an unutterable prig. I just wanted some fun, is all. And she deliberately took it the wrong way. But having said that, you are right. There is absolutely no good to be gained from falling out over Foolata. As a party, in the wilderness, we have to stay together now even if we do not want to. It is far too dangerous not to. That is all there is to it at the end of the day, so we will. But I shall not forget this, and we shall have to go our separate ways when we get back to Cape Town one day, as I am sure we will. I just hope we will never have to meet after that."

37

Beside Water

ON THE OTHER SIDE OF THE RIVER was what looked like a huddle of poor huts, a village of some sort perhaps, and some natives from there came across the river in canoes the next morning. They said they were from the local tribe called the Batuana, and James found he could talk with them reasonably easily as their language was a dialect not too unlike the Sechuana he had been learning. They guides said their tribe had a new young chief called Lechlulatebe, whose town was near the Great Lake out of which the river flowed. They said the river was called the Botletle (although one man claimed it was called 'the Zouga'), and the town was on the other side of the river to where James' party was. Their chief would be sure to welcome the party, so two of them said they would act as guides to his town. They also said he would almost surely want to trade elephants' teeth in return for guns or indeed anything at all. He had a great quantity of ivory as well because his country abounded with elephants. Lewis thought to himself that at last he had reached the right place to get rich. This was why he had put up with James all this time. The opportunity to trade for ivory, that was why they had suffered in the desert, and he was going to make the most of it now. James, the prig as Lewis thought of him all the time now, might think he was the better shot but he Lewis was, in his own opinion of course, the better and more experienced trader. James with his love of curiosities was just an amateur. Lewis' idea of trading however was not the same as James', because one of them had different standards of honesty to the other. Lewis was more than a little put out therefore, and indeed not a little surprised, when they discussed their prospects for trading to find that James wanted ivory which could be turned into cash quite so urgently as he now said he did. But their new guides, self-appointed again as before, were sure their new chief would be very welcoming to all the macooas (white men) in the party.

While James pondered the opportunity of trading and of recovering the money he had paid to Adriaan Beck and for the rest of his Cape Town debts, he walked over to the gigantic baobab tree he had seen the previous evening, and found his eyes had not deceived him. Sure enough there was indeed a rough wooden box fastened to the trunk at a height of about five feet off the ground. It was securely made with metal nails, and so not made by a native, thought James, and had a metal hinged lid for access. The tree trunk next to the box was carved with a large letter "A", which letter was six or seven inches high. Inside the box were a few tattered shreds of paper, which seemed to have been largely eaten by some insect, but on one of which was written, in rather crooked writing, what appeared to be the word "Carl". There was nothing else. When he had closely examined all the tatters, one by one, James put them back in the box, and left them for someone else to find, and wonder at. In fact, there were two giant baobabs in the group of four trees, and James measured both at a height of one yard off the ground and found them to be seventy-six and eighty feet in girth. It was to the larger tree that the box had been affixed. When he returned to the camp to get ready for the onward journey he described what he had found to an uninterested Lewis.

The onward journey from the river west towards the Great Lake was, compared with what had gone before, very soft and easy. There was the river beside them with plentiful crystal clear drinking water available whenever they wanted it, and grass and forage for the oxen was all around in huge quantities. But as the Botletle appeared to abound with crocodiles, Argos' caution earlier was understood. James absolutely forbade anyone and everyone in the party to go in the water for any reason. Lewis, stirred by thoughts of crocodiles, and the sight of them which he described as abhorrent to men, told

James a version of how his friend Robinson had met his death by crocodiles. James might have had concerns had he but known the other versions Lewis had previously told.

Since however the banks of the Botletle abounded with places where animals had gone down to the water to drink, as big a danger as the crocodiles were the game pits, which natives had dug in many of those places in the hope that animals would fall in, and then once trapped they would be able to kill them. These big pits they had artfully covered over with small branches and reeds, then they had sprinkled sand, animal droppings, and a few dried leaves on top for good measure, so the pits were very well concealed. After various members of the party including the dogs had fallen in a few times, James, John and Lewis took it in turns to ride on ahead of the wagons' intended path, to see if they could uncover the game pits. Lewis' horse fell in one pit which he had not seen. The consequence was serious, as it took most of one day to dig the horse out, although Lewis himself was able to clamber out up a tree trunk which James and John cut and lowered to him for that purpose. After that incident, and because it was so very hard to spot the game pits in advance, the party soon gave up the idea of trekking too close to the river and moved well away. After all the water was still so close as to be easily accessible. And game still abounded such as steinbuck, leche, koodoo, buffalo and waterbuck, so there would be no problem with obtaining meat for the pot. Another real problem for them if the wagons stayed too close to the river was the closeness together of a large number of trees of all sorts, which meant that they had to cut down a great many of them to make room for the wagons to pass. But still they went on westwards, and now they were parallel to a very reliable water supply. The spirits of the party were high, almost festive.

On the third day of this stage, a large group of thirty Baloba men and women came up to the wagons. The Batuana guides with the wagons explained that the Baloba were servants to the new Chief Lechlulatebe, and asked if the Baloba could be fed and taken to him at his town. They said he would be pleased at the return of these people, but this request lead to a furious argument between Lewis and James. Lewis wanted to return them, but James disagreed. James thought they were really slaves, not servants, and so did not want to force them back. This argument lasted on and off for two days while they were travelling west, but it was resolved shortly before they came to a place where their guides said they could cross the river by boat, because the Baloba decamped in the night and were never seen again. In the meantime the guides pointed out to them that if they went on another week or so they would have distant views of a large lake. Although it had taken such a dreadful and prolonged effort to get there, James was in no rush to take those last few steps, and see what he assumed was the fabulous Great Lake. He could go another day, any day. The lake was real and that was all that mattered, but that fact they had realised, even if only unconsciously, ever since the party had reached the river. A last needful step was something of an anti-climax after all that effort.

The boats the guides had referred to were in fact canoes made from hollowed-out tree trunks. They had all seen numbers of these canoes in the distance but now they were apparently close to the town they saw a good number. Some were straight as arrows but some were made from trees which had twisted trunks so that the canoes made from those trees necessarily had a bend in them, and looked most ungainly to say the least. None had sails, all were paddled. "Take a boat, my boy." The words of Sir Roderick Murchison rang in James' ears. James thought Sir Roderick would be so very pleased to know that his advice had been right, but when he gave it he could hardly have known how hard it would be to get to where boats were actually needed. Later, much later, they saw several quite wide rafts that natives had made for the purpose of transporting cattle or indeed anything larger than a human being across the river. A canoe of the type he saw would have been of no use at all in trying to take a wagon across the river.

38

Lechlulatebe

AS THEY LOOKED AT THE RIVER, a group of canoes came over to them, and a tall, very dark-skinned native (who the guides said to James was called Nkese) walked up the bank to James, and solemnly raised his right hand in a peaceful greeting. Carrying three spears and an animal skin shield, coloured black and white, with a spectacular single white ostrich plume attached to the warrior ring on his head, he was wearing an extremely large kaross coloured a strong red with ox blood, and a tsecha, and fine masekas or bangles of brightly burnished brass, one on each upper arm, and many on each leg below the knee. His sandals, with thongs between the toes, stretched back around the heels and entwined a little up and around the ankle, so that they were of an almost Roman design, thought James. He was physically very imposing, and his deep bass voice gave him the authoritative air of a person of considerable importance in his tribe. James did not fully recognise the language he spoke, and nor did Lewis, but it seemed to be a variation of Sechuana, and so James could manage well enough. Lewis, who was standing next to James, privately agonised that James had been approached and then addressed by an ignorant native as if he were the leader of the expedition, and not himself.

Nkese said that his chief, named Lechlulatebe, had heard many months ago that three macooas were approaching, coming from across the desert, and he wished them to visit his town, and that he would make them welcome when they came. He hoped they would trade with him. He had heard that white men always wanted elephants' teeth, of which, said Nkese, his chief had many. Would they go to visit his chief now please? Thus spake Nkese (somewhat peremptorily, thought James), on his master's behalf.

After their earlier experiences with Sechele and Sekomi, James and Lewis had a good long talk about trading and the best way to do it, and decided that they should not appear too eager to visit, or to trade. Having thus earlier decided on the reply, James told Nkese that they would wish to cross the river on the following day if Nkese would provide a raft to take them, and would then need guides to show the road to Lechlulatebe's town. Then, they might trade, but that would all depend on Lechlulatebe. Nkese made a high-flown speech by way of reply, and offered both the raft, or more than one if needed, and more guides, and said all would be ready to convey the party over the river early the next day.

The next morning there was a problem because when Nkese eventually appeared, mid-morning, he and some fellow nobles came by canoes and not by raft, and Nkese had with him in an accompanying canoe a small goat, which he offered to James by way of gift from his chief. Lewis wanted to kill and cook the goat, but James had heard from Livingstone that chiefs sometimes made insulting gifts of low quality and worth as a way of showing the importance of the giver by comparison with the status of the intended recipient. So James told Lewis that they could not accept, because the offer of a goat was a test set by Lechlulatebe, and to accept a mere goat would have been to admit a loss of face to Nkese, and through him to his chief. So James told Nkese that they had enough meat, and did not want a goat, and accordingly they proposed to untie the goat and let it wander away where it willed. He said that if Lechlulatebe wished to make another present, then they would accept a good ox, but if he could not do that they would be unwilling to impose the burden of their visit on such a poor chief. James and a quietly grumbling Lewis then sat down, and when the camp fire was well and truly alight, started to brew coffee. They had their backs to Nkese all the while. Nkese was obviously upset by this show of indifference, and he clearly understood that the offer he had put forward as required by his chief, of an insultingly small gift to strangers, was shameful, and that as a result the long-awaited visit to his chief by these white men might not happen. He got back into his canoe in a very subdued manner and said as he did that he would convey what they had said to his chief as soon as he could.

Very early the next morning John roused the camp with a great shout, crying out that a raft was coming to the bank, and on it was a large party of natives and a garlanded ox. Hurrying to the bank James saw that Nkese was standing next to a very young man, of obviously immense physical strength, tall, and with a handsome appearance. He had two magnificent white ostrich feathers attached his head ring and was wearing an ample blood-red kaross, with violent streaks of black across it. He, like Nkese, wore brass rings on his upper arms and legs, and his sandals were the same pattern as those Nkese wore, but were gold in colour. Himself unarmed, he was surrounded by older men who were all armed with spears and shields, shaped and coloured like Nkese's, and who were being very deferential to him. This man, guided by Nkese, walked up the bank straight to James, and raised his right hand in greeting. James rose to his feet and did likewise. The man did not look at or acknowledge Lewis in any way, presumably having been told by Nkese about the rejection by James of his test present the day before.

Nkese was with him, and hailed him as chief. Lechlulatebe, for it was he, said he wished to welcome them to his kingdom. He had met one other macooa many months before he said, but James and his party were the first he had seen since then. He hoped they would honour his town by visiting it. James, who was privately delighted that he was able to understand what was being said, replied that they would be prepared to do that. So the next few hours were taken up with the ferrying over the river by raft of both wagons and their oxen, all the party of servants, the animals, plus all the impedimenta that they had accumulated to date. This was noisy and a dangerous business, because the rafts were not built to take any real weight, and could well have sunk had they been over-loaded. So the wagons had first to be emptied of their contents to make them as light as possible, and the contents had to be ferried over separately just as the oxen were. It was mid-afternoon by the time everything and everyone had been ferried over the river, order had been restored on the northern side, and the wagons had been properly repacked, so after a very short haul of about two miles, James ordered a halt for the day, saying to Lechlulatebe that they would set off towards his town early the following day. This plainly pleased the chief, and the day ended with a quiet meal for the party of travellers by the camp fire, sufficiently far from the river to avoid the mosquitoes. Lechlulatebe meanwhile went on ahead to his town to prepare for their arrival.

When, next day, led by their new guides, the party reached the town after a leisurely journey across loose sandy ground, James ordered a halt about a mile short, and hence outside it. There they made camp, surrounding the wagons with prickly thorns in order to keep the most acquisitive natives from coming too close, and thereby having the opportunity of maybe obtaining goods from them otherwise than by trade. That evening the party had a long talk as to the way they should conduct the actual visit, which was not something they had done before – when they met Sekomi for instance – and because of that experience, they knew that they must keep guard on their wagons and their contents. So John was put in charge of the camp with Martinus and Dedderich the two wagon drivers in charge of their wagons and their contents. Edward and Jessa were to look after the other livestock and make sure no one entered the perimeter hedge. The oxen would remain fastened to their trek-touws and Edward and Jessa would also be responsible for feeding and watering them. As the discussion ended Foolata appeared at James' side, wearing a European dress she had been given by Ma-Mary, and asked if she could go into Lechlulatebe's town with them rather than staying in the camp. James agreed to that, despite the objection Lewis made. But to placate Lewis, James made it very clear to her that she must stand behind the two of them, and say nothing at any time.

When the party of James and Lewis, with Foolata, who had Argos with her but walking behind them, entered the town, it was in a state of disturbed and quietly anxious upheaval. James, when they approached Lechlulatebe's house, asked Nkese why that was so. It transpired that they had that morning received news that a large party of Arab slave traders had arrived at Chief Sebituani's town, which was a few weeks' journey north, and were offering him guns in return for slaves. The Arabs wanted, said Nkese, as many slaves as they could get. And they had said that if they did not get the slaves within a very short time then they would burn the town down, and take Sebituani away as a slave himself. Sebituani was, said Nkese, the most important neighbouring chief, the head of the clan, and Lechlulatebe owed him loyalty and military help if and when called on. He was being asked for that help by Sebituani now, with the implicit threat that if Lechlulatebe did not give it, he would be in serious and irrevocable breach of his tribal responsibility. The penalty for such a breach was certain war. And, Nkese added, Sebituani also wanted guns so as to be able to defend his tribe from the Boers who had lately been robbing his outlying villages of their oxen, and taking their very young children off. At the moment Sebituani had only a very few rather old muskets which were not much good against the new rifles the Boers now had. He was certain to hold Lechlulatebe very strictly to his tribal loyalties.

Lewis was impatient to trade, and did not really want to listen to all the problems Lechlulatebe had, and so he suggested, without offering any support or sympathy, that he wanted to acquire elephants' teeth by trading. But the chief made it clear that he did not want to trade until the problem he had been landed with in relation to Sebituani had been dealt with. He asked, said Nkese, that James and Lewis should stay with them and discuss the problem, and then if they agreed what to do, perhaps they might trade then. He said they were going to hold a pitso to decide formally what to do, and James and Lewis were asked to attend and perhaps to offer advice.

Lewis ignored what was said and repeated a little too insistently that he wanted to trade for ivory, and said he did not want to attend the pitso. James could see that young Lechlulatebe was impatient with what Lewis said. That was after all tantamount to disagreeing with him about the importance of what had happened, so James offered to stay and do whatever he could to help. Lechlulatebe crossed the enclosure in front of his house and put his right hand on James' shoulder. "You are my honest brother," he said. But he said nothing to Lewis, who, seeing what had happened and how he was being apparently deliberately ignored by the chief, petulantly turned on his heel. Saying nothing, he sulkily walked off, back towards their camp, on his own.

That evening when James returned to the camp with Foolata, Lewis' wagon had gone. John told him that Lewis had returned from the town in a towering rage, and had claimed that Lechlulatebe had insulted him and refused to trade with him, so he had resolved to go off and shoot ivory on his own, and to hell with James and the natives. James could join with the natives, and be damned to him as well. John was very worried because, he said, after Lewis had returned he had been drinking cape brandy all afternoon as Dedderich got ready for their departure, and so when he left he had to ride in his wagon as he was too drunk to ride his horse. Dedderich had in-spanned, and was driving the ox team. Lewis had taken a large box of James' ammunition with him, and according to John, had said he would meet James where they had first found the Botletle river, on the south side, in exactly five weeks' time. By then, he had promised, he would have enough ivory. And then they could both start for home. James was very concerned for their mutual safety as the party which he had been trying to keep together had now split, and both of them were now that much more defenceless in what it appeared was a very disturbed country.

39

The Pitso

THE PITSO WAS TO BE HELD THE NEXT DAY, in order that everyone from the outlying villages could attend. From first dawn the next morning the warriors gathered in groups to discuss what was to be debated at the coming pitso. Groups of warriors sang war songs threatening death to the Arabs slavers, and to the Boers, and their bloodcurdling cries mingled with the shrill clamours of the women and children. So it was that in the bright mid-morning light, in a tense and frightening mood, the whole tribe gathered noisily in the large circular enclosure in the middle of the town fenced in with a very rough hedge, which was the place exclusively for public assemblies. This site was not allowed to be used for any other purpose except a pitso, or council of war. It was about one hundred and fifty yards in diameter James guessed, and along one side the numerous naked warriors squatted on the ground in densely packed rows, with their shields of bullock hide to their front, and in the same hand behind their shields each held six or seven assegais, bristling up above their heads like a dense wood of bright spears. A few, James could see, had old-fashioned muskets. Many had quivers full of arrows on their backs and some also clutched battle axes.

The men who were too old to fight, and the women and children, squatted the other side of the enclosure facing the warriors. The two groups together formed a horseshoe-shaped gathering, and the centre was, at the start of the pitso, reserved for the privileged, meaning those who had killed another warrior in battle, as it was there they could sing and dance in celebration of their deeds of valour. This they did as a prelude to the debate about Sebituani's

Pitso or War Council at Lake Ngami (1862).

Oil painting by Thomas Baines now in the MuseumAfrica collection. Painted more than twelve years after James' visit, by which date a trader had a store at his town; this painting shows Lechlulatebe seated in the middle, in his new European clothes, and Nkese beside him. By this date also, the tribe had managed to acquire some rifles as opposed to muskets, demands. When the brave warriors, and there were a lot of them, had eventually finished singing their war songs and dancing their war dances, they rejoined the warriors waiting patiently at their side. The entire crowd of warriors sang in harmony, and their war songs were deep, vibrant and resonant and filled the air with a throbbing wildly aggressive harmony.

Lechlulatebe himself sat on a large cube-shaped grey stone facing the horseshoe-shaped tribal group, with his warriors on his right. He wore a very large dark-coloured lion skin kaross which was highly polished on the inside, and a necklace with three rows of lions' claws. He had a large flat rectangular copper ornament suspended from his left ear to signify his rank, and the grease ring on his head, which shined with sibilo, sported a fine spray of pure white ostrich feathers. Shining brass rings glittered on him as before. He clutched his wooden-shafted battle axe in his right hand. At his feet was his bullock-skin shield coloured black and white, like many among the warriors, and his bundle of assegais was in his left hand. James sat on a small and low wooden log next to the chief with his rifle across his lap. Foolata, in her best Ma-Mary dress, crouched with the women and children of the tribe to their side of the enclosure, under an animal-skin awning. After all the preliminary dancing and war songs had ended, silence gradually fell while the whole tribe waited for their chief to speak.

James could not say exactly when the pitso started, and he knew he would never recall exactly what was said or declaimed by the many and various participants, but it started, as far as he could later recall, with Lechlulatebe standing in the empty middle of the circle, and demanding silence. The warriors replied with a deep throaty groaning noise, to signify compliance with his will. He then pointed an assegai north in the direction of Sebituani's town, and uttered a blood-curdling curse on the Arabs who wanted slaves. This drew a great roar of approval. Then he denounced the Boers in equally ferocious terms. Blood-drinking eaters of women and children was the least of his angry descriptions of them. He said they were worse slavers than the Arabs because they mostly stole children. He told his own people that they themselves were a strong and conquering people, and that they should not be afraid of any of their enemies. He claimed the Arabs would have to leave soon because they had come from far away, so they could not stay long. They were not to be afraid of the Arabs like that coward Sebituani; the real hazard lay with the threat from the Boers who were, he said, advancing on them at that very minute. It was a long denunciatory speech, full of boastful references to the feats of arms of his tribesmen warriors, and then, even as he sat dazed by the violence of the speech, James heard his name shouted out by Lechlulatebe in acclamation, but he did not understand completely what was being said amid all the noise. The chief finished with a final oratorical flourish, waved his battle axe to the sky, and cried out "poola", in an heroic shout. He wheeled around, returned to James' side and raised James up, and then lifted his right hand holding the rifle, amid more savage shouts of acclaim. Then he left James, and sat back on his stone throne, with the repeated shouts of his warriors ringing around the assembly.

James remained standing, and when the shouting gradually died down, he waved his rifle in the air. Why he did this he could not later recall, but overcome by the excitement of the occasion he felt driven by the spirit of what Lechlulatebe had said. Then, holding his rifle aloft, and to a growing roar of cheering, still waving his rifle, he walked slowly to the centre of the circle where the Chief had stood. When he reached the position at which Lechlulatebe had spoken, all the warriors fell utterly silent. Not a sound was to be heard.

He shouted out his speech to the assembled tribe, in his poor Sechuana, and he hoped they would understand well enough. He said that they were all free men, as he was himself. He owed no one any duty, save only his own chief. His chief was the greatest and most powerful chief anywhere. His chief had made a law that no one anywhere in the world should be a slave, had freed all slaves and said that to take slaves was punishable by death. The Arabs, he said, were spineless cowards, who were thousands of miles away from their own lands and because it would take them very many months to get back to their own country they could not stay long. If the Arabs did not leave at once and without any slaves from Sebituani's tribe, he had no doubt that his chief would send thousands of warriors to free their slaves, and kill them. They had to escape quickly or they would die. A messenger must at once be sent to tell them that this was what the English macooa, who was a friend of Lechlulatebe, and at his town, said. As for the Boers, he knew them and their ways, and he would himself stay and help the tribe to fight them. He had no love for the Boers (he glanced at Foolata as he said that), they were the enemy of his chief and they would be defeated. As he finished, James shook his rifle above his head, and shouted out "poola" at the top of his voice, just as their Chief had.

The roar of approval that greeted his shout was, if anything, even louder than had been given by the warriors to their own chief. Even as the shouting and cheering continued, Lechlulatebe walked dramatically forward and clasped James in his arms. Drawing back a little he gave James his battle axe, and in a daze James passed him his rifle in return. The cheering was so loud that James was deafened, as well as frightened and embarrassed.

The pitso continued with many nobles speaking, and ordinary warriors too, particularly the older men, and they followed each individual speech with shouting and dancing and much waving of weapons of all sorts. It concluded with another speech by the chief, who declaimed dramatically that with the brave English macooa alongside who would fight with them, they would have nothing to fear from anyone. James was not at all sure what would be involved in this, and was already beginning to regret what he had said. But it was far too late for regrets.

More war songs and dancing followed, and at length the gathering at the pitso gradually calmed as the day drew to a close. Lechlulatebe beckoned James to him and led him through the town to his house, where his wives had ready large bowls of boyalwa native beer and wooden platters laden with chunks of half raw meat, and fish from the river, with fresh fruits. James sat on the ground to eat, and noticed Foolata had followed them to the chief's house, and was sitting at the back with the women. James repeated to the chief that they must send that warning to Sebituani immediately, although privately he was very far from certain that his own chief, whom he had not disclosed was a woman, would send any soldiers to help. Even if she or Sir Harry Smith on her behalf did, they would be months and months too late to be of any use anyway. But Lechlulatebe told James he had already sent tribal elders as heralds to Sebituani with the message, and he was sure that once the Arabs knew that the great and famous English macooa, who was a friend of his own great chief, was with him and had the support of his chief, that they would disband and flee. He was at least as much worried, it transpired, about the Boers as anything else.

At that point, as if only just realising what he had done, he asked James for his battle axe back, and when James promptly gave it to him, he smiled broadly and immediately returned James' rifle to him. James knew that he was extremely lucky to get it back, and thought to himself how stupid he had been to let himself get carried away in the heat of the moment. He should never have risked losing his favourite Blisset. He could not recall exactly what he had said, but he knew it was very rash. He realised that his bravado had exposed an aspect of his own character he had not fully understood before, and he felt drawn to the position that he must live up to his own expectations. He found an unexpected strength in his own utterances, and in his own ambitions, and knew that with what he had done and said at the pitso he had changed himself as much as others.

The feast gradually drew to a close in the still warmth of the rapidly approaching night. Lechlulatebe said that it was too late for James to go back to his wagon then and so he should stay in his town instead; he said he had already had a house prepared for James. He would send a message to James' party to say he was staying in town and that that would be all right. James said he was quite happy to stay and shortly after he was shown to a new house, newly erected in his honour as he later learnt, circular like all the others, with walls of wooden stakes and a thatched roof, the floor of which had been laid with fresh grass, which smelt sweet as if newly cut. "And you must have your wife with you," said the chief, and as he parted the kaross entrance curtain, he firmly pushed Foolata inside.

Inside, Foolata said nothing. She unfastened her dress slowly, which slid to the ground around her feet. She stood motionless facing James, naked, smiling a quiet, cautious smile. Her warm brown eyes were shining, and she looked at James as if to say that this was the moment of real decision for both of them, and one that she at least had been awaiting, and hoping for, for many months. James moved towards her and she looked up at him, almost shyly. Face to face with her, James saw her then as if he was seeing her properly for the first time. He saw that she was serenely, darkly beautiful. He understood then that up till that moment he had not really looked at her, had not really considered her. He had been unthinking and far too self-centred, he now realised. Slowly he took her in his arms and held her close, gently, and with an inward understanding that now at last he had found what he realised he had so long been looking for, peace and genuine love he could and did want to return. Her young warm body was firm and gracefully pliant, and welcoming in his arms, and she responded to his touch with an embrace from which he knew without doubt that she loved him, and that what he now felt was what he had always thought he would feel with the woman he loved. They stood together in a silent and long embrace. Foolata's face glowed, and softened gently. Her copper-coloured skin reflected the dim light filtering past the kaross across the entrance. At last, after so long, Foolata knew she was with the tall, young and handsome Englishman she had loved ever since he had saved her from that beating in the street by the cruel Mynheer Beck. And now they both knew they would become the real lovers that spiritually they already were. She could see the light in his eyes, and at that moment they both knew that they felt the same way about each other, and the future. After a while they kissed.

That night James and Foolata both lay naked on the warm dry grass inside the house, in perfect harmony, with an ease and complete happiness which neither had known before. They made love together slowly, and repeatedly, and with great joy. Their differently coloured skins seemed almost to fuse together with their sweat. They both felt their lovemaking was so perfect, so right, that they felt and hoped it would never end. It seemed as if they were the only people in the world, no one else mattered, or even existed. Where they were was unimportant, as was the threat hanging over the tribe from a possible war. Everything else but their love for each other was irrelevant, forgotten. The only thing that mattered was that they were with each other, and with the light of love in their eyes, they found complete happiness. All night long, a warm gentle wind stirred the kaross across the opening to their house.

40

Plans for Defence

As the sun rose over the waking town, the pale early morning light falling through the narrow doorway was darkened by the appearance of Lechlulatebe who, drawing the entrance kaross aside, stood and peered in at the two of them lying together on the grass floor. He was smiling. "Come," he said, un-embarrassed at seeing them together and naked, "we have much work to do." And with a quick but unpleasantly sharp pang of regret for all his bravado at the pitso, James roused himself, and when they had dressed, they both went and joined Lechlulatebe who was waiting patiently outside, to go and "make preparations for war" as he put it.

James walked with the chief back to his house, with Foolata and Argos following behind them, and on reaching it Lechlulatebe, with a quiet smile, calmly pushed Foolata inside, and told his wives to look after her while James and he went out to prepare for battle.

James explained to the chief that in order to advise him properly, he needed to see the lie of the land, to understand how any attack might reach them, so the chief, Nkese and James rode north on salted horses, in the direction of Sebituani's tribal lands. Nkese explained that the horses were special as they had survived the sickness which the flies caused, but pointed out that any horses James or Lewis had, having no resistance, would more or less inevitably die from being bitten. It always happened to horses new to the lake area. Argos ran behind James now, and did not seem to get tired despite the distance they covered.

To their west as they rode was a broad river called the Tamunakle which the Chief said flowed into the Great Lake, and which therefore with its crocodiles protected their left flank, and ahead and east lay very rough and high ground. On closer inspection the ground gradually became steeper and rougher as they moved north, and after about four hours' hard, difficult riding, the party came to a place which formed a narrow rocky defile through the hills, which James thought, with his totally inexpert eye, would make a good and easy site for an ambush. Any army trying to move on Lechlulatebe's town from the north would have to move down through the pass, and James imagined to himself that a small but determined resistance at this site could well halt any such advance, if it were determined so to do. He explained his thinking to Lechlulatebe and suggested that first they should reconnoitre another position a few hours still further north to find a point from which advance scouts could observe any approaching enemy, and from which they would at once, when they did see such a force approaching, retire to warn the main defence force of the impending attack. That would be waiting at this point of defence at the pass. The location was sufficiently close to Leclulatebe's town for waiting warriors to be supplied with food and water easily enough, thus enabling it to to stay indefinitely sealing off the approach, however long it took for the enemy to come.

The chief thought that this strategy was quite unlike anything he had ever heard of before. But he accepted that the macooa might well be an able warrior, so he would think about the plan. (James wondered to himself if Lechlulatebe would be so happy to even listen to what he was saying if he knew that James had no experience of war at all.) Lechlulatebe himself had no plan, but to fight whenever and wherever he could, with all his tribe's strength. The enveloping horns of a buffalo was the only military tactic he had ever heard of, and he drew a plan of the formation in the dirt for James to see what he had in mind. He said all the tribes used it, and so he was interested in James' new idea as something that he was sure Sebituani's tribe would never have met before. That might well make it harder for them to counter it, he thought. James refined the idea as they talked. He found himself thinking about the disposition of warriors and their concealment as the enemy approached, and suggested that the flanks of his suggested site of ambush should be secured as well, in order to prevent the defenders being outflanked. Lechlulatebe said that was what he was saying when he described the enveloping horns of a buffalo form of attack, but he now understood how his scheme could be used in defence as well. After all, he argued with himself, he could not attack his tribal superior, which Sebituani was, but he could and should defend himself and his tribe from unjust demands for the provision of slaves, or tribute in any alternative form. He told James he would give the whole plan further careful thought, after they had all slept on it, but he could see that James' plan might be a winning tactic from a fighting point of view. It would have changed James' view of Lechlulatebe had he known that he, like many others, indulged in slavery when he wanted.

Nkese, who had kept very quiet while these discussions were going on, suggested that the tribe should post the forward scouts as quickly as possible, even while they were still waiting to hear the reply from Sebituani. He was pessimistic as to what the reply would be and said they should prepare quickly. The chief said nothing, but listened carefully.

It was early evening with the light just starting to fade by the time they returned, and James, parting from the others, went immediately to the house he had shared with Foolata the previous night. She was there, waiting for him. He sat Argos down outside. Their feelings for each other at that moment were of intense, deep and warm but unspoken pleasure that they remembered rightly how they had felt about each other the previous night. They knew their feelings for each other were certain. James and Foolata had discovered each other.

Before James and Foolata became too settled for the evening, the chief sent a servant to ask them to eat with him that night, and so before they had time to make love they had to go and rejoin Lechlulatebe and his wives for their evening meal. A number of goats had been roasted and had, somewhat unskilfully in James' opinion, been cut up. Sitting on the ground around the fire at the entrance to his Lechlulatebe's, the meat was passed round to each person in turn, by hand. Bowls of milk and beer were all around, and the lively chatter of those eating and drinking made for a convivial evening. In fact it was quite late before James and Foolata could politely get away to the house that both now regarded as their home. They wandered back through the small town, hand in hand, passing peacefully chatting family groups sitting in the doorways to their houses, and exchanged quiet greetings with many people. They all seemed to watch James and Foolata with curious, but friendly, and sometimes sad, interest. Everyone knew a battle was coming with all that might entail.

When they reached their house, they entered and held each other closely. They just wanted to be alone together, and to be that way always. They lay naked together, facing each other, and talked. It seemed as if they must have lain talking for hours, but eventually their talk slowed and they made love again as if there would be no tomorrow, as if nothing and nobody else mattered, or even existed. They had each other, and all they wanted was for that happy state to last, unchanging. They knew the threat of war was hanging over the town, and the dangers that lay ahead if war were indeed to start, and that made the sharp sadness of their position more striking. James would be the prime target for any enemy attack, they both knew, and also that Lechlulatebe's warriors were far fewer than the likely attackers. And in such native wars, as they also knew, defeat meant a mutilated death, if you were lucky. It was certain that the enemy would make directly for and try to kill the macooa who had inspired Lechlulatebe to defy Sebituani. With this thought in his

307

mind, James took his ring off, and gave it to Foolata, and when it did not fit, suggested that she wear it around her neck on a necklace.

The next morning John appeared at the enclosure in front of their house, and called James' name out, a bit timidly thought James. James went outside and realised at once from John's obvious distress that he had completely ignored John and the other servants with the wagon, and had not talked to them or explained what was going on. So with fulsome apologies for his hurtful thoughtlessness, he told John everything that had happened. Everything, that is, except for the new relationship he had with Foolata. He told him about the threat of war and the detailed preparations being made for it and said there could well be a delay in the town for a month or even more. He instructed John to move the wagon back over the river to another camp beyond the mosquito belt, and make it secure there. He had been told there was better and higher ground there. When that had been done, he wanted John and Martinus to bring any and all spare rifles they had, with ammunition, back to him at the town, leaving only one rifle and a small supply for Edward and Jessa, who would have to stay with the wagon and look after it and the oxen. John was also told to bring the latest of James' journals back to the town, with adequate writing and painting material, as he wished to bring his journal up to date, not having written his journals for at least a week now and to paint a picture of the house he and Foolata shared. John said he would do all this as quickly as he could, and was soon on his way back to the camp.

The chief's wives had left a variety of cooking utensils and foods in the house the day before, and so Foolata made the first breakfast of their new life together. She did so happily, singing quietly to herself, while James sat contentedly beside her, and happily watched the light of his heart.

About the middle of that morning Lechlulatebe and Nkese came across to James' house, sat down on the ground at the entrance and started without any more ado to talk about James' plan for the defence. They said that the forward scouts had been posted, as Nkese claimed he had suggested, and arrangements had been made for their periodic relief. "What more," asked Nkese, "should we be doing?" The the most important thing, James said, was to explain to the warriors that this was going to be a different way of fighting, and that they would not be washing their spears in the blood of the enemy until after they had so reduced the attacking force as to render it impotent. The chief would have to instil this new form of warfare into his warriors. Absolute and complete discipline was essential, urged James. There was to be only a small group of warriors fighting and stabbing with assegais, which was he knew their usual way. Meanwhile, said James, he had to go out to the pass again, and see where on the surrounding higher land his, Johns' and Martinus' rifles, together with any muskets that the chief might have, could best be sited.

The need for all his warriors to follow and accept the new tactics and style of fighting they would use was critical, agreed Lechlu-latebe. He and Nkese undertook to get the tribal elders together to explain the need for discipline. The chief thanked James for his advice and said he was glad that he had a great and wise macooa who was so skilful at warfare with him and his tribe at this perilous time. Because of that they would certainly not need the help of James' chief's warriors said Lechlulatebe, a remark for which James thanked his God, privately.

But Lechlulatebe had news of the Boers on his other flank to the east. "The Boers have," he said, "according to a fleeing villager, completely burnt down two small villages, and carried off a large number of children, and driven over three hundred cattle away. I hope that will satisfy them for the time being as I do not want to have to fight two wars at the same time. The main pity is that another of the fleeing villagers who has come back said he had seen Lewis' wagon nearby in a very perilous place, in the path of the Boers."

James inspected the pass again with the chief and Nkese that day, and having taken a sketch pad with him, he drew a small picture of the site in pencil so as to help him remember the lie of the land. Then the three of them set off back to the town, riding quite steadily, but not as quickly as James would like. "I know why you want to get back so quickly," said the chief. "It's that wife of yours. I have seen the way you look at each other, I know about these things." James considered that, but said nothing, and only the faintest blush beneath his tan showed the chief was right. He had discovered so much about himself, mainly accidentally, that he was not surprised at what the chief said.

41

Peace and Goodbye

THE NEXT FEW DAYS PASSED VERY QUICKLY. The chief and Nkese were everywhere explaining to the tribe what the plans were. A number of the young warriors who had not yet washed their spears were very disdainful of the plan. It had to be explained to them, accompanied by quite severe threats, that the plan was going to be followed, to the letter. If they were not prepared to follow the plan, and in particular the style of fighting, then they would be driven from the town and south over the river and then into the Kalahari, without any food or weapons. They all knew that meant probable death, so despite muttered disagreement from a few, the training of the warriors and the instilling of discipline into them continued apace.

Meanwhile James and the chief awaited news from Sebituani. That did not arrive for another week, and when it came it was not good. Sebituani demanded the handing over to him, as a prisoner, of the macooa called James who had persuaded Lechlulatebe to be so disloyal as to defy him. James was by now spending a lot of time with the chief trying to teach him and the tribal elders, and through them the warriors, how to set the ambush from hiding, a principle which the warriors did not seem to understand at all, and how to fight once the trap had been sprung. His ability to speak their dialect had much improved, and this helped greatly, but it was not until after the chief had replied to Sebituani that he told James of the threat, and of his reply. The chief said he had told Sebituani that if he wanted the macooa James, he would have to come and get him, and he would have to hurry as the macooa's own chief was sending his own warriors in their thousands to help put a stop to slavery. The chief said this would stop Sebituani from making any more threats, and also from attacking them. James doubted all this, and just thought that as long as the threat was hanging over the town, and himself, he could not leave. Perhaps the new self he had discovered at the pitso was not as brave or as wise as he had hoped. This other new self was really centred on someone else, Foolata.

A week after the reply to Sebituani another messenger came from him, and this time the news was very sweet. The messenger said that the Arabs had decamped just as suddenly as they had come. It seemed they had decided that they did not want to fight as they had too many slaves to be safe if a fight happened. As a result, Sebituani now had no need for any help, or guns, or even slaves, from Lechlulatebe. No mention was made of tribal disloyalty and the matter seemed to be as if it had never happened. Forward patrols were still sent out by Lechlulatebe as a precaution, and they reported back that they had seen the Arabs retreating eastwards together with their many slaves in long coffles, so the tribe knew that what the messenger said was true.

To say that James was relieved by this Arab retreat was an understatement. He was, however, regarded as the hero of the hour by the whole tribe, who now ascribed their remarkable escape from attack solely to his military advice. James was certain he did not deserve that accolade. But the more he disclaimed responsibility, the more Lechlulatebe, and Nkese and the elders, all ascribed his denials to that modesty suitable to a proper military man, even if they never practised modesty themselves.

Lechlulatebe decided that he wanted to reward James (and his wife) for what he had done, and said that he wanted to give them elephants' teeth, as many as their wagon could carry. James was also given various personal gifts such as a large collection of brass masekas (which he later quietly gave to Foolata), several very highly decorated assegais and a shield with three trailing lion tassels, this last from the champion warrior called Xamla. John being also a macooa, and therefore plainly (they assumed) a warrior, was also laden with presents, and was offered a wife, indeed a choice of several wives. It was very embarrassing all round as John was a young and innocent man, albeit of fine physique, and was much admired by the local girls, who made their views and offers of matrimony very plain. John, however, declined all of them as gracefully as he could, much to the general public amusement.

James' party's preparation for leave-taking was an excuse for much singing and dancing. Their last night in the town Lechlulatebe gave a general feast in their honour, and in recognition by the chief of her rank, Foolata sat between him and James, if a little behind them. The chief's wives were placed very much to the rear of the gathering, so Foolata's place of honour so close to the feast was very notable. A number of whole oxen had been roasted, there was fish from the river in round wooden bowls, a mush of potatoes was on flat slabs of wood into which one dug one's hands for a helping, and boyalwa was plentiful. As they sat eating and drinking on the ground to one side of the roasting fire, the most notable warriors came and danced in front of them. They danced lithely and with wild jerky gesticulations by the light of the flickering flames of the fire, waving their weapons over their heads with fierce stabbing motions, and with spear-washing movements, the firelight casting leaping shadows over the scene. Their barbaric, almost shouted, singing, and the wild war cries from the dancers, were accompanied by strange ululations from the watching women. The women seated at the back of the gathering did not take part in the warriors' celebrations, and many of them looked enviously at Foolata, who was still wearing a Ma-Mary dress. Near the end of the evening James, who had in advance prepared an extravaganza, as he thought of it, fired off some six rockets into the dark star-crossed blue-black sky, much to the startled and even frightened amazement of the tribe. The rockets were all blue in colour as it happened, and the colour reflected on their skins and made them seem of a much darker hue than they were.

The next morning a long procession wound out of town with James and the chief leading, with Foolata behind them, and a long train of porters beyond, each of them carrying one elephant's tooth. Edward and Jessa had brought the wagon back to the far bank of the river, to the old camp site, and after the cargo had been ferried across to them by canoe, it was loaded up with the newly gifted ivory.

At this point Jessa came to James somewhat shamefacedly, and asked if he might leave the trek as he had met a girl, and he said he wanted to marry her, and stay. This sounded rather sudden to James, but Jessa told him that one day while he and Edward were waiting at the wagon the other side of the river, and doing nothing in particular (James did not believe that), the girl had turned up apparently out of nowhere, and had made "advances" to him, and he said he now loved her. Although that seemed a bit sudden to say the least to James' way of thinking, and plainly the story was merely an excuse, what it was an excuse for James did not know and could not think. Apparently the girl had said she loved Jessa, and he said he loved her, and in his present love-filled mood and thinking only about Foolata, James was not going to deny Jessa, or the girl. He did think about saying that all this business of staying behind was ridiculous, but then he saw Foolata looking at him, and so he gave his agreement that Jessa could stay with the girl, and marry her if that was what he and she both really wanted; it was, apparently, so Jessa and the girl stayed behind in order to get married.

When the wagon had been fully loaded, and once they had in-spanned, James and his party said their goodbyes to Jessa and all their many new friends in the town, and the wagon set off on the long trail back which would eventually take them to the Cape. With everything that had been going on, James had quite forgotten that he had not even seen the Great Lake, but when John reminded him that was the case, pointing out how near it was and how easy it would be to go there, and indeed that had been the reason for the expedition, James said that he did not care about that any more now.

He had other seriously important thoughts now about his return. Not least of all was what would happen to him and Foolata when they returned to civilisation. The first place they would reach would be Kolobeng where Livingstone might, indeed was certain to, mention his view in somewhat forceful terms. James could well imagine what that might be. Livingstone knew he was married, and would surely express himself forcefully when he learnt about James' relationship with Foolata. He was after all not simply married, but a married white man who had a coloured lover. It would be very hard, he knew, to persuade Livingstone of the genuineness of his feelings, but he knew he had to do this.

James now started the trek back towards their rendezvous with Lewis. The meeting place with Lewis was the point on the southern bank where they had first reached the river, but when they got there after a further few weeks' travel, Lewis was not there, nor was there any sign that he had been there but had moved on. They could do nothing except wait for Lewis and his wagon to appear.

James thought about his and Foolata's position continually, and their love for each other, and then felt bound to write a brief note about it to no one in particular. He did this and put it in the wooden box on the baobab tree. Just a few words, with his and her names and the date on it. The remains of the original note he had previously found were still there. As he placed the note in the box the foliage above him moved quietly in a passing breeze. Meantime while he waited for Lewis to arrive, James relaxed and took most of two days to paint a careful and vivid watercolour of the river with all its varied colours, clear, almost translucent waters and waving reeds with overhanging trees. When it was completed he stowed it in his clothes trunk, having first wrapped it in a shirt. He thought his mother might like it when he got back; it would look good in the morning room at Highsteignton.

Lewis and his wagon arrived on their side of the river after they had been waiting five days. The picture he and Dedderich presented was not a happy one. Lewis told the story of what had happened to them, which matched the sorry sight he presented. Apparently he had been, he said, very successfully hunting elephants, and had managed to collect quite a good haul of ivory, all of which he assured James was of good quality. But one evening quite late as he and Dedderich were sitting by his camp fire, a party of twenty Boers had ridden up. They had shouted at him and insulted him, being quite deliberately very offensive to him because he was an Englishman. Some of them had then climbed into his wagon, despite his trying to stop them, and when they saw the ivory he had there, they went "mad with anger". They said it was their land, not part of the English colony, and Boers and only Boers, were entitled to shoot the elephants as they, the Boers, were sovereign there, but he had no permission from them or from their government to shoot any at all, and he should have had that. As he had no permission they said they were confiscating what he had illegally shot. At first he and Dedderich had tried to physically resist, but that had only seemed to make them more aggressive, and anyway they were outnumbered by the Boers. The Boers then started teaching him and Dedderich "a proper lesson". A group of ten beat them both severely, and blacked one of Lewis' eyes, they may have broken a rib or two he did not know, and they lashed poor Dedderich with a jambok so badly that his back was a mass of blood. Lewis and Dedderich had absolutely no chance to fight back, they were so totally outnumbered. When the Boers had finished the beating and whipping, they threw all Lewis' ivory out of his wagon, bundled it up, and loaded it up onto a number of his oxen, and then drove them off with them after they had first emptied the wagon of pretty much everything else of value, including all his guns and ammunition, and most the food he had left. It was only because he now had an almost empty wagon that his reduced number of oxen could draw it at all. They had left untouched the two side boxes bolted on the outside of the wagon, so he still had his medicine chest and a few tools, but that was about all. His bad luck had continued, he said, as even his horses had died, but he did not know why. Two of Lewis' surviving oxen were very sick and would not live in his opinion.

Lewis said he did not know how he and Dedderich had managed to survive after that robbery, but after a few days a group of Batuana from Lechlulatebe's town had come across what they had thought was an abandoned wagon, and found them inside in a state of collapse, and given them some meat and fresh water, and had then, after a short rest, helped them and their wagon back across the river. They said they had done this as an indication of the respectful thanks that they said was due to the English macooa to whose party they said Lewis belonged, having seen him with James at the chief's town earlier.

By reply, in his turn James then explained all that had happened after they had separated. He was perhaps too modest in the telling of the tale, and in particular he said nothing about his relationship with Foolata: his excuse to himself for that was that Lewis was his wife's brother after all. A passing feeling of guilt for that omission remained with James for days.

He realised that silence was shameful, and might have told Lewis all but for Lewis being so full of the story of his being beaten up that he would not stop talking. The main thing that upset Lewis, and it really made him bitter, was the theft of all his ivory, which as far as he was concerned meant the whole purpose of the trek had been lost. And he had no way of getting any more now he had no guns. His anger at the Boers only increased and turned towards James when he learnt, as part of the story James told, of the present of a wagonload of ivory which the chief had freely given him as thanks for his help, and without even trading. Lewis at once got into James' wagon and inspected the ivory. To begin with Lewis was friendly and congratulated James on the size and value of the load, which he estimated as worth at least £1,000 sterling, maybe more, looking at the quality. Then getting more angry, he said that James should give him half of that ivory because he would never have got there without him leading the expedition. But James was angry at this calculated insult and so he refused to share it, saying that as Lewis had chosen of his own free will to go off on his own, especially to hunt ivory, and had left James to deal with the Sebituani crisis in the town, that he did not agree to sharing. James said that if Lewis had shot a collection of ivory he, James, would not expect to share in it; they were not shooting halves after all. The argument became quite heated, but James was adamant. He would not simply give away half of the ivory that he had been given by Lechlulatebe. It was his and he was keeping it. Lewis said with a sneer he was sure that James' wife Francesca would want him to share the ivory, but this threat did not move James in the slightest.

Then, after the argument had died down, Lewis and Dedderich were cleaned up and fed by James and his servants, although not by Foolata. When they were all safely and peacefully settled down around the fire for the evening, and the party was still talking about what had happened to Lewis, James commented that there was nothing that the Colonial Government could do about the Boers and their attack on Lewis anyway, as its writ did not extend north-wards beyond the 25th Parallel.

42

The Return Starts

THE RETURN JOURNEY was easier and quicker than the outward route had been, not just because they knew it, but because they could slightly shorten it in places, and in many others the water holes they had dug on their way north were still partly open, although the sides were a bit crumbled in. This meant that there was not nearly as much work digging water holes as there had been on the outward journey. Digging was usually time-consuming and back-breaking work. The salt pans when they passed them were just as bleak as the last time, and the eastern outskirts of the Kalahari desert were as unwelcoming as before. The sand river when they followed it again still had traces in places of their old tracks which made the going clearer and a bit easier. Shooting game was much harder with no horses, but with men to drive the animals to James' gun, he managed to shoot enough for Foolata to keep a store of biltong of sufficient size to feed them all.

Lewis was obviously still angry and unhappy at not being given a share of James' ivory and he watched James and Foolata, who now openly slept together in his tent, normally pitched near his wagon, for all to see. Lewis made several very sarcastic remarks to James about married men who were unfaithful with the servants, but James ignored him and them. Lewis however persisted in making these remarks, and when she could hear them, they upset Foolata considerably. Eventually James was provoked into muttering about Lewis' night-time visits to various establishments in Cape Town, but Lewis simply pointed out that he was not married and James was, and to his sister. It eventually turned into another full-scale row with raised voices between the two of them, and if it had not been for the fact that Lewis now depended on James and his men in order to continue the journey, maybe the argument would not have ended as peacefully as it did. The main result of Lewis' sarcastic remarks was to emphasise to James that he and Foolata would have a difficult time living together as a couple in Cape Town, or indeed anywhere. But it was impossible for him to think that they would not live together as man and wife at some time in the future.

As they neared the Bamangwato Hills, which they could see from a great distance, they diverted westwards, at James' suggestion and with Lewis' agreement, in order to go round them and hence speed up the trek. Strangely, water did not prove a problem and the diversion saved them many miles. James tried to work out how many but failed. He was still keeping up his journal on an almost daily basis, and in it he set down the truth about how he felt about Foolata, and he expressed his doubts about what would happen when they got back to Cape Town. Would she be able to stay at Parke's with him he wondered? He had no answers to this and many other questions, and indeed the nearer they got to Kolobeng, which would be their first approach to civilisation, the more uncertain he became as to how he and Foolata would manage their life together. He knew that he had to find answers to all these questions. He also understood that the answers to these questions were not important in themselves: what mattered, and was critical, was that they were together, and in love.

Lewis, using antimony, made a number of rockets "just for fun". He asked James at one point if he could have some more antimony, which he used for making them, as he had run out. James supplied it freely although it was his last, and hoped that the request might herald a better relationship. But it did not. It seemed to James that their relationship had entirely broken down. They were barely on speaking terms as the wagons at last neared Kolobeng.

James had decided that he needed to get to Kolobeng and see

Livingstone before Lewis did, and try to break the ice with him, as it were, about his new relationship with Foolata. They had seen Livingstone on the way up country, and he knew who Foolata was, and that James was married. So, James decided, without telling her, that he would walk on ahead of the wagon when they got near enough to the mission station for him to do just that. He thought that a day's walk, which he was not unused to, would be about twenty or twenty-five miles or so, and he would take John with him for company, and to carry the rifle and any supplies such as food for the day's trek. It would be easy walking, and he would leave the wagon with its ivory safe with Martinus, Edward and Foolata. In quiet moments, he tried to work out what he would tell Livingstone about his new relationship with Foolata, but however hard he tried he never found a formula which sounded absolutely right.

Lewis had formed a plan with Dedderich's help, a plan for him to get his rightful half share of the ivory, as he thought of it. It was a simple plan, but it had to be put into effect before they reached Kolobeng, for two reasons. Firstly, at that place James' haul of ivory would be seen by Livingstone and by any gentleman visitor or trader who happened to be there. So, if Lewis was to get hold of that haul, or any of it, then that must be done before then. And to get it he would have to separate James from his ivory. James would not share it: Lewis had asked him, nicely as he thought, and James would not share it. So it would have to be stolen. But they, that is Lewis and Dedderich, would only steal half of it, namely Lewis' share. So, he reasoned, it wouldn't really be stealing anyway. They would take it from James' wagon and put it in Lewis' for transportation to market somewhere. Once they had it, Lewis doubted that James would even try to get any of it back; he would have enough after all. To separate James from his ivory they decided that they would unfasten his oxen from the trek-touw one night just before they got to Kolobeng. The oxen would then surely stray, after all they usually did if left unfastened overnight. In the morning they would suggest to James that he and John walk on ahead while the oxen were recovered, and Lewis and Dedderich would persuade Martinus and Edward to help them do the rounding up. Lewis would steal half the ivory while they were doing that and while James with John was on his walk to Kolobeng. But in reality, Lewis said, James must not get to Kolobeng, or otherwise he would know if he did and saw his wagon, that his ivory or some or all of it had been stolen. Knowing as he did that Lewis had none, he would obviously accuse Lewis of theft. The problem was how to stop James from seeing that the theft had occurred when he got to Kolobeng. Martinus and Edward could both be dealt with after the oxen had been rounded up, and before he could take the wagon onwards.

Lewis realised that this plan involved killing James and maybe John as well. If John did die that would be incidental and unavoidable. To follow his plan to the letter, when the wagons were about twenty-five miles from Kolobeng, he would pack some biltong in a knapsack along with a large flask of coffee, and to the coffee he would add a lethal quantity of antimony. On the morning of the final day, as he came to think of it, all he would then have to do would be to persuade James to walk on ahead of the wagon with John because his wandering oxen could not immediately be found. When James agreed, as he surely would, he would be given the poisoned coffee to take with him for that walk. Then when it killed him, Lewis was not going to shed any tears. It would simply mean more ivory for him. If James didn't take it, or if it didn't kill him, then the fact that it had been poisoned was irrelevant. Martinus and Edward would either agree to cooperate or they would kill them. If they had to do that, then Dedderich would drive James' wagon to Kolobeng. Foolata they ignored, as a native woman would be disbelieved in any claim she might make against a white man like Lewis. Anyway, he could claim that any story she told was invented out of spite because he had rejected her sexual advances.

On that last night in camp James had stayed up a little later than normal writing up his journal, and after he had checked that the out-spanned oxen were all safely tied to the trek-touw, he went to Foolata in their tent. She was waiting up for him, and had been mending a Ma-Mary dress. It was blue – a colour which she loved, as James knew. The light from the lamp was very poor and she could not see very well what she had to do. The dress was in tatters from the heavy wear she had had to make of it, after all she now had no other. She was in tears because she felt she could not mend it well enough for her to wear it decently any more. She wanted to look at her best when they got to Kolobeng. It was no use James trying to console her by saying that he did not want to see her in any dress anyway, he liked her better naked – she said she felt as if she was getting farther and farther away from being "presentable". She told James not to be so childish, she wanted to look decent, and asked how she could if she had no proper clothes.

As James and Foolata lay down to sleep, James told her that having thought long and hard about it, he had decided he ought to walk on ahead to Kolobeng the next day expressly to talk to Livingstone about their new relationship. He would take John with him. Foolata said she understood that what James proposed was for their mutual good, and inwardly she was pleased at his foresight. She said she would not be worried by being alone with Lewis, she would have Martinus, Edward and Argos with her, and they would look after her. They both agreed his talk with Livingstone would be important to their future together, not to say critical. Kolobeng was only one day ahead now. As he lay beside Foolata, James wondered to himself what excuse he would give to Lewis for wanting to walk on to Kolobeng the next morning. He had no idea that, as it happened the Livingstones and family had already left for Cape Town following the death of their baby daughter.

Then, as Lewis' preparations were complete and he could see

that the light in James' tent was extinguished, Lewis cautiously crept out into the dark night, and in execution the first part of his plan, went across to James' team of oxen which were securely tied to their trek-touw, and untied the various rheims fastening them to it. The stolid creatures stirred silently, moved, and started to wander.

43

Ivory and Death

J AMES ROSE EARLY THE NEXT MORNING at about four o'clock. As
soon as James left the tent he saw at once that his oxen had
strayed. He could not understand it as he had himself checked the
fastenings the night before, and he could see that Lewis' oxen were
still fastened to his trek-touw, securely.

Exasperated, he called out to Lewis to tell him the oxen had
gone, and he came over at once, even though half dressed, and the
camp was soon fully awake. The straying of oxen was not that
unusual an incident in itself, it had happened often enough in all
conscience. But it was a nuisance, and obviously they had to be
recovered or James' wagon with its heavy load would be going no
further. James said he wanted to get on to Kolobeng without this
latest delay, and said he would walk on ahead. He did not tell Lewis
why he wanted to do this as it was none of Lewis' business, he
thought. Lewis of course merely assumed, because that was what
he had planned for, that the reason was the straying of the oxen.
James merely said he was frustrated by the delay that fetching the
oxen entailed. Lewis happily agreed that since walking and the pace
at which oxen hauling a laden wagon across soft sand was not that
different, it was perfectly all right for James to walk on ahead to
Kolobeng. He and his wagon driver Dedderich would stay with
both wagons and would wait while Martinus and Edward went and
followed the spoor of the missing oxen. When they had been
recovered, they would catch James up. He did not mention Foolata
or John. And then, remembering that Foolata had said she was
uncomfortable with Lewis around her, James quickly suggested

something slightly different, namely that his man Edward, and Dedderich too, would track and fetch the missing oxen, Foolata and Martinus would stay with his wagon, and Lewis with his, and he and John would walk on ahead to Kolobeng. Then when the oxen had been fetched back Martinus, Foolata and Edward would bring on his wagon to the mission station. Lewis made one or two apparently helpful suggestions about the details of this arrangement and James was quietly pleased (if surprised) when Lewis handed him the knapsack with the provisions including the coffee, that had been readied. James privately hoped that this friendly talk and even assistance might mean that now that they were so close to civilisation perhaps Lewis was becoming more reasonable. Maybe, he mused, Lewis had really come to accept the ivory was not for sharing. James thanked Lewis for his help and thoughtfulness, and said a quick goodbye to Foolata. Edward and Dedderich set off on the spoor of the oxen and James and John set off on foot for Kolobeng. They had no map with them because they knew the way, they had travelled it before in the other direction, but James had a compass "just in case", and he and John would share the burden of the rifle as they walked.

James and John set off along what they could see from the old tracks of their own and other travellers was the right way, and walked steadily, with James taking first turn at carrying the rifle and ammunition and John having the knapsack. They walked for about an hour like this and came to a small pool of water, where they stopped and made a fire, and taking long sticks from a bush nearby, fried some of the biltong and ate it, and they warmed the coffee as best they could and drank some but not all of it. John thought both tasted revolting and James agreed. Then James sat and smoked a pipe of tobacco and chatted with John about Highsteignton. Their thoughts were of home. After their rest, they restarted their walk and after another fifteen minutes came across a bush which had some common wild fruit on it. They both ate some as they walked, and after a little while they again sat down to rest. As they chatted they decided to go back and pick some more of the fruit so John went back and fetched some. After eating the fruit, James again smoked a pipe and then they moved on. Their trouble started soon after that, when first James and then John took ill, and started to be sick. It was a fierce retching and griping, and it left them both very weak. James was reduced to lying down, and was doubled up with the sharp, prolonged pain of retching. After a short while, all he could vomit up was bile, but he still strained and retched. He had not the strength to move. John was no better. He too was seriously ill, vomiting and violently retching continuously.

Dedderich and Edward followed the spoor of the missing oxen for over eight miles before they saw them, trying to graze unsuccessfully on the poor feeble bushes they were among. It was not hard to get them together and start heading them back towards the camp. But Dedderich had privately been given instructions by Lewis before they set off, and as he was going to share in the ivory according to the promise Lewis had made him, Dedderich proceeded to carry out the next part of the plan. So, while they drove the oxen from behind in the general direction of the camp, when they neared the camp Dedderich picked up a heavy but hand-sized stone, and very quietly creeping up behind Edward so as not to make any sound, without warning hit him hard on the back of the skull. Edward fell heavily to the ground unconscious. Dedderich knelt over him, and drawing his bush knife, he slashed Edward's throat. His lifeblood gushed out. The dumb oxen walked stolidly onwards towards the camp.

After James and John had been gone only about an hour or so, Lewis asked Martinus who was sitting in James' wagon to help him unload some ivory, and to transfer it into his.

Martinus protested, "But this ivory all belongs to Mister James, not you. I really should not help you. And you must not touch it anyway. It is his."

Lewis said, "He agreed with me last night that we would share the ivory so it will be quite all right. I am not asking you to do anything wrong."

"I am very doubtful about that. I think it would be sensible to wait till we get to Kolobeng and then we can ask Mister James." He looked questioningly across at Foolata who was standing nearby.

Foolata shook her head vehemently. "Mister James would never have agreed that. I know."

And so, fatefully, Martinus added, "I am sorry Mister Lewis, but I really cannot help you, and you must not touch the ivory on any account."

Lewis angrily turned on Martinus. "How dare you speak to me like that! I am your employer, and you must do as you are told. I am going to take the ivory whether you like it or not. All of it. If you get in the way I will have to take the jambok to you. You can do what you like but the ivory is mine by right, as leader of the expedition, and I will have it. You can help transfer the load, which is heavy, and ungainly as well, and can have a tusk as payment."

Martinus and Foolata were very frightened and argued as strongly as they could against Lewis doing anything so foolish, but he was obviously very determined. Ignoring their protests, Lewis climbed into James' wagon and suddenly picked up James' spare rifle. Foolata saw what he was doing and backed well away, as she knew (as did Lewis) that the spare rifle behind the fore-chest was always kept loaded with one round in case of emergencies. James had taken only his beloved Blisset on the walk, so the spare was ready and to hand as a weapon. Foolata called to Martinus that Lewis had the rifle, and Martinus started to run towards her and away from Lewis who was now standing on the fore-chest. Whatever else he was, Lewis was now a good shot and it was easy for him to sight on Martinus, and then shoot him in the back as he ran. Martinus was only wounded however, and not apparently mortally. He fell, and shouted to Foolata to get away as he did so. Lewis crashed into the back of James' wagon looking for the ammunition box. He needed to fire another shot. But Foolata knew that James kept the box locked and had done so ever since his last row with Lewis. Knowing she had a bit of time before Lewis could fire again as he would have to force the lock, she turned and ran for her very life. As she did so the last thing she heard behind her was Lewis cursing at the lid which was resisting his efforts. She did not know what had happened to Martinus, or if he was alive or dead. She just ran, with Argos beside her, for herself, and for their unborn child.

Dedderich returned with the missing oxen mid-morning. He and Lewis tied them in to James' trek-touw, and then began the arduous task of transferring the ivory from James' wagon to Lewis'. It was a hot and sweaty task, and every so often they had to rope the tusks together to stop them working loose when they came later to move the wagon. When they eventually finished, they started to discuss how they would split the haul. Dedderich wanted half and said that as he had killed Edward he should have at least that, but Lewis said that as the leader of the expedition, and he had shot Martinus as well, he should have the bigger share.

While this argument was still unresolved, they went across the camp site to where Martinus was lying. Martinus had bled to death from his wound, his blood flowing only a short distance as it dried in the strong sun even before it could sink into the sand. He had twisted as he fell and was lying on his back, open-mouthed, and hundreds of black flies were all around the blood and his mouth and eyes. Lewis waved them away, but only for a second as they came back almost instantly. He closed Martinus' eyes, as he thought they were looking at him. They started there and then to dig a grave right beside him. The ground was surprisingly hard once they dug below the surface, so after the grave was three feet deep they mutually decided that that was deep enough, and they tumbled the corpse in and quickly shovelled the sand back over him. Then they looked around for Foolata but could see no trace of her hidden in the scrub. They knew she could not have run far, she was not strong, there was no need to bother about her. The sun and lack of water would finish her.

James and John eventually stopped being sick, and simply lay on the bare open ground where they were, in amongst their vomit, exhausted. They were too weak to talk. As the day drew on they lay beside each other, for comfort as much as anything. Neither was strong enough to do much for the other. James reflected that his medicine chest was full of cures for sickness, and then alarmingly called out, "Oh my God, John, I think we have been poisoned. I wish I had my medicine chest here with me. I would give a hundred guineas this very minute if I had it, it would put us both to rights in a few minutes." As well as vomiting sporadically and violently they were both attacked now with horrendous, vicious diarrhoea. The spasms lasted for whole minutes at a time, but after just a few minutes all the straining in the bowels was simply muscular contractions, but it felt just as painful. They were both very cold, and had no blanket so that night they slept no more than fitfully after their bodily spasms lessened, and in the cold grey light of the early dawn they felt as if they must somehow try to struggle on. If they did not, they would certainly die.

James and John desperately wanted to try to walk as far as they could on that second day, but they were much too weak, and were both frequently sick, and troubled by retching and attempted diarrhoea. James thought they should try to eat the last of the biltong, so they gnawed at the last barely edible cold strips and drank the last of the poisoned coffee, barely more than a mouthful each. After the momentary ease of having something in their bellies, they were sick again, and the constant griping in their bowels was agony. James tried to smoke again, and imagined it helped dull the pains in his stomach for a few moments, but then they returned more strongly. He shivered and sweated in rapidly alternating attacks. The rifle felt so heavy that neither could properly and safely carry it. James dropped it several times, and they were tempted to abandon it. Every movement was painful, and took an age and terrible physical effort. They managed to stagger a few hundred yards until James looked at the compass uncertainly, and exclaimed that they had taken the wrong road and were walking straight into the Kalahari desert. He said they must turn back or they would certainly die of thirst. John had no idea where the road was, so they straggled on a few yards more to a hollow in what might have been the bed of a sand river. James dropped his hat there, somewhere, and after he had, he could not find it.

Once, they were sure they heard a whip cracking, which could only mean a wagon, perhaps theirs coming on, but no wagon appeared. They tried firing all their last bullets save one, to attract attention, but when they did, leaving themselves defenceless, no one came, no one replied with a gunshot. They lay down close together, and waited for the inevitable. They fantasised that their wagon had got to Kolobeng and a search party would be sent out to look for them, but as the second night drew on and nobody came they knew that they were reaching the end.

James said a brief prayer, "Let us pray to Almighty God to have mercy upon us lying down to sleep."

John said, "Amen."

James cried out, "What would mother say if she saw us like this?" He started to gabble incoherently, apparently in Sechuana. He knocked the gun over accidentally, and it fired the last shot against a rock nearby, uselessly.

When the sky started to lighten as the sun rose, neither saw it. Birds circled high above.

*

Dedderich climbed onto the fore-chest in James' wagon, and cracking the whip, started the wagon off to Kolobeng. He was a day late starting but that did not matter, it was a simple straight trek, and after a little he realised he could no longer see James' spoor in front of him. He knew from that that James and John must have wandered off the right course. He did not stop to look for them, it was unimportant to him and their plan. He carried straight on to Kolobeng which he reached as the evening light of the day after the murders was also fast dying. He took the wagon to where it had rested on the way northwards, watered the oxen, and left them fastened to the trek-touw. No one saw him in Kolobeng: the place seemed completely deserted that evening. Then Dedderich simply abandoned the wagon and left it, full as it was with James' belongings, but with no ivory, and walked away. He headed west away from the station and toward his agreed meeting with Lewis. It is a matter of record that they never met.

44

News Reaches England

From Graaf Reinet

To Sir Marshall and Lady Eleanor Duffield

13th Feb 1852

Highsteignton
Devon

Dear Sir Marshall,
I was much shocked today to learn from my correspondent in Colesberg of a tragedy in the interior of the colony which has personally distressed me greatly. There has been a dreadful event, the precise nature of which is presently unknown, but the outcome of which is that I am left with the very melancholy task of having to write to you and inform you of the sad death of your son, James, and also that of his English servant John Coleman. I thought I should write to you instantly I heard the news, and I shall endeavour to get the full details of the disaster and shall write with them to you when I have them. Whether or not you consider this intelligence is sufficient to announce his death to his friends I leave to you to judge, but I am perfectly sure that there is no possibility my correspondent Mr Charles Orpen of Colesberg would have given me these sad tidings were they not all too true. I must add that his story has been independently confirmed to me by a certain Captain Bladen Shelley who was, he has told me, near at hand when the sad event occurred. He will be writing to you, he has assured me. I too shall write again as soon as I can properly do so.

Believe me, yours very truly
H. D. B. Dyne.

From Captain Bladen Shelley

c/o Hamilton Ross and Co, Cape Town.

Friday 27th Feb 1852

My Dear Sir Marshall,

It is with very great sadness and a strong sense of personal loss that I write to inform you that your unfortunate son and my good friend James met with a very sad death near Kolobeng on or about the 26th of December last. His servant John Coleman met the same fate.

It would appear that they were nearing Kolobeng, when for some unknown reason James and his servant decided to walk the last few miles to the Mission Station. Little is known until it was realised at that place that James' wagon was waiting patiently in the town, laden, but abandoned by the servants, and James had not arrived. Search parties were sent out along the route he should have taken, but at first no trace of him could be found. After a more systematic search was undertaken, his remains were discovered, and very strangely they had not been greatly mauled by lions. A bullet mark and other remains such as his hat and torn clothing nearby showed that it must be assumed that James had tried to drive off a lion, and presumably failed.

His servants are missing, and a great mystery surrounds his death, not the least of which is the present whereabouts of his travelling companion Lewis Trevanion. I believe you know the family. Lewis, whom I know of, is not to be found, and I have to assume a degree of suspicion attaches to his absence. Not the least reason for this is that James told me before he set off that he would keep a daily journal, but although there were writing utensils in the wagon, there was no journal found. Natives do not read, so they would not have removed his journal.

I must add that I got to know James well when he first came to Cape Town, and I am quite sure I am right in saying that one of the principle reasons for his trek to the far interior beyond the boundaries of the colony was to have the opportunity to make some money by the shooting of elephants in order to gain their ivory. It is however a melancholy fact that there was no ivory on the wagon when its contents were inventoried by myself and two others.

Your son's body has been buried in the cemetary at Kolobeng mission station, and his grave is tended by a native living nearby called Foolata, I believe.

I think it imperative that a member of the family comes out to the colony in order to understand the full circumstances of the two deaths. I know from what James told me in the past that you might well find the journey over-taxing physically, but perhaps James' wife (whose name I am most sorry to say I cannot recall) could visit, and you may rest fully assured that I will personally escort her so that she sees everything that requires to be seen, safely. I would welcome a visit from her at the earliest opportunity, and will escort her from her point of landing to wherever she wishes to go. I assume she will wish to go to the cemetery. I am presently quartered at the castle, and if James' wife were to stay at the very respectable nearby Parke's Hotel, where James stayed, the lady proprietor, with whom I have spoken, will alert me the moment she arrives. In the meantimes her arrival is expected and Mrs Parke has some of James' belongings in safe custody awaiting her arrival and instructions as to disposal.

I am respectfully and sorrowfully yours,
Bladen Shelley (Captain)

45

Francesca's Visit

ALTHOUGH SHE WAS STILL VERY WEAK, Francesca's health had improved in the last months, and she was living a solitary life after her father had died. She was very lonely, she rarely saw the Duffields and she pined for the child she had lost. More and more, her thoughts centred on James and his abrupt departure. The Duffields were very solicitous, but out of choice and despite their wishing her to live with them, she lived alone in her father's old house. When the Duffields received the letters about James they sent Coleman over to fetch her. He had strict instructions not to say anything of the content of the letters, but from his guarded words, and grim face. She knew the news was not good. But she also knew beyond reason that James would return to her. She was so sure that he had had no intention of deserting her when he left for the Cape. Strangely, the longer she waited for his return the more certain she became that he was coming back to her. She still received her allowance and she had thought that it would be stopped if James died, so she thought that its very continuance meant he was still alive, even if so far away that he could not write. She kept the memory of their wedding night closely to herself, and waited patiently, yearning for his return.

And then the Duffields showed her the two letters. She read them both in silence.

"I must go there, as soon as I can arrange it," said Francesca. "This Captain Shelley suggests that I go. I have to go, I should have gone long ago."

"But will you be strong enough for all that travelling?" asked

Lady Eleanor. "We could not manage it, we are far too old, and getting very unsteady, so unless you go, no one can. We will pay for everything of course, but will you be well enough, do you think?"

"Right now, perhaps I am not. But the long sea voyage will strengthen me, I must hope. The air will do me the world of good, so I will go. Now. Right away. There is no choice about it. I should have gone after James, chased him really I suppose. Oh, I miss him so."

It was nearly a year after she had been shown Bladen's letter that Francesca arrived at Kolobeng after a long and dispiriting journey. Bladen had accompanied her all the way from Cape Town, and during the arduous journey she had learnt from him much more about James than she had known before they got married. She had also managed to get the truth about James' relationship with Christina out of Bladen, and he had also told her about the native girl, of whom he said he knew very little save for her name and that she had once worked for the Becks. That morning Francesca had asked Bladen to leave her and simply point out the cemetery to her, as she told him that she wanted to see James' grave, her husband's grave, where he had been buried, on her own. And so it was that shortly before ten o'clock Francesca approached the rough brown patch of waste ground where three grave mounds were protruding sadly, from the red sandy earth. The bleak and arid landscape around felt strangely welcoming. The air was almost still, hot already although it was yet early in the day.

At first Francesca thought she was alone at the cemetery, but then she could see a poorly dressed young native woman in a faded, tattered blue dress, standing at a lone grave which was a little apart from the others. An old grey dog lay on the ground near her. She had a baby in her arms, and was rocking slightly back and forth. She was crying.

Francesca did not want to disturb her, but she needed to know which was James' grave, so she quietly approached the woman, who, hearing Francesca approach, looked round, saw her and stood still. She tried rather ineffectually to dry her eyes on her stained sleeve. Francesca saw the woman was young and as she thought, very pretty. She was lightly copper skinned, but her baby, now Francesca could see from closer to, was very much lighter skinned. Francesca felt the air stir, but she herself could hardly breathe.

Francesca smiled at her and gently reached out a hand to touch the baby. The woman, smiling away her tears, let her touch the baby, which did not flinch. "What a lovely looking little baby. Please tell me, what is your baby's name?" asked Francesca very quietly, smiling still.

"I call him James," she paused, "after his father." She fingered the necklace she wore. Francesca saw the sun glint on the ring in the sunlight, and remembered the occasion of it being given to James.

"And you are Foolata," said Francesca, not asking, but knowing already what the reply would be. The air around them moved very slightly. "We have both lost James, you know, and your baby is his son, I can see, and the name of course."

"Francesca? James always said you would come if anything happened to him. I have waited for you."

"Yes, I am Francesca."

"He said I was to tell you when I saw you that he was so sorry for everything."

"I know he was."

"I found an envelope with your name on it among his papers. There is a letter inside, I think."

She reached inside her shawl and pulled out a grubby envelope, more of a slim packet really, which she offered timidly to Francesca. Francesca took it, and looking at it, she saw her name on the outside in James' handwriting. There was no address, just her name. She said nothing. She opened the packet, and inside was the letter she had long awaited from James. Foolata stood and waited patiently while Francesca read it. It gave a frank account of the last weeks of the journey, and in it James told honestly of his relationship with Foolata. When she had read it, Francesca looked at the girl. She was grieving like herself, she could see. "I loved him," said Foolata, "I loved him so much. But he was your husband, not mine. There was always a part of him that was yours. I miss him every single day." She paused, and looked at the grave. "And what is to happen to us, me and the baby, now?"

"We both loved James, I know, and you have all that is left of him now. The baby. Foolata, although we have never met before, I feel as if I have known you for a long time. I want to help and love you and your child, James' child. This baby is all that is left of James. Will you let me do that, please?"

"He would want me to, I know, so yes, I would".

"I could best help both of you if you and little James would come back to live with me in England. Would you be prepared to do that, please? I would look after you both as my family, in truth you would be my only family. I have no other."

Francesca was not afraid of the answer, and briefly felt a soft warm breeze on her face, like a caress, and saw it lightly touch the sleeve of Foolata's dress.

"Yes. We will come."

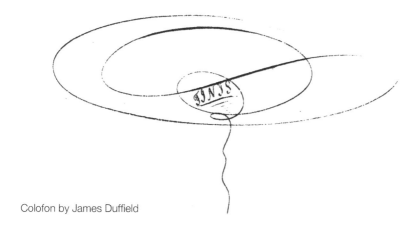

Colofon by James Duffield

Water pit in the Molopo.

James Duffield's ring.

The cemetery at Kolobeng today . There are three graves. The larger in the picture is that of Elizabeth Pyne Livingstone who was buried on 18th September 1851. The other two seen in the picture are those of John Coleman and of James Duffield.

Acknowledgements

THE STORY derives from James' actual murder which occurred on 26th December 1851, in the manner and for the motive described. Both he and John Coleman are buried at Kolobeng. Naturally, many but not all characters have been renamed, even if one only derives existence from a single mention in one of Livingstone's letters. I have however, simplified and changed many figures, dramatised and invented many personal details. The main events in Africa, did however all occur precisely as described.

This book recounts many incidents of travel in the wilds of Africa in 1850–51, most happened to James, and all are derived from one or other of the sources listed in the Bibliography, some have been embroidered, but only slightly. In particular I apologise to Frank Vardon for changing his first name to Harry, he was one of the noblest and finest men travelling in the Colony at that time. I apologise also to Livingstone and Oswell who in real life jointly discovered Lake Ngami in 1849. Otherwise, I have accurately, if very briefly, described both Kuruman and Kolobeng and their Ministers. They are far too famous to do otherwise.

James' brother has been changed greatly from family tradition. I have changed the relationship they had with each other, and I apologise to both of them for that. In real life they were devoted to each other.

James' dying words were spoken almost exactly as they are written. John Coleman who was also murdered was James' valet in real life, I have given him a background. Christina existed, as did her father, the dramatic story I have given of James' relationship with her is as right as I can get it after so long, even with the benefit of court papers. Everything else about James relationship with the Becks is completely imagined. The engagement did however end up exactly as written. I now have the ring.

I have changed Lewis' name. He led an 'adventurous' life in the Colony, and beyond. I have tried to find any descendants but have been unsuccessful. He was described by Livingstone as an "inveterate liar."

I acknowledge that I have had trouble with the spelling of names and places. Some have changed names since the events occurred, and I have tried to keep to the old names. Spelling then was never consistent. I have altered the geography in one place only (although quite considerably), for which I hope I can be forgiven, I have had trouble with guns, which at the time the story took place used powder and shot/bullets, and not cartridges. Hunting then was far more dangerous than might be imagined.

I am deeply indebted to Fiona for her editing work, and to all at The Choir Press including Miles and Adrian for their assistance in getting me to understand my role as author in the complicated world of publishing. My thanks are due to Julie Davidson for the photograph of the Cemetery at Kolobeng which appears with her permission. I must also thank Richard Stott for his production of photographs of James' ring and the other pictures which are all from my own collection. I am very grateful to Steve Greybanks and his colleagues at Central Building Design for production of the map of the trek, which is based on the Unfinished Proof map given by John Arrowsmith to James Duffield which is in my possession.

As a young boy I was entranced by stories of James' exploits in Africa, and of his untimely end, all as told by my Great Uncle John. When I inherited the collection from him, and had myself retired, I decided to write the story down as I had long threatened my wife Susan I would. She was very patient and helpful, if a little critical at times, and the result of her help is this book, which if not completely as she would have wished, exists nevertheless as a result of her loving assistance. My thanks are most certainly due, and are now most happily offered, to her.

Julian Dolman

Bibliography

Newspapers, periodicals and offical/military records

Blackwoods Magazine, Travel and Adventure and Sport

Breutz, P L. *The Tribes of the Districts of Kuruman and Postmasburg.* Govt Printer, 1963

Cape of Good Hope Almanack and Annual Register for 1846. B J Van de Sandt, 1846

Cape of Good Hope Government Gazette 1850

East India Register and Army List for 1847. Wm H Allen, 1847

Primary sources

Baines, Thomas. *Explorations in South-West Africa.* Longman, Green, Longman, Roberts and Green, 1864

Baldwin, William Charles. *African Hunting from Natal to the Zambesi.* Richard Bentley, 1863

Browne, G Lathom and Stewart, C G. *Reports of Trials for Murder by Poisoning.* 1883

Cumming, Roualeyn Gordon. *Five Years of a Hunter's Life in South Africa.* John Murray, 1855

Harris, Captain William Cornwallis. *The Wild Sports of Southern Africa.* John Murray, 1839

In the Footsteps of Livingstone. Bodley Head, 1924. Ed. J. Irving

Livingstone, David. *Missionary Travels and Researches in South Africa.* John Murray, 1857

McSymon, R M. *Fairbridge Arderne and Lawton.* Juta and Co, 1990

Moffat, Robert. *Missionary Labours and Scenes in Southern Africa.* John Snow, 1842

Northcott, Cecil. *Robert Moffat, Pioneer in Africa 1817-1870.* Lutterworth Press, 1961

Oswell, W Edward. *William Cotton Oswell , Hunter and Explorer.* Heineman, 1900

Pama, C. *Bowler's Cape Town, and Life at the Cape in Early Victorian Times 1834–1868.* Tafelberg, 1977

Secondary sources

Andersson, Charles John. *Lake N'Gami.* Hurst and Blackett, 1856

Bell, N. (N D'Anvers). *Heroes of South African Discovery.* Walter Scott, 1899

Blaikie, William Gordon. *The Personal Life of David Livingstone.* John Murray, 1882

Bruce, Carlton. *The Boys' Friend, or the Maxims of a Cheerful Old Man.* John Harris, 1835

Bruce, Charles. *Stirring Adventure in African Travel.* W P Nimmo Hay and Mitchell, 1840

Carruthers, Jane and Arnold, Marrion. *The Life and Works of Thomas Baines.* Fernwood Press, 1995

Galton, Francis. *Narrative of an Explorer in Tropical South Africa.* Ward Lock and Co, 1889

Gordon-Brown, A. *The Cape Sketchbook of Sir Charles D'Oyley 1832–1833.* Balkema, 1968

Holden, Rev William C. *History of the Colony of Natal.* Alexander Heylin, 1855

Methuen, Henry H. *Life in the Wilderness.* Richard Bentley, 1846

National Portrait Gallery. *David Livingstone and the Victorian Encounter with Africa.* 1996

Schapera, I. *David Livingstone Family Letters 1841–1856.* Greenwood Press, 1975

Schapera, I. *Livingstone's Missionary Correspondence 1841–1856.* University of California Press, 1961

Thompson, George. *Travels and Adventures in Southern Africa.* Van Riebeck Society, 1968

Wallis, J P R. *Thomas Baines, his Life and Explorations 1820–1875.* Balkema, 1976

Walters, Rev William. *The Life and Labours of Robert Moffat.* Walter Scott, 1882

Williams, C. *Narratives and Adventures of Travellers in Africa.* Ward Lock, no date

Williams, Wilman. *The Rock Engravings of Griqualand West and Bechuanaland.* Deighton Bell, 1933

Lightning Source UK Ltd.
Milton Keynes UK
UKOW07f1343070115

244078UK00013B/106/P